PANDORA RISING

Reincarnation Series: Book 2

To my Lizzy Liz

Rochelle Purdy

Loves you!!
&

Chelley

Copyright © 2016 by Rochelle Purdy

All rights reserved. No part of this publication may be reproduced, distributed, or transmitted in any form or by any means, including photocopying, recording, or other electronic or mechanical methods, without the prior written permission of the publisher, except in the case of brief quotations embodied in critical reviews and certain other noncommercial uses permitted by copyright law.

This is a work of fiction. Names, characters, businesses, places, events and incidents are either the products of the author's imagination or used in a fictitious manner. Any resemblance to actual persons, living or dead, or actual events is purely coincidental.

ISBN-10: **1539771202**
ISBN-13: **978-1539771203**

Cover Illustration: http://www.selfpubbookcovers.com/Viergacht
Editing by Jeremy Koedam

Published by Createspace.com

DEDICATION

To Jeremy, my true partner in crime.

Table of Contents

Chapter One 3

Chapter Two 10

Chapter Three 21

Chapter Four 39

Chapter Five 52

Chapter Six 78

Chapter Seven 92

Chapter Eight 115

Chapter Nine 128

Chapter Ten 139

Chapter Eleven 158

Chapter Twelve 180

Chapter Thirteen 194

Chapter Fourteen 220

Chapter Fifteen 243

Chapter Sixteen 267

Chapter Seventeen 289

Chapter Eighteen 320

Chapter Nineteen 354

ACKNOWLEDGMENTS

I would like to acknowledge Janette McMahon for being an awesome librarian and editor who encourages me to go to workshops. Of course my family who always enjoys my work.

CHAPTER ONE

Slinking back against the empty stone, Courtney felt utterly defeated. Avarie was right, he wasn't in there at all and God knows how long that tomb remained empty of its humanly contents. Sasha leaned down and put his hand on Courtney's shoulder. "He's been gone a long time, Courtney. We can't do anything about it right now." Sasha sighed heavily as he looked around the room. In his heart, he wished that Avarie was wrong and that only dust would line the inner marble. Instead, it was only wasted space.

Courtney put his head in his hands, *"We have to find him, Sasha."*

"We don't have to do anything, Courtney." Sasha felt the frustration rise through his body. *"He's left you alone for many years now. Going after him at this point is mute. We need to focus on what needs to happen now."*

Avarie held her eyes downcast. She felt the defeat as much as Courtney did. The evil creature who taken her family from her, was alive and that didn't sit well with her. Picking up her Rossi Ranch Hand, she left all four of them alone in the crypt. Sprinting upstairs to her bedroom, she slammed the door and threw herself on the bed. This was all too real. A headache was forming at her temples as she tried to wrap her mind around the fact that hers and Courtney's destinies were entwined. *Synchronicity* is what Sasha called it. There are no accidents in life.

Her door opened, snapping her from her thoughts. Sasha entered the room quietly and closed the door behind him. Sitting on the edge of the bed with her, he brought her into a slight hug. "Luscious, is past." His deep voice filled the room with his broken English. "You are present." He said tapping her heart with his hand. "Move forward, Avarie." Tears slipped down the sides of her cheek. Gently, Sasha wiped them away.

"How do I move forward knowing that he's still out there?" Her voice shook as she spoke. "He's committed horrible deeds, Sasha."

Rocking her gently, he answered in his broken English, "He has, and he pay for them. Justice is in universe." He just had gotten done explaining this to Courtney before he came up to see her. "If you trust in the universe, it's love send you justice."

Avarie was tired, but her head hurt too much and she was still shaking. "How'd you learn our language so fast?" she asked.

"Internet." Sasha said while making jazz hands in the air. "It not perfect, but I learn, yes?" He grinned at her.

"It's good enough." Avarie responded as she patted his back. "What now?"

"You rest." He demanded. "Head hurt?" he asked as he poked her forehead.

"It does a bit."

Gently leaning in, he pressed his soft lips against her forehead and they lingered there a bit. A warm sensation passed from that spot and into him. Pulling back, he let out a breath of icy cold air. "Better?" he asked. Avarie nodded. "Good! You rest."

Putting her feet up on her bed, he threw the covers over her. Georg bounded up the side of the bed and batted at his shoulder as Avarie closed her eyes. Making a shush motion to Georg, he signaled him to follow Sasha out of the room. Once out, Sasha closed the door behind them.

They both looked down the hall and went to Matthias' door. Without knocking, both he and Georg entered. Finding Eva and Matthias just sitting on the bed in silence, he joined them.

"Don't you knock?" Matthias asked.

"I knew you not naked." Sasha quipped. Eva chuckled as the cat jumped into Sasha's lap and started purring.

"Wow, he somewhat speaks English." Matthias said being a smart ass. "How'd you have time to learn that?"

"You sleep too much. I use Internet." Eva busted up in a full blown laugh. Sasha's broken English was nice to hear. He wasn't awake long and he's already explored the Internet to learn how to communicate with them.

"Well Sasha, as you can see we have a problem. Now Courtney will want to hunt down Luscious. It'll be like finding a needle in a haystack. I have a man coming to train the girls and I can't even reach him." Matthias tried in his downtime to contact Gill McCullum, but the phone just kept on ringing.

"I handle Courtney. You focus on projects." Sasha stated as he crossed his arms. Sasha was right; Matthais still had work to do on his programming machine for Eva.

"Where's Avarie?" Eva asked Sasha.

"She resting for now."

"Is she alright?"

"She has much on her mind." They all needed for Avarie to get her rest. There were too many revelations for one day and she had to take time and embrace them. Sasha patted Georg's belly as he rolled around on his lap. There was silence for a while as Georg's purrs filled the room. Their heads turned towards the doorway as Courtney stomped through the halls and slammed his door shut.

"*Jesus*, he's gonna shake all the stones out of place." Matthias exclaimed as he shook his head. "We need to snap him back to reality." Matthias' exchanged glances with Sasha. Rolling his eyes, he placed Georg on the bed and stood up. Sasha knew that he was the only one with common sense in this house. Apparently, Matthias didn't want to deal with Courtney right now and he didn't blame him. At the same token, neither did Sasha. Making his way out the door, he motioned for the cat to stay in the room. At Courtney's door, he tried to open it, but it was locked. He tapped lightly and waited. When there was no answer, he tapped harder.

Throwing the door open, Courtney yelled, "What!" Sasha took a step back. The room reeked of weed and his eyes were bloodshot. Sasha just folded his arms across his chest. "Oh for fucks sake Sasha!" Allowing him in, Courtney looked down the hallway, then slammed the door.

"*What? Are you going to tell me something deep?*" He picked up the joint and took a puff. "*Are you going to tell me things will work itself out? What the hell do you want?*"

Sasha expected this. It's not easy to come to the realization that your life was duped by a man who gave you a miserable human existence, then turning you immortal. "*Courtney, I understand your frustration, but you need to stop feeling sorry for yourself. Yes, he's still out there, but don't let that suede you from your goal.*"

"*What would you have me do, Sasha?*"

"*Go back to work. Let the girls train.*" He took a deep breath. "*The Mossad is still outside your doors just waiting for a chance to grab Avarie. We don't even know who tipped them off about her existence.*"

Courtney took another drag of his joint and put it out. "*So, you want me to go back to work and act like that sick fucker is still dead?*" Sasha nodded. "*You know, I'll still have that in the back of my head for the rest of my life. I can't live like that.*"

Courtney's phone started ringing. He picked it up and answered. "Boss?" It was Gerhart's voice.

"What's going on, man?" Courtney was feeling the effects of the weed and his head was starting to swoon. He plopped himself down on his couch and put his feet up.

"I know I only had a chance to speak to you briefly, but the Mossad broke into Alex's apartment the night we took care of her. Her electronic devices are gone." Gerhart wasn't happy to be giving him this information.

"Shit, there's a lot of company business on that laptop. Knowing her, she didn't have any safety nets on it either." Courtney responded.

"There's more."

"Alright."

"There's another player involved in this game."

Courtney's heart started to race. Looking over at Sasha, he motioned for him to take a seat. "Who?"

"We don't know. One of my guys who were tracking the Mossad found one of their burnt out vans by the river with their bodies in it." Gerhart didn't like this game at all. "Either somebody else is trying to protect us, or they want her bad enough to take out the competition."

"Fuck." Courtney yelled into the phone.

"This shit is serious, Courtney." Gerhart took a breath. "Look, I think the best thing for us right now is to lay low. Nobody leaves the house without protection, and that includes you."

Courtney knew that Gerhart had his best interests at heart. "Have they gone after Jude or anybody else?" he asked.

"No. I don't think they're aware of Jude at this moment. If they are, they haven't made any moves. We'll keep him close, though."

"Alright, why you think they went after Alex?" Courtney was curious.

"I think it's because they knew she was your personal assistant. She's the one who sent that video of you and Avarie around the company. It's possible somebody uploaded it on the Internet and they saw her. Plus, she has all the company information."

"Well, what's your suggestion at this point?"

"Come back to work starting tomorrow. I'll have my teams posted at your house. If Avarie feels like a ride, I'll have one of my boys escort her around. I don't want anybody's home to feel like a prison. I can send a car for you in the morning, if that's alright."

"That's fine." Courtney sighed in defeat.

"We still need to finish up our new center in France. Let's remember the main purpose for its existence right?"

"Yep."

"Good. I'll see you in the morning." Gerhart hung up and Courtney put the phone down.

Sasha sat there patiently with a smirk on his face. "You heard it all didn't you?" Sasha nodded. "Guess I don't have a choice but to go to work then huh?"

"You go to work, I watch the castle." Sasha said in broken English.

"So, you learned English?"

"Enough."

"Good. Now get the hell out of my room so I can go to bed. I have to work in the morning." Courtney said motioning to the door. Smiling, Sasha made his way out and into his own room. Leaving the door open, Georg wandered in. Sasha took off his shoes and threw them on the floor. As he undressed, the cat bounded up on his bed and meowed at him. "Give me a minute." Sasha cooed at him.

Cats were such curious and smart creatures, Sasha thought as he climbed into bed. Grabbing the laptop, he sat up as the cat made himself comfortable on the pillow next to him. "Well Georg, what topic should we explore tonight?" The cat just meowed at him. "Of course, we can find videos of cats for you." Sasha giggled as he pulled up YouTube and played funny cat videos the rest of the night.

ϒϒϒ

He stared out the window of his office in Moscow. Leaning back in his chair and putting his feet up on the window sill, he watched the politicians pass by on the busy street. He was expecting a call back from the Russian President; he needed the okay to drop more weapons to the American Militia. Three hangars waited with military cargo planes and they were already full and waiting for the word. Once they left, they would stop in Ireland to refuel and then make their way towards the drop zones in the States.

He grew impatient. He was tired of waiting around when this could've been done already. The Thirteen families of the New World Order could be wiped out in one fell swoop and humanity could start over. But no, President Konstantin didn't want an all-out war yet. He wanted to wait and weaken their defenses just enough and give the American's a chance to beat them back some more.

"Prime Minister?" He swirled around in his chair to face the man calling his name.

"Yes?" he hissed.

"A package came in for you." The small man sat it down on his desk. Opening it up, it was a flash drive. He inserted it into his computer and opened the files. The small man stated, "It's what you waited for and your brother is already on it." His eyes twinkled with joy.

Videos streamed of a young lady on a bike and in a pool naked. Leaning closer to peer into the screen, he opened another file. This one had her information and place of residence, date of birth and so on.

"Are we sure this is the one?" he asked.

Without hesitation the man answered, "Our Seeker found her. She resides with Courtney Cambridge. Somehow, he managed to find her after the escape." The man sat back pleased with himself.

That *stupid fucker*. He was supposed to bring her to Russia and he kept her all to himself. "Why isn't she here then?"

"Your brother says that the Mossad wants her and they've been stalking her. Naturally, Courtney's kept her locked up for the past two weeks."

He slammed his hands angrily on the desk. "Why am I just now hearing about this?" he screamed. "My brother better clean up this fucking mess or by God I'll chop him up in pieces and let the fish eat his body!"

"Calm down Kirill. Your brother is the best and it just so happens that the same could be said about Courtney's security team. Mikhail just can't take her in the middle of the night. We need to be diplomatic about this."

Kirill sat back in his chair. His anger seethed through him. Interrupting his thoughts, a call came through from the President giving him the go-ahead for the air drop team. Picking up the receiver of his phone again, he called the hangars and gave them their orders. Placing it back down he motioned for the man to sit.

"What do you suggest, Peter?" He had enough time to calm himself down as he waited for the answer.

"Your brother has already taken out one of the teams." Peter handed him a picture of a burnt out van with scorched bodies inside. "Let's just say he left a message to any Mossad left that they're in the wrong territory."

"What about the girl?" Kirill hissed in his direction.

Peter took off his glasses and cleaned them with his shirt, never taking his eyes off the man in front of him. "Call Courtney and bring him here to explain himself or you can just give him a call. It's quite obvious he's having some fun with her." Putting the glasses back on he continued, "Remind him that the plans haven't changed and she comes here to train."

Kirill thought about it. "Are the Mossad still in Freiburg?"

"Mikhail is cleaning them out as we speak. It seems they didn't send their best this time around."

"We'll contact Courtney when the Mossad is completely gone. I don't need those fucks meddling in our affairs. How did they know about her in the first place?"

"It's hard to say. They plant themselves everywhere these days."

"Can we go around Courtney? Who's the guy living with him? Is that his boyfriend of something?" Kirill questioned.

"That is Matthias. He's relation to Courtney. I believe a nephew of sorts." Peter sighed. "I can try to make an appointment with him."

Kirill thought about it. "No, let my brother handle the Mossad first. When we know she's safe, I'll contact Herr Cambridge."

Peter nodded in agreement and stood up. "Anything else, sir?"

"Yes. Make sure my brother doesn't fuck this up for me." As Peter walked out, Kirill kept watching the videos. He knew Courtney wouldn't give her up that easily. He was in love with her and that was obvious. The thought made him laugh. Too bad, he made a deal, and this girl was coming here with or without his consent.

Pandora Rising

CHAPTER TWO

As Gerhart promised, the car was there to pick him up in the morning around 6am. Leaving a note for the others he grabbed his coffee mug and headed out. The ride to work was without incident. As soon as he came into his office, Gerhart followed him in.

"Her family reported her disappearance. I need you to expect policemen today. They showed up yesterday, but I told them that you were indisposed at your home." Gerhart told him in a quiet whisper.

Courtney nodded. "Well, I have an alibi so I should be fine."

"And what's that?" Gerhart cocked an eyebrow in his direction.

"I was at home fucking my girlfriend." They both busted up laughing. They were both glad Alex was gone. Gerhart was more than happy to pick up the extra responsibilities. "What's on the agenda today?"

"I believe her family is coming in to pick up her personal belongings. They asked if they could and I gave them permission. They'll be calling before they get here. I could put you in a meeting with the engineers, or you can help me plot demographics."

Courtney thought about it. With everything that was going on, it would be a good idea to be distracted. Gerhart took care of more than Courtney could ask for. He was a good man. "How about I help you with your demographics? We can talk more in privacy then."

"Sounds like a good idea to me." Gerhart agreed.

Courtney grabbed his laptop, poured himself another cup of coffee, and they made their way to an empty conference room.

ΨΨΨ

The others woke up late. Sasha was already in the kitchen drinking hot tea and reading the newspaper. He didn't bother to wake them up after Courtney left. He liked the peace and quiet afforded him while they rested. The cat hardly left his side the entire night. Now Georg was underneath the chair, rubbing his body against Sasha's feet. He reached down and scratched his ear as Eva came into the kitchen.

"Did you make breakfast, Sasha?" she asked while reaching into the fridge.

"No, I don't cook." He said as he looked at her from behind his paper. Not far behind her was Matthias. He turned on the coffee maker while rubbing his eyes.

"Is Courtney awake yet?" Matthias asked Sasha.

His eyes never left the paper when he responded, "He went to work. He left note."

Picking up the piece of paper, Matthias read it to himself. "By God he did. You convince him to go?"

Shaking his head Sasha responded, "No, Gerhart did."

Eva started making four plates of food as Avarie entered in her workout gear. "Before you ask, your boyfriend went to work and he sends his love." Matthias said.

Avarie stopped dead in her tracks with a confused look on her face. "Wow, I didn't expect that. I thought maybe he'd be plotting revenge or something without me." She thanked Eva for the plate of food as Matthias handed her a cup of coffee.

"Revenge not in cards today." Sasha stated harshly. "Neither for you, or Courtney." He folded down his newspaper and started to eat. "Matthias work in office, we work downstairs."

Eva smiled over at him. "You planned our day, Sasha?"

"No, it business as usual, goal not change." He smeared butter onto his toast and took a bite. Avarie peered over at him. He was definitely ready for something. He wore sweat pants and one of Courtney's t-shirts that were a size too small for him. Avarie thought about how handsome his electric blue eyes were. They really brought out his toned olive skinned body and black hair. Catching her watching him he asked, "Why you look at me like that?" Avarie broke her gaze and looked away.

"Because you look like you're going to break out of that shirt, Sasha." Eva quipped. Oh thank God for Eva. Avarie picked at her food and Matthias watched her with a sly grin.

"You know, I'd like to go back to the time when you didn't notice guys." Matthias couldn't help himself. "I think that was for the first two weeks you were here." He let out a soft chuckle and Eva nudged his ribs with her elbow.

"Shut up! For God's sake she can look! Lord knows I am." Avarie noticed she was watching Sasha as he ate too. Avarie blushed and quickly cleared her plate. She left without saying a word as the cat followed.

Sasha watched her leave as he took a bite of his toast. "What does that mean?" He asked Eva.

"It means she was checking you out and she got caught." Matthias answered for her. "She finds you attractive and obviously so does Eva." He turned in her direction. "Maybe I should supervise training today?"

Sasha still looked confused. "No, I work with them; you work on your....machine." He waved Matthias off.

"I guess your job as a cleaner is done. I'm sure your last paycheck will come in the mail." Matthias changed the subject.

"I guess." Eva said as she put her plate in the sink. Her job didn't really matter anymore. She had to call in so many times because of Avarie, it was probably a good thing she quit. Avarie was almost a full time job within itself, but she wouldn't have it any other way.

Sasha clapped his hands together as he stood up, "We go now." Waving towards Eva, they headed downstairs. Matthias cleaned up the dishes and headed for his office.

Watching the monitors, all was quiet on the grounds. He debated about walking around outside, but decided against it. Sasha was right; he needed to work on his machine so Eva could have enhanced strength. Feeling a bit safer, Matthias got to work, but first, he needed to get a hold of Gill. He checked online to see if he made his flight and he wasn't listed. Picking up his phone, he dialed and it just rang. *Fuck.* He'll try again later.

ϓϓϓ

Sasha had the girls sitting on the mat with their legs crossed. He wanted to teach them meditation. The ancients used this to align their strengths and gather the forces of the universe within them. That was until the Elite bastardized it to the point that it was seen as evil. The ancient art of Kabbalah was used as a force to become closer to the universe and it was being used as evil. He wasn't having any of that. Eva had a very powerful force within her and he wanted her to harness it. She was a spiritual being and her heritage was passed down through her ancestry.

He spent the rest of the morning showing them yoga poses. It didn't have much to do with fighting, but that was okay. The point of all this was to ready their bodies for any battle. He was sweating so much; he had to take off his top. He rubbed the sweat from his body using his shirt and caught the eyes of both girls who stared at him making stupid faces. Avarie was blushing and Eva didn't even bother looking away.

Looking at himself he asked, "Is something wrong?"

Eva cracked a huge smile and said, "You're just so damn beautiful." Sasha busted up laughing. He'd never understand the human female. Looking at himself again, he almost forgot about the tattoos that the warrior had when he passed on. They complemented his body well. Avarie kept her eyes to the floor as Sasha prepared them for the next round of yoga. Getting back on the floor, he explained the 'wheel pose' and bent his body backwards. Eva followed as did Avarie. Her heart raced faster as she turned her head towards Sasha and watched all his muscles flex. He turned to look at her and smiled. *What the hell is wrong with me? s*he thought.

Her thoughts were interrupted by a high pitched wail and Matthias walking into the room. "Alright, the monitor is working again, but I don't know who it's going off for?" he yelled in annoyance. Dropping back to the ground, all three sat up as Matthias waved his wand around Avarie, then Sasha.

"Well I'll be, it's Sasha." He declared as he shut the alarm off. "At least

I know it still works." Walking across the room, Matthias grabbed towels and threw them at each person. "It's time for lunch."

They dried off and went upstairs. Sasha still had his shirt off as he bit into his sandwich. The cat came and joined them. Giving him bits of meat and bread, he meowed his thanks to Avarie. A phone went off. The girls left their phones in the kitchen as to not be disturbed. Matthias picked it up and answered with a full mouth. It was Courtney and they chatted for a bit. Hanging up the phone Matthias looked at Avarie. "It turns out that you have a visitor coming in about an hour. When you get done here, you need to go upstairs and put on your riding gear. Same with you, Eva." He said between bites.

"What about Sasha?" Avarie asked.

"He's coming too." Matthias replied. Sasha looked around confused. "We're going on a bike ride, Sasha. You ever heard of a motorcycle?" He shook his head.

"He doesn't even have riding gear." Eva quipped. "He can't even ride a motorcycle, Matthias."

Matthias looked around and a doorbell rang. "He does now. I'll be right back ladies." He said as a smile crossed his lips. He ran out of the kitchen to the front door. It wasn't until a few minutes later that he came back with a large box.

"Here Sasha, Courtney didn't forget about you." Opening the box, he pulled out chaps and a leather jacket. Sasha looked even more confused at the crotchless leather pants. "You wear jeans under it." Matthias said as he rolled his eyes and pulled out a pair of jeans. "Courtney said you're the same size in the waist but a few inches taller. If you need too, I'll help you put on your gear."

Avarie's hand went to her mouth as Eva nudged her elbow into her. Matthias gave them a sharp look. "Oh for *God's* sake! Sasha, I don't know if I like the idea of them two alone with you." Sasha just threw up his hands in the air. "Damn perverts." Matthias shook his head.

With lunch finished, they all changed and met downstairs in the great room but had to wait on Sasha. "Well, is he coming down?" Eva asked.

"He better." Matthias replied.

As soon as he spoke those words, Sasha carefully descended the stairs. Avarie's eyes went wide. *This man was not their Sasha.* Eva and Avarie exchanged looks. Sasha trimmed his goatee and his hair while he was upstairs and the sunglasses that came with the delivery were sitting on the top of his head. The riding gear was almost like Avarie's: white and black. As Sasha joined them at the bottom, Avarie quickly looked down, but noticed he also had the boots to go with it. "Are we ready?" Matthias asked. Everybody nodded and walked down into the garage.

Avarie was excited to take Black Betty out again but a realization hit her, "What about the Mossad?" she asked Matthias.

"Don't worry; we have company with us today." He gave her a wink. Opening a door to where the motorcycles were stored, Sasha walked in first. "Who's he going to ride with?" Eva asked. "He can't fit on Avarie's bike, he's too big."

Sasha looked around while Avarie pulled out her bike. "Can he even drive one?" Eva asked. Avarie just shrugged her shoulders. Sasha found something interesting and pointed at it. It was a Yamaha Tesseract. Pulling the keys from the holder Matthias threw them at him and Sasha smiled as he caught the keys and pulled the bike out. Naturally, Eva went for Big Red.

"I bet he could. Never know what this guy knows for sure." Matthias said as he slapped Sasha on the back.

Sasha smiled as he put the key in the ignition and fired it up. He looked behind him as the girls stared in awe. Sasha climbed on and kicked it into gear and moved it forward, but it jerked to a stop. He repeated the process and they all thought he was having issues. Turning around to face them, he brought his sunglasses down and yelled, "Just kidding." as he did a burnout in the garage.

Avarie's heart skipped a beat and Matthias busted up laughing. "He's got the internet remember?" Matthias and Eva got on their motorcycle and started it up. Avarie hopped on and joined them as they drove out. Meeting them in the driveway was none other than Xander.

"Nice to see you feel better." He said on top of his bike. Avarie was elated to see him. They all introduced themselves and drove down the road. As they neared the end of the driveway, a whole gang of motorcyclist met them on the highway. "I brought my friends with me, if you don't mind. Courtney explained the situation so I rounded up my people. They wanted to ride with the Renegade."

Excitement rolled through Avarie as she looked over the sea of people. There had to be at least 50 of them. Eva laughed with excitement and so did Sasha. It would definitely be hard for the Mossad to get to her with this many people.

"Are you ready?" Xander asked her. Nodding her head, she revved up her engine and they were off down the highway. This was going to be a great day, Avarie thought as the wind blew through her hair. Sasha was doing great on his ride. He didn't do any tricks, but he handled that bike well. If he learned that off the internet, she wondered what else he learned. It was strange because it seemed like he processed information quickly. Picking up English and communicating with everybody was somewhat obvious. That was a necessity. Soon, she knew he'd learn German and many other languages.

She watched the other riders around her as they claimed the highway, shielding her from whatever harm would come. Avarie almost felt like crying. These people didn't know her and they were willing to put themselves in harm's way just to keep her safe. Refocusing, she shifted gears through a curve with Xander beside her. The landscape changed and the day grew dark. Her headlight focused in front of her through brush and debris. She didn't know where she was and the people disappeared. Bullets flew by her head as she dodged them while leaning low into her motorcycle. Hearing voices in the distance, she turned to find them.

"Avarie!" Snapping back to reality, it was Xander. The landscape changed back to the present and she was riding the ditch. *Oh fuck!* Pulling her beast back onto the road, Xander signaled the other riders to pull into the nearest field. As they did, Xander jumped off his bike along with Eva, Matthias, and Sasha.

"Are you okay?" he asked. "It's like you just zoned off into the distance after we hit that curve." Avarie had no clue what was going on inside her head. Certain things set off memories of her past life and she couldn't control it."

"I'm fine, Xander." Avarie said.

Eva pulled Avarie to the side and whispered, "What did you see?" After explaining the image to her group, Sasha chimed in. "How often this happen?"

"It happens more than I like." Avarie admitted. She saw the other riders gawking at her concerned. "How do I control it?" she asked Sasha.

He went deep into thought. "You focus on what you do. When surroundings change, you change them back."

Xander came back up to them. "They're ready to ride when you guys are. I just told them you were recently sick and gotten light headed for a minute. They understand." Avarie nodded.

Back on the highway, they rode for three hours straight and Avarie didn't have any more vision issues for the rest of the ride. Relief swept over her as they took a small break at a lake.

"Is it better?" Sasha asked. Nodding her head, he patted her back. Somebody brought a guitar with them and they started a sing along. One person begged Avarie to sing and they all joined in. Giving in, Avarie took a request. Xander was a fan of Don Henley and his buddy knew all his songs. She sang *Last Worthless Evening* for them. Everybody joined in on the chorus and Avarie looked in Sasha's direction as he bobbed his head up and down.

Eva asked the question that was on both their minds. "Sasha, can you sing?" The song was over and all eyes were on him. "Not very well." He stated in a matter of fact tone. "There is reason I only sing in shower." Laughter filled the air as another song started up. There were ladies in the group who moved closer to Sasha and Avarie blushed. They knew he was damn good looking too. He looked like a different man all up in that leather.

After their break was done, the entire gang headed back to the castle. Once there, they all bid each other a good night and safe ride home. Yes, this was a good day.

ϒϒϒ

Courtney was waiting for them all in the kitchen when they arrived. Avarie spotted him first and ran into his arms. He gave her a long lingering kiss and asked, "Did you miss me, *Schatz*?"

Avarie started laughing. "I thought you were plotting revenge without me!"

"Oh no, I have to work and keep a roof over your heads." He winked at the others as he hugged Avarie tight. "I brought food home so we don't have to cook." Courtney said setting out Chinese takeout on the table. "How was your ride?"

"It was awesome! I didn't know Xander had an entire army out there." Eva exclaimed as she started to set the table. Avarie nodded in agreement.

"I take it you rode too, Sasha?" Courtney asked him. Nodding his head, this was the first time that Courtney got a good look at him. "Holy shit, I did good when I picked out your gear."

"Don't worry, the ladies noticed too." Matthias said glaring at Courtney.

"Which ones?"

"The ones in this room." Matthias started handing out the silverware. "Avarie was practically drooling once he walked downstairs."

Courtney cocked an eyebrow at her and she quickly looked away. Turning his head towards Sasha he said, "Really?" Sasha just shrugged. "I don't think Sasha notices these things." Courtney said as he picked up his chopsticks and took a seat at the table. They all sat and dished out food onto their plates.

"I don't think he's that clueless about women." Matthias met Sasha's eyes. "He knows when the girls are looking at him." Matthias threw out a hint of jealousy. Eva slapped him on the arm.

"Don't get jealous, Matthias." Eva kissed him on the cheek. "He's easy on the eyes, what can we say?"

"Shit, if I were a chick, I'd fuck him." Everybody looked in Courtney's direction as he shoveled Lo Mein noodles in his mouth. "What?"

"Don't get them started, Courtney." Matthias warned. "Before you know it, they'll have strange fantasies that I really don't want to indulge in."

Courtney almost choked on his food and busted into laughter. "I don't think I want to put him through that." Sasha slowly shook his head back and forth. "Welcome to the family you poor bastard." Courtney said as he raised his wine glass. They all raised their glasses and toasted Sasha.

Finishing their meal, Matthias suggested that they go swim. They had to get Avarie back into her routine. Once at the poolside, Eva and Avarie stripped down and went in first. Sasha watched them in wonder.

"Strip down, Sasha." Matthais was already taking off his clothes and the girls turned around. "No ladies! New person at the pool, turn around." They both huffed a bit and giggled. Courtney shook his head as he stripped off his business suit. Jumping in, he grabbed Avarie and floated with her.

Matthias motioned for him to hurry up. He was still in his riding gear and had problems taking off the chaps. Matthias shook his head in annoyance and started to help him get them off. The girls turned around and started cat calling, "Woo hoo! Take it off for him, Matthias" Courtney turned them both back around and told them to behave themselves.

"Fucking women man!" he said. "Everything is sexual with them and Eva's the worst." The chaps were off and Sasha could finally strip down. Courtney herded the ladies together and covered their view. Sasha jumped in with Matthias right behind him.

Sasha stayed away from the women. He wasn't sure what to expect from them. "Are they always this way?" Sasha asked Matthias. "When I first came here, the women weren't like this at all."

"I'm telling you man, there's a difference between women in your day, and women in ours." Matthias answered and shaking his head. "Better keep your distance from these two."

Sasha started laughing and swam towards the deep end. Courtney reached over the ledge to grab pool noodles and the boys joined together for a noodle fight while Eva and Avarie watched on. They were glad the boys weren't getting too rough. Sasha was a natural swimmer and it seemed as though he was part of the water.

"Avarie, what're we going to do with all these men?" Eva asked her with a strange twinkle in her eye.

Avarie chuckled and answered, "I know what I'm going to do with one." Diving underwater, she opened her eyes and came back up instantly. "Oh my God, Eva." Avarie pulled on her. "Take a peek under there." Avarie said in a hoarse whisper. Giving her a strange look, Eva dove under and came back up.

"If you're talking about Sasha, let's just say he's blessed in more ways than one." The girls were giggling to themselves.

The pool noodle fight stopped. "What are you ladies giggling about?"

Courtney turned in their direction with a noodle in the air.

Eva answered him with, "Avarie just said your hair looks nice." And they continued giggling.

"They're laughing at us." Matthias whispered to the guys. Sasha had another confused look on his face. "Maybe we should teach them a lesson." He said as he whipped his pool noodle in the air. Courtney nodded in agreement and Sasha went along with it.

The girls were too busy talking to notice the guys behind them. Picking them up out of the water, the boys dunked the girls in. Avarie wasn't prepared and she inhaled water into her lungs. When she came back up, she coughed it out while clinging to Courtney's wet body. "I'm sorry, *Schatz*. I didn't mean to drown you." Avarie still went into coughing fits Sasha came up to her and with one deep thrust, jammed his hand into her rib cage. The rest of the water was expelled into the pool. "Thanks, Sasha." Avarie said breathlessly.

"Maybe we should get out of the pool before we kill each other." Matthias suggested as he started climbing out.

Kissing her forehead Courtney looked into her eyes. "Are you alright, *Maus*?"

Taking in a deep breath she answered, "I'm fine; I know you didn't mean it." Every one climbed out of the pool and wrapped towels around themselves. Courtney went into the pool house to grab some beers.

Pulling up a fifth chair to the table, they all talked about their day and Courtney announced he was visited by the police for questioning in Alex's disappearance.

"Is she dead?" Eva asked

Courtney thought about it before answering. "I don't know. If she is, we know who to look at and it's not me. Somebody broke into her apartment stealing the company laptop and her electronics. I wouldn't do that." He didn't want to tell them the truth, but Matthias knew. "Besides, I was here when she disappeared." He took a swig of his beer. Avarie looked concerned. She didn't want Alex to get hurt, even though she almost cut her throat that one day. She only shook her head.

Sasha downed his beer quickly. It wasn't like the type he used to drink. It was thicker and had more of a wheat taste to it. The others could only watch him in awe. "You want see trick?" Sasha asked in his signature broken English. They said they did and he made his way to the side of the pool. With his presence, the water started making small waves towards him. They all watched in astonishment as Sasha made a parting motion with his hands and the water parted all the way down to the concrete floor.

"Holy shit!" Matthias jumped out of his chair as Sasha let the water return. "How the hell did you do that?"

"I can only do with water." Sasha winked at them and sat back down.

"Now wait a minute!" Eva waved her hand at him. "What else can you do with water?"

He turned over in her direction and started waving his hand again. Behind him, they watched as the water turned into a fountain and then back down again. Eva spun towards Avarie. "He's a damn water deity." That explained how he was so good with water.

"Well, he isn't called a gargoyle for no reason ladies." Matthias took another swig of his beer and finished it off.

Courtney did the same with his and finished Avarie's too. "Well ladies, I'm ready for bed and I have to work in the morning. If you want, you can watch the water show, but I have business I have to take care of." As he stood up, Avarie joined him. She was tired and missed Courtney today. They grabbed their clothes and walked hand in hand out of the pool area.

Courtney walked her all the way to her bedroom door. "I'd bring you into my room tonight, *Schatz*, but I don't sleep well when you're in there." he said giving her a sly smile. "Don't worry though. I'll make a half day so I can spend time with you." She stood on her tip toes and kissed him on the cheek.

"Night, Courtney." She said as she opened the door to her room. Grabbing her arm he pulled her back out.

There was something he was meaning to ask her. "About yesterday, I'm sorry. It was a lot to hit you with. Are you doing okay?" Courtney's facial expression turned to concern.

Taking a deep breath she answered. "I don't remember it all, you know. Everything comes in flashes and in the most strange moments." Her voice trailed off. "It just seems like I don't remember anything *good*. The life I live now feels good and I like it." She was trying to be honest with him. It was true that she didn't remember much. She didn't even remember what the guy named Jace looked like. It was a different world and a different time. Courtney snapped his fingers in front of her. She spaced off again.

"Where'd you go this time?" he asked softly.

She started to shake her head, "Just lost in my thoughts, I guess." Her face turned sad and she looked like she was ready to cry. Courtney had an idea. "Wait here. I have something for you."

Quickly going to his bedroom, he threw his clothes on the floor and went into his closet. Turning on the light, he dug through Nikita's trunk. Finding what he was looking for, he brought it back to her.

"Before the shit hit the fan in the States, you had a beautiful life, Avarie." Folding the picture in her hand she brought it up to her face and studied it. It was her with three small children laying in the grass and smiling. He hoped it didn't upset her too much, but these were her old memories of a life she once lived and she deserved to see them. Holding it to her chest, tears broke free and rolled down her cheeks.

"Thank you, Courtney." She whispered and pulled him into a hug.

"I want you to try and pull good memories through the veil. Don't let the sad ones creep in." He kissed her again. "Now get some sleep." She nodded as she turned for her door and he for his. "Hey Avarie?" Courtney said.

"Yea?"

"I love you." He meant it. He truly loved every part of her. If anything ever happened to her, he'd lose his mind.

"I love you too." She whispered back with a smile. Entering her room, she took deep breaths and wiped her eyes. Carefully, she placed the picture on her nightstand. Putting on a t-shirt and panties, she crawled into bed and hugged her pillow. It wasn't fair that her flashbacks were of sad and scary shit. She really wanted to dream about something nice for once. Staring at the picture, she asked the universe for one good dream. As her lids grew heavy, she nodded off and for once, the universe granted her wish.

CHAPTER THREE

It's been three days and no sign of the Mossad. Gerhart still had no clue who burnt out the van by the river and it bothered him. His entire field team has combed the city and the outskirts for any sign that may show other factions are involved. Regardless, he still had Courtney and his group remain on high alert. Gerhart was in the office building when he received a message from Damian. The new building in France is almost ready and they're doing a test run of the servers.

Courtney wanted to get them online within a week so he can continue his espionage efforts against the Elite. With better decryption chatter, they can decipher information faster and more accurately. Damian and Jude were at their stations and they telecommunicated to France to fire them up. Within minutes, the servers were capturing information. Courtney stood behind the two with Gerhart at his side as they watched the monitors filter binary information through.

"It looks like they're working." Gerhart said to Courtney. "What do you think they're gathering?"

Courtney thought about it, "I don't know, but it's a lot of chatter." He didn't expect this much information to come through so quickly. "We need to shut it down."

Damian and Jude turned their chairs towards him with a look of shock. "Why?" Jude asked.

Courtney swallowed hard and answered, "I don't think the system can handle that much information. Plus, we don't even know where all this is coming from." He stared at the screens as data filed through.

Jude gave the order to shut it down. Damian was lost in thought as he punched codes into the system. "I think we can make a program that can filter out the nonsense. We can build another server room just for the information we need, and leave our current one alone for pure communications." Damian grabbed blue prints of the system and threw them down on a fold up table. "Gerhart, see this room here?" Damian pointed at a box like shape. "We can put the servers in here."

"Alright, so how do we retrieve the information?" He asked. Courtney was wondering the same thing.

Jude chimed in, "We can filter the information through another computer out of the country and make sure the information doesn't ping back to the location that it's coming from."

Courtney cocked an eyebrow at him, "So we block the source location?"

"Exactly, this way, your information can only be found on one database and if you have a breach, nobody can know where the information is coming from." Jude wore a shit eating grin. He knew how this game was played. Courtney and Gerhart exchanged looks. The only problem was, they'd have to get another permit to install servers and keep that room temperature controlled.

"How do we bypass the permits?" Courtney looked at Gerhart for the answer.

"Fuck the permits. I can have my boys in France work on it and nobody would be the wiser."

"Keeping people out of the room?"

"Ever heard of hidden doors?" Oh he was good. Courtney knew all too well about hidden doors.

"You two agreed?" Courtney looked over at the other two.

"Let's do it." Damian became excited and the game plan was on. All four spent the entire day planning out more secret servers.

ɤɤɤ

On his way back to his office, Claudia handed Courtney a message. "They didn't leave a name, just a number." Claudia walked back to her desk and sat down. Opening his office door, he sat behind his desk. Unfolding the message, his heart stopped. *Oh fuck no.* The number was to the Russian Prime Minister's office and he knew this couldn't be good.

Hesitantly, he picked up the receiver and dialed the number. After a few rings, a man picked up.

"Prime Minister's office."

"This is Courtney Cambridge, I was told to call." He tried to keep his cool but inside his chest, his heart thumped against his ribcage.

"Just a minute." said the man with the thick Russian dialect. Courtney was placed on hold until another man answered.

"Ah, Herr Cambridge. Nice of you to call back." *Fuck*, it was Kirill, the Prime Minister of Russia. Whatever he had to say to Courtney wouldn't be good. This man had a temper of a hungry snake.

"What do you need?" Courtney calmed himself.

"I need the *girl*!" The Russian hissed at the other end. "You promised Russia that she'd come here as soon as she was ready so we can train her. Why may I ask, isn't she here?"

Good God, Courtney shook his head. "Because she isn't *ready*!" Courtney quietly yelled into the phone. "Why now? I kept in contact with your men while she was in stasis and for the last thirteen years, heard *nothing*." He breathed deep. "You *fucks* dropped the ball on me. I had to shift my life around to accommodate her and now you want me to just send her over there? Not a snowballs chance in Hell, Kirill."

"We shut down communications for a reason." Kirill's voice started to boom over the receiver. "It was my men who guarded the stasis room and allowed her escape."

"Well congratulations, she was in the damn wilderness for three days before we found her."

"I don't give a shit. She's alive and we want her."

"She's being trained here, so you can fuck off."

"And, who's supposed to train her?" Kirill was pushing his buttons. For a man Courtney has never met before, this guy got under his skin.

"Gill McCullum." There was silence on the other line.

"Irishman?" Kirill asked finally.

"Yes, the Irishman."

"He'd be good if he wasn't found dead in his home four days ago." Kirill laughed on the other end.

"How?" Courtney was becoming seriously pissed.

"The same people who are after you."

"It seems their interest died down."

"No, they're still interested, Herr Cambridge." Kirill sighed. "My brother has been keeping them at bay for you." Alright, Courtney thought. This is why there haven't been signs of the Mossad. "Now, you owe me for keeping all of you safe and sound, don't you think?"

"I've kept her safe since she arrived."

"Yes, I've seen the evidence of you 'keeping her safe'." Kirill laughed heartily on the other end of the line. "Letting her run away and fucking her isn't exactly what I would call safe."

Now Courtney was pissed. "Are you jealous that I got to taste the goods, Kirill?"

"She's not my type." He hissed. "Besides, you're weak and you fucked up. Soon, I'll come to get her." He threatened. "When I do, you better remember your contract." The line went dead.

Courtney put down the receiver as panic flooded his body. Collecting his things, he rushed out the door. Calling Gerhart on the way to his escort vehicle, he filled him in. Gerhart wasn't only looking for Mossad agents, but now the FSB.

ϒϒϒ

He came into the great room and found it empty. He hoped he would run into Matthias before he found Avarie. Speed walking towards Matthias' work area, he spotted him setting up a strange machine. "Matty!" Courtney hissed and motioned for him to come here.

"What man, can't you see I'm in the middle of something?" Matthias gave him an annoyed look.

"They're coming for her!" he hissed again. Matthias met his gaze and almost dropped his tools on his foot. "He called me today at the office, he knows she's here and he wants her now."

"Did you tell them that I have Gill coming to train her?"

"Gill's dead!" Matthias' face went pale. "That's why we couldn't reach him, Matty."

Striding over towards Courtney, he said, "*Jesus Christ*. Avarie has no clue does she?" Courtney shook his head.

"They've dropped contact over thirteen years ago. I assumed they weren't interested in her anymore and that's why I hadn't brought it up." Courtney kept shaking his head. "The deal was never made with Kirill; it was made with Konstantin way before he became President."

"So what now?" Matthias was running his hands through his hair. "Kirill is bad news and he always takes what he wants. You know how they are."

"I can hide her." Courtney said defiantly.

"The Hell you can! You don't hide from these people, Courtney." Matthias kicked a garbage can across the room in anger. "They're coming to our damn doorstep to take her."

"Take who?" Avarie asked as she stood in the doorway wiping her face with a towel. Simultaneously, Courtney and Matthias' hearts stopped. "Well?" she asked again.

Looking into each other's eyes, they silently agreed to tell her. With a heavy heart, Courtney led her and Matthias out into the great room. Rounding up Sasha and Eva, they sat down at the sitting area near the fireplace.

ϒϒϒ

"Avarie, before you were created, Matthias and I made a deal with the Russians. We would code your information and set you up in the research facility in the States under the guise of a project for the Elite and for the Russians cooperation; they would protect you while you were there and ensure we could get you out." Courtney waited for a response. She looked at him blankly and he continued. "The deal was, I set you up here and when you were ready, you go to Russia to train with their FSB."

"Why do they want her so soon?" Eva asked.

"Because they know the Mossad is onto her and they want her out of danger." Matthias answered for him. "They know that Gill McCullum was killed too."

Sasha listened to the conversation quietly. The cat jumped onto his lap and he stroked Georg's fur.

"Avarie, they're coming here to get you. I don't know when, but the FSB are just as dangerous as the Mossad. I can't hide you away from them." Tears from anger were forming in Courtney's eyes. "When you were almost six years old, they dropped all forms of contact. That's when Matthias and I made alternate plans for you. Had I known they were actually going through with this, I would've told you sooner."

She didn't look happy. In fact, she was raging pissed. Matthias looked at his monitor and realized it didn't work on her anymore. He made a mental note to take it off.

"So you're telling me that I have to go into another strange land, with strange people, in order to be trained because it was a *deal* that you guys made over twenty years ago?" Courtney sadly nodded his head. Slowly standing up, she acted like she was going to walk away. Instead, she slapped both Courtney and Matthias across their heads. "I told you that you should've just let me run." She hissed while bounding up the stairs for her room.

Matthias rubbed his forehead. "I think she took that well." A door slammed overhead, vibrating through the castle walls. "In fact, I think she's feeling alright about going to Russia." He said sarcastically.

Eva and Sasha sat silently staring at the other two. Breaking the silence, Sasha said, "I can hide her." He crossed his arms. "I can take her back to my world if you want." He was being serious.

"They won't stop looking for her, Sasha." Courtney put his head in his hands. "While she hides with you, we'll all be in danger. They'll take down everything I built just to get her back."

"Then she has to go." Eva said softly. She didn't want that for Avarie, but Courtney made it clear, these are people you don't mess with. "Will they at least treat her well?"

Neither Matthias nor Courtney had that answer. "Put stipulations on them. Otherwise Avarie will find a way to run if she can." Sasha looked straight at them. "You have a bargaining chip. If she gets harmed, they get exposed." *Damn, Sasha can play this game too*, Courtney thought.

"You've been in this situation before?" Courtney asked.

Sasha took in a deep breath. "I have. However, that was another life and I don't want to recall the details. Right now, we need to prepare her for the inevitable." His language skills were improving like crazy. If he could pick up on English this good, imagine how well he'd do with more complicated speech patterns.

"Alright, but until they come, nothing changes. They still have to abide by their contract. When she gets done training she comes back here." Courtney didn't sound very confident.

"Yea, but how long will she train?" Matthias wasn't sure about this plan at all. "Will this guy give us a date?"

"I don't know. But when he gets here we'll find out his intentions."

"When is he coming?"

"Sooner than later."

"*Oh Hell.*" Matthias stood up and walked out. Avarie didn't have a chance to prepare. The Russians dropped the ball years ago and now they want her. Eva followed him into the kitchen while Sasha looked at Courtney.

"She's stronger than you know." Sasha said reassuringly. "Now get upstairs and apologize to her." Sasha stood up and stretched out. "She may be mad at you, but these are circumstances beyond your control." He patted Courtney's shoulder and headed for the kitchen.

Courtney went upstairs and knocked on her door, there was no answer. He opened it and found her on the bed, hugging her pillow tight with blank eyes. Sitting next to her he dared to wrap his arm around her shoulder.

"Avarie, I'm sorry. I had no clue this is what they wanted. I haven't heard from them for thirteen years and here they are out of the blue, wanting you now." Her body felt warm against his. She laid her head down in his lap and he stroked her hair. "It's alright to be mad at me. I tried for years to get somebody to respond. Their excuse was that they had to drop contact because the Elite were onto you."

"Did you ever think this was a possibility?" she asked through hot tears.

"I did at first. They knew you were out of the facility. The guards in the stasis rooms were put there by the FSB. I had no phone calls and no contact from Agent Zero. If he died, nobody told me." Courtney was being honest with her. "That's why you got the choice to either live a normal life here, or go on to fight. The Russians wouldn't give you that choice."

"Do they know who I really am?" she asked softly.

"Hell no. And you don't tell them either." Word about her reincarnation didn't need to get out. "Pandora dealt with the Russians before. I know this from her friend Jace. So, if you meet a man named Konstantin, that's who you dealt with. He was a former FSB agent also. He supplied you with the tools and I did the communications."

"Did I actually meet him face to face?" Avarie asked. Courtney knew she didn't remember her full past. Maybe it was for the better.

"That I can't be so sure of. So he may not recognize you or maybe he will."

"That's not good." She said as she turned her head into his stomach. Even when she was vulnerable, she managed to turn him on. Right now, he wanted nothing more than to take her right here. However, his stomach told him that he was hungry and he couldn't do much on an empty stomach.

"Avarie, you're more than ready to go with them." It broke his heart, but he needed to build up her confidence. "As much as I'd hate to be without you and not knowing what's going on, you have to go."

"If I didn't, you'd all be in danger." She closed her eyes and wiped her tears with Courtney's expensive suit shirt.

"That's right." God he hated this. "When they do come for you, be on your best behavior. Don't flip them shit and don't try and run." *Fucking Russians.* "Do what they say or else they'll pay you back tenfold."

"What if they ask things of me that I'm not comfortable with?" She turned around and looked up at him.

"Like what?" Courtney had no clue what she was getting at.

"Like…the things we do." Wow, he didn't think about that.

"Let's say if you're asked for sexual favors, make them work for it." Courtney winked at her. He didn't think that was how the FSB operated, but you never know. He hoped that isn't something that they would ask of her. "I'm hungry and I could use some food. Would you come back downstairs and eat with us?"

Pushing her ear into his stomach, she heard rumbling sounds. "Alright. Your stomach is growling at me." Sitting herself up, she hung her legs over the edge of the bed. "We can talk game plan over supper."

Courtney felt little relief. He was glad Avarie wasn't too terribly pissed at him. On the other hand, he knew he had little time with her and he'd break down after she left. He decided as they walked down the stairs to make the most of their time together.

ϒϒϒ

None of this felt real to Avarie. To her, it was another illusion. Two days ago, things were fine. The Mossad was off their backs and her and Eva trained with Sasha. She asked Courtney if he knew when the Russians would show up and he always told her the same thing, "I don't know." The prospect of leaving scared her and she would be on her own. She debated on running off and how she would get away with it. But it was no use; she couldn't hide from these people without dire consequences.

It was the weekend and Courtney promised to spend as much time with her as possible. Tonight, he was taking her out to eat. Eva called it a "real date" considering that he'd never taken Avarie out before. She had no clue where she was going. Eva helped her get ready and she was excited for Avarie as this would be a milestone for her. Courtney picked out a black see through bra with black crotch less panties. She would wear a tight black dress with a matching garter and thigh high boots.

"What's with the underwear and bra?" Avarie asked Eva as she looked in the mirror.

Eva started chuckling. "Obviously, he's got plans for you *after* dinner." Eva helped her slip on the dress and zip it up, careful not to mess up her hair. She added a pearl necklace with matching earrings. "Better make sure you have condoms."

"Oh no….." Avarie didn't even think about it the last time. Eva warned her that she could get pregnant and even though she didn't quite understand the concept, she knew Eva would be disappointed.

"Don't tell me he didn't wear one the last time either?" Avarie could only shake her head in shame. "Well this time, he will!" She decided that Matthias could throw a box in Courtney's room for later. "Alright, all done. Now turn around." Avarie spun around for her as the black dress lifted up to reveal the garter on her left thigh. "Perfect. I think he's waiting for you downstairs."

Eva walked with her down the staircase. Courtney came into sight in a gorgeous tuxedo and shiny black shoes. Matthias and Sasha were waiting for her also. With a shit eating grin, Courtney took her arm in his. "Damn, maybe we should skip dinner."

"No you don't!" Eva scolded. "You treat her like a lady before you even think about taking her back upstairs."

"I was just kidding." Courtney started laughing. "Shall we?" Avarie nodded. She was nervous. This was her first date ever and she had no clue how she was supposed to act or where she was even going. Courtney walked her outside and Avarie gasped. A huge black limo waited for them in the driveway and a man opened the door for them.

Riding in the backseat, Courtney opened a bottle of wine and poured them a glass. Every now and then, he'd kiss her cheek or stroke the dark tendrils of her hair. His eyes never left her body. "I think I did well when I picked out that dress for you."

"I think you did good picking out your suit." Avarie said with a smile. He was extremely handsome with his hair trimmed and spiked up a bit. He shaved yesterday, but he had some scruff and that made it that much sexier to her. The limo finally pulled up to the restaurant and the driver opened the door for them. It was an exclusive place by reservation only. Walking in, they were greeted by a server. Courtney gave his name and they were led to a private table outside on a terrace.

Another server came and poured wine. Everywhere she looked, there were people dressed up just like they were. Courtney explained that it was a black tie affair and the cheapest thing here was a $5 glass of water. Before he made the date with her he told her that he didn't want to talk about Russia or anything else that had to do with training. This was their night and he wanted her to enjoy it. Still, it was on the back of her mind. This could possibly be the last night they have together and she prayed that it would last.

"Why are you so sad?" Courtney asked as he took her hand in his. Avarie felt like she was on the verge of tears. "Don't cry Avarie. This is our night, remember?" When she looked up at him, he looked the same.

"I'm sorry." She said as she swallowed a lump, forcing it back down into her throat. The server came just in time to take their order. He was a small enough distraction for her to calm herself. A band started up and Courtney asked her to dance.

"Don't we have to wait for our food?" she asked.

He chuckled. "No, we can dance for a few songs. We'll know when they bring the food. Don't worry." Escorting her to the dance floor, he pulled her close. Wrapping his hands around her waist, she brought hers around his neck. Avarie had to stand on her tip toes because Courtney was so tall. He laughed at her and said, "Maybe I should've gotten you high heels instead."

"If you did it would hurt worse when I accidently step on your feet."

"*Touché.* I never figured you for a high heel kind of girl anyway." Avarie smiled at him and blushed. She looked around the dance floor and noticed people looking at her and Courtney. Suddenly she became self-conscience and stared at her feet. Courtney brought her back to attention by lifting her chin up with his finger. "Don't worry about them. They just know a beautiful woman when they see one."

It made Avarie feel a bit better. After two more songs their food was ready. Leading her back to the table they ate in silence. Avarie looked up every now and then to find men occasionally looking in her direction with soft smiles. The women didn't look so happy at her. Leaning back against his chair Courtney swirled his glass of wine and took sips as he watched her carefully eat. He glanced around too and noticed the reactions of the patrons around them. Avarie started to look out into the night sky to avoid their stares.

"Hey." Courtney said with a smirk. "All those men are looking at you because they know you're the most beautiful woman here tonight. And those ladies, they know it too. It seems you're the only one who doesn't know how beautiful you are."

That was the sweetest thing he's ever said to her. She didn't feel pretty at all. In fact, she felt out of her element. Eva always bitched at her when she noticed Avarie avoiding the mirror when she brushed her teeth or to just to pull back her hair. "Are you sure it's because I'm pretty or because I'm with you?" Avarie asked slyly.

Courtney thought about it then answered, "Maybe it's both." The server came back around, bringing them another wine bottle. Courtney said he didn't order it and the server explained that a man at the bar ordered it for them. Pointing in the direction of the bar, the man lifted his wine glass towards them and they followed suit. He was an older gentleman with dark graying hair and light green eyes. He smiled sweetly at both her and Courtney.

"Do you know him?"

"I don't, but he was nice enough to order us another bottle of wine so let's not let it go to waste." The server uncorked it and filled their glasses. After they were done eating, Courtney took her back out to the dance floor.

"I have another surprise before we go home." He whispered in her ear.

Excitement grew in Avarie. "What is it?" she asked.

"Oh no, you have to wait." Bending down, he kissed her softly on the lips and she blushed.

When the band stopped playing, Courtney paid for the bill and they entered the limo again. Avarie's head was starting to swoon from all the wine. "Are you alright?"

"I think I may be getting a little drunk." Avarie admitted. She's never drank so much before. Grabbing a bottle of water, he handed it to her.

"Drink this. I don't want you puking all over the place before we get there." Avarie downed the bottle and it made her feel a little better. Again, the limo stopped and the driver let them out. Walking up huge steps, they entered a building. It was an art gallery. Courtney showed her around and brought her to a painting. It was one of hers. He must've hijacked one of her pictures from under her bed. It was the canvas of Sasha's room she painted a while back. "See, now your work is displayed in an art gallery."

Tears of happiness streamed down her cheeks. Courtney pulled out a handkerchief and wiped her eyes. "Thank you." She whispered. "How'd you do that?"

"I just brought it in and they liked it."

"Really?"

"Really."

Avarie's heart welled up with joy. There were many emotions that were fighting inside her and she didn't know exactly how to feel. "Shall we look around some more?" he asked. She nodded and he led her down more hallways and corridors explaining the artwork on the walls. It was around midnight before they left for home.

Once there, Courtney picked her up in his arms and carried her all the way to his room. Kicking open and shutting his door, he quickly set her down on the bed. He glanced at his nightstand to see a box sitting there and started laughing. "I think somebody knew my plans for tonight." He gave Avarie a wink as he handed it to her and it was a box of condoms. Yep, this was Eva's work alright. Avarie started laughing. "Let me guess…Eva?" he asked smiling.

"Eva."

"That woman knows me too well…unless somebody was telling secrets." He said as he slowly took off his tie and blazer. Avarie looked guilty as she sat silently on his bed. Seductively leaning over her he whispered in her ear. "I hope you didn't tell her how you took advantage of me." Avarie started laughing.

"I think that's the other way around."

"Oh no, I recall the first time, somebody came to my door in the middle of the night sopping wet. The second time, that same person just wanted to nap and it turned all naughty."

"That was all in your head." She responded with a giggle. She stood up and unbuttoned his shirt. Slowly sliding it off his body, she grazed her lips over his chest. He moaned softly. "I think you like that." She whispered as she undid his belt and pants. They slid to the floor and she slowly followed the soft trail of hair that went from his chest all the way down to his boxers. Carefully moving them to his ankles, his member was already throbbing. "Ah look." She said as she grasped it with her right hand. "He's all ready for me too."

"My god woman, when did you learn to talk dirty?" The look on his face said he was enjoying this immensely.

Avarie carefully cupped his balls with her left and said, "Eva." She was on her knees as she stroked him and looked up into his eyes with a naughty grin.

"Damn that woman is a pervert." Courtney said hoarsely as Avarie took him in her mouth. Her tongue lapped at the bead of wetness that formed at its tip. Courtney brought his hand to the back of her head, getting a handful of hair. She brought him in further and he could feel the warmth of her mouth as it gently stroked him. "And where did you learn this?" he asked between harsh breaths.

Stopping to look up at him she answered, "The Internet."

"Oh, thank god for the internet." He moaned. He fought back the urge to put too much of his cock into her mouth. Her tongue stroked the vein while filling up her moist lips. It was almost too much and she wasn't even naked yet. Carefully, he reached down and removed her necklace, putting it on the nightstand. He wanted her to stop so he could enjoy her, but it was too late. He was on the verge as she stroked him with her right hand up and down his shaft while licking the tip. "Avarie, I'm going to cum if you don't stop." A sinister grin formed on her lips.

"That's when you keep going." She said while lapping at him. Oh damn, she used his own words against him and he was going to pay. Both hands were now at the back of her head as he started bucking almost wildly into her. Moans of pleasure escaped his lips as he spilled into her mouth and she didn't let up. He grabbed handfuls of hair as heat rose to his core. When he was done, he started shaking and let go. Avarie swallowed everything he gave her and ran her tongue up and down his shaft, sending shivers up his spine.

"Alright, you need to give me a break." Gently, he pulled back from her. He was still shaking a bit as she stood up and kissed him gently on the lips. She was like electric heat. Any small touch sent shockwaves through him. Turning her around, he unzipped her dress and let it fall to the floor. He slowly looked her up and down. Her nipples poked through the soft fabric as he lightly grazed them with his fingers. The panties were crotch less lace. Slowly, he traced a line from between her breasts down to her wet lips. She was almost dripping when he stroked her clit. Moaning softly, she wrapped her arms around his neck and played with his hair. Dipping a finger into her entrance, he found her wet and hot. He continued stroking her while she kissed his chest and lapped at his nipples. He was starting to stand at attention again as he thought about entering her.

He laid her down on the bed and kicked off the rest of his clothes that were at his ankles. Taking the garter off with his teeth, he ran his lips up and down the inside of her thighs. She moaned in delight as he made his way back and parted her legs. Gently, he glided his tongue along her nether lips and found the hot little bud. He lapped at sucked at it while she bucked herself into him. The heat and musk of her thrilled his senses as he made long strokes, up and down. Avarie breathed heavily. Pleasure built up within her core and radiated through the rest of her body. She wanted him inside her.

"Courtney, please." She moaned.

"Please what?" he answered softly while sucking on her clit.

"I want you." She whispered hoarsely as she worked her pelvis into his tongue. Lifting his head up, he decided that he would give her what she wanted. Covering her with his warm body, he met her lips and sucked on each one before driving his tongue into her. Avarie wrapped herself around him as he ran his tongue around hers, taking in her heat. His right hand found her lush mound as he pulled and pinched at her nipple. She moaned harder while he moved to suckle her ear. His member was touching her belly as she rose up to him. "Please." She begged softly in his ear. He obliged as he grabbed for the box of condoms. If Eva found out they did it again without them, he'd have to grow a new dick and he didn't want that.

Tearing open the box, he quickly grabbed a condom. Ripping the plastic open with his teeth, he quickly put it on. Avarie was flushed as she breathed harder. Letting the tip slide over her, she whimpered. Smiling down at her, he guided himself in. She was wet and tight so he had to go slow. "Oh god, Avarie." He said as he went deeper. Avarie felt him fill her up. He shifted on top as he ground himself into her. She ran her fingers up and down his back and it sent shivers up his spine. He propped himself up as he lapped at her nipples and she moaned even more.

It wasn't enough for Avarie. She moved her hand to his hips urging him on. Wet heat spilled over her as he moved faster. With each stroke, she rose up and met him. Sitting up, he lifted her legs and shouldered them.

Avarie was almost breathless. Courtney could feel small contractions inside her as he started to buck harder. He bent down, almost bringing her legs to her ears as he met her lips. She felt his entire weight on her. Within seconds, liquid heat filled her body as an orgasm raged through her. Throwing her head back, she moaned so loud, she could've woken up the entire castle. Courtney didn't care; he was on the verge as her excitement rolled through him. Bucking faster, his hips jerked as he came into her. Burying himself into her neck, he moaned with pleasure. He sank into her body as the waves passed. They were both shaking as he rolled over onto his side. Sweat covered his body as he tried to cool down. Avarie's eyes were half closed as she struggled to breathe.

"See, I told you it gets better every time." He reached over and kissed her ear.

"No, you're not lying." She said between breaths.

Courtney ran his fingers across her abdomen and up to her breasts. "I think you get louder each time too." He whispered into her ear.

"I don't mean too, it just happens." Tears formed in the corners of her eyes. She was sweating as her lips quivered. "I blame you." She said jokingly.

Courtney pulled off the condom and threw it into the trash. "Want to see if you get louder?" he teased into her ear. Avarie nodded with excitement and pulled him to her. It was a good thing Eva grabbed a box of ten, because that night, he used five. They fell asleep in each other's arms around 8am. This was the best night they've had together and he prayed for a few more.

ϒϒϒ

Going downstairs for breakfast, Matthias found poor Sasha asleep on the couch. His feet hung off the edge and the damn cat was lying on his back. Since Sasha's room was across from Courtney's, Matthias could only imagine what sounds he heard throughout the night. Even Eva slept with a pillow across her head. Stirring Sasha from his sleep, he offered to make him breakfast. "Are they done yet?" Sasha asked sleepily. Matthias assured him that they were while laughing so hard, his ribs hurt.

With everybody awake for the exception of the love birds, Matthias took the other two into town for food and to grab Sasha some necessities. They arrived back around 3pm and no sign of Courtney or Avarie. Matthias rolled his eyes as he went to Courtney's room. Pressing his ear to the door, he heard Avarie giggling and Courtney's voice. Obviously they were awake and they could join the living.

Without knocking, Matthias busted in, surprised that Courtney left his door unlocked. "Alright, you two need a break." He announced as Avarie threw covers over her and Courtney. They were still buck naked wrestling around on his bed like two teenagers. Matthias walked further into the room and opened up all Courtney's windows.

"Matty, don't you remember how to knock?" Courtney said as he removed the covers from his head. Matthias flipped him off just as Eva walked in. "Seriously? You too?" Courtney sat up smiling as Avarie hid herself from view still giggling.

"Seriously, Courtney, it's time to get out of bed." Eva demanded as she stood in the doorway and crossed her arms with a smirk on her face. "It smells like both of you need a shower too." She said as she waved her hand in the air. His room smelled like sweat and sex. No wonder why Matthias opened the windows.

"We don't want too." Courtney said as he dove back under the covers for Avarie. Matthias glanced over at Eva and had the go-ahead nod. Quickly, Matthais jumped on Courtney's bed and tore the covers from both of them. Avarie fell off the side laughing so hard she couldn't move and Matthias was wrestling Courtney. "Dammit Matty!" Courtney yelled with high pitched laughter. Avarie grabbed her clothes and ran towards Eva who escorted her out of the room. "Look! You let her get away!"

"Get dressed you Asshole!" Matthias demanded while chuckling. "She'll be back. Jesus, she's no use to anybody if she can't walk. Give her a break."

"Oh damn, that's a good idea! Bring her back here. The Russians won't want her then!"

"Courtney!" Matthias said snapping his fingers in his face. "You know as well as I that they'd fix her regardless. Now get your ass in the shower." He pointed towards the bathroom.

"Fine, party pooper." Courtney was giddy as he made his way towards the shower. "You better leave my room!"

"I'm not leaving till you're dressed. God only knows what's going on in your perverted head right now."

"Speaking of perverted..." Courtney started to say as he turned on the shower. "You know that Eva taught Avarie how to talk dirty? It's your woman who's the pervert."

"I can't help what Eva teaches Avarie." Matthias yelled into the bathroom. He wasn't wrong, she did talk dirty. Sometimes it was downright porn language, he thought as he laughed to himself. He walked over to the nightstand to find a completely empty box of condoms. Damn, where the hell his stamina came from, Matthias thought. "Really? The entire box of condoms are gone?"

Courtney busted up laughing in the shower. "Well, somebody had the bright idea to try and make balloon animals. Just so you know, it wasn't me."

"We created a monster!" Matthias exclaimed. "I claim no responsibility for any of this. I blame you *and* Eva." The shower turned off. A few minutes later, Courtney stepped out with a towel wrapped around his waist.

"You can leave now."

"Nope, you're still naked."

Courtney pulled clothes out and rolled his eyes at Matthias. "You do realize I'm a big boy now right?" He asked as he pulled on boxers and socks.

"Yes, you're a big sexed up teenager. Now get dressed so you can go downstairs and eat."

It was almost an hour before everybody gathered in the kitchen. Sasha sat at the kitchen island drinking tea. As soon as he saw Avarie and Courtney, he flashed them a funny look of disgust. Poor Avarie looked like she rode a bull all night by the way she was walking.

"Next time, you two use inside voices." Sasha said as he took a sip. "Some of us like our sleep." Eva and Matthias cracked up laughing. Sasha didn't have a good night.

"I'm sorry, Sasha." Avarie said as she scooted next to him at the island. "I'll make sure to gag him next time." She joked as she patted his back.

"I didn't know Courtney could scream like a girl." Everybody lost it. Sasha was definitely a smart ass. Matthias gave him a high five while Avarie blushed with embarrassment. Eva started to get items out for supper while the others helped. Avarie knew she'd miss this. There was no way the FSB would be as fun as these guys.

The rest of the weekend was spent riding bikes and running errands in town. Every night, Avarie slept in Courtney's room with him. Sometimes they slept, and sometimes not. Russia was never mentioned the entire weekend, but they all knew it loomed somewhere in the near future and secretly, they were all fearful of what would come.

CHAPTER FOUR

It was a hot Monday in August when the black limo pulled to the front door of the castle. A big man stepped out. Dressed in a business suit and black shades, he knocked on the door. He didn't bother to call because he didn't want to warn Courtney that he was coming. There was no answer and he knocked again. *Jesus, don't they have a butler to answer the door*, he thought. Finally, a sandy blond man answered.

"You must be Matthias." The man said in a thick Russian accent. "I'm here for the girl."

Slowly, Matthias opened the door and stepped aside to let the man in. Two other men joined him. They wore business suits just like his. Sizing them up, Matthias thought the one Russian had to be at least six foot three and two hundred and fifty pounds. He knew he couldn't take him even if he wanted too.

"Where's the girl?" He demanded.

"She's downstairs training." He answered. "I think you should wait for Courtney to get home. He'll be here in a few minutes.

"I believe that's fair." The man stated. The other two walked numbly around the great room.

"May I ask your name?"

"I'm the Russian Prime Minister." The man just looked around. Matthias knew he was anxious. "My name is Kirill Borowitz. I already spoke to Courtney about this matter."

"I understand. However, you didn't speak to Avarie about it. Haven't you ever considered her feelings?" Matthias dared to ask.

"No. Her feelings don't matter to me, and neither do Herr Cambridge's."

"I need you to understand that you're taking her away from everything she knows. She's been awake for a little over two months. This could be a lot to process." Matthias wanted to appeal to this man's heart, that is if he had one.

"I don't give two shits." Kirill said. "A deal is a deal and she comes with us." He pushed Matthias aside and went towards the fireplace. "Your boss would do good to remember that."

"Well, I'm the one who created her."

"Congratulations. I hope she's as good as promised then."

Damn, Matthias wasn't getting anywhere with this prick. Georg came bounding down the stairs. He took one look at Kirill and scattered for the cellar. Possibly to warn Sasha and the others. That cat was damn smart.

Courtney's car could be heard in the driveway. Within minutes, he was in the great room. Courtney slowly examined Kirill. His heart skipped beats when he realized what Kirill was. *Annunaki*. Carefully extending his hand, he introduced himself, but couldn't look away.

Bending his head down to Courtney's ear, Kirill whispered, "You know my kind, don't you?" He pulled back smiling. Courtney nodded. "How do you know?" Kirill was curious. There wasn't a human alive who could decipher their kind from humans. Courtney sat him down on the couches and he gave a summary of his story. "So this being, Luscious... he gave you immortality?"

"He did."

Kirill chuckled. "Describe him to me." Courtney described him with as much detail as possible. Kirill's face turned serious as he leaned in to hear more of Courtney's story.

"Do you know him?" Courtney asked.

"Let's just say, he's not a friend of ours." Kirill said honestly. "But I'm not here to tell bedtime stories. Where's the girl?"

"She's downstairs."

"Take me to her." Kirill let them know he was in charge. With Courtney leading the way, the others followed.

ϓϓϓ

Avarie and Eva were busy working on their martial arts. Sasha as it turned out, was pretty good at actual fighting. They were distracted when the cat rushed by them and found Sasha. Georg literally climbed up his sweatpants and into his arms, meowing the entire time. They've never seen a cat act this way. It looked as though Sasha listened to him intently as Georg told his story. Stroking his fur and putting him down, Sasha glared in the direction of the doorway.

"What is it, Sasha?" Eva asked frightened.

Pandora Rising

"They're here."

Panic filled Avarie's entire body. She looked at Sasha, but she knew he couldn't do anything about it. "Calm down Avarie." He said quietly. "You show them no fear. They feed on it." Avarie faced Sasha as she took in deep breaths and counted to one hundred. Letting her heart rate slow down, she was able to focus.

Suddenly, the energy changed in the room. Whatever just entered was not of this world. She felt the heat of the entity several feet behind her. She could smell him….expensive cologne and sweat. Rage started to fill her.

Kirill looked around as he entered. A small woman had her back to him. She had to be no more than five feet tall and a little over a hundred pounds. Another woman stood in the corner with blazing red hair and greenish blue eyes. However, his eyes fell on the black haired man with electric blue eyes. He had a presence and Kirill could feel it. This one was not human.

Courtney was completely silent as he stood between the other two men in suits. Matthias made his way around them towards Avarie.

"Well?" Kirill said impatiently.

Slowly, Avarie turned around. Kirill was completely taken aback. Her beautiful dark brown hair spilled over dangerous deep green eyes. She looked like a panther ready to strike. Her eyes told him she wasn't going without a fight.

"Are you Avarie?" he asked looking down at her.

"Are you the asshole who's going to take me away from my home?" she asked back.

A sinister grin crossed his lips. "Yes, I am exactly that asshole." He answered.

Avarie let her eyes sweep across him. She looked him up and down. She could hear Sasha in her head, telling her to knock it off, but something took over her. She looked into his eyes. She knew those eyes, but they didn't belong to Luscious. No, these eyes were flat brown. It seems the cosmos died in this man's eyes a long time ago. "You're one of them." She hissed. "I know those *eyes*."

"Good, then you know what I'm capable of." He hissed back.

"I *know* what your kind do." Avarie walked over to the weapons wall and pulled down two short swords. Courtney's heart raced, *Please don't let her do this…he'll kill her.*

"Put them back!" Kirill's voice boomed. "I'm not here to fight you."

Eva watched in panic as Avarie defied him. She was as light as a dancer as she moved towards him. He shook his head and grabbed a long sword from the wall. "If this is how you want to do this, that's fine by me, little one. But know this; I won't be easy on you."

As soon as he was near, Avarie started at him. She was quick and fast. Nobody has ever seen her move like this before. Kirill was having a hard time blocking her thrusts. Courtney's blood pressure dropped as he silently pleaded Sasha to do something to make it stop. Sasha caught his eye and shook his head no. *Let her fight him*, he seemed to say. When it looked like Kirill was about ready to slice into her, sparks flew from both short swords and she cut his in half. He sat there on one knee, looking up at her smiling. She was out of breath and shaking with rage. His smile turned devious as he threw away the rest of his sword, pulling his hand back, he was about to slap her across the face. That is, until Sasha quickly caught the man's wrist midair.

Kirill could feel numbness setting in as a bone chilling cold swept through his arm. Letting go Sasha said, "You lost." and turned away.

"The fights not over unless I say it is." He hissed at Sasha.

Sasha just turned his blue eyes at Kirill. "If you want a fair fight, I'm right here." Sasha dared him over without even moving. Avarie was blown away. Sasha could take this man if he wanted. She looked for Eva and found her wrapped in Matthias' arms in fear.

"Like I said, I'm not here to fight. I'm here for her."

"You can't have her." Sasha said.

"Why not?"

"Because she's bound to me." he said nonchalantly. "I took her sacrifice and she's mine. It's as simple as that."

"The deal was made with Courtney. Not you."

"Then let's make another deal." Avarie had no clue Sasha was in the bargaining business and neither did Courtney as he shrugged at her, unsure of what was happening.

"If you take her, I have to go with her." Sasha said taking the swords out of Avarie's hands and putting them on the wall. "If you take her without my consent, I'll slaughter you where you stand." The look in his eyes said he wasn't joking. "I will allow her to go with you. That's what you want isn't it?" he asked.

"It is."

"Good." Sasha said as he strode up to the man. "Then let's go upstairs and negotiate the terms."

ϓϓϓ

Nobody had any clue what was happening. In an instant, Sasha turned into a negotiator for Avarie. Courtney suspected that he had an ace up his sleeve, but he didn't know what it was just yet. Tea was made and everybody sat near the massive fireplace to get comfortable. Sasha stood at the mantle. His eyes looked aglow as the light from the fire reflected around him.

"What are the terms?" Kirill asked Sasha.

"I go with her and am a part of her training. Even if I'm not there, I am aware of what's going on." Sasha said with quiet confidence. "She gets to contact home every day. You remember you're taking her far from what she's known and that's not fair to her."

"No. It's better if you contact home for her. Any messages anybody wants to leave, they can do it through you. I'll give you the access, but not her."

"And why's that?" Sasha asked.

"Because she'll become homesick and not able to concentrate on her training. I don't want thoughts of home distracting her."

Sasha glared at him. "I'll add a stipulation."

"What's that?"

Sasha looked over at Courtney. "She at least gets to talk to Courtney once a month. You understand, she needs to hear his voice. If she doesn't, she won't know if you had him killed while she was away."

"Now why would I kill Courtney?

"It isn't the fact that you would have him killed, it's that in her head, he would be dead and there would be nothing worth fighting for." Sasha had him there. Flames kicked up a bit, even though there was little wood in the fire place. Sasha glanced at it, but looked back at Kirill.

"Fine, but there will be a time limit of only thirty minutes once a month." Kirill glared at Eva and said, "It still stands that only you can contact them once every day and pass messages to Avarie."

"Agreed."

"Good, now my stipulations." He rubbed his hands together. "She lives with me. However, I only planned for one, so you two will have to share a

Pandora Rising

room." Sasha nodded his head. "My brother will do most of the training and I have a mentor for her. She will obey every order given without question. If she defies them, she pays the consequences."

"And what are those?" Sasha cocked an eyebrow.

"It depends on what orders she didn't follow." Kirill gave Avarie a dirty smirk. "The punishment will fit the crime." Avarie cringed. "There will be times that she will have to follow orders that she won't be comfortable with. She will not argue, she will do what she's told."

Sasha didn't like the look he was giving her. His eyes fell on Eva. She was staring hard into the fire. The flames flickered up again and didn't let up. Sasha carefully backed away from the fireplace. He looked deeper into her eyes and saw the reflection of the fire.

"You're asking a lot of a nineteen year old." Sasha said as he moved behind Avarie. "She tends to be stubborn and she's not your average human."

Kirill said harshly "I am aware."

"However, I will be willing to allow you a concession." Courtney was wondering where Sasha was going with this. Nobody has ever spoken for Courtney before, but he had no choice, Sasha wouldn't allow it. "This Annunaki, Luscious…you track him down." *There it is...* now Courtney realized that he was using Avarie to get to Luscious.

Sasha noticed that Avarie was sweating. The heat of the fire was getting hotter and Eva hasn't turned away from it. Kirill was silent. He was mulling it over. Sasha motioned with his eyes to Courtney and Matthias towards Eva. She sat on the couch, lips moving with silent words at the flames as it licked the fireplace stones.

"Alright, I'll track him for you. Just know that he is part of the Thirteen."

Courtney nodded. If Avarie was going to leave he damn well better get something out of it. It broke his heart that she would only talk to him once a month for thirty minutes. Sasha was doing the best he could for all of them.

"How long will she train?" Courtney asked.

Kirill hissed at him, "We're putting years of training together in a matter of months. FSB agents train for years so don't expect her back next month. Possibly a year, but it depends on how she progresses."

That's what Courtney was afraid of. Avarie is strong and a quick learner, but he had no clue what she would be trained in. He swallowed hard. The moment that he was afraid up had come, and he had to give her up. He felt confident that Sasha would be with her and keep her protected.

"Are we good with negotiations now?" Kirill was anxious to get going. Sasha looked at Courtney and Matthias, neither had anything to add. "Good, now get packed little one, we're burning up precious time."

"I want to take my bike." Avarie said defiantly.

Kirill laughed. "Oh my precious one, I don't need for you to have an escape vehicle on hand. I've seen you ride that monstrous thing and I know better than to let you take it with you." He liked this one already. He knew she was trouble, but he'd break her down eventually. "Now, go pack."

Standing up, Avarie went to her room and Eva followed. Kirill watched her intently. He'd take her with too, but there wasn't any room. Sasha excused himself and went to his room. Matthias met him at the doorway as Sasha packed a duffel bag.

"Is it true?" Matthais asked, "You claimed her as your own?"

Sasha stuffed clothes into his bag. "It is."

"Then how come she's with Courtney?"

"She's with Courtney because she loves him. One day, she might have his children."

"I don't understand, where does that put you? I mean, you claimed her, so why aren't you…. You know?"

"Having sex with her?" Sasha asked while laughing.

"Yea."

"It's because we don't work like that. When we claim humans, it is in the form of family or friendship only. Nothing sexual." Sasha went into the bathroom to grab toiletries.

"But it can be?"

"If we wanted, I guess." He zipped up his bag and motioned to the door. Avarie was still packing while Eva was in the room helping her. He could hear Avarie sniffling behind the door. "Right now, Avarie needs somebody who can watch out for her best interests. I don't trust this man and neither should any of you until he proves himself. That is why I'll be calling you every day, plus, Courtney would want to make sure she's alright. He's not taking this any better than she is and I need you to make sure he keeps his head."

Pandora Rising

Sasha knocked on Avarie's door. Matthias was amazed how he took complete control of this situation. He was right though. Courtney wouldn't be able to keep his wits together.

Eva opened the door as Avarie put the last of her stuff away. Saying good-bye to Georg, they both left the room. Sasha kept a careful eye on Eva. She was firing on all pistons and he could tell she was getting hot. He needed her to keep her cool also.

Back downstairs, Sasha and Avarie were ready. They said their good-byes as Avarie tried to control her tears. Kissing Courtney deep she told him she loved him and would be back as soon as humanly possible. Before her and Sasha were escorted out the door to the waiting limo, Kirill had one last thing to say to Courtney. "I swear to God if I find out this girl is pregnant, I'll send your unborn child to you in a *fucking* jar."

His eyes went wide with shock. This guy was a monster and he couldn't believe he was even allowing Avarie to go with him. The flames in the fireplace shot higher, but Kirill didn't notice as he looked at Eva. "As for you, I'd take you with me too, but I only have just enough room for these two." He grabbed her chin and shook it, but pulled back with a hiss. Heat blisters formed on his fingertips as the fire behind her turned almost into an inferno as the flames spilled out, filling the entire fireplace with intense heat He'd never seen green eyes burn before, until he saw hers. "Well, I see you guys have a fire pagan!" His eyes turned sinister as he looked at Matthias. "Good luck with this one, you only fan her flames." He turned around as he put his fingers in his mouth to cool the sting on his fingertips.

All five left, slamming the door behind them. Turning around, the boys watched as the fire behind Eva died down. "What the fuck is he talking about, *fire pagan*?" Matthias asked Courtney.

"I don't know." He shook his head. "I think it's time to break out the old tomes and see what the hell we're really dealing with."

ϒϒϒ

Once in the limo, Avarie held to Sasha tight as he cradled her in his arms. Kirill kept giving both of them dirty looks. He sat across from them with the two men on either side. He looked at his watch and peeked forward. "It's a four hour flight to Moscow. Once we get to my home, I'll give you both time to settle in. I apologize that you have to share a room, but like I said, I was only expecting one." His demeanor was a little nicer. "I'll let you call Courtney and the others tonight when we arrive." He said to Sasha. "You are the only one who will have access to the cell phone." He pointed at Avarie. "If I find out you were on the phone without my permission, I'll have you punished."

Without thinking, Avarie kicked him hard in the shin. He cried out in anger. "You little shit! You're lucky we're in the limo and you have *him*."

Sasha chuckled at Kirill. "I told you she's defiant and stubborn. It would do you well to remain polite." He warned him. Avarie buried herself deeper into Sasha's warm embrace. He stroked her hair and held her tighter. Pulling out her iPod from her pocket, Avarie turned on her music. She didn't want to listen to this hideous man sitting in front of her. He disgusted her.

The day turned dark as they pulled into a hangar. Sasha and Avarie were escorted onto a big plane surrounded by armed men. She could hear the metal clacking at they walked up the ramp. A lady showed them to their seats and informed them of the amenities the plane offered. The chairs were big and comfortable. Once they took off, Avarie laid down on Sasha's lap and fell asleep.

ϓϓϓ

After almost four hours, the plane landed and they were escorted out by another limo. Avarie stared out the tinted windows as they zoomed by a foreign landscape. It was just as beautiful as Germany, but in a different way. Sasha still held onto her as Kirill stayed silent.

It took almost an hour to pull into the Prime Minister's home. The black limo took them into the massive double oak front door. Avarie and Sasha noticed security men stealthily moving around the perimeter. Those same security guards escorted them inside carrying the luggage in for them. Being led into a dining room, Kirill already had a late dinner made. They ate in silence until Kirill spoke of his plans to them.

"After you eat, you will be taken to your room. The door will remain locked until 6am." He said as he bit into a piece of meat. "Since it is late, you will be allowed to sleep in." A man stepped forward with a cell phone and handed it to Kirill. Looking it over, he placed it in front of

Sasha. "All calls home will be monitored by the FSB. Thirty minutes a day is your time limit. After we eat, you can call Courtney." Sasha nodded in agreement.

Avarie was bone tired. She was overloaded for the day and she wanted nothing more than to sleep. It was almost midnight when they arrived and it was nice to know they were allowed to sleep in. Kirill's demeanor seemed a little nicer since he was home. She hoped he really wasn't the bad guy that she first met. "*Mishka*, you'll have only a day or two of rest. My brother won't be back from Germany yet. You'll already be started in training by the time he arrives."

Wonderful, he has a brother, she thought to herself. *I bet he's as big of a prick as this guy*. Avarie didn't meet his eyes as she moved food around on her plate. She felt his nasty gaze burning into her body sending shivers up her spine.

With dinner being done, Kirill walked them to the third floor of the big mansion. Leading them into a big room with an oak door, he pushed it open. "The bed is big enough for both of you. I'll leave you both to work out the sleeping arrangements." Once inside, the room had a dresser, wardrobe, sitting area, and large bed. He showed them the large bathroom. "You have all the creature comforts of home here. Anything you need, you'll be given." Avarie just wanted this guy out. She was emotionally drained.

Looking at Sasha he said, "You can call Courtney now. As for you..." He pointed at Avarie. "You come with me." She cringed. What the hell did this guy want?

"Where you taking her?" Sasha asked in his deep voice.

Kirill squinted at him. "She has a punishment waiting."

"Not without me present." Sasha crossed his arms in defiance.

"No! The deal was that you were present when she trained, not when punishments were dealt out!" He grabbed a handful of Avarie's hair. "That indiscretion in the limo will not be tolerated!" Forcing Avarie from the room, he slammed the door before Sasha could protest. He walked her into the room across the hall using her hair as a leash. The back of her scalp burned as he threw her to the floor.

Lifting herself up with her arms, she turned to face him. Fear flooded her system and she was ready to fight. "Don't fight me, *Mishka*." He read her mind. Pulling the belt from his suit pants, he whipped it into the air with a crack. "Take off your clothes." A sneer crossed his lips. He looked like he was going to enjoy beating her. Avarie didn't move. She hoped any minute now, Sasha would break through the door. Again, he grabbed her by the hair and pulled her off the floor. "If you don't take them off, I'll do it for you." He hissed.

Taking his threat seriously, she ripped off all her clothes. Standing naked in front of him, she didn't bother to shield herself. Sasha wasn't coming to save her so she had to take his punishment. Motioning for her to turn around, she did so. She wasn't prepared as the first lash hit her shoulder and flinched. He ran his finger across the streak and it sent shivers up her spine as his touch scorched her body. The second was harder when it hit her other shoulder. She expected him to touch her but he didn't.

Tears welled up in her eyes. She never felt so violated in her entire existence. Suddenly, he broke into wild lashings onto her back and ass. Some even went across her thighs. She held back muffled screams as she bit into her bottom lip. The hot tears rushed out as every lash felt harder than the last. Losing count at ten, she struggled to remain in control. "Turn around." Taking a deep breath, she did as he said. "Raise your arms up." Slowly raising her arms, she realized he was going to do the same to the front side of her body. "Spread your legs." *What the fuck?* She thought. Slowly, she let a gap open between her legs. Looking him up and down, she noticed that he was aroused. If he thought he was going to fuck her after this, he was out of his damn mind.

Out of nowhere, the lashings started again. He was beating her with such force she felt he would break her ribs. Still, she bit her lip and closed her eyes, trying to hold back the tears that would eventually break the barriers of her lids. Every crack vibrated off the walls and into her ear drums. Two lashings actually went between her legs, finding her sensitive area. She was breathing heavily and prayed that he would stop before he bloodied her. One last lick went straight across her breasts, making her nipples feel sore and tingle with pain. "Now, are you going to behave yourself?" he asked, pleased with himself. She nodded her head. "I can't hear you." He said throwing the belt on his bed and unbuttoning his shirt.

"Yes." She said quietly.

He smiled. "Yes what, *Mishka*?"

With a shaky voice she said, "Yes, I'll behave myself, you dirty *fuck*."

He was taken aback with wide eyes. Her body burned with rage and he started laughing at her. "I think you like my punishments." He quickly grabbed her by the arm and led her towards the huge bed. Sitting on the edge he threw her over his lap and started spanking her ass so hard it was on fire. "Go ahead and scream. I hope that fucking water sprite hears it!" She wiggled to get away from him but he was too strong. Screaming with anger, she struggled against his blows. When he had enough, he threw her to the ground. He wiped sweat from his forehead with a handkerchief. Her body was severely sore as she tried to get up. Again, he grabbed her arm and stood in front of her. This man towered over her and his flat brown eyes met hers. She had a hard time standing on her own and he steadied her with both hands.

He leaned into her ear and whispered. "My god, I hope you misbehave more often. I love feeling your subtle skin under my hands." She fought back the urge to punch him. Slowly, he moved down to her neck and kissed it but with a bit of teeth and it made Avarie jump. She could've sworn she felt fangs.

Shoving her clothes in her arms, he marched her out of his room. Once back into hers, Sasha stood up in shock while viewing her condition. He threw the phone on the bed and took Avarie into his arms. "You had your fun?" He asked Kirill in disgust.

Kirill was breathing deeply while looking Avarie over. "I could've had more, but I didn't think she was willing."

"Well, your fun is over." Sasha motioned for him to leave. "She needs her rest."

Good night, *Mishka*." Kirill said tenderly as he left with a dirty smile on his face.

Her skin burned and Sasha's hands felt nice and cool on her naked body. He looked down on her with pity. "Please don't piss him off anymore." he pleaded. "He is a sick man and men like him get off on power."

"I'm ready for bed." Avarie whispered. She didn't bother getting dressed as he helped her get under the covers. The fabric irritated her almost blistered skin. Sasha put on sweatpants and climbed in next to her. Avarie shuddered with pain. Every time he shifted, it hurt. Gently, he pulled her into him. His skin felt cool and it relieved the burning from the lashes. "He called you a water sprite. What does that mean?" She asked him sleepily.

He softly chuckled. "It means that my element is water. I can control it and am a part of it." He kissed her forehead. "You'll heal quickly, Avarie. By morning, the pain you feel will be nothing more than an irritation. Now sleep." He cooed. It wasn't long before Avarie nodded off. She was too tired and in pain to think about home. Sasha lay awake, staring up at the ceiling with her in his arms. He made the conversation with Courtney short. He didn't want him to hear Avarie screaming from across the hall. It seemed Courtney was on the verge of freaking out. Sasha calmed him as best he could. He reassured him that he'd watch over her. He left out the part of Avarie's punishment from Kirill. He didn't lie; he just didn't tell him everything. Sometimes, people needed to be protected from themselves and Courtney was no exception.

Somehow, he needed to get through to her about not messing with creatures like Kirill. He decided that avoidance was the best answer for now. He looked down at her. Tears still flowed even though she was asleep. His skin soaked them in and he felt her sadness wash through him. The poor girl has been through enough. She wasn't Pandora this time, she was Avarie. He took a deep breath as he shifted her onto her side. Putting her feverish back against his chest, she winced in her sleep. He was glad to be here with her. She needed all the help she could get and he planned on pulling out as much magic as he possibly could. If she didn't survive, his whole world would fall apart for the second time.

CHAPTER FIVE

Courtney woke up to his alarm at 5am. Rolling over, he realized Avarie wasn't there. He became angry. Their future was unsure at this point and he wanted time to fly by while she was gone. His head roamed aimlessly as he showered and dressed. The car was waiting for him when he finished his cup of coffee. Once at the office, he called Gerhart in to speak with him about the new situation.

After he explained what was going on, Gerhart responded. "*Jesus*, Courtney." He said in frustration. "They took her just like that?"

"They did. Thank God Sasha's with her."

He nodded in agreement. "We still need to keep watch. But that answers the question of the Mossad I guess." He put a hand on Courtney's shoulder. "I'm sorry man. She's a strong girl and she'll survive them. We need to keep you busy while she's away." He took a sip of his coffee. "They promised to bring her back?"

"After her training is done, and that could take up to a year." His eyes were forlorn. Gerhart never seen him this heartbroken. It was obvious he was upset. Courtney had bags under his eyes and had a hard time keeping his composure.

"Would you like to take some time off?" Gerhart asked softly. "I can handle things from here. I have a safety net thrown around everybody, so you don't have to worry."

Courtney thought about it. Taking time off would only give him time to think about Avarie. "No. I need to work. Think you can help me with that?" His eyes were downcast and it looked as though he was ready to cry.

Gerhart felt for him. Avarie really had ahold of this man's heart strings. It's almost like she died and he has to fight his way through this. "Courtney, I'll help you with whatever you need." Gerhart reassured him.

Around 10am, Gerhart announced that Courtney had a visitor and needed to meet with him right away. Escorting the man in, he made a double take. This man looked exactly like Kirill, but with an unshaven face and longer jet black hair that was spiked up. He was the same height and wore a blue business suit. His smile was gentle as he reached for Courtney's hand. "I'm Mikhail, Kirill's better half." He was chewing a piece of gum. "I apologize for my brother Herr Cambridge. He's a prick and this situation could've been handled better."

Gerhart stayed in the office and had no intention of leaving until being asked. "What can I help you with?" Courtney asked. He looked defeated and Mikhail wasn't going to push that dagger in his heart any farther.

"I wanted to meet you personally and reassure you that Avarie will come to no harm." He pulled a package of gum and offered it to each of them, but they refused. He shrugged and put it back in his pocket. "I helped keep the Mossad off your doorstep for now. I apologize for not warning you of our presence. I thought it would be better to keep things quiet." Courtney understood that all too well. The FSB were like ghosts in the night: only appearing to spook you when needed.

"A heads up would've been nice." Gerhart answered, holding his cup of coffee away from him. "Your people could've been caught in crossfire."

Mikhail waved him off. "I trust your people Gerhart. No harm would've come to either of us."

Courtney wanted to get on with this meeting. "So, what's going to happen to Avarie?" he asked impatiently.

Mikhail looked back over at him. "When I get back in a couple of days, I'll start training her. I've convinced my brother to give her a short respite. I understand she has a friend with her?'

"His name is Sasha." Courtney answered.

Mikhail dared to ask. "Is he…her lover?" he asked carefully.

"No, she's mine."

Mikhail almost spit out his coffee. "Well, then I guess we don't have to worry about much from him." He looked Courtney up and down. "No wonder you pissed my brother off so bad. So why is this Sasha with Avarie?"

Courtney didn't care to explain but knew he had too. "He has claim on her."

"Come again?" Mikhail was confused. Waving Gerhart out of the office, he left and closed the door.

"Sasha is…I guess an immortal from the other side. Avarie found him and gave up a blood sacrifice. How it happened, I didn't bother to ask. So in the end, he is tied to her and wherever she goes, he goes too." Frustration followed Courtney's gaze outside.

Mikhail understood what he was saying. "I want to make this process easier for her. The faster she's trained, the faster she comes home to you." He meant it. He hated this part of his job and the look on Courtney's face said it all. "I need you to give me as much information on her as possible. I know she's strong, the men at your house last night told me she almost beat Kirill's ass." He winked at him. "He's not good with weapons, but brute strength is another matter." He took a breath. "The point is, she knows our kind somehow and when she meets me, I don't want her to be afraid of me…or want to kill me on sight for that matter. I'm not that type of demon."

Courtney mulled it over in his head. "I think it would be easier to discuss this in my home if you don't mind. This way you can see how she lived and understand what Sasha is."

Mikhail nodded. "Of course. When can we go?"

"Right now." Courtney stood up and Mikhail followed him out of the office. Calling Gerhart, he let him know he'd be out for the rest of the day.

ϒϒϒ

Courtney rounded up Eva and Matthias. Mikhail met each one and offered them a piece of gum. They declined. Mikhail studied Eva as they talked. She looked like she'd set him on fire any minute. He was able to get her alone in her and Avarie's room. She only spoke when she needed and showed him the downstairs where Sasha was. He looked around in awe and realized that Sasha was a water deity. The gargoyles gave him away. He explained to Eva what Sasha's abilities were and how they were lucky to find him. She was somewhat hostile towards him in her body language.

"Eva, I'm sorry for my brother's actions. He can become belligerent sometimes. I am not him and I will never be him. He may be my twin, but that doesn't mean we're the same person." He needed to win her over. "Eva, do you know your ancestry?" he asked curiously. She nodded. "Good, then you know that your ancestors were pagans who used the elements. Yours happens to be fire." He smiled at her. "That's how you burnt my brother. They don't call you fiery redheads for nothing you know?"

Eva thought that was just coincidence. Maybe she was just so pissed she brought her body temp up. She couldn't explain what happened last night. "What else did my brother say to you?" he asked.

"He said that Matthias should be careful with me, he just fans my flames or whatever that means." She said in a huff.

Mikhail started laughing. "He's right." He walked her back up the stairs. "Oh my young lady, you have a lot to learn. I can give you the resources if you need." He looked back at her. "I wish I could train you also. I'm sorry Avarie was taken from you like this. It wasn't my idea. I wanted to give her time and I see that your heart is broken for your sister." He said sadly.

"She's not my sister." Eva was confused by the way he spoke.

Mikhail was back up in the room already. Raising a finger to her in a tisk-tisk motion he said, "But she is, you don't need to be blood to be family. You've given her sisterhood when she had none. From what you've told me, you've taught her many things. You have a bond that can never be broken. For this, I'll allow her to write to you. I won't even read the emails." He promised.

"Really?" she asked with a cocked eyebrow.

"Really." He said. "But she'll be busy with training and will have little time for contact. I'll give her the access when I can."

They walked out of the room and shut the door. "What about Courtney?" she asked quietly. "You know he loves her and this is breaking his heart."

"Truth is it breaks my heart too. I'd let her talk to him every day, but Kirill has to be allowed his exceptions. If I fight him, it'll be a hard battle and nobody wins." A thought came to him. "Eva, if I could build up your skills, would you accept my offer?" he asked sincerely.

She thought about it. "What do you mean?"

"I mean, you have the power of fire within you. I know…somebody who could teach you how to harness your power. I understand Matthias is building a machine to help your body adapt to fighting skills, but in times of need, it won't be enough." He stopped in the hallway. "Entities like Sasha exist around the world, although rare, I know one who can help you."

"Now why would you want to help me?" Her tone was skeptical.

Pandora Rising

It was better to be honest now than to drag this game on. "Because war is coming. This shit has to end sometime and you're in this battle whether you like it or not. We're taking on the Thirteen. These are the powerful illuminati families and the heads of their table are just like me and Kirill. We are unnatural creatures who came to this world and there are only so many of us left who fight for humankind. The more allies we have, the better."

Eva was in shock. This was a huge revelation and it shook her to the core. "Alright." She said softly. "If the boys approve, I'll take the help."

"Good!" he said smiling. "I'll send them your way as soon as possible."

They met Courtney back in the great room. Matthias was talking to Courtney in hushed tones. He was frustrated. "Are you both alright?" Mikhail asked.

Matthias pulled Courtney towards him. "Tell him Courtney." He urged.

"Tell me what?" Mikhail asked. "Are we missing something?"

Courtney was hesitant but Matthias nudged him on. "There's something else you need to know about Avarie." He said quietly.

"Well?" Mikhail was growing impatient. It was hard to win the confidence of these humans and he was only trying to help ease their pain.

"Do you believe in reincarnation?" Courtney asked seriously.

Mikhail thought about it. "I know it happens from time to time. However, those who become reincarnated don't usually come back until centuries later only to live an opposite life that they once lived. Why?"

Courtney looked dismayed. "We have something to show you. Follow me."

Mikhail thought that this better be good and have something to do with Avarie. They all hoped that she was their ticket to winning this millennia long war. Mikhail followed them all the way into the chapel and stopped at the crypt door. "Have you seen Avarie yet?" Courtney asked him.

"No, I haven't." he answered carefully.

Courtney pulled out his phone and showed him pictures of her. She was a pretty young lady with deep green cat like eyes, button nose, pert lips and dark brown hair. Every picture he saw, she was smiling with Eva or the other two guys. Seeing her face made him happy. He even gotten a glimpse of Sasha and this made him feel better knowing what they look like..

"What I'm about to show you is a bit morbid." Courtney started to open the door. "Keep in mind, this is all about her and I wouldn't show you this if I didn't feel you had her best interests at heart." Courtney's eyes implored him.

"Alright." He said softly. "Let's see what you have to show me."

Turning on the lights, Courtney led him to the mahogany coffin in the corner. "You may not believe this story, but Sasha can confirm it for you when you meet him." Mikhail nodded.

This is the second time Courtney had to open it up. Mikhail asked, "So you came down here to show me a corpse?"

"It's not just any corpse. Look." Matthias told him. Daring to peer in, he looked the woman over. She appeared to be in her 50s, but still beautiful for her age. He dared to touch her body and move the graying hair away from her forehead.

"Let me see that picture again." Mikhail demanded. Matthias pulled his out and Mikhail looked at the picture and looked at the corpse. "How is this possible? If she's dead, what's she doing in Russia?" He was still confused. "Would you tell me what's going on?"

Courtney explained. "When I created Avarie, I took DNA from this woman. You know who she is?" Mikhail shook his head no. "Look at the engraving on the lid." Courtney closed it again.

"*Nikita Judith Stormwall.*" Mikhail's eyes grew wide. "You have *Pandora*?" He almost whispered her name.

"Not exactly." Eva answered. "Now, *you* have Pandora."

Mikhail's eyes locked on each person in the crypt. He was trying to add two and two together but it wasn't happening like he wanted. "Okay, I think I might have this together but bear with me." he said as he paced the stone floor. "You, took Pandora's DNA and created a new person. This new person who is Avarie, is now...Pandora...again?" All three nodded. "Now. No." He said waving his hand in the air in an unbelievable manner. "Let me try this again." Courtney was smiling watching Mikhail's frustration. "Are you saying that you took Nikita's DNA..grew her a new body..." They nodded as he kept going. "And she is *fucking* reincarnated?" His eyes were wide with disbelief. "I need to sit down."

Matthias started laughing as Mikhail looked for a spot to sit. His reaction wasn't exactly what they expected it to be. He sat on the lid of Luscious' tomb. He put his head in his hands as though he were stressed out. Running his hands through his jet black hair he just shook his head. "Fuck, Courtney." He said in frustration.

"Is there a problem with that?" Courtney asked between giggles.

Mikhail gave him the evil eye. "She was a pain the ass to deal with years ago!" He threw up his hands. "And somehow, the damn universe plucks her to come back into a new body and raise Hell again."

"If it's any consolation, she's different now." Matthias said nonchalantly.

"Is she still stubborn as Hell?" he asked.

"Since the day I picked her up." Matthias answered with a grin.

"Then she isn't any different." He stood up and looked at Courtney. "I blame you!" He hissed. "Did you know she kicked Konstantin's ass when they were in Colorado? She threw him to the ground and broke his ribs." He exclaimed. "I personally never met her, but the stories I heard were enough to scare any man away." Mikhail wondered the tomb and looked around. Suddenly, he stopped in his tracks. "Who's in here?" he tapped on the lid.

"Nobody anymore." Courtney answered. "He's gone like the wind." The smile from Courtney's face left. Mikhail looked at the markings and hieroglyphs.

"Who was supposed to be in here?"

Matthias answered for Courtney. "A man named Luscious." He corrected himself. "Actually, he was a man like you."

Mikhail studied the lid. "I know that dirty son of a bitch." His eyes grew wide with hate. "He bragged to Kirill that he killed her children and husband." He put his fingers in quotation marks. "He told him how he beat her within inches of death and he enjoyed every minute." He ran his fingers over the lid. "He's still out there you know." Mikhail whispered. Courtney looked like he was ready to rage and Eva wanted to hold him back. "This one is *vicious*. He's had so much human blood, he's Satan himself."

Mikhail glanced over at them. He knew he hit a touchy subject. Silently, he looked from Courtney to Pandora's coffin, then to the tomb. A wonderful realization hit him and he felt almost overjoyed. He rubbed his hands together in pure delight. He smiled as he observed all three standing before him.

Letting out a maniacal laugh he declared, "The universe has aligned my children!"

They all looked at him like he went crazy. "What the Hell are you talking about?" Matthias asked.

"Don't you see? The universe brought this all together. It's ready to shake the demons off this planet like fleas on a dog." Mikhail was still rubbing his hands together.

"Please talk sense, Mikhail." Courtney pleaded.

"Courtney, before you met Nikita, did you know that Luscious killed her family?"

"No."

"Did you use her DNA knowing that she'd come back into her new body?"

"No."

"Did you know that Luscious was still alive?"

"Not until she told me."

"Did she have any clue you knew her families killer and that she was under the same roof that he lived?"

"No."

"Do you see what I'm getting at?" He said with wide eyes. "The universe sent her back for a reason and put you two together. There is no such thing as coincidence." He shook his finger at them. "Yes, a beautiful war is coming, and this time, we'll win."

Eva shook her head at him. "He's gone mad, Courtney."

Courtney smiled at her and said, "He sure has, but he's right."

"There's work for you to do." Mikhail said as he paced the room, filled with hope. "Matthias keep working on your machine. Courtney, I know since you're the communications guru, keep us informed on any chatter that comes from the Elite." He looked over at Eva. "And you, I'll have your trainer here as soon as possible." He motioned for all of them to leave the crypt and they followed. Mikhail was extremely excited. "I won't tell my brother any of this about Avarie." He said pointing to the crypt. "He doesn't need to know anything. I'll have her trained as soon as possible."

Mikhail sat down at a pew and the others gathered around him. "It won't be easy for her." His tone changed. "I can't give her shortcuts." He

Pandora Rising

put his hand on Courtney's shoulder. "She'll have good days and bad ones. I need you to understand that I'm condensing years of training into months. She has a good mentor when I can't be there. I'll work with Gerhart to keep you guys safe." He assured them.

"What about your brother?" Courtney asked. "I don't trust him."

"As you shouldn't." Mikhail replied. "I'll do my best with him. If he harms her intentionally, he's going to deal with me and Sasha. It seems he's become her guardian."

"He's helped us more than you know." Eva said softly.

"He's a pure spirit. His intentions are always for the greater good."

"How do you know?" Eva asked. "You never met him."

Mikhail laughed. "I know his kind. The ancients called them forth all the time, hence all the gargoyles."

"Did they return?"

"Yes, they went back into the universe. Sasha is the first I've ever heard of staying behind for so long."

Courtney was glad that Mikhail had some answers for them. He didn't have to come and meet any of them. His obvious interest was in Avarie, but he gotten a whole lot more. This man wasn't tainted like his twin brother. Mikhail actually cared about people and it showed. "I have to get going. I'll meet with Gerhart tomorrow then I'm off to Moscow. I have a hard job ahead of me." He stood up. "I thank you very much for allowing me information. Like I said, I won't tell my brother. The less he knows about her history, the better. Let him assume whatever he wants. I'll be in contact with you Courtney. I know Sasha gets to contact you every day, but that may not be enough. I don't need you dying of a broken heart before she comes back."

"She's a hard one to earn trust with." Matthias told him.

"I understand. I'll try my best with her. In time, she'll learn to trust me." They walked him to the front door. He had one last message for Courtney, "I know you love her. I see it in your eyes. It is my hope that she comes back stronger and ready for anything that comes. Until then, be brave for her." He turned around and left.

"Jesus, I wish it was him that came and got Avarie. Not that piece of shit that was here last night." Eva stated. "He really is the better half."

"Isn't that the truth?" Matthias agreed. "Damn, I'd go anywhere with that guy. He seems pretty cool. Does he make you feel any better?" he asked Courtney.

Courtney just stood there staring at the door. "He does, but control is just an illusion. Knowing his brother, he'll try and fuck us somehow and Mikhail will be fighting him tooth and nail."

"What is he anyway?" Eva asked.

"That dear, is a long story." Courtney sighed. "Just know that he's pretty much the last of his kind."

"But he said there were more like him"

"The Annunaki have a strange history. They were supposed to be Watchers but instead, became destroyers. This one it seems is still a Watcher."

"Like an angel?"

"Sort of, but not quite." Courtney responded. "Well, let's just hope he keeps his word. He's pretty confident that he's got good hand."

"Where's that leave us?" Matthias asked.

Courtney answered with a devious grin. "With a full house."

ϒϒϒ

Avarie and Sasha were woken up by the alarm clock. Its annoyance buzzed into their sleepy ears. Sasha shut it off and stirred Avarie awake. Her bruises were healing quickly, he noticed as she moved around. The day before, Kirill's men showed them around Moscow and let them take in the sights. It kept Avarie's mind occupied. They found out the only time that they'd see Kirill was at supper.

Today, they would be taken to the FSB training center. They had thirty minutes before the automatic lock on their door would open, letting them out of their room. Sasha hustled her into the bathroom so they could clean up. "I'm moving, Sasha." Avarie said sleepily. He chuckled at her. "We have half an hour, *Maus*. So you better hurry up." He turned on the shower and quickly got undressed and hopped in.

Avarie brushed her teeth and she could smell the manly soap in the water vapor. She didn't bother looking towards the shower because it was see through glass. They developed a routine already. Sasha would wake them up at 6am. Avarie brushed her teeth and used the facilities while Sasha showered. He'd leave it running when he got out, giving her an opportunity to get in quicker.

She heard his wet feet hit the bath pad and she knew it was her turn. With her eyes to the ground, she peeled off her shirt and panties to step in. As she showered, she heard him brush his teeth and dry off. The water felt nice on her body. The bruises were fading and she was thankful her body wasn't as sore as it was yesterday. She washed her hair and body with the fruity soap. "Hurry up, Avarie." Sasha coaxed. She looked through the glass of the shower and saw that he already had jeans on. Rinsing off the rest of the soap, she shut off the shower and toweled dry.

As she got out, he already had her clothes lying out on the bed. She shook her head. "Get dressed." He told her softy as he patted her shoulder walking by. He threw on a tank top with a red checkered button down shirt.

Her hair was still wet as she pulled on her clothes. "Why are you so anxious to get out of here?" She asked

He looked her up and down. Grabbing a towel, he roughly dried her hair. "Because when that door unlocks, we're expected to be ready. You have five more minutes." Avarie huffed as she pushed him away. "Now get in there and pull your hair up." He pointed to the bathroom.

She didn't feel like arguing with him. Within two minutes, she had her hair pulled up and barely looked at the mirror as she did so. She met Sasha at the door. He looked down at her and said, "You don't even have to try do you?" He asked in jest.

"What's that mean?" she asked defensively.

"It means you throw your hair up and you look put together." It was a complement. Her hair could be a complete mess and she'd still look good, he thought to himself.

Avarie was about to say something, but the lock unlatched itself for them. She let him open the door first. They were met by a man in a suit who looked patiently upon them. He nodded and they followed him down for a quick breakfast. They ate in silence. Avarie was extremely nervous and Sasha could feel it. Once done, they were escorted into a limo.

It took twenty minutes to pull into Lubyanka Square. It was a massive square building with Russian architecture. Another man met them and escorted them inside. He talked to both Sasha and Avarie in Russian. Sasha nodded in understanding as Avarie kept her eyes to the floor. Handing her a badge, he led the way down long corridors. She was thankful she had Sasha. Confidence flowed from him and the others saw it. As for Avarie, she was scared shitless. He whispered to her, "He says if you misplace or lose the badge, you need to let someone know as soon as possible. The badge allows you access into the training and classrooms. There's even a swimming pool here." Sasha smiled.

"It's like a labyrinth in here." Avarie told him. "How will we remember which way to go?"

The man stopped in his tracks and turned around to face her. "Well, *Mishka,* you learn the say way we do. Walk the halls enough and you'll know where you're going." The burnet man smiled nicely at her. "If you do get lost, and it has happened before, there's a button on your badge." He showed her where it was located. "Press and hold it. Someone will find you and take you to where you need to go."

That made her feel better. She didn't want to be in a place where she shouldn't. He continued on and showed them a classroom. "The first class is weapons training. You learn about every weapon we have and how to use it. The firing range is off site. There'll be days when we take you there."

Going into a lower floor, he opened up a massive training facility. "This is where you'll learn hand to hand combat. If we feel confident enough, we'll put you in groups with the men and women who train here. Rest assured, that won't be for a while."

"Who's her trainer?" Sasha asked politely.

"She'll have one mentor, one trainer, two classroom teachers, and multiple instructors." He said as he looked her over. "I'm going to assume you'll be joining her since you're her guardian?"

"I will."

"Good. You'll be a great confidence booster and cheerleader for her when she gets down. Not everybody has a good day here." He brushed a strand of hair back from Avarie's face. "We train hard here. I know it's scary at first. I was scared too. The people here are wonderful. We bring them from around the world to help train some of the most elite agents."

This man was nice. He wasn't like the other agents who just scowled at her and Sasha. "I am one of your classroom trainers. We'll start with basics and work our way up depending on how fast you excel." He walked them around the room and pointed out different areas. "Well, let's go to the swimming pool and you can meet your mentor."

Avarie grabbed onto Sasha's hand and squeezed tight. He reassured her as they walked farther along the hallway. Using the badge to let him in, he ushered them to the pool area. The scent of chlorine filled her nostrils almost instantly. It was an Olympic sized pool. Two diving boards flanked the deep end. There was a diving pad that reached almost two stories. Heights were not her thing. She preferred to stick to the terra. He pointed out a massage area in the corner and a massive hot tub with a strange hose. Avarie eyeballed it. "What's that for?" she asked.

He walked over to it and informed her that it was therapy for sore muscles. They called it a water massage. It was like a shower, but only better. The head could be adjusted for different sprays. Now that was cool, thought Avarie. She wanted to try it out as soon as possible.

A door slammed shut and they turned in that direction. A tall blonde woman strode up towards them. She was extremely tone and fit. Wearing a one piece bathing suit, she was putting her hair up in some type of rubber cap. "Do you swim?" she asked Avarie in a thick Russian accent.

Avarie nodded but Sasha had to add, "She hates the deep end though." The woman looked her up and down.

"Ah, those who hate the deep end must've had an near death experience with water in a past life." She chuckled. "My name is Viktoria, but you can call me Tori." She extended her hand and Avarie took it. She had a strong grip.

"I'm Sasha and this is Avarie. She's here to train." Sasha said as he shook her hand. Thank God Sasha did most of her talking for her.

"Well then, you're my protégé. Welcome to the FSB Avarie." Tori said with a smile. "My uncle will meet us later in the afternoon. He's still in Germany cleaning up some business with bad guys." She shoved the rest of her hair under the cap. "If you like, you can leave us now Valentin." He bid his farewells and left. "Do either of you have a swim suit on you?" She asked.

They both shook their heads no. "Well, I'll have to remedy that." She dove into the water with the grace of a swan, did a lap and then came back. "Did you pack any swim suits at all?" she asked politely. They both shook their heads and Avarie gave her a shy smile. "Oh, you swim naked don't you?" Sasha nodded. "Well," She said clapping her wet hands together. "Get undressed and get in. Nobody will be in here for a while." Avarie hesitated as she looked around and at the door. "Ah, *Mishka*, don't worry. I booked the pool for us for the rest of the day."

Avarie took off her clothes as did Sasha. He was the first to jump in next to Tori. He had no issues swimming around naked in a public pool. Tori looked onto him. "You're a natural." She said to Sasha as she laughed. "Let me have a look at you, Avarie. Turn around." Even though it was awkward for Avarie, she did as she said. "Very nice. You may be small, but you look very strong." Slapping the water she urged Avarie in. Bounding in, Avarie wasn't as graceful as Tori. She allowed them to swim around for a while.

Tori led them in swimming exercises. She was careful to avoid the deep end for Avarie's sake. Already having earned her trust, Tori decided to let Sasha go to the deep end and dive off the boards. They both watched as he had a good time by himself. "Where'd you find a handsome thing like that?" Tori asked her jokingly.

"He's my guardian." She answered shyly. "He protects me from evil."

Tori understood. There was no relationship between them. He was there to be her guardian only and make sure she stayed safe. "You must be one lucky girl to have someone like him." Avarie wanted to change the subject.

"Who's your uncle?" Avarie asked curiously.

"He's one of the heads of the FSB. More like a shadow if you will. His name is Mikhail. He's Kirill's brother."

Avarie shuddered at the thought. They spent a few more hours swimming. Tori wanted to see how strong Avarie was without her knowing. They managed to play around with Sasha a bit before getting out. She took them to the cafeteria and then back into the training room. Sitting down on the mat, they joined her.

"Now there's somethings I need to know." She looked at them seriously. "Did you have a routine when you lived with Herr Cambridge?"

"Somewhat. I woke up, ate, trained, ate lunch, trained some more, ate, then went swimming."

Tori nodded. "Okay so we have some work to do." She leaned into them. "I understand that Kirill has you both locked down once you go back to his place." Sasha nodded. "All training starts here at 7:30. You'll have classroom time first so be there promptly. You'll have a few breaks depending on the teacher. After that, it's lunch time around 11:30. You only get an hour, so use it wisely. At 12:30, you'll be in here with me. There are multiple trainers in different disciplines. We'll start off with basics and progress. We'll stop around 5:30 so you can snack and rest up. After that, we go to the pool so your muscles can relax." She looked around for objections, but there were none. "You'll end training here at 8:15. At 8:30, your driver will be waiting for you to take you back. You'll eat supper and go to bed."

Avarie dared to ask. "Do we get weekends off?"

Rolling her head back, she thought hard. "I think that depends on Kirill. If he hears that you're progressing, he may indulge you." She clicked her hands against the mat. "If I were you, I'd avoid that man like the plague. Make him happy, please." Worry crossed her face. "He's not a very nice person, Avarie. I'm sure you already discovered that." She said as her finger grazed the bruises on Avarie's abdomen. "He has a mean temper and it just gets worse."

A door opened in the background. Avarie didn't look up because she felt a strange presence and she couldn't put her finger on it. It wasn't until the door opened and she knew instantly it was Kirill. She cringed inside her skin. "I see you met the little one, Tori." Kirill's voice boomed through the training room. Sasha nudged her to get up. She did but kept her eyes to the floor. He stood next to her and the other man followed. All she could see were their shoes.

"She's a strong one, Kirill." Tori gave him a bit of attitude. "She'll be just fine."

Somebody was chewing gum in the background. She could hear their lips smacking around. "I know she's strong." He said defensively. "With strength comes stubbornness so you need to watch out for her."

"I can handle her just fine." Tori spat at him. "Why don't you go back behind your desk where you belong you *fucking* lizard."

Sasha started chuckling and turned away. Avarie held back a laugh. Tori could handle her own.

"*Oi*! That's no way to talk to your uncle." Kirill said. "Especially in front of company."

Avarie watched Tori's shoes as they met head to head with this evil man. "I'm sorry you're a fucking lizard. Now get the hell out of here." She pushed him towards the door while he laughed. He gave her a kiss on the cheek and left just like that. Clapping her hands together, she announced. "Now Uncle Mikhail, this is Avarie."

Daring to slowly move her head up, she thought she was looking at Kirill again. The realization hit her that this man was his twin, but he was different. Taking steps back beside Sasha, he watched her with a pleasant smile. She carefully looked him over. He had jet black hair that was as long and thick as Sasha's. He wore a goatee and had hazel eyes. They weren't flat like Kirill's. No, there was magic behind them. He wore a black ops suit like he just came back from a mission and a Krinkov strapped on his back. He took his time as he chewed his gum and looked them both over.

Pulling a package out of his pocket, he offered Sasha a piece of gum first. He shrugged and took it. Popping it into his mouth, he looked down at Avarie and nudged her again. Mikhail held it out to her. Hesitantly, she took a piece and put it in her mouth. Tori stood beside him with pride, but worry overtook Avarie's face and she noticed.

"*Mishka*, he is nothing like Kirill." She assured her in the beautiful thick Russian accent. Sasha smiled down at Avarie again.

Excitement worked its way through Mikhail as he looked at them both. A bigger smile crept onto his face as he chewed his gum with fervor. The gun on his back made clicking sounds as he extended his hand towards Sasha and he took it. It looked as though they were having a mental conversation. Mikhail crossed his arms and walked around Avarie, the smile never leaving his face. He could tell she was nervous and it didn't help that he looked like his brother who she thought was a major prick.

"They made you so little." He exclaimed with sarcasm. "Tori, this is the little one who gave Kirill a run for his money. You believe that?" He cocked an eyebrow in her direction.

Tori giggled. "He underestimated her it sounds like." They both laughed.

Avarie averted her eyes. She didn't know if she should feel shame or delight. Mikhail crouched down to meet her gaze. He was inches from her face. "*Mishka*, I understand you're a force to be reckoned with." Avarie felt like she was going to cry being this close to him. "I won't intentionally hurt you. You're here to learn and you're with the best." He lifted her chin towards him with his finger. "Training starts in earnest tomorrow. I want you rested and prepared." He stood up and slapped Sasha's arm. "Make sure she's ready my friend." He turned around and walked out the door. In the hallway, they could hear him yell extremely loud. "We're going to win!"

Avarie just shook her head and Sasha giggled. "He's very excited about you, Avarie." Tori said. "Now, let's get you both home."

ϒϒϒ

Back in their shared bedroom, Sasha ushered Avarie into the bathroom and drew her bath. "I need to call Courtney. You stay in the tub until I come get you." He winked and left. She strained to listen to the conversation from the extremely large soaking tub, but it was all mumbled. She knew Sasha did that on purpose and it made her angry. Thirty minutes later, he came in and told her she could come out.

"What'd he say?" She asked anxiously.

"He said he loves you and wants you to behave yourself while you're here." Sasha motioned for her to get into bed. It was late and she needed her sleep.

"Is that all?"

"No, the other things he wanted me to say to you were very naughty and I don't wish to repeat them." Sasha said in jest. "Just know that he's already missing you and so are Eva and Matthias."

Avarie wished she could talk to them just to hear their voices; but she'd be in trouble if Kirill found out. "What do you think of Kirill's brother?" She asked Sasha as she pulled her covers over and turned off the light.

"Mikhail has your best interests at heart. Courtney told me that he visited them yesterday and apologized profusely about his brother."

"Do you like him?"

"I like what he is, yes. He knows what I am and that I'll protect you from harm." Sasha propped himself up on his elbow. "Most of all, he knows who *you* are."

Avarie snuggled a pillow into her. "What's that mean?"

Sasha explained. "Courtney can't hide the fact of who you are. Last night, Mikhail got the whole story. Needless to say, he's extremely excited about your presence. At the same time, a little apprehensive."

Avarie tried to put two and two together. "So he knows I'm …her." He nodded. "So why's he apprehensive?"

He laughed and rolled on his back. "It seems in your past life, you were very stubborn and hard to work with. He's hoping it'll be better this time around."

Rolling on her back she huffed. "Fucking Russians." Sasha chuckled and leaned over to kiss her forehead.

"You need to sleep. Tomorrow is a big day for both of us." He shut off his light. Avarie rolled over to face the wall. Closing her eyes, she pictured Courtney. After a while, she finally fell asleep.

CHAPTER SIX

Courtney has managed to stay busy. After talking to Sasha last night, he felt a little better. Avarie met with a woman named Tori and she was finally able to meet Mikhail. Sasha was confident that she'd get along fine as long as she followed the rules. He had no choice but to trust Sasha.

In the office, Gerhart let him know that the servers were running and there was a lot of chatter. Damian and Jude were hard at work deciphering everything. Excitement grew inside Courtney. "Good, how long before it gets decoded?" he asked.

"I don't know, it depends on the programming." Gerhart said honestly. "We know they're on the move. I think they're trying to overwhelm the militia."

"Let's hope Russia stays on top of that."

"Speaking of the Russian's, how's Avarie doing?"

Courtney sighed and said, "Sasha said training starts today. He's excited for her and he likes the people he has training her. I'm glad he's with her."

"Me too." Gerhart took a sip of his coffee. "How are the others holding up?"

"Eva is quiet for the most part. Without Avarie, she seems to have lost her spark. Matthias is still working on his machine. I might have to send Jude over sooner than later to help him."

"I can arrange that." Gerhart assured him. "Besides, those boys get antsy just staring at a computer screen all day."

Courtney laughed. He knew all too well what happens when you stare into a screen for too long. Back when the internet first came out, he was completely enthralled. He decided to let Gerhart make the arrangements.

ϒϒϒ

When Courtney arrived home later, the house was completely silent. Matthias texted him earlier letting him know that they were having supper with Xander so they could explain Avarie's situation. The last thing Courtney wanted was to be alone. He made himself something small to eat. Going up to the attic, he dug out old Tomes that he promised Eva and brought boxes of them down to the library. He thought to himself, Avarie would love these. Tears started to flow and he broke down crying. He was glad nobody was there to see him become a weak pussy. He never intended for any of this to happen and he didn't know when he'd see or speak to her again.

Mikhail promised him that he'd let him speak to her once a month. If he stepped on his brother's toes too much, Avarie would pay the price. In the darkness, his phone rang. Plucking it from his pocket, he answered to Sasha's voice. They spoke their ancient German so Avarie wouldn't understand. She's not supposed to be in the room when they talk.

Sasha spoke of how training went and his first time holding a rifle. Avarie had already impressed one of her instructors on her combat skills and Mikhail has grown very excited about her abilities. "So far, she's doing what she's told." Sasha assured him. "Tori is very much in love with her...and me."

Courtney laughed. "You mean this woman has a crush on you?"

"It's not funny. Women are strange creatures." He whispered into the phone. "I don't know what to do with them. It's bad enough I have to watch out for Avarie. Do you know how hard it is to get her out of bed in the mornings?"

Sasha was so funny. In his entire existence, he'd never had a full-fledged encounter with a woman. This was going to get interesting. "No, I let her sleep in."

"Therein lies the problem." Sasha sounded frustrated. "How do you handle these females?"

"Oh Sasha, you let them handle you, that's the trick." Courtney would have to tell the others about this conversation. "Just go along for the ride."

"I don't want this one to expect things from me." Sasha hissed. Talking about women made him uncomfortable. "I'm not that kind of entity... I mean I could be, but I'm not."

Courtney busted up laughing. Poor Sasha, he had no clue what he was in for. "Alright, calm down. Mikhail can help you in that department. I'm stuck over here in Germany so there's not much I can do."

"Fine, but just know this; I'm not happy about it."

Courtney was still laughing. "I'm sorry, Sasha. You're a good looking man and women can't help themselves. Maybe this Tori girl could teach you a trick or two."

There was silence on the other line. "I'm changing the subject." Sasha demanded. He talked of other things and let Courtney respond. When the timer buzzed, Sasha wished him good night and hung up. Courtney couldn't help feeling jealous towards him. He wished he was the one with Avarie right now.

Eva and Matthias arrived home and they went through the old Tomes. Courtney found one that explained what Sasha was and how he worked. Then he dove right into the conversation they had on the phone. Eva thought that was the funniest thing she ever heard. "How do you get through life avoiding females?" she said

"In his time, females were much different." Matthias pointed out. "They weren't as open as you are now."

"Still, he had to come into contact with many of them." Eva had another thought. "Think he likes men?"

Courtney and Matthias looked at her like she was crazy. "No!" Both insisted.

"Damn, I was just asking, *geez*." Eva said defensively. "Question a man's sexuality and they jump down your throat."

"Eva, he's not a sexual being, that's the thing." Courtney said smiling. "That isn't something that's required in the existence he comes from."

"But he can if he decides he wants too?" Eva asked. "I mean, you don't wonder around this world a virgin unless you're a priest."

"Eva, how many priests do you know are really virgins?" Matthias asked with a sneer.

"Fine!" She grew frustrated with the conversation. She looked through more Tomes. "Are these supposed to help us somehow?" she asked Courtney.

"They might. It's about all the magic in the world. Mikhail called you a fire pagan. So before this person gets here, maybe you should look through these and try to find something interesting."

"When's this person supposed to arrive?" Matthias asked Courtney.

"Monday, and it's a *he*." Courtney responded quickly.

"Oh." It sounded like Matthias' heart sank a bit. Courtney chuckled.

"A he?" Eva didn't sound so sure about this now. "Where's he going to stay?"

"*He* is Ivan." Courtney looked up from the Tome. "And Ivan will stay in Sasha's room for now." He pulled a smaller Tome from the stack and flipped through it. "He's an entity like Sasha."

"Wow, another Sasha." Matthias quipped.

"Oh hush." Courtney bopped him on the head. "Sasha isn't that bad."

"No, Sasha is pretty cool, this guy better be just as cool." Matthias rubbed the top of his head. "Where's he from?"

"The Ukraine." Courtney responded. "He speaks English and a bit of German so he can communicate with all of us." He added another piece of information. "He's much younger in this world than Sasha. He was brought over in 2015 when the Ukraine-Russian crisis hit. I don't know what faction brought him over so don't ask."

"Wow, so he's all caught up compared to Sasha then?' Eva asked.

"Woman, I don't bother with details." Courtney shook his head at her. "All I know is that Mikhail vouched for him. So do me a favor and be on your best behavior please."

Eva pouted at him while Matthias laughed. They spent the wee hours of the night going through as many Tomes as possible. Courtney bookmarked the pages that he thought would be interesting and they discussed a game plan. He fell asleep thinking about tomorrow being Friday and Courtney hoped the weekend would get here soon. He needed to get drunk and Gerhart promised him a night out.

ϒϒϒ

Avarie was on her second day of training. The classroom time wasn't so bad. She was in a room full of other agents. They looked upon her kindly. Out of fifteen total, four were women and it seemed she was the smallest one. Sasha sat next to her as Valentin went through weapons training. They had to learn every mechanism that made up each gun and they were quizzed on it. Avarie was never in a school setting so this was new to her. Sasha sat patiently and answered questions that were asked of him. He was quick to ask about wind resistance and range when it came to the sniper rifle.

A picture came up on the screen of a Barrett .50 Cal and Sasha looked like he was in love. "You like that Agent?" Valentin asked him. He nodded excitedly. "Good, because sometime next week, you'll get to shoot one." Sasha rubbed his hands together. "Some men say shooting this rifle is better than sex. The power in this thing is what wet dreams are made of." Sasha cocked an eye brow. Valentin laughed at him and moved on. Avarie nudged him in the ribs and gave him a 'what the fuck?' expression. He shrugged at her.

Valentin skimmed through some other rifles and automatic machine guns. Some had videos on how they fired. That was the best part for Avarie. "Can anybody tell me the difference between a clip and a magazine?" He asked. Sasha nudged her because it was her turn to answer. She raised her hand. "Yes, Agent?"

"A magazine is a container that holds cartridges while a clip is more like a strip that holds the cartridges together at the butt of the bullet." She answered.

"Very good! Our late comer may make a good agent yet!" he declared. The rest of the class laughed with him.

A guy next to her leaned over and jokingly called her an ass kisser. She whispered back to fuck off. Sasha giggled at them both. They took a short break from their class to stretch and walk around the room. There were facilities right there along with refreshments. Avarie was happy for that. She was getting hungry and needed to pee. The next instructor would be in soon. His name was Karl and he was from the Ukraine. His class taught situational awareness. She grabbed some food and gobbled it down. Watching the others, she noticed the ladies were gathered in a group and checking out Sasha. They whispered and giggled to each other. One burnet one motioned for Avarie to come over. She looked around and went to meet the ladies.

"Is he your boyfriend?" She asked. Avarie knew her as Julia. She shook her head no. "We understand you two came together right?" She nodded. "Then, is he family?" The other ladies were anxious for the answer.

"Sasha is my guardian." Avarie whispered. "He has to protect me." The ladies looked at her confused.

"So, he's your caretaker?" Julia asked.

"Yes, he's my caretaker." Avarie just let it go. She didn't expect them to understand.

"He's handsome." One of the ladies said to her. "You're lucky." Avarie looked over at Sasha as he mingled with the Russian men. He was in his element here.

"He's a pain in the ass." Avarie said. "I don't consider that lucky." she joked. Avarie was able to get a snack and use the restroom before the instructor entered the room and motioned for the rest of them to sit down.

Pandora Rising

Yesterday, they went through the OODA Loop. It means; Observe, Orient, Decide, Act. Those who can cycle through this loop the fastest wins. Karl showed videos yesterday on this loop and decided to go through the first step today. He talked about using all your senses to observe the environment around you and the color coded system that goes along with it. They were forty minutes into the lecture and something changed with Avarie. She heard clicking sounds out in the hallway, but they were a distance away. Her heartrate elevated and she softly touched Sasha's shoulder. He leaned in and whispered, "What is it?"

"I don't know, something's happening and it isn't right." She whispered back. Karl was still talking as he went through seemingly innocent scenario's in which situational awareness was needed for agents. He was oblivious to what might be going on out in the hall. She realized that maybe he couldn't hear it. The sounds became a little louder and she recognized the sound. It was a machine gun clicking. The rules of the building were no guns allowed on the third floor. The sounds of footsteps were almost at the door. She feared they found her and somehow gotten into the building.

Running to the door, Karl looked at her in surprise. The door was unlocked and she debated on locking it. "Agent Moeller!" He said to her. Putting her finger to her lips, she motioned for him to be quiet. A confused look gathered on his face. The person was at the door. As they opened it, Avarie slammed her fist into their nose, and then swept her foot under them, knocking whoever it was on their backside. She took the rifle out of his hand and slid it over to Karl.

It was all over within seconds. Standing up shaking, Avarie looked down at the man. *Oh fuck, it was Mikhail.* He was laid out on his back and he looked up at her stunned. Sasha jumped up from his seat and helped him up. Karl grabbed tissues for the bloody nose while the other students looked on in shock. She knew she was in trouble. In less than a week, she would receive another belt beating from Kirill.

Mikhail wiped his nose and looked down at Avarie. He started laughing at her. Sasha looked at him like he lost his shit and was running with it. Karl announced to the class. "Thanks to Agent Moeller, the lecture by Direktor Borowitz will be postponed for a bit." God she felt horrible. Karl pulled all three of them into the side office and closed the door.

"Agent Moeller, how'd you know he was coming?" he asked curiously.

Tears started to fall down her cheeks. "I'm so sorry, I didn't mean too. I know we're not supposed to have guns on the third floor and I heard the clicking sound first." She tried to control herself before she sobbed all over the place.

"Don't be sorry." Mikhail said calmly. "You got me good." He looked around for his rifle. "Oh shit, you took that from me too didn't you?" She nodded. "Karl, we have a gem here!"

"More like a diamond in the rough." He corrected him. Karl looked over at Avarie and handed her another tissue. "I didn't know she was already trained." He told Mikhail.

"She isn't." Sasha stated. "She has heightened senses and they kick in. Sometimes in the most awkward of moments too." Avarie could hear chatter from the classroom. She already managed to embarrass herself and she didn't want to go back in there. She could only imagine how bad high school would've been.

"Why don't you go back out Karl? I'll handle this from here." Mikhail coaxed. "Go calm them down a bit. I'm sure they'll be talking about how the new person kicked their Direktor's ass." Karl nodded and walked out.

Sasha pulled Avarie into him. He cooed into her ear that she was alright and Mikhail wasn't hurt as bad as she thought. Mikhail pulled a bottle of water out of the mini fridge and splashed it onto a paper towel. "My God, you're good." He said as he smiled. "I'm not even sure you need this class." He handed her another tissue. "Oh, I'm not mad. You did exactly as you were supposed to." He blew his nose into a clean paper towel.

"And what was that?" Sasha asked him, confused about the situation.

"She disarmed me." He stood up and threw the bloodied towels in the trash. "She's right; we're not supposed to have guns on the third floor. This is the floor for new agents only and we're supposed to check our guns in." He reached out for her, but she stepped back. "We just need to polish your skills, that's all." He winked at her. She felt a little better, but not by much. He was all cleaned up and ready to go back into the classroom.

Avarie hesitated. Mikhail looked down at her. "Don't worry, *Mishka*." He whispered. "You have no need to be embarrassed." She looked up at him like he read her mind. "What you did was the whole point of this class.

Now go back out there." He coaxed. She didn't want to get into any more trouble so she went back out with Sasha and sat down. Her faced burned with shame and she avoided eye contact with the other Agents.

He came to the head of the class in all smiles. "I guess we know which agent we shouldn't be sneaking up on." He announced. The classroom roared in laughter as did Karl. He went straight into a lecture about how using all your senses and establishing a baseline of everywhere you go. Avarie avoided looking at the front of the room. This was the last class before lunch and she couldn't wait to get out of there.

ϒϒϒ

After classroom time was over, she quickly grabbed Sasha and headed for the cafeteria. He laughed as she pulled him along. "Slow down, *Maus*." He said smiling. "You're going to run people over." She wanted to get away from the others as quick as possible and she didn't care who was in her way. She looked like a child tugging a mule along a dirt road.

Finally making it to the cafeteria, she felt safe. That was until she noticed people looking sideways at her. She rolled her eyes and drug Sasha along to get something to eat and they sat down. The other agents from the classroom were whispering in her direction. She was getting unwanted attention and she couldn't hide in here. Ten minutes later, Tori joined them at the table. "So, I hear you kicked Mikhail's ass." She said as she bit into her apple. "In front of an entire classroom too. Impressive." Now Tori was handing her shit.

The scent of the sweet apple hit Avarie's nose. It reminded her of something, but didn't know what. Shaking off the thought, she went to poking her food around. "*Mishka*, you have great senses. Karl can help you tame them." She said taking another bite of the apple. "Mikhail is very impressed with you right now. He's up there bragging at the lunch line how you broke his nose." She started laughing.

"I didn't mean to." Avarie said finally. "I already feel bad." She had to fight back tears. She didn't want to cry in front of hundreds of strangers.

"Don't cry and don't feel bad." Tori patted her back. "I'm just curious as to why you saw him as a threat."

Avarie took a big swig of her milk before answering. "I thought they were coming for me." She whispered. "I heard the sound of the rifle shuffling on him and footsteps. I honestly didn't know it was Mikhail."

"You mean to tell me you heard all that in a classroom while he walked down a hallway outside?" Tori looked amazed. Avarie nodded. "Who are *they*?" Tori asked.

"The Mossad." Sasha answered for her. "They've been stalking us for the past few weeks."

"Well, they sure as shit won't get in here." Tori said with wide eyes. "They'd be lucky to get past the security, let alone to the third floor." Tori looked around and watched as people stared and whispered in their direction. There were at least four high powered officials in the cafeteria and they looked in Avarie's direction. "Now you have the attention of all the Direktors'." Tori said. "They'll be watching your progress now, too. Let's not disappoint them." She patted Avarie on the hand.

"Wonderful." Avarie shook her head. "My second day here and I already have all kinds of eyes on me." she huffed. Sasha grinned at her. Avarie didn't want to hear or see anymore. Pulling out her iPod, she plugged it in and ignored them.

Deciding to give Avarie space, Tori engaged Sasha in conversation. Avarie was distracted to a song and bobbed her head up and down. She didn't notice Mikhail sat down across from her until he stole one of her fries she wasn't eating. Looking up at him, he smiled at her. She kept bobbing her head and looked away. He tapped her foot and he looked at her again. He started to mimic her and bobbed his head up and down, still smiling at her. He was trying to get her to smile. It worked and she blushed when she realized that he made her do it. He was incredibly handsome when he gave her a full grin. His eyes were full of life and she found them appealing.

He looked around and picked up his walkie. He said something into it, but she couldn't hear because she still had her earbuds in. Tori looked at him and shook her head and he nodded. Sasha asked, "What's going on?"

"Tradition." She answered. "When a new agent happens to kick the ass of a direktor, they turn up the music in the cafeteria. Usually something fast and Mikhail likes to embarrass the person. It's funny, just watch."

Avarie watched as Mikhail pointed up to the ceiling and she pulled out her earbuds. The crowd gathered around her table and Mikhail heard the first few notes of *Take on Me*. He started to squirm in his seat and Avarie could only watch as he started to lip-sync the words to her. He put on a whole production as the entire cafeteria clapped along to the song. He got up and the people made space while he danced for her. He was actually a damn good dancer. Avarie couldn't help laughing at him. Sasha was entertained and Tori hooted and hollered for her Uncle to bring it home. God this was even more embarrassing than having broken his nose in the classroom, Avarie thought. Her face flushed red hot and prayed for the song to be over soon.

After it was done, the cafeteria erupted in applause and Mikhail bowed. When everybody settled down, Avarie looked like she was ready to bolt. Mikhail sat down across from her again. "It's very rare that a new one takes out a direktor within the first week, let alone the second day."

"I told you I'm sorry." Avarie pleaded. "I thought I was in danger and I didn't want anybody else to get hurt if they were after me."

"Shh, *Mishka*." He said calmly. "You were in the right. I broke the rules and that's on me. I deserved that beating."

"You aren't going to tell your brother are you?" Her eyebrows furrowed with worry. "He'll hurt me again and once is enough."

"No, I'm not going to tell him." He smiled at her. "I'll tell him that you're progressing as you should. Nobody but me and your direct teachers report to him about you and that's the way it should be." He looked at his watch. "We need to get ready for our combat training." He stood up and they followed. All eyes were still on Avarie and Sasha as she walked out with Tori and Mikhail.

ϒϒϒ

In the training room, they started off with hand to hand combat. Mikhail would use Sasha as his volunteer. He still hadn't won Avarie's trust and knew he had to work slowly at it. Sasha was his way in and he planned on using him to his fullest potential. Sasha grew on him and they had a mutual friendship. It was nice to find somebody like him in this world.

As Tori watched them simulate moves, she whispered to Avarie, "How do you sleep next to him without wanting to touch that sexy body?" Avarie concealed a giggle. She hadn't really seen Sasha in that way. He was just her buddy and nothing more.

"He steals the covers, but he blames it on me." She said back. "That helps."

"Girls!" Mikhail yelled. "Pay attention!" He shook his head. "Damn women." He said as he took his stance and looked at Sasha. "I swear I'll never understand human females."

Sasha threw up his arms in frustration. "That's what I tell everybody." Tori covered a smirk as they watched them simulate a conflict. Avarie and Tori followed suit. Some fights became aggressive, others not so much. They continued until break time. In the locker room, Sasha grabbed water and a power bar. Mikhail sat down next to him on the bench while he toweled off.

"Tori really likes you." He said to Sasha as he shook his head. "I tried explaining to her that you aren't that kind of being, but she doesn't care. It's like the harder you are to get, the more they try." He started laughing. "Maybe you should come onto her and see what happens; then maybe she won't like the hunt so much."

Sasha smiled at him. "No thanks. Avarie is enough to handle."

"Oh, so you do have a relationship with her."

Sasha corrected him, "No, Avarie has a relationship with Courtney. She won't even look at me twice and I prefer it that way." He downed his water and grabbed another bottle.

"Ah, she's not into you."

"No." He shook his head. "It isn't that our relationship is complicated. I protect her and she understands that. She's never asked anything of me that I couldn't handle or outside of my comfort zone."

Mikhail put down his towel and looked down. "You know, there will come a time when she will be asked to do things outside of hers and we need to push her along." He sighed. "It won't be for a while yet so we won't worry about it right now." He patted Sasha's shoulder and led him back to the training room.

Sasha didn't want Mikhail to elaborate on what he said. He understood too well what he meant. Avarie would have to warm up to the idea and it wasn't going to be easy. Mikhail needed to earn her trust before even going down that road.

ϒϒϒ

It was Monday already and Courtney was completely shitfaced all weekend. Gerhart made good on his promise to take him out. They went to a casino, two strip clubs, ten bars, golf course, another casino and the rest was a blur. That man knew how to party. Matthias was ashamed of him when he came home. Eva about slapped him when Gerhart carried him in singing and laughing on Sunday afternoon.

Gerhart and Courtney took that Monday off to recover from their shenanigans. Avarie was running around in his mind so much, he needed to drink her away for a while. He felt guilty, but he had to cope somehow. Shit, even Matthais was getting laid and it wasn't fair to Courtney.

Late afternoon, the doorbell rang. Matthias answered it and it was their guest. A very stunning and buff red-haired man stood in the doorway. "Is this the home of Herr Cambridge?" he asked slowly in a Slavic accent.

"It is, are you Ivan?" Matthias asked politely.

"I am." He stepped inside the house with his bags and introduced himself to Courtney, who was still semi drunk and sitting at the piano just clapping keys together with sunglasses on. Ivan whispered to Matthias, "Woman problems?" Matthias grinned and nodded. "Figures." Ivan shook his head in disgust. "Only a woman could drive a man to drink that much."

"Speaking of women..." Matthias spotted Eva coming up from the training room. "This is Eva. She's the one you're here for."

She met him and shook his hand with a shit eating grin. She was almost giddy as she gotten lost in his light blue eyes. Matthias just shook his head in wonder and took Ivan's things to his room. When he came back down, Ivan and Eva were at the sitting area. She explained what happened last Monday and he listened intently. Matthias joined them in the conversation. Ivan had a game plan together for Eva.

"If you would like, you could join us if that would make you comfortable?" Ivan asked Matthias. "I wouldn't mind."

Matthias thought about it. "I'll join on some, but I have some projects to work on." He looked over at Courtney who fell asleep stretched out across the front of the piano. "And somebody has to babysit him while he wallows in his sorrows." Ivan laughed at him. "I'm hoping he goes into work tomorrow."

"Is this over the young lady, Avarie?" He asked softly. Matthias nodded. "I heard she didn't go quietly."

"She was quite pissed if that's what you mean?" Eva said with anger in her eyes. "They just came in and took her from us. It wasn't fair."

Ivan sat back in the seat. He understood exactly what she meant. "They took somebody you care for without warning." He thought to himself. "We can use that to your advantage. It seems you all love her very much."

Matthias and Eva nodded. "Good, love is a wonderful spark to start with." Ivan's blue eyes became soft as he sat forward again. "We can get to work tomorrow. Right now, I'd like to see the castle."

Matthias was more than happy to give him a tour. Walking by Courtney, Matthias slapped him behind his head. Courtney shot up and looked at him. "Go upstairs and sleep it off, drunkie!" Courtney was in no condition to argue and he lumped up the stairs. They watched as he lumbered like a groggy bear.

Ivan turned to Matthias and asked, "She doesn't drive you to drink does she?" He asked in jest.

"No, she just drives me crazy." Eva slapped his arm. "Ow, woman." He rubbed his arm. "It was just a joke." Matthias continued with the tour. He knew he was going to like this guy as much as Sasha.

ϒϒϒ

Watching footage from the Mossad, Shimon was not happy. The damn Russians were swooping in everywhere and they wanted to keep things low key. Fucking Kirill and his twin brother Mikhail were onto them. Calling one of his top officers into the office, he pushed the laptop out of his way.

A large man about six foot four stepped in, dressed in a military uniform. His blonde hair swept across his flat brown eyes. "Sit down Luscious." Shimon demanded. He did as he was told and made himself comfortable.

"Please tell me, how the *Hell* the Russians knew we were in Germany?"

Luscious acted uninterested as he picked a stray thread from his uniform. "Possibly because you sent in newbies and they weren't properly trained. I warned you."

Slamming his fists on his desk in a rage, Shimon yelled, "You stupid fuck! You said that Courtney didn't have a Russian task force."

Luscious just stared at him with a blank face. "He doesn't. He has the grandchild of a militia member who works with him and acts as head of his security." He started to laugh. "You remember he has ties to other factions."

Shimon was not enthused. "Where's the girl?" he asked as he opened his hands. "We were supposed to have her, and now she's gone."

Luscious shook his head at him. "Courtney probably has her hidden somewhere. After your pansies were attacked, maybe he decided that she needed to go into another country or go back to the States." He was getting annoyed. "Why is it that you always underestimate humans? They're very smart." He hissed softly. "Courtney is no exception. Yes, he has his faults, but he's defiant. You've seen him strike against us over and over again. Too bad the Thirteen has never figured out his game."

"We let him slide because he's one of yours." Shimon shook his finger at him. "You told us to leave him alone and we have. Without knowing it, he's been a great ally and an even greater enemy. You taught him well."

Luscious smiled. "Yes, he was a beautiful disaster and still is. Unfortunately, he thinks I'm still dead. So making a pit stop is out of the question." He sighed and shook his head. "I love that boy but I hate him. In the end, faking my death was the best for each of us. He got a great treasure out of it." He said waiving his hand. "My castle, fortune, history, you name it."

"We aren't here to reminisce about old times!" Shimon's voice boomed. "We're here about the girl! Project 314! Can we please focus on *her*?"

Luscious didn't even budge from his seat. This man didn't scare him one bit. He's seen it all. "Well, tell me about her. I wasn't aware of her until six months ago." He lifted his cap off and put it on his knee.

"So, an executive rummaged through files and found hers incomplete, so they put a termination order on her. However, another brought the subject up to Verinus and he decided to run with it. He gave the order to the executives to keep the termination order on her but; he had an order to implant an IUD device inside her. Don't ask me why? He has his reasons." He continued. "The next time around, the executive looked through her file and found something interesting…" He threw a file folder in Luscious' direction.

He opened it up and flipped through. "It says that the Mossad ordered her. I don't remember that." Luscious said.

"Exactly." Shimon hissed. "Somebody wanted to hide who she is and the real intentions for being created."

"So please tell me what this has to do with Courtney." He threw the file back at him. "He's not one to meddle in affairs like that. He's more of a playboy than a political player. Sure he's helped the militia from time to time, but a man with immortality needs excitement every now and then."

Shimon was growing weary of this conversation. Pouring himself a glass of whiskey, he handed one to Luscious. "We believe your *Courtney*, is the one who funded her."

He shook his head, "Maybe he wanted a fuck buddy."

Shimon threw his empty glass against the wall and watched it shatter. "Maybe Courtney wants to help the damn Russians! He isn't exactly on our side either!" He paced the room. "This girl he created, possesses special abilities, Luscious. We had it set up that she be terminated and on that date be released to us." He shuddered. "Somehow, she escaped. Some asshole programmed her to run north, and she did. Now, she's in Germany and we don't even know how Courtney got a hold of her."

"What the fuck do you want me to do about it?" Luscious stood up and poured himself another glass and hissed at Shimon. "Go knock on his door and tell him to give us the girl?" He swirled the brown liquid in his glass. "Good luck." He took a drink and let the fire rage in his throat. "He's smarter than that. He'd put himself in harm's way for the cause."

Shimon grabbed the empty glass from his hands. "Why don't you deal with him like you dealt with that woman from the States? The one who tried to expose us all."

"Which one?" he asked. "There were many people I took out from the conspiracy movement, so you have to be specific."

"Fucking Nikita Stormwall!" Shimon had enough of this shit. "Tear him apart like you did to her, I don't care how you deal with him, just do it." He demanded.

"I didn't kill her. I murdered her family. That was fun by the way." He snatched the empty glass again and filled it. "I can't just walk into his house like I did with her. He has protection." He took a long drink. "I haven't had any contact with him since I left."

"Yes, and you disappeared from his life like a fart in the wind…" Shimon shook his finger at him. "You will figure out how to deal with him and get the girl."

"Fine, but it won't be immediately." He put the empty glass down. "We'll watch Courtney closely and look for signs of the girl. If she doesn't show up…let's say in a few months, we'll deal with him." He picked up his hat from the chair and placed it on his head. "These are matters we have to deal with tenderly, Shimon." He started for the door.

"We wouldn't have to deal with it tenderly if he wasn't one of yours!" He hissed after him.

"You're absolutely right." Luscious put his hand on the knob. "That's why you'll let me deal with him and if I find out you so much as touch him, there'll be a coup de ta on your hands. You don't want that now do you?" Shimon looked away. Luscious winked at him and slammed the door shut.

ϓϓϓ

Sasha was more than excited to be at the shooting range. His eyes were wide with excitement. Avarie could only shake her head at him. There was something about males and firepower. Sasha never held a gun in his life and he looked like he was about ready to ride the best rollercoaster out there. By God, he almost skipped off the bus. Valentin couldn't wait for this day. The men were all pumped to be using sniper rifles and the ladies would use the handguns with another instructor if they liked.

They were all given gear over the weekend. Avarie looked like a short shadow compared to the others. She was all dressed in black and had a utility belt. She tried to remember what she wore when she was Pandora, but she couldn't remember. Strange how that worked. Mikhail was there with them. He wanted to watch Sasha shoot the Barrett since that was all he could talk about. Mikhail managed to get Avarie's weapons from Courtney. Her Rossi and Beretta were in a case for her. He knew she would be okay with them but wouldn't let her have them yet.

Mikhail whispered in Avarie's ear, "Please don't show them up too much."

"I don't have a lot of experience with weapons yet." She said honestly. "I think they'll be showing me up. But I can't wait to see Sasha's reaction after he shoots the Barrett."

"He might actually get a hard-on." He said as he nudged her ribs. Avarie laughed. She was starting to get a little more comfortable with him. Not knowing exactly what he was, she still wasn't sure about him.

At the shooting stall, Valentin and the other instructor set up the rifles. Sasha kept rubbing his hands together in anticipation. He really wanted to get his hands on it. Valentin decided that Sasha needed to build up anticipation and go last. He wasn't happy about that. His eyes turned a sad blue and he sat next to Avarie with ear protection on. He grew jealous as the men shot round after round. There were only four set up and it took almost an hour before Sasha took his turn with Avarie.

Sitting down at the table, he blew into his hands like they were cold. Mikhail stood back and gave instructions. As Avarie felt the metal, she knew this baby. It was like a long lost friend and she couldn't wait to shoot rounds into the target in front of the huge berm. She remembered that it had a nasty recoil so she steadied herself as she looked through the scope. In German she told Sasha, "Steady yourself, these things hurt if you don't anticipate the recoil." Mikhail let them know that the firing range was hot and Sasha let loose one round before Avarie. Fuck, he wasn't even pointing, he just squeezed the trigger to hear it go boom. Avarie lost her shit as did the rest of the class. "Damn Sasha." She said between breaths. "At least aim the thing."

He blinked oddly at her with a strange expression on his face. He looked at Mikhail. He shook his head. "Valentin told you, better than sex." He patted Sasha's shoulder. "Now please actually aim this time, it makes the experience so much better."

Calling for the range to be hot, Avarie aimed and hit her target, but the recoil was nasty. The vibration shook her to the core. She had nine more rounds to go. Saying what the hell, she made a smiley face. Valentin and the others thought that was hilarious. Sasha took his time aiming. He only missed three shots, but it was good. Letting go of the gun, he stepped back with a shit eating grin. She didn't even want to know what was going through his head right now. He tasted the sweet power of a .50 Cal and he liked it.

He joined the other guys as they high fived him. The ladies joined Avarie and they chatted while the handguns were being set up. This is when Mikhail gave her the case and unlocked it for her. He brought out a bag with ammo. "Some of this was hard to find. The .45 Colt, we had to get a company to make for us, so use it wisely." he winked.

Valentin cleared the range and everybody fired at their target from 25 yards, and then moved it closer. Avarie did pretty good and Sasha did alright. He was enjoying himself. The instructors wanted to see the range everybody had and that was alright by her. It was three hours and they took a break. Nobody broke a range rule and they were intact. Some of the women were good shots with the handguns.

A lady asked Avarie about the Rossi. She explained what its original intention was as a rancher gun and how they shot it from the hip. The sights weren't the best and you needed to aim low. Mikhail was curious about this one. They lined up again and Avarie yelled. "Permission to walk the range!"

Valentin looked at her oddly and Mikhail asked her, "Why walk the range?"

"I need to move my target further out."

"How far?"

"At least to fifty yards." She stated.

Valentin and Mikhail conferred with each other. She didn't want to break any rules or get anybody in trouble. The Rossi demanded attention and it's been a long time since she shot her baby.

"Alright, since this gun isn't standard issue, we'll allow it. We want to see how it works." Valentin answered. "How do you intend to shoot it?" He looked it over.

"The way the cowboys did" she winked. Loading it up on the table and inserting extra rounds into their holders across her body, she was ready. "There's different ways you can hold this gun. Just watch."

They were curious. "Is it just you on the range?" Mikhail called out for her.

"Yep. Keep them guns off me. I'll show you how Betsy fires." She grabbed her Rossi and jumped over the table. Yelling for the range to be hot for Avarie only, she let loose, holding it in her right hand with her arm outstretched. Every round that went out, she expelled the shell by twirling the lever in the same hand and coming up again. She walked the range as she fired each round. It only held six fully loaded. Once those rounds were gone, she reloaded and walked with it on her hip, cocking it the same way over and over again. Mikhail and Valentin watched in awe as she had complete control over this strange weapon. She hit the target each time. It was like she didn't even have to aim. Sasha yelled. "Show off!" She didn't pay any attention to him. She was with her girl right now and they needed some time alone. After every shell was spent, she called for the range to be clear. Everybody stared at her wondering what the Hell just happened.

Mikhail was lost for words as was Valentin. She handed him the Rossi back, careful for him to not touch the barrel. "Thank you." She said. He

Pandora Rising

smiled at her and gave her a wink. Valentin wiped his brow and looked at Mikhail.

"Alright everybody, the range is hot!" Valentin yelled. Avarie grabbed a bottle of water and sat down as the shots were fired. Mikhail watched as she smiled with pure pleasure. He needed to make sure that she had thousands of rounds at her disposal. Mikhail knew for sure that she didn't need this class. He decided to upgrade her next week to the sniper and handgun classes with the intermediate learners. Valentin took care of those classes also. He'd work with Sasha personally with his shooting skills so he could move him up. "What are you thinking, boss?" Valentin asked him.

"I'm thinking she needs to be moved up a class." He said nodding. "She's very skilled with assault weapons it seems. I'll have to work with Sasha. He seems to be enjoying himself."

"Well, I can move her up next week if you like."

"I'd like that." He said softly. "Karl wants to fine tune her situational awareness and I think that's a good idea. Do you see any potential problems with her?" He asked honestly.

"I've read the file that you gave me. The only problem that I could see is her hot dogging. But she asked permission to own the range before she did so." Valentin looked over at Sasha. "It seems that Sasha fills her with confidence, but he can't be there all the time. Is there something we can do to build that up?"

"I think we need to get her alone more often if we can and see how she does. This is only the start of the second week and we're already advancing her." He smiled. "It's a shame really. I enjoy having her and Sasha."

"There's still much more to learn, we've only scratched the surface with her." Valentin said. "Besides, there may be other areas that she could be lacking."

"I'm sure there are. Especially when it comes to the 'honey pot'."

"Oh yes. She's no exception to the rule." He smiled. "I see her killing though, not seducing."

"Don't be so sure." Mikhail said. "She has potential in that department." He watched down range. "We'll cross that bridge when we get there." He patted Valentin's shoulder and cleared the range.

ϒϒϒ

It was a long day and they were back at Kirill's house. Avarie was in a good mood and he could tell. He liked getting good reports about her progress and it made him glow with anticipation for the next week. He made it a habit that they talk about their training with him every night. Sasha told him about firing the Barrett and using the handguns. Avarie was mostly quiet. He hated that Sasha did most of her talking for her.

"Avarie, how was the firing range for you." He asked

"It was fine." She said with a mouthful of bread. She looked tired though. She didn't exactly have the best weekend. It was spent doing extra hand to hand combat with another trainer.

"I heard you were the best at the range." He swirled his wine. "Mikhail and Valentin are planning on advancing you."

"That's fine." She said as she finished her food.

"Aren't you excited?"

"I'll be excited when I get to go home." She said defensively.

"*Mishka* there's still more training to be done. If you think it's all about weapons and situations, you're wrong." He polished off his wine. "You have more months ahead of you."

"I know." She said quietly. Standing up, she was ready to go to her room. A man escorted her in. Fifteen minutes later, Sasha arrived. He kicked off his shoes and gear. He was still smiling.

"Geez, Sasha." Avarie exclaimed. "You jizz in your pants over that rifle?"

The look on his face said it all. "If that's as close as I get to sex, I'm alright with that." Avarie busted up laughing. That boy had no clue what he was missing but she wasn't about to tell him.

"You had to show off with your fancy guns." He said teasing her. "Everybody was jealous. You made me look bad."

"You made yourself look bad. You need to aim before you fire, dummy." She teased him back. "You'll get the hang of it." She plugged in her iPod and headed for the tub. Her body was sore and Sasha needed to check in with Courtney. It was the same routine. They babbled in their own ancient language while she soaked her body. Her shoulder hurt and it was bruised up a bit. Sasha laughed while he was on the phone with him. She hoped that she could talk to Courtney soon. She really missed him. She needed to talk to Mikhail about contacting Eva. He said it was possible and he would let her.

Sasha opened the door to let her know it was time to come back in. Drying off, she threw on her t-shirt and panties. She climbed over him, making sure she dug her knees into his stomach and he pushed her off of him while giggling. "You shouldn't be mean to the person who takes your messages for you." Sasha said haughtily.

"Let me guess. He loves me and can't wait for me to come home?"

"That was easy."

"It's the same every time." She said while throwing on her covers. "Are the Mossad gone?'

He put the phone on the night stand. "They aren't sure, but it's quiet for right now. Eva has her new trainer. His name is Ivan and he's from the Ukraine. He's going to teach her how to work with fire." He sounded excited.

"Ivan huh?" Avarie asked. "Is he like you?" Sasha nodded. "How many of you guys are there?"

"Could be many more. The universe is busy it seems." He shifted onto his side. "I can feel the energy building slowly. It's getting ready for war I believe. It will call reinforcements when needed for this world."

"Good, because I can't do this shit on my own." Avarie sounded relieved.

"You aren't expected to either. You know that right?"

Avarie wasn't so sure. It seemed a lot of attention was focused on her. She shut off the light and pulled the covers over her head, avoiding Sasha's question. "There are more people in this fight than you know. It's not all centered on you." He lifted the covers and kissed her forehead. "Sleep good, Maus."

CHAPTER SEVEN

Within a month and a half, Eva was learning quickly with her mentor. Ivan was very patient and kind towards her. It also helped that he was easy on the eyes. Many times he invited Matthias in on the sessions and he was more than happy to join. Ivan explained how each element was worshiped by pagans and what they did.

"How does that help us?" Matthias asked.

Ivan gave him a funny look and answered, "Matthias, the universe never gives its creations things it cannot use. You must be creative with the use of these forces."

"Can you give me an example?" he asked.

Ivan laughed tenderly. "Let's talk about the power of the wind. You like to fly don't you?" Matthias nodded. "Well then, you use the wind to your advantage by gliding across it." He continued. "Wind can also be a destructive force, by fanning the element of fire, or pushing water into waves."

"So your main element is fire?"

"It is." Ivan answered. "Fire is considered a masculine force as it changes things. Just because it's a masculine element, doesn't mean that females can't harness it." He winked at Eva.

"Alright, I want to see what Eva can do." Matthias said rubbing his hands together. She wanted to slap him for putting her on the spot. "Please." He begged.

In Sasha's room, Ivan placed a candle between them. "Now concentrate." He told Eva. Closing her eyes, she pictured the light in the room setting the wick aflame. It took some time, but it lit up. Matthias looked at it and teased, "I could use the element of wind to blow it out."

"Don't you dare!" She said giving him the evil eye. The flame flickered with anger.

"See how the flame changes with your emotions. You need to control its destructive aspect."

"You guys down there?" Courtney yelled as he walked down the steps.

"Yes!" Matthias yelled back.

Courtney looked flustered as soon as he reached the stone floor of Sasha's room. "Have any of you heard from Sasha or Avarie?" They shook their heads. The last time Eva heard from Avarie, was a week ago through an email.

"Has Sasha called?" Matthias asked.

"Not yet." Courtney looked around the room.

Ivan asked "Why're so worried?"

Courtney took off his blazer and sat down with the others. His eyes were heavy with worry. "It turns out; the Mossad is really looking for her. It's not just the Mossad either." He rubbed his hands through his hair. "My guys picked up chatter from the Elite. They're getting ready to move in the States to push back the militia and their generals."

"What about us?" Matthias asked. "Are we okay for now?"

"I don't know. Mikhail called me not too long ago. He said we need to shut down all contact and sever ties for now. They don't want Sasha and Avarie in danger and they don't want to give them a reason to come for us." Ivan could feel Courtney's heart pounding.

Eva shook her head, "That's just gonna drive Avarie crazy. She'll try to find a way to escape, Courtney."

"I know." He said as he rocked back and forth on his haunches. "Mikhail assured me that he's got tabs on her and Sasha is helping." He heaved a large sigh. "Jude told me that somebody tried to get into the castle security cameras. That's twice in two weeks. They know she's not here." His eyes went wide. "I don't want to scare any of you, but one of us might become bait if they get ahold of us. Instead of actually finding her, they know she'll come running if any of us are in danger." He held Eva's hand. "Avarie can't send you any more emails and Sasha won't be calling me anymore. They belong to the FSB now." Tears were welling up in Courtney's eyes. "Mikhail told me that Avarie's hit a roadblock in her training and she's fighting them tooth and nail right now."

"What's happened?" Ivan asked. "We thought she was doing well?"

Courtney shook his head. "She's homesick. The last time I talked to Sasha, he said her nightmares are becoming worse. Mikhail can't get her to trust him and she's taking steps back." His brows furrowed. "I think I fucked up guys."

"No, you didn't." Ivan said defensively. "It sounds like it's in her nature to fight. She is a whole new being that the universe created. Her

DNA is almost pure, but her soul is old. She didn't come with a manual, Courtney."

"How long has she been there? A little over two months already?" Eva asked. "She didn't exactly go on her terms nor did she volunteer. Of course she's going to have trust issues and fight them. What did Mikhail tell you, Courtney?"

He stared blankly at the ground. "He said that we have to go back to normal and act like Avarie never existed. He told me that I have to forget about her and she has to do the same for me. This was just a stop in the road for her and she moved on to the next point. He's afraid that she's going to do something stupid and get us all killed."

"So, they really do belong to the FSB now." Matthias said softly. "He didn't give details on what she's fighting them on did he?"

"He did. They're trying to hone her abilities and it's too much for her right now. That's why he doesn't want any contact. He said it's like an obstacle for her and she can't remove it." He leaned up on his knees. "He said that it seems extremely easy for her to fight, but the way he described it, she has problems letting go."

"Oh." Ivan said. "I understand now. Her past holds her down. Instead of learning from it, she harbors it inside her like a haunted vessel." He clacked his fingernails on his teeth. "Eventually, that ship will hit land and she'll have to disembark, you know."

"So, you agree with Mikhail?" Eva asked.

"I do. Her past is full of fear. She didn't have the greatest past life and she tried to save many of those she loved. It's quite possible her nightmares are a warning to her and she fears them instead of embracing the lessons they showed her. When you fear, you cannot trust anything, even your own senses."

Matthais was blown away by this revelation. "Wow, that's deep man." He went through every interaction with Avarie and thought about the ways he had to earn her trust and not fear him. "What can we do for her in the meantime?" He asked sincerely.

"Do you believe in the power of prayer?" Ivan responded smiling. "Words have meaning you know. They're magic and the most powerful magic in the world is love."

"I believe somebody gave us a spiel on how that works." Matthias pointed at Eva. "She told us about karma and paganism."

"It's very true. You can create anything you want within your world." Ivan said. "Do you understand your word 'imagination'?" They shook their heads in confusion. "This is a beautiful word. Break it down into its parts. I meaning you." He pointed at them. "Magi meaning magic. Nation meaning people. You are a nation of magicians. Think about that. You are created from the universe and as I said, the universe never gives you anything that you don't need in your struggles. Use your imaginations."

Courtney picked a stray thread from his pants. "That just leads to more questions you know?"

"And we will address them when we get there. For now, you all need to focus your positive energy in other places. If you don't want the Mossad or the other dangerous factions to come here, don't imagine what you don't want, imagine what you want and it'll come to you."

ϒϒϒ

Avarie had a bad week and it was getting worse. She's been in Russia for over two months and it's not getting better. Two weeks ago, Kirill beat her with this belt again because she blew up at him. Her body was tired from the strenuous training. Mikhail tried to get her into the deep end and Tori was pressuring her to get in there for longer than ten seconds. In her situational awareness training, she managed to take out two guys who were supposed to be allies, but mistook the signals, again. Nobody was happy with her, not even Sasha. She managed to piss him off by not taking his advice about her nightmares.

She knew she was fighting everybody. She hated it as much as they did and she had no clue what was happening to her. Advancing through classes was supposed to be a good thing. Secretly, she thought she'd glide right through them. All this frustration might have happened when Mikhail told her that they had to cut off contact with Courtney and the others. The situation was becoming dangerous and the Mossad and their minions were snooping. She belonged to the FSB now and she had to follow *every* order that was given regardless of how she felt about it. So many emotions swirled inside her head and she couldn't shut it off.

ϒϒϒ

Mikhail was at the firing range with Valentin. Weapons training was always fun, especially for Sasha. He was becoming better with his Barrett and even gave her a name, Ivana. Whenever they walked by Sasha while he was firing, he said naughty things to it. Valentin joked that every time he spoke dirty to Ivana, he hit his target. Avarie wasn't doing so hot today. Both men could tell something was wrong. She could barely concentrate in Situational Awareness, it was like her mind wandered somewhere in the distance. Karl became concerned and feared that it would only get worse if they couldn't break her walls.

Watching Avarie fire her Beretta, she lacked enthusiasm. Shit, she didn't even have to aim anymore. She wasn't allowed to have her Rossi until she behaved herself. That just pissed her off even more he noticed. They decided to have only Avarie and Sasha out here for the day with nobody else. They'd let her take out some aggression and Sasha could have some time with his rifle. He hoped she'd blow off some steam along with the rest of them. When he reached out to touch her, she backed away in fear. He still didn't have her trust and it was killing him.

Avarie was aimlessly pointing her gun. The echoes of gunshots rang out in the distance. Even though the weather was starting to turn to Autumn, sweat still poured from her head. Out of nowhere her senses kicked up and the smell of smoke filled her nostrils. Looking around the berm and the shooting tables, she saw that the others weren't even aware. This wasn't gun powder, it was actual smoke. The scenery changed before her eyes and she was swallowed by plumes of smoke on the range and lost sight of the men. Flames shot out from behind the berm and Avarie felt the heat against her skin, making her sweat even more. Fear filled her body. Screams and shouting were heard in the distance. Grabbing her gun, she walked out on the range looking for whoever was her target. The screaming became louder as she walked stealthy towards the flames, ready to fire upon whoever was there.

Avarie, wake up. Everything was back to normal, but she wasn't at her shooting table. Standing in the middle of the live firing range, she looked behind her to see Mikhail running after her and shouting her name. He grabbed her elbow, but she pulled back. He had enough of her shit and he threw her over his shoulder and brought her back. She started screaming and kicking at him. *Damn he was strong*, she thought.

He threw her down in the dirt with Valentin and Sasha hovering over her. "What the fuck do you think you're doing going out into a live firing range like that!" he screamed at her. "Sasha could've killed you. If there were other people, *they* would've killed you!"

Avarie started shaking as she looked at Sasha. "It happened again." She whispered to him. "I couldn't stop it."

"Stop what?" Valentin demanded. He watched as storm clouds gathered in her eyes. "Answer me." he hissed.

"I saw a fire and people screaming. I felt the heat and saw smoke." It was no use in explaining. "I'm sorry. Maybe we should cut out the firing range for a while." She said softly. Mikhail offered to help her up, but she shrugged him off. He locked her guns away from her and they rode back to the FSB in silence.

Valentin could tell that she scared herself out there. He knew who she was. All her instructors did. Yet he kept her previous life on the down low from the other agents. She was having strange flashbacks and they needed to find a way to control them. He watched as Sasha cooed in her ear and told her reassuring murmurings. She only put her head on his shoulder and closed her eyes.

They put her back in situational awareness training with Mikhail keeping a close watch on her. They let Sasha have a break and join Tori with exercises and whatever else she could keep him occupied with. On the second floor, they had their simulation going. Avarie processed every sound, sight, scent, and taste. They went through Coopers Colors with her and the team. They really enjoyed working with her, but today was different. Her mind went in another direction again and she was the one who ended up getting hurt because she went all the way to Black. Nobody wanted to be in Black. That was panic mode and she couldn't respond to any of the stimuli around her.

"Avarie!" Karl boomed. "You just ended up dead! You're better than that. What happened?"

She stood up and bolted out the door in a panic. Mikhail ran after her screaming her name. She didn't stop. She was already at the ground floor and he had a hard time keeping up. She swiped her badge and went into the swimming area and then the ladies locker room. Mikhail was there just in time to catch the door before it shut. His badge didn't work in this area.

He found her in a shower stall, sitting with her back against the tile and her feet up against the other wall. She was shaking like a leaf and turned beet red. He carefully walked up to her, not knowing what she was going to do. She was a threat now and he had to handle her carefully.

"Avarie." He stepped inside the stall and shut the door. "I'm getting really tired of your *shit*." She looked like a rabid dog about ready to bite, and he just locked himself in the stall with her. He couldn't deny she looked hot in her black combat pants and white t-shirt with her hair pulled back all crazy like.

He sat down across from her and waited for a response. "I'm getting really tired of my shit, too." She whispered softly. "I can't stand to be me right now."

"I can't help you if you don't tell me what's going on." He put his head in his hands. "You have to let us in, Avarie." He reached out for her but she kicked him away. "Are you homesick?"

"That would be the first thing that comes to mind." She said leaning her head back against the white tile. "I'm here against my will is another thing."

"Then let's work through them."

"How the *fuck* am I supposed to work through them? You told me last week that we couldn't have any more contact with home." She sneered at him. "I don't know if they're dead, alive, in danger, or having the time of their lives."

"I cut off contact for a reason!" Mikhail was losing his temper. He never hit a woman who didn't deserve it and she was getting close. "We have to keep everybody safe. That was the deal and we'll take every measure necessary to ensure that." He glared at her. "You belong to the FSB now."

"I didn't agree to that!" She kicked the wall and a tile cracked. "That deal was made without my knowledge."

"Too bad! Why don't you cry me a *fucking* river!" He yelled. "You're here now and you have to cope with that."

"How can I cope when you've taken everything that I know away from me?" She screamed louder. "I got Sasha, that's it!"

"And if you listened to him, you'd be doing fine." Oh he was on the verge. She frustrated him to no end.

"So I'm supposed to act like everybody is dead and go on with my life like it never existed?" This was becoming a full blown screaming match and Mikhail's anger grew.

"If it keeps them safe then yes!"

"Well fuck you too!" She stood up and he brought her back down. A knock came at the door of the stall.

"Avarie?" It was Tori. "Are you alright?"

"We're having a one on one conversation my dear." Mikhail said through the door. "I would suggest you give us some private time."

"Uncle Mikhail! You're not supposed to be in here!" Tori hissed through the door.

"Go the fuck away, Tori!" He said with a smile. "She needs a come to Jesus moment and you're not involved."

"Fine!" She yelled and stormed off.

"Now, I'm trying to figure out the real problem with you but it's not easy. You wage wars in your head and you're losing every battle." He sighed. "Forget about Courtney and the others for the moment and just talk to me."

Tears streamed down her eyes and she tried to brush them away before he saw, but it was no use. "I can't fight what I don't know." She said honestly.

"But you know all this." He said waving his hand in the air. "I don't understand what exactly you're fighting against. You're great with weapons; your hand to hand combat is getting better. Yes we hit a roadblock with your situational awareness but we can overcome that."

"I don't know what keeps blocking me." She said sternly. "I can't clear my mind enough to even concentrate anymore."

He reached out to touch her again, but she kicked him back with more force. "Don't *fucking* touch me." She hissed. Her green eyes burned with anger as she stared him down. Her black combat gloves rolled into fists. "Touch me again, I'll fuck you up."

He had enough. He quickly jumped up and turned the shower on full blast to cold. Avarie tried to roll about of the way, but he had her under the full spray. She punched him in the thigh and he came down next to her, getting wet in the process. The cold water stung Avarie's skin as it produced goosebumps.

"You need to fucking cool off." He screamed at her. She tried to sit up but he held her there, letting her clothes drown in the water. She looked like a raging bulldog and she was using the water to her advantage. She slapped at him and threw him into the tile wall, letting them break with a thud against the floor. For what seemed like an eternity, he finally had her pinned down at the shoulders. He could feel the heat come off her body as steam rose from her chest in the wetness. He straddled her body with all his might.

Avarie looked up in his eyes. It seemed the green of the hazel swirled as they looked down on her. His hair was soaked and it dripped onto her. His hands dug into her shoulders. If he didn't let up, they'd break under his weight. Shaking from exhaustion, she let herself relax, allowing her arms to fall to her sides. This fight was over and she lost, again.

He lowered himself on top of her, giving her shoulders a break. His body was warm against the freezing water and for a split second, she welcomed the shelter. He looked her over with curiosity. She didn't like him this close to her and she squirmed a bit.

"What's wrong?" He whispered in her ear. He was practically touching it with his warm lips. "Does being this close to me make you uncomfortable?" She had no choice but to nod. He breathed on her neck and ran his nose up and down it softly. It gave her the chills but she held still. He lifted his head up and went to the other side. "Why won't you let me touch you?" He whispered into her other ear.

Small sensations of pleasure started to well up inside her and she fought against them. "Answer the question. Why won't you let me touch you?" He kissed her earlobe and worked his way to her neck.

"Because I don't know what you are." She admitted. "You *scare* me." The water still splashed on her face. It ran off his body onto hers. She concentrated on the water and let the cold sting her skin.

He lifted himself off her and looked down at her body. Her hair was beautifully strewn behind her in went entrails. Tears still ran down her cheeks. She was breathing heavily and he watched her chest rise and fall. He could see everything though her white shirt. She wore a white lace bra that allowed the pink of her hard nipples to be exposed. He was getting excited. He had her where he wanted her. Absolutely vulnerable.

He ran his right hand from her neck to the soft mound and gave her a gentle squeeze. She gasped softly but never left his gaze. "You scare me too." He brought his lips over the fabric of her shirt to nip at her soft flesh. He didn't know if she was shivering from pleasure or the cold water. He left it on as she wasn't done raging just yet. He went back to her left ear, letting his body crush against her breasts. God she had so much heat flowing through her, he couldn't control his arousal. He knew she felt it because she winced under him. "I don't think you're just scared of me, *Mishka*." He said as he ran his lips over her outer ear. "I think you have fear that lives inside you, and it blocks everything out."

She put her hands on each of his shoulders and shifted under him. "Your fear of the unknown holds you back and we have to challenge it every time." He kissed her neck and made his way slowly to the underside of her chin, forcing her head back.

She couldn't fight him like this. His body felt extremely good on hers. The water felt colder and her lips quivered. For some reason, he still chewed his gum. It was a strange thought as she started to focus on her situation. His hot breath smelled like spearmint as he made his way around to the right side. He didn't chew it as he grazed her sensitive skin. She took deep breaths under him and his weight shifted on her. She expected him to keep talking, but he didn't. After a long silence of him just exploring her with his lips he said, "Do you still fear me?" in a soft whisper. Desire built up in her and she had no clue how to stop him. She wanted him, but didn't. It was a strange battle. She nodded and said, "I still fear you."

"What is it that makes you scared of *me*?" He lunged for her breasts again. He pulled up her shirt for better access and ran his tongue along each nipple. Her head was swooning. "Answer the question." He breathed on her. He wasn't letting up.

"Because you make me lose control." She said loudly. "If you touch me, I know that I have no control over what I do." More tears streamed down her cheeks. "I don't know if I need to fight you, run, or just leave it alone." He came back up to meet her face and he covered her mouth with his. She could taste the sweet gum on his tongue as he probed hers. Her heart raced and she let her hands flow to the small of his back. He cradled her head in his gloved hands. Sucking on her bottom lip, she felt his teeth graze it. Her head felt light and she lifted up his wet shirt only to feel the tender scars on his back. She wanted to rip it off him and see the sexy full sleeve tattoos that ran from wrist all the way across his chest and back again.

He felt her giving into him. This wasn't a standard issue agent and she definitely didn't fall into that category. This wasn't protocol and he didn't care. He joined her mouth again and pulled her up against the white tile. He knew he had to back off before he stripped her down right here in the ladies shower room. He reached up and shut off the water, pulling down her shirt, he kissed her one last time. A confused look crossed her face as she started chewing his gum. He smiled as he thought he finally made headway with her. "Let's get dried off. I don't want you catching your death because of a cold shower." His voice was as smooth as caramel. He helped her get to her feet and unlatched the door and opened it.

She debated on bolting again. "Don't run from me." He said as he clasped her elbow. It was like he was reading her mind. "I'll find you and we'll have to do this over again."

"I've heard that before." She said quietly as she stared into the distance. Her wet boots squeaked on the floor as they walked. He handed her a towel and she dried herself off the best she could.

"I'll meet you at the pool." He said and walked out the door. Avarie hung her clothes up to dry while wondering what the Hell just happened.

ϒϒϒ

He sat on the bench next to Sasha as he pulled off his wet boots in the locker room. Mikhail was completely soaked in cold water. "What did you do to her?" Sasha asked curiously.

"I found out what the hell is going on in her head, my friend." He stripped off the shirt and threw it down.

"I could've told you what was going on." Sasha looked at him. "All you had to do was ask me. You know that."

"I had to hear it from her. She needed to say it out loud." He pulled off the combat pants as they stuck to his legs. "I had an inkling that she was scared, but I didn't really know what she was scared of. Did you?"

"Not really, just that she's scared." He gave Mikhail a strange look. "How did you get her to tell you anyway? She avoids you like the plague." He asked surprised.

"My friend, we call that the 'honey pot'." Mikhail pulled on his tight swim trunks. "You ever hear of it?" He shook his head. "Sasha, we Russians have perfected the art of seduction. When you make a person vulnerable, they'll tell you anything."

Sasha smirked at him. "You got her to touch you?" His eyes went wide. "I can't believe that."

"Well, there was a struggle and such…but what matters is that she spoke to me and we can now see eye to eye." His gaze caught Sasha's swollen ankle. "What the hell happened to you?"

"Tori caught me by surprise." He said with a laugh. "She's a crazy fighter."

"Have you been hiding from her?" Mikhail smirked.

"No, I just don't want to walk on it yet." Sasha looked down at his foot.

"If you want, I can drag you to the pool."

"Works for me." Sasha rode piggy back to the poolside. Tori thought they were a sight to behold. They looked like two boys who were ready to start a water fight. Mikhail gently put him down and Sasha stuck his feet in the water. Tori strode over with an ice pack and gave it to Sasha. She and Avarie worked on their water exercises in silence. Mikhail noticed that the tension that Avarie had built up was relieved for now. However, his was another story. Being in the shower stall with her gave him naughty thoughts. No wonder Courtney was so in love with this girl. She was feisty as Hell and she wore it like a second skin.

Sasha nudged him hard. "Stop it! I have to sleep next to her you know." Mikhail laughed at him. Poor Sasha, of all the people that could wake him up from the great beyond, it was this girl. "I have my hands full you know. Between her and Tori, I don't know what to do."

"Wow, so Tori is making some moves on you?" Mikhail asked amazed.

"Yes, look at my foot!" Sasha wiggled it in front of him. He was frustrated. "You know, I was told that the females were very magical, but now I know why."

"Because they could love you and kill you in one strike?" Mikhail enjoyed joking with Sasha. In his time, females were mystics and held sacred. To come into this age, the females were allowed to be more open. They were still sacred, but in a different way.

"They confuse me, that's all." He wanted to end this subject.

"Sasha, you're part of the agency now and you'll have to be put in some awkward positions like Avarie is. You know what that means?"

"Fuck you; I'm not learning the honey pot." He crossed his arms around his chest, like it would protect himself from Mikhail's words.

"Sasha, there was a time when I was scared of women too, but not anymore."

"Congratulations."

He slapped Sasha's leg. "They're very beautiful creatures. Look at those two work together. See their grace and companionship."

"See them walk onto a live shooting range or break windows during a bad dream. Oh look, she stole your covers again." Sasha mimicked. "Oh no, I twisted your ankle, let me get you an icepack." He talked with his hand. "I'm sorry Sasha, I didn't mean it." This time it was a high pitched voice and Mikhail busted up laughing.

"You have to take the good with the bad."

"I'll take the good, you can keep the bad." He watched Avarie as she swam. It looked like she was chewing on something. He leaned closer; it was a piece of gum. "You're not supposed to chew gum while swimming." His eyes rolled over to Mikhail. "Did you give her a piece?"

"Oh yes I did." He said smiling. Sasha slapped him upside the head and gave him the evil eye. Mikhail kept laughing as he clapped his hands at the girls. Pool time was over.

ϒϒϒ

Avarie was in the room with Sasha. The week of training was done and they were waiting for Kirill to come up with a weekend schedule. Normally, they would train more in combat or swim, but this weekend was different. Kirill wasn't in a good mood and Avarie knew they were going to feel his wrath. Sasha warned her not to piss him off today. He noticed that her demeanor changed over the week since Mikhail had her alone. Sasha didn't mention anything because they were too tired at night to even talk.

"Avarie, you think he'll make us train some more?" Sasha asked breaking their silence.

She shook her head. "No, I think he wants to kick somebody's ass tonight. Knowing him, he'll probably give me the belt." That thought made Sasha cringe. Kirill's lashings were worse each time.

"Behave and he'll have no reason to punish you." He said softly laying on the bed next to her. "I see you're getting along better with Mikhail."

"Yea, I don't think I have a choice at this point." Her eyes stared at the ceiling. "You and Tori are getting along."

Sasha propped himself up on his elbow. "Why did you have to bring her up?" he asked. "You know I'm not interested."

Avarie gave him the look. "You so are! You're just scared of her!" She started laughing. "You're a virgin entity and you're scared of women!"

"Shut up! It's very awkward for me. Especially when Mikhail brought up that I have to learn 'the honey pot'." He cringed.

"What's that?" She asked curiously. "I've never heard that term before."

He sighed. "Remember your 'heart to heart' with him?" Avarie nodded. "That was the honey pot."

"That *mother fucker*..." Avarie said in wonder. "I'm gonna punch him."

Sasha laughed at her. "And you fell for it!"

"Well if I can fall for it, so can you." Avarie smacked him with a pillow. "So you watch your junk."

"Nobody is stealing my precious seed." Sasha exclaimed jokingly. "I think that's what women really want."

"Not really." Avarie nudged him. "There's more to life than sex. Mainly about being with the people you love."

"Oh yes, and fighting them every step of the way." He quipped.

"I don't do it intentionally." She stated. "I just don't understand what holds me back is all."

"Fear."

"Like you fear women?"

"I don't fear women. I think the female human is alright. Nothing against them, it's just that they confuse me is all."

"And men don't confuse us?" Avarie said defensively. "Believe me, you guys aren't exactly that easy to read either."

"What's the confusion, *Maus*?" Sasha said with exasperation. "We only require a few things in life and we're fine."

"And what's that?"

He looked at her. "You hand us things that go boom and something fast, I think we're alright." He laughed. "Look at me, I'm awesome." He slapped his muscular belly.

"Yes, you're so awesome you steal the covers at night and you take all the hot water." She shook her head. "Let's not forget, you named your rifle Ivana. What the hell does that mean anyway?"

"It means, 'Ivana pull your trigger'." He laughed at his play on words. *Man, he even laughs at his own jokes*, Avarie thought.

"It's pretty bad you have a loving relationship with your gun."

"It hasn't let me down yet. And she only talks back when I let her." He rubbed his hands together.

"Go fuck yourself, Sasha." She slapped him again with the pillow.

"I don't need to. However, I think somebody else does." He slapped her back. "Why don't you go release your frustrations." He pointed towards the bathroom. "Maybe you'll feel better."

"Maybe you'll feel better if Tori releases yours." She quipped back and slapped him again with the pillow. That was a sore subject for him. He slapped her again with the pillow but harder.

"At least I didn't get honey potted!"

"At least I'm not a fucking virgin!"

"At least I can get along with people!"

"Yea but you're scared of Tori!"

"You're even more scared of Mikhail!"

"Oh fuck you!" She swung the pillow at him and their shouts became louder.

Kirill was walking down the hallway with the schedule for them but he stood outside their door. It sounded like they were fighting and yelling. Something was knocked over. "Look what you did you shit head!"

"You did it. I hope Kirill beats your ass!"

Kirill didn't realize he had two children in his guest bedroom. The yelling and fighting were getting louder as he busted open the door.

"What the hell is going on in here?" He boomed at them and they stopped swinging pillows at each other. "I didn't know I had two overgrown children in my house. If I did, you'd both be in daycare!" He shook his head in rage when he saw the vase in pieces on the floor. "Sit down now!" They both did as they were told with wide eyes. *Yea, papa caught you two fighting*, he thought.

"Sasha!" His head snapped towards Kirill. "Pack an overnight bag you're going with Tori tonight." Sasha didn't move. "*Oi*, did I fucking stutter?" Sasha jumped up and packed his clothes. Avarie knew she was in for it. "Go down and wait for her in the foyer." He pointed towards the door and Sasha left in a hurry.

Kirill's eyes met Avarie's and they grew soft. He sat on Sasha's side of the bed and made himself comfortable. He patted for Avarie to join him. She was too exhausted to fight so she scooted closer. It was amazing how much he looked like his brother. The exception was that Kirill was clean shaven and kept his jet black hair closer to his head. "I've been told you've had a bad week." He said softly.

"No, it's been a bad month so far." She admitted not looking at him. She felt the heat of his body next to hers. "I'm sorry." She said softly. She was too sore to take a beating from him.

He looked over at her with a bit of sorrow. "I know I didn't grab you in the best of circumstances. Those who join the agency do so of their free-will. We need you. Actually, the world needs you."

"And the weight of the world is on my shoulders. Nice." She said sarcastically. "That's a lot of pressure you know."

"Don't talk to me about pressure. I've been fighting this shit for years." He huffed. "Don't sit there and think the world revolves around you."

"It sure fucking seems like it." She knew she was copping attitude, but she didn't care. "Why haven't you won yet?"

"Because the circumstances were never right." He sighed. "We beat them back and then they come again."

"What's changed?" She asked as she slid down further into the huge bed.

"The fact that the universe has finally had enough. We're seeing all kinds of changes in the world right now."

"Are you sure that isn't just CERN fucking around?" Avarie laughed. "I've heard they can open portals and mess with dark matter."

She got Kirill to laugh. "I never thought of that, but you didn't come from CERN did you?" She shook her head no. "That may be a good idea you know, having Courtney go back to CERN." Mentioning his name hit her heart strings. He noticed the change in her. "I'm sorry, *Mishka*. I didn't mean to bring him up."

She dared to ask, "Is he okay?"

"He's just fine. Mikhail is having them watched and protected if needed. You don't need to worry about him right now." He patted her hand. She dared to look at him. His eyes started to change, almost like Mikhail's. "I know it's useless to tell you that, you'll always have him on the back of your mind."

He changed the subject. "I've been told that Mikhail had to give you a talking to." God, she could almost hear him pulling out his belt.

"Yea." She said softly. "So why aren't you beating my ass right now?"

"Because he already did."

"Bullshit!" Avarie almost jumped up from her bed. "You call wrestling me in a shower stall an ass beating?"

Kirill started laughing at her. "Sometimes words hurt worse than beatings." He put an arm around her. "Now you have to decide who the bigger asshole is; me or Mikhail."

"You're both assholes." She crossed her arms and nudged him off. "I don't know if there's a difference anymore."

Kirill sighed and pulled her closer. "I'm going to tell you a secret." She rolled her eyes but he ignored her. "I'm the political one and he's the shadow. The others know who we are. It's a long story and I'll save that for another time." He continued. "When the others have some bullshit spiel for us about how they're going to defeat our forces and what not, they come to me."

"Whys that?"

"Because they love pissing me off." He winked at her. "You see, it's against the rules to kill your own kind, but some did anyway and they turned into unholy monsters."

"You've never killed any of them?"

"Oh, I have. That's why I'm such a bitter asshole."

"What about Mikhail?"

"No, he just beats down their forces." Avarie leaned back into the pillows and thought about it. She was still confused about what it all meant, but in time maybe he'd tell her. He leaned back into the bed next to her so their faces met. She could feel him breathing on her. "*Mishka*, all I want for you right now is to put everything out of your mind and go with your training."

She turned to look at him face to face. Their noses almost touched and the aura in the room changed. "I'm trying my best." She whispered. Suddenly, he didn't seem so scary anymore. He was acting funny. "Are you trying the honey pot on me?" She gave him a crooked look. Damn he looked as good as Mikhail right now.

He busted up laughing. "Who uses the honey pot anymore?" Sliding a hand under her neck, he brought her closer. "No, this is me being very sincere with you. I need you to break through these barriers because there's more ahead. It may not seem fair of me, but in order for you to go back, you have to fight me in hand to hand combat and win." *Nope, that wasn't fair at all*, she thought. "You may not think it, but you have all the resources available to do it. Beat me, and you go home, but it still won't be for a while yet."

"Thanks for the warning." She said in defeat. "Why do I have to beat you anyway?"

He looked her over and she watched as his eyes changed. "Because we have to change the battlefield. If you guys want Luscious, I'm giving him to you." She looked at him in confusion.

"You know where he is?" she asked.

He nodded. "He's been watching Courtney. That's why we cut off contact. If he knew you were here, it'll put us in danger."

"Is Courtney aware of this?" Avarie asked in shock. Without knowing it, she was feeling the soft arm of Kirill's sleeve in a fidgeting motion.

"No and its best that he doesn't. We like to keep things quiet."

"Well, thanks for letting me know." She said quietly and laid her head back in his arm. "Now I just feel helpless."

He pulled her head back up to him. "Don't, there's nothing you can do about it right now. Let them play their games." His fingers danced on her collar bone. "You belong to the FSB now."

"And I keep hearing that phrase." She flicked his hand away. "So why's Sasha going with Tori? I thought she was *my* mentor."

"As it turns out, Sasha needs a little more help than you do in specific departments, but she's still yours."

"What about me?" She asked not really wanting the answer.

"As much as I'd love to lay in this bed with you, I have a late night function."

"So you're going to leave me here to my own devices? I'm told that's not smart."

"I'm not that stupid. You're going with Mikhail. He'll be here in about thirty minutes." He said looking at his watch.

"Wonderful, I get to train more." She threw her head back in frustration.

Kirill shifted himself closer to her. His button down shirt was thin enough that she could feel his muscles against her skin. "We have time to try the honey pot if you want?" he said teasingly. He kissed her nose and she gave him a stupid grin.

"You know, I wouldn't mind that if you acted like this all the time." She pushed him away from her but he pulled her back down. "Oh my God. Your brother already did this."

His eyes grew wide. "Well that asshole." He exclaimed with a fake surprised expression. "Sometimes I swear we're the same person."

"It wouldn't surprise me one bit." She huffed. Her body grew warm under him and the pleasure sensations were moving through her like a snake. She wanted something to save her from him right now. "You know, I haven't seen you two in the same room very often." She ran her hands through his thick black hair. "Makes me really wonder." She said thoughtfully. "You're working the fucking honey pot on me aren't you?" She asked with wide eyes.

His smile grew large and sincere. He shook his head. "No, I think it's the other way around. I'm not doing shit." He leaned in and kissed her neck. "You ever had twins?" She busted up laughing and pushed him off her. He stood up wearing a shit eating grin.

A knock at the door snapped her back to reality. Kirill opened it and Mikhail stepped in. He looked different. He wasn't dressed up in the usual gear. He wore a plain gray tee with jeans that hugged his body and a black ball cap. She could still see his eyes though. They spoke to each other in Russian and Avarie didn't care to pay attention. For the exception of the clothes and Mikhail having the longer hair and goatee, they looked the same. She felt better knowing that it wasn't just an act for her sake. They turned towards her and laughed in her direction. God, she felt stupid.

"*Mishka*! Get your things, you're coming with me." She jumped up from the bed and packed an overnight bag. She'd rather stay in her room, but they knew better. "Don't look so glum. We aren't training this weekend anyway." He smacked her ass as she came out of the room.

They waited at the elevator and they stepped in. "So, you tried the honey pot on my brother huh?" Mikhail busted up laughing. "I didn't think you had it in you."

Now she was embarrassed. "Shut up. He tried it on me."

"No, he tells it the other way around." Mikhail wasn't going to let up and she couldn't go back upstairs. He wrapped his arms around her and kissed her forehead. "Oh, *Mishka*. We don't win every battle so you better get used to it."

The elevator pinged the parking area and he escorted her to his SUV. "What are we doing tonight?" She asked.

"I think you need a well-deserved break. So I have you the entire weekend. Kirill has a full schedule for himself so he can't entertain you two." He said as he pulled out of the garage.

"What about Sasha?"

"You don't worry about Sasha, or anybody else for that matter." He turned on his lights and zoomed out. "You're going to have a nice weekend with me and that's it."

Wonderful, Avarie thought. More troubles, more guilt and more of this guy. Just great.

ᖯᖯᖯ

The cool Moscow night air filled his nostrils. Luscious couldn't wait to see Kirill. He loved fucking with him in any way he could. He knew he couldn't get into the FSB and the people working for the Prime Minister's office wouldn't give his men any information whatsoever. He'd love to run into Mikhail, but in battle only.

He knew that Kirill was supposed to show up at a dinner party and he had his tickets. Priming up his tux, he stepped back and checked himself out. He looked like a real gentleman. More like a wolf in sheep's clothing. He went to the plaza and gave his ticket to the man at the door. It was a meet and greet for Russian parliament. Luscious was in the shadows so much, nobody knew who he was.

Mingling generously, he found out that he missed the meal, no big deal. He wasn't hungry anyway. He looked around the room for Kirill and spotted him talking with some committee members. Konstantin was in the corner with his mistress drinking wine and snacking on an appetizer. He smiled to himself. These stupid fucks don't even know I'm here, he thought. He snagged a wine glass from a passing waiter and drank tenderly.

The wine was sweet and dry, just like the dead bodies he left behind when he helped conquer land for the Roman Empire. Those were the good old days. The rivers flowed with blood and the air smelled of sweet iron mixed with dirt. He could almost taste it on his lips.

His focus moved to Kirill as he walked out to the balcony with a cigar in hand. He put down his empty glass and made his way outside to the cool air. Kirill was leaning over a balcony smoking his cigar with a wine glass in his hand. It sparkled in the moonlight. God, it'd be so easy just to throw him over the edge.

"I wouldn't do that if I were you." Kirill answered. Fuck, he should've masked his thoughts better. No matter, he thought as he moved next to him. "What the hell are you doing here?"

"The ball was open to the public, so I bought a ticket." He hissed. "Oh, and it's been a long time since I've seen your smiling face."

Kirill turned to face him, full of confidence as he flicked ashes from his cigar down below. "Well, aren't you a *bold* fuck." He said in his thick Russian accent. "You know the rules, you stay on your side, and we stay on ours."

"The game has changed, Kirill." He looked him up and down. "You see, we're tired of the same old shit as much as you are. Maybe you and I can come to terms."

"Fuck your terms, Luscious." Kirill said as he puffed on his cigar. "Why don't you be a good demon and tell me what you really want?"

"Alright, I guess it's no secret that we lost a package of ours and we think that you may know where it is?" He cocked an eyebrow at him. Kirill knew better, he was trying to get information.

"And what would this package contain?"

"Let's just say, she is running around somewhere."

"She?" Kirill laughed. "She must be something special if you guys want her that bad."

"She is." Luscious pulled out a smoke and lit it. "I'm not stupid; I know you guys are snooping for her too."

"Please explain." Kirill was enjoying this.

Now he was getting angry. "We know you're in Germany. A group of my men are dead and your FSB are watching Courtney Cambridge. Now why is that?"

"Now why are you in neutral territory?" Kirill asked happily. "You know the rules."

"Fuck your rules, Kirill." Luscious hissed. "Now, where is she?"

"*She,* is somewhere not in Germany. That I know for sure." He had to relight his cigar. Luscious looked at him suspiciously and sniffed his suit. "You like my cologne you dirty pervert?"

"You've had a woman earlier didn't you?" He laughed. "Now that's against the rules."

"Fuck your rules, Luscious." Kirill sipped from his wine glass. "That one was dropped ages ago, that's why we're still here, remember?"

"Oh I remember well" He threw the butt of his smoke over the balcony. "So, if she's not in Germany, then where is she?"

"Oh, so you didn't ask Courtney then?" Kirill patted Luscious' back. "I figured you'd ring his doorbell and ask by now."

"That bridge was burnt eons ago." Luscious looked out over the darkened skyline of the city. "Besides, even if I did, you think he'd tell me? Maybe you're the one he'd tell."

"No go." Kirill said. "He doesn't like dealing with us and we already tried."

"I thought you guys had some sort of relationship with him, then again, I could be wrong."

"You are very wrong." Kirill wanted this fucker away from him but he loved getting him going. "How about you and I have a contest? I know you love a challenge."

Luscious' eyes became large and he rubbed his hands together in excitement. "Alright. What is it?"

"Let's play, 'who can find the girl first'." He chuckled. "Whoever gets her, wins."

"Oh Kirill, now that's not fair. Just because either one of us gets her, doesn't mean they win."

"Well, they win the *girl*." Kirill finished his wine. "It doesn't mean they win the war. How about it?"

Luscious thought about this little game. Kirill liked to make things interesting and he liked that about him, but that was about it. "Can we have one little rule?" He asked wiggling his index finger in the air.

"And what rule would that be?" Kirill laughed.

"Whoever finds her gets to keep her?"

"Oo, that's good." Now Kirill was getting excited. "So, if you find her, we can't go after her and vice versa?"

Luscious rubbed his chin. "Exactly like that." He giggled with excitement.

"Alright. If you get the girl, you need to let us know. If we get her, we'll tell you." Kirill was thinking Luscious was getting way into this. "Should we shake on it?" He extended his hand. Luscious almost looked like he was going to back out, but took his hand greedily.

"Now, I'm going back inside. Feel free to say hello to Konstantin. I'm sure he'd love to hear you brag about slaughtering Nikita's family again." Kirill turned his back on him and walked inside.

Luscious decided to leave. When Kirill felt that he was long gone, he sent a message to Mikhail telling him the game was on.

CHAPTER EIGHT

Mikhail had a flat inside the city square. He traveled all the time, so there was no need for a bigger space. Usually, he hoofed it to work when the days were nice. It was only a half an hour walk. He showed Avarie around the small space. There were only four rooms so she couldn't get far from him. Kirill wanted them off his hands. He felt like something was up and having them separate seemed like a good thing. He knew Sasha grew weary of Avarie's shenanigans.

"So, we can watch movies and have popcorn." Mikhail suggested. Avarie sat on the couch next to him.

"Are you going to paint my toenails too?" She asked sarcastically. "How about I give you a makeover?"

He grabbed the remote and clicked the TV on. "My name isn't Eva. As much as you miss your sister, I'm not filling in that gap."

Great, now he had to bring her up. She missed them more than they knew. This wasn't much fun but what did she expect of him? It was like hanging out with Matthias in his workspace, plain boring. "Well, what's there to do here in Moscow?"

"Watch TV. We aren't going out tonight." He turned his cap backwards on his head and stretched out.

"You know, I could just go to bed. I'm tired anyway." Her voice sounded somber. He flipped through the channels and found the news. She stood up and grabbed her bag. "Where do I sleep?" she looked around the flat.

"Bedroom is in the back." He answered. This shit was last minute and he had nothing planned nor did he clean properly. Kirill was insistent that he take her and he couldn't tell him no. She headed towards the bedroom. There was a bunch of stuff on the bed and she pushed it off to the side with a loud thump. "*Oi, Mishka*! Be nice to my stuff!" she heard him yell. *Fuck him*, she thought.

Her body was tired but she was happy it'd get rest. She bounced up and down on the bed and realized that it had water in it. It was soft and had clean sheets. That's the most she could ask for. Peeling off her clothes, she stuffed them in the bag. She climbed in and covered herself up. The room smelled like him. Courtney's room smelled like him too. Shit, she did it again. She's not supposed to think about him or the others. She reached into her bag and felt around for the iPod. Putting the earbuds in she cranked the music. She needed a distraction from everything and this was the closest thing she had to nirvana right now. Sleep took her easily and she was out like a light.

ϒϒϒ

Around midnight, Mikhail received Kirill's message. He shook his head in disgust. Luscious was a rotten fucker. He knew he'd renege if he found out they had Avarie. No matter, she was in his room sleeping, he hoped at least. Getting off the couch, he walked into his bedroom and flicked on the light.

He felt relief knowing that she was lying in his room, sound asleep. He flicked off the light and went back to the couch. He debated on sleeping on the couch tonight or on his bed. If Luscious was in Moscow, then he'd be snooping. The bed it is. He wasn't tired, but he didn't want Avarie to be stolen in the middle of the night either.

He walked back into his room and turned on the lights. He watched her as she slept. Her music player was going in her ears. He wondered if he should take them out but decided against it. It's probably how she always slept. He kicked off his shoes and socks. Getting down to his boxer briefs, he pulled back the covers and climbed in. Before he brought the covers up, he watched as she breathed softly like she didn't have a care in the world. Sasha said that she always slept in panties and a t-shirt. This one looked like it was worn thin. He could see the birthmarks on her stomach and left shoulder. She was flat on her back with her thick brown hair spilled on the pillows. Maybe she was an angel. He wasn't sure, what he was sure of was that she was a disaster waiting to happen. She didn't even know it. He was about to switch off the light when she stirred. He prayed he didn't wake her up. Waiting a few moments, he switched off the light and pulled the covers around him.

He lay there awake, trying to ignore the fact she was there, but at the same time, being aware of her presence. It was so silent; all he could hear was the soft sounds of her breathing and the music from her earphones. He rolled over to face her because he couldn't take his eyes off her. He was afraid that if he blinked, she'd go missing.

It took almost an hour for him to close his eyes for good, but he heard something and opened them again. He looked for the source and found it was Avarie. She was mumbling something in her sleep, but it wasn't loud enough to make out. She shifted her head slightly and licked her lips. He thought it was done, but that was just the beginning. Kicking the covers away from her, she started to squirm. A moan escaped her lips and she went quiet again. Bringing her hands above her head, she lifted up her hips slowly and brought them back down. She lifted her head back and down again.

His eyes were wide with excitement as he watched her move her right hand slowly down her toned abdomen. Her fingertips went to the top of her lace panties, and she stopped. He felt like he got gipped. He was awake now and he wanted a show. *"Keep going."* He whispered to himself. Just like that, she did. Sliding her hand inside her see through panties, she found her core and started rubbing. She moaned in her sleep while her legs opened up a bit so she could let more of herself in.

Mikhail was getting turned on. He'd never seen a woman do this before in their sleep. His cock throbbed against the fabric of his boxer briefs and he told himself to settle down. Before long, Avarie looked as though she was ready to explode. Her face flushed and her hips were bucking against her hand. Letting out a soft cry and throwing herself back on the pillow, she was spent. He felt like applauding. She really worked him up and now he'd have to take care of it. Removing her hand, she pulled the covers back up and went to sleep again.

He got up and went to the bathroom to splash cold water on his face. He seriously debated on jerking off, but he decided it was best to calm the Hell down. A bead of moisture rolled down his back and he wasn't even aware he was sweating. Checking his watch, it was almost 3am. He needed to get to bed. Suddenly, the bathroom door clicked open and Avarie walked in. It was as if she wasn't even aware of him as she pushed him out of the way. She sat on the toilet to pee. When she was done, she scooted him over and washed her hands. "Move, Sasha." She mumbled and dried off her hands. She left the bathroom without giving him a second glance. He followed her there and she laid down and went right back to sleep.

Pandora Rising

He checked to make sure the alarm system was on and the doors were all locked. He came back into bed and pulled the covers around him. Once he calmed himself down, he closed his eyes. *Damn her*, he thought before sleep over took him.

ϒϒϒ

It was 10am when he woke up. Remembering that Avarie was with him, he looked over. She was still there and sleeping soundly. Flooded with relief he made his way to the bathroom. Turning on the shower and shutting the door, he undressed and got in. He relived last night's show and decided this was a good time to take care of himself. If she did it again tonight, he hoped for an invitation to join. Being washed up, he toweled off and his cell phone beeped. Tori sent him a text checking in. She wanted to make sure Avarie was alright since she heard Luscious was in Moscow. They texted back and forth for a bit. In the kitchen, he made a breakfast of cinnamon buns. He was still in his towel, but he didn't want to wake Avarie until breakfast was ready. She beat him to it. She walked out with sleep still in her eyes and looked around. "You slept out here last night?" He nodded. "I'm sorry. Maybe I should've taken the couch." She said with a yawn.

"That's fine. Did you sleep well?" She nodded and went into the bathroom. Popping back out, she looked at the couch.

"You didn't sleep on the couch last night did you?"

"How would you know?" He asked pulling out the cinnamon rolls.

"There are no covers and the clothes you wore last night are in your room." She went back into the bathroom. *Touché*, he thought. He heard the shower turn on. Five minutes later it was off and she popped out in a towel. She went back into the bedroom and dressed in jeans and a tight t-shirt.

Joining him at the table she looked at him funny. He scooped up a roll for her. She picked at it with a fork. Taking little bites, she decided she liked it enough to eat. He went back and got dressed.

"Do all you guys steal the covers?" She asked with an evil eye.

She had zero clue what happened last night so he played along. "I'm sorry, *Mishka*. Men like covers too." He held onto his poker face for dear life as she downed her orange juice.

"Are we doing something today?"

He thought about it. Maybe it wasn't safe to take her out. "I'd love to take you out, but I need to get the all clear first, alright?" Avarie approved.

Pandora Rising

"Is Sasha alright?" She asked. Something was up and he wasn't letting her in on it.

"He's just fine. Tori is a good host." Avarie still looked at him suspiciously. "What?"

"Why are we separated?" She cocked her face to the side.

"To keep you safe." He answered.

That wasn't enough and she pressed him. "From what? And why did he go with Tori and I with you?"

He took a deep breath and rolled his eyes. "You're with me because if anybody were to come and find you, you'd be safe. Sasha is with Tori because he has things to learn."

She wasn't buying it. Her eyes grew wide with fear. "Mikhail, I can run you know." She whispered softly. "I'll make sure they won't find me and everybody could be safe." He shook his head. She went back into the bedroom while he cleaned up after breakfast. With his back turned, she unlocked his doors and ran down the hall. He caught up with her this time. Picking her up, he threw her back in the bedroom.

"I told you. Stop running!" Rage filled his veins. God he wanted to hit her. "Running away doesn't make things better, it makes them worse." His voice went hoarse. "That's how we found out about you. You ran from Courtney and it was all over the place. You can't do it quietly."

Avarie lay there defeated on his bed. Her hair fell around the pillows and tears welled up in her eyes. He felt bad for her. "*Mishka* let us be the ones to keep you safe. It isn't your job to protect everybody. It never was." He shook his head and lay down next to her. "I can't tell you how to feel, but there are forces out there much stronger than you and you need us." He pulled her close to him as tears fell onto his shirt. "When we get the all clear, we can go out. I'll take you anywhere in Moscow." He let her cry on him. It was hard to believe that this girl was only nineteen. She seemed so old, yet so new. "Please Avarie, let me do my job." He pleaded. "Can you do that?" He lifted her chin so he could look in her eyes."

She gave him a nod through her tears. *Those green eyes*, he thought to himself, they almost looked blue. It was an hour before he received the all clear from Kirill and the FSB.

True to his word, he took her out into the square and showed her around. He stayed armed the entire time. They ate kababs and walked through the stores. He bought her strong coffee and she tried new foods besides the shit at the cafeteria. It was nice to get fresh air. The days were getting colder and soon she'd need a jacket. That thought wasn't lost on him as he bought her a few hoodies because she told him those were her favorite types of clothes. Later, he took her to a movie and she got to experience Russian cinema. He told Tori earlier in the day that they were to remain separate the entire weekend until they went back to Kirill. He made sure to stay close to the FSB and his flat the while they were out. For supper, he took her into a café and they ate on the balcony.

Back at the flat, Avarie said she was tired and went to bed. He stayed up a bit and watched the news. It was the same shit over and over again. A news report came up about Courtney's new company in France opening up for communications. He was pictured with a smoking hot lady on his arm that wasn't Avarie. *Good, he's following orders.* He shut it off and went into the bedroom. Avarie was out and had her earbuds in again. He stripped down and lay next to her. Crossing his fingers in the air and grinning from ear to ear, "Please, give me another show, just one." He whispered quietly in the dark.

He knew that was bad of him, but she's so much trouble and this would make it all worth it. She mumbled again and he looked over. She started moving her head, but it was to the beat of the music in her ears. Maybe he wasn't specific enough. Her eyes opened up a bit and she said, "Shh, you're too loud." and went back to bed. No, this would not do.

"Seriously, I want the show I got last night." He whispered quieter. Her eyes opened up and she looked at him. "You say something?" She asked.

He shook his head. Her green eyes almost glowed in the dark. She went right back to sleep. Nope, not going to happen tonight. He got comfortable, careful not to stir too much. Facing her, he closed his eyes and nodded off.

It wasn't until sometime in the night that he woke up to movement. He thought somebody was in the flat, but it was just Avarie again. It looked as though the show was back on. Rubbing the sleep out of his eyes, he watched intently as her hand went into her panties and rubbed her soft little nub. He reached over for her, but he pulled back. *Would I regret this*, he thought. *No, first instinct is always the right one.* Covering his hand with hers, he found his way in. Finding her soaking wet, he rubbed the hard little pebble until it felt swollen. She pushed his hand down further and allowed him access into her.

It was hot and wet as he swirled two fingers round. He scooted closer to her as she moaned with pleasure. His cock throbbed against his boxer briefs and he pushed it into her thigh as she moved against his hand. Her nipples poked through the fabric of her shirt and he ran his free hand across them. It was almost too much. He could feel her heart race under his hand. Her free hand went to his chest and worked down to his member. She found it and started stroking. He wasn't expecting this and went with it.

Her grip was easy as she went from shaft to tip. He started to moan, he kept working her as she stroked him faster. Her breathing increased and so did her stroke. Sensations started to flood his system and he wanted to hold out until she came. He worked her faster and swirled his fingers around until he found her sweet spot. He felt the contractions inside her start to build up. She increased her pace on him as she came and moaned so loud, he thought she'd wake up the neighbors. He finally came in her hand, making a mess of himself and her. When he settled down, he grabbed a towel and cleaned up the mess. He gently wiped up her hand before she could run it through her hair. He scrunched himself back into sleeping position and he could see she was already asleep with both arms around her head in sweet slumber.

Closing his eyes he almost fell asleep until she bolted upright. He looked up at her in surprise. Her eyes were definitely blue now. With shock on her face, she pulled out her earbuds and asked, "Are you sure you didn't say something?"

"Go to sleep, *Mishka*. It's 3am."

She lay back down putting her earbuds in. He watched as her eyes closed and she slept for the rest of the night. Damn this one was strange and Sasha had to share a room with her. Every night had to be a new adventure for him. Talking in her sleep, nightmares, dancing around, masturbating, and God knows what else. She's got to be the reason Sasha fears females, there's no other explanation for it.

ϒϒϒ

The morning was interesting for him as he observed Avarie. When she woke up, she continuously shook out her hands. He asked her what was wrong and she explained that they felt like she slept on them wrong. He worked hard to conceal a smile.

He asked Avarie what she wanted to do that day and she said that she wanted to know if Moscow had a music store. It was an odd request, but he indulged her. In the center of town, he took her inside a store that sold music and instruments. Avarie looked around at their music selection and Mikhail never let her out of his sight. There were a few FSB agents in the store that he ran into and they chatted.

He watched from the corner of his eye as Avarie found the pianos and sat down at a big black grand piano. Pulling her hoodie over her head, she tinkered with the keys. Before long, a soft tune came from her fingertips and he watched intently. The other two agents turned in her direction. They had no clue what she was playing but it was a haunting melody. Mikhail grabbed his phone and hit the record button. Courtney never mentioned that she could play the piano.

"She's playing *Gloomy Sunday.*" A woman whispered to them. "Can she sing?" She asked looking at Mikhail.

"I don't know." He said honestly. "But I'd like to find out."

Ironically, a light rain drizzled outside the windows with a soft pitter patter. She started to sing, but it wasn't the Hungarian version. He stood with the other agents and goosebumps ran across his body. He'd never heard a voice like that. The store was busy and it seemed everybody stopped in their tracks as the soprano angelic voice rose and fell, filling every gap in the air. *"What are you?"* he whispered to himself.

When she was done, he sent the video to Kirill. He'd find this interesting for sure. Five minutes later, all agents had a mass message for high alert. Quickly, Mikhail grabbed Avarie and they rushed for the flat.

"What was that about?" Avarie asked once he locked the doors.

He didn't want to scare her so he answered. "It could be a drill, I don't know."

"Bullshit." She quipped. "Really, what's going on?"

He forced the words from his throat. "They're snooping around, Avarie. I don't know if they know what you look like, but we can't give them a chance to find out."

She nodded and was about to say something but he cut her off. "No, you aren't running. Fuck those assholes." He threw his jacket on the couch. "Remember, if you run, you put all of us in danger."

He flicked on the TV to watch the news and wait for the all clear signal. The same news as last night was playing on the screen. "Go pack up your stuff, *Mishka*." She ran into the bedroom as he sat down on the couch. The clip of Courtney's new company played as the news agency gave off information. The picture of him with the lady on his arm came up again. A loud thump of something dropping behind him grabbed his attention.

Avarie stood behind the couch, watching the screen as it stayed on that picture for what felt like an eternity. She stood there as her face went pale. He started to stand up, but she ran for the bathroom and slammed the door. It sounded like she was puking. "*Mishka*!" He yelled. "It's not what you think!" Oh God, he should've turned the TV off. Now he was fucked.

He knocked on the door and pleaded. "Avarie, please open the door." She didn't answer him. The toilet flushed and he heard crying. His heart broke for her. He went into her bag and grabbed her toothbrush. "I have your toothbrush if you want it." He said softly. "Please, *Mishka*, open the door."

She opened the door only a crack and held her hand out for the toothbrush. In defeat, he gave in. It was an hour before she came out. Without a glance in his direction, she went to the bedroom still looking like she seen a ghost. She flopped down on his bed with her head in her arms and he followed suit.

"I'm sorry, Avarie." He said as he pulled her hair back from her face. "You weren't supposed to see that."

"What has been seen can't be unseen now can it?" She said defensively. "He's already moved on to another woman and he's forgotten about me."

Mikhail shook his head. "It's all a ruse. We're throwing them off your trail." He grabbed a tissue and dried her eyes. "That woman is an FSB agent. She shows up to publicity stunts with him and keeps him safe."

"He sure looked fucking happy if you ask me." She buried her head deeper into her arms. "Guess I don't have a home to go to now do I?"

Oh man, she was throwing this all out of proportion. "Avarie, he loves you. He's fought me tooth and nail on everything I've asked him. He's not sleeping with her."

"How can you be so sure?" She asked him.

"Because that isn't her job." He sighed in frustration. "This is why we cut off contact. What happens in Germany stays there. What happens to you in Russia stays here. Don't you understand? These are two separate worlds and you both stay in them separately." The look on her face says she didn't get it. Damn these nineteen year olds! "You belong to us. I've said it over and over again."

She pushed him away from her. There was no point arguing, her heart was broken. He reached out for her again and she slapped him away. Not this game again, he thought. He cracked her on her ass and told her to behave. She slapped his even harder and it stung like a bitch. The slapping match turned into wrestling but it was over within seconds. He had Avarie pinned under him and she squirmed.

"I told you, behave." He said grinning. "We've been through this before and I don't want to do it again."

"You don't have cold water on your side this time." She spat out.

"*Oi*, Why are you so feisty? It's so easy to do what I say." He let go of her but kept her down by covering her body with his. "You know, we could try the honey pot if you want." He said laughing in her ear.

She busted up laughing as he smiled at her. "No thanks." She patted his back but he wouldn't move.

In a way, she didn't want him to either. He was warm and soft so she wrapped her arms around him in a hug. For now, he was her safety net and that was okay. He hugged her back. "You confuse me so much. When I think I've gotten into your head, it goes another direction. I don't understand this."

She could smell his spearmint gum as he breathed into her hair. "I don't understand it either. Just when I think I have my shit together, it falls apart all over again. I've just come to the conclusion that we're all fucked."

He laughed into her and said seriously. "I don't know what you are and it scares me. It's like you're an angel and demon wrapped into one." She was stroking her hands up and down his back. Her face was relaxed and the tears have long been dried up.

"Are you working the honey pot on me?" She asked with a sly smile. "If you are, it's not working."

He looked her over. "I think we're beyond the honey pot at this point." Her eyes were turning blue as she ran her finger across his face. He quickly kissed her before she could protest. He turned away from her to spit out his gum in the trash. "I can't have you stealing on my gum." He kissed her deeper and forced his way into her mouth. Avarie flooded with warmth as she ran her hands faster up and down his back. He wasn't letting up on her and she didn't want him to. He ran his lips over her face and neck with a fever that she never experienced before. He leaned up suddenly and pulled off his shirt and came back down to her. He spread her legs so he could feel the heat between them. Avarie was losing control and she ripped off her shirt under him. His fingers pulled and pinched at her nipples as she moaned.

Her hands went for his pants and unbuckled his belt. She ran her lips across his chest and lapped at his nipples. "*Mishka*, that's naughty." He whispered hoarsely. Electricity ran from his chest to his member, making it even harder. She kicked his pants off, exposing his black boxer briefs. He continued exploring her neck with his tongue as he pulled down her pants along with her panties. He ran his hand into her nether lips and found her wanting. She was so slippery; it made a wet spot on the sheets beneath her. She was getting him too excited as she bucked against his hand.

He pulled his underwear down and she grabbed his cock. "Easy, it's really excited." He whispered into her ear. "So am I." She whispered back. "Don't make me beg." It was almost a whimper. His hand fumbled in the nightstand drawer for a condom. He didn't find one. Oh fuck it. He entered her slowly, keeping in mind that he needed to pull out before he came. She was so wet and hot it sent shivers up his body. Avarie felt every inch of him as she dug her nails into his back. He filled her up and started to hit her sensitive areas as he rubbed her clit. Heat pooled in her core and she moaned louder. That only stirred him up. He put her legs on his shoulders and ground into her deeper, each thrust harder than the last. "Don't stop." She yelled. He felt her tunnel starting to contract. He wanted her to come before he did and he tried his hardest to make that happen. His eyes were watching her soft breasts bounce up and down under his thrusts. He covered them with his lips, bringing her knees almost to her ears.

He was so deep inside her she felt the tip in her stomach. The orgasm built deep inside as she almost screamed into his ear. It was just in time and with a few more thrusts, he pulled out and spilled his seed on her abdomen with a loud grunt. She shook under him as he laid his body down on hers. The room smelled like sex and sweat. He rolled over to the other side, taking deep breaths to calm himself down. "You totally honey potted me." She said as she looked up at the ceiling. He busted up laughing and kissed her nose.

Pandora Rising

A text message came in. The all clear was given and he could take Avarie back to the Prime Minister's house. "I have to get you back. Get cleaned up." They left his flat almost an hour later.

ϓϓϓ

He parked the SUV in the parking ramp. Before she got out, he kissed her one last time. He was sad the weekend was over, but he'd see her tomorrow. They came in the back way and Tori met them with Sasha just in time. Kirill waited for them at the door and looked them over. They stared blankly forward with no expressions on their faces. "My God, I've never seen such forlorn faces in my life." He exclaimed. "I told you both no training this weekend." Kirill looked at both Tori and Mikhail. "Jesus, I'll just send food up to your room for tonight." Two armed men escorted them to their room and they didn't look back.

Kirill looked at both of them. "What the Hell did you do to them?" He said accusingly.

"Nothing." Mikhail answered. "It was a boring weekend." He turned and walked out with Tori behind him.

"You'd think we killed their spirits with the way Kirill acted." She whispered to him and giggled.

Mikhail looked down at her and laughed.

ϓϓϓ

Sasha and Avarie threw their bags down on the floor and plopped on the bed. They said nothing to each other for what felt like an eternity. Both their eyes stared at the high ceilings with their arms behind their heads. "Was your weekend boring?" Avarie finally asked quietly.

Sasha heaved a deep sigh. "Not really." He answered softly. He looked spent and his eyes turned a softer blue. "I'm tired." He admitted. "I'm not even hungry." Avarie snuggled into him and held tight.

"I'm tired too." She said sleepily. They both fell asleep as they were. A knock came at the door, but nobody was awake to answer. The food stayed outside the room for the rest of the night.

Kirill softly opened the door to their room and found them sound asleep. He smiled to himself as he went and pulled off their shoes. They were so tired they didn't even bother to get ready for bed. He could only imagine how their weekend went down. He swallowed hard as he thought about Luscious getting his hands on either of these beings and cringed. Soon, they would become a great team. He pulled the covers over them and shut off the light.

ϒϒϒ

The week after having stayed at Mikhail's place guilt started to eat her alive. She tried hard to push it away from her mind and it wasn't easy. Every now and then the images of that day would come forward and remind her of her guilt. It ate away at her soul. She didn't enjoy being an agent for the FSB nor being around the twins. However, Courtney did warn her that she would have to follow orders and she may not like them. But the issue wasn't following orders. It was the fact that she slept with Mikhail willingly.

Speaking of following orders, she started to rebel again against Kirill and Mikhail. It wasn't the fact that she was doing much to them; it was the fact that she was ignoring them and trying hard to keep her distance. Much to the annoyance of Kirill, it frustrated him. Even after their talk, he felt they had broken a small barrier. Now it seems she rebuilt that section of wall. The twins both regretted having taken her the way they did, but they couldn't undo what has already been done.

Kirill felt somewhat heartbroken. He was angry with himself because he allowed his emotions to get involved with Avarie. He finally burst the day of their monthly check-ups with Dr. Alex. The second story of the Prime Minister's house was broken down into a doctors office like Matthias' back home. It also had a large workout room where Kirill spent most of his hours after work and before supper. On that very same floor was the lock up for the weapons room along with a break room for the security guards.

Dr. Alex was busy with Sasha downstairs while she read "Behold a Pale Horse" by William Cooper. She tried to drown out the sounds of Kirill and Mikhail yelling below her. Normally, things were quiet when they worked out together on Fridays. She didn't discover that there was actually a workout room under hers until a month ago. She was never allowed on the second floor. It was off limits to her and Sasha unless they were getting their checkups.

Avarie strained to read because this was actually a damn good book. She tried to pretend they weren't yelling about her, but she knew better. Those two didn't know how loud they could be when they fought. The constant clanking of the weights along with their annoying banter pissed her off and she wanted nothing better at this point than to either run away or for them to shut up. At this point, she already had her time with Dr. Alex. He drew her blood and checked her over meticulously, giving her a clean bill of health. He'd take longer with Sasha. Hell, Sasha had only been gone fifteen minutes and it felt like an eternity.

A loud crash snapped her from her thoughts as she looked down at the floorboards of her room and she heard a click. This fight was becoming pretty intense. Avarie had no clue what she did to make them so angry other than the fact that she'd been blowing them off and avoiding them since last weekend. Avarie rolled her eyes and looked towards the door and noticed something odd, it was ajar. Whatever they threw, it knocked the doorjamb out of its lock....

ϒϒϒ

Kirill was pumping the barbells as Mikhail was working the punching bag. "You know, I honestly thought we gotten through to her!" Kirill yelled as he furiously pumped 500lbs while dripping sweat from his brow. "Now she receded back down into her own head again." His face contorted with each set. "I swear we'll be the first to kill her before she has a chance to return to Germany!"

Mikhail rolled his eyes. "*Oi*, she hates us that's for sure." He pulled off his gloves and toweled off his face. "She wasn't ready for any of this. We pushed her too hard." He grabbed a bottle of water and dumped some on his head. "She's like nothing we've ever dealt with before."

"We should've let her live with Konstantin like he offered!" Kirill screamed. "Of course she'd give him a fucking heart attack within the first three months. Now I'm wishing she would run away."

"*Oi*! Kirill! For Shame!" Mikhail yelled back at him. "You be careful what you wish for!" He grabbed at the pull up bar and went to work. "If the others get her, we'd be in serious trouble."

"Like we aren't already?" Kirill put the barbell back in place and sat up. "She's a fucking mess! We should put her out of her misery and tell Courtney and Matthias to start over!"

Suddenly Mikhail stopped in his tracks and shot Kirill a deadly look. "Are you so blind that you can't see what she's going through? You and I both know that she didn't start off with a clean slate..."

"That's because Courtney didn't tell us she was broken out of the research facility! We could've had her at the very beginning!"

"But we didn't, Kirill!" Mikhail was beyond frustrated. "This is why I'm the one dealing with new recruits and agents, not you! Since the beginning you have always dealt with the political aspects. You forget yourself when you deal with her. There's nothing political about her! You cannot just give her a burn notice when things don't go your way." Mikhail ran a hand through his jet black hair. "She's not an unfeeling super soldier."

Without warning Kirill grabbed the barbell and flung it across the room, making a huge crash against the wall. "That's exactly what we were supposed to get! That was what was promised to us by them!" Kirill kicked the bench over. "We got a damn midget with muscles and half a brain!"

"*Oi*, look at you! Losing your temper over a midget!" Mikhail retorted. "You remember that in her past life, that midget crippled the New World Order in the US. She can do it again." Mikhail threw a dumbbell at Kirill. He managed to duck out of the way before it struck him in the face.

A brawl was about to ensure until one of the security guards opened the door. "What?" Kirill yelled.

"Dr. Alex and Sasha were wondering where Avarie is." The guard answered.

"*Oi*, she's in her room where she's supposed to be." Kirill answered. The guard shook his head no. "No?"

"No, she's not there. We're wondering if she went to another room of the house with your permission."

"Her door was locked."

"It was when Sasha went back."

"How did she get out?"

"We're not sure."

"What are you sure about?"

"We're sure she's gone, sir."

"Is she anywhere in the house?"

"No, sir. We checked already." Mikhail's heart sank so far into his chest he felt as though he could puke. Avarie was gone and she had a head start. Kirill calmly sat down on another bench and folded his hands together. "What's our orders, sir?" Kirill looked at Mikhail and a devious smile swept across his face. "Sir?"

"Call the FSB and see if they can't hunt her down. She is their agent after all." Kirill answered and turned to Mikhail. "Let's see how well you guys trained her to hide."

ϒϒϒ

Avarie had her duffel bag and scampered from rooftop to rooftop. She wasn't stupid. She knew the city had cameras on every street corner. When she couldn't jump a rooftop, she shimmied down a drain pipe or stairwell into a darkened alley only to climb back onto more rooftops. Every now and then, she'd scan the darkened horizon to find the freeway.

Twenty minutes into her escape, she felt as if somebody was following her. There was no way in hell the FSB could find her so damn quickly. For a moment, she thought it could be Sasha. She shook the thought away from her head. Avarie felt horrible for leaving Sasha behind. Truth was, this escape wasn't very well thought out. It wasn't until she was a mile from the freeway that she actually thought about turning around. What did she exactly have to go back to? The twins didn't really want her and Sasha could find comfort in Tori.

Avarie stayed in the shadows of the night and made it to the freeway. She started to flag down a car when gun shots rang out in the night. She ducked, but it was too late, a bullet caught her in the shoulder and another in the thigh. She tried to stand up, but the pain was horrific as it snaked through her nerves. How could she be so stupid? Avarie was about to pass out from the pain until a Mercedes pulled over to the side of the road and the passenger side door was opened.

Struggling to her feet, Avarie gladly accepted the ride as more bullets shot out in her direction. "Hurry and get in!" the man yelled. She managed to drag herself into the car and slammed the door shut as a bullet hit the back windshield. Tears rolled down her cheeks as she held onto her left leg. "Keep your head down!" The man demanded as he tore off the side of the road and sped down the freeway.

Avarie didn't keep track of how long they traveled until the man pulled over somewhere. He flicked on the cargo light so she could see his face. He pulled a bag out from the backseat and pulled some items out. "Take off your pants." He demanded. Avarie hesitated. "Now!" She was in no condition to fight him and did as she was told. After she battled with the pain her pants were removed and he tied a makeshift tourniquet to her thigh. "I can't do anything with your shoulder right now. We have ten more minutes till we get to my place. Can you hold on?" Avarie nodded as she clenched her teeth through the pain. "Good. Now sit back and breathe through it."

He shut off the light and drove onward. It wasn't long before they pulled off into a wooded area with a long driveway. His headlights beamed onto a small cottage. He got out and went to her side. He opened the door and gently lifted her and her bag out. As he reached the door he punched in a code. Immediately he took her into the bathroom and set her down into the glass shower. "Take off all your clothes. I need to make sure all the bullets are out and tend to your wounds." Avarie was close to blacking out but willed herself to hold on. He helped get her shirt off. He was nice enough to leave her panties on. He turned on the shower and sprayed the blood off her body. "You're doing good, *Mishka*." He cooed. Her eyes were blurred from tears and she couldn't get a good look at him. However she knew he was strong and had no intention of running off. He ordered her to sit on the shower floor and he left the room, only to come back with doctors' tools. "This is going to hurt. I have to take the bullet out of your shoulder first so I can sew you up."

Avarie nodded and let him go to work on the backside of her shoulder. She screamed out in pain as he took some sort of strange tweezers to pull what was left of the bullet that entered her. She was becoming woozy from the pain and blood loss. Without warning Avarie puked in the shower and blacked out. When she awoke, she was curled up in a large mahogany four poster bed. Lifting the covers, she found herself completely naked. Quickly, she threw the covers back over her body.

"I see you're awake." The man said as he entered the room with a tray. He set it on the bedside and turned on the lamp. "It's just crackers and milk. You should get something in your stomach." Avarie sat up careful to conceal her naked body. She was extremely groggy but hungry. Ironically she didn't feel any pain. "You heal quickly little one." He said. "I gave you a pain killer to help you sleep. You've been out for almost four hours."

Avarie looked suspiciously around the room, expecting more bullets to fly at any minute. "Are you one of them?" she asked quietly. "Am I safe?"

"I think that depends on what you mean by them and being safe." He sat down across the room and Avarie focused her eyes on him. If she could put an age on him, it would be late forties. His dialect wasn't Russian. He didn't even look Russian, more like Arabic. His eyes were a grayish brown and he seemed about six feet tall. He definitely had a muscular build as she could tell through his t-shirt and blood stained jeans. His short jet black hair was sprinkled with silver at his temples. He was most definitely handsome for his age. "Before I answer any of your questions, why don't you tell me what you were running from? You owe me at least that."

"A bad situation."

"It seems you ended up in a worse situation don't you think?"

"It seems so." Avarie answered honestly. "I don't even know your name."

"It's Omar."

"I'm Avarie."

"Well Avarie, maybe I should call up your bad situation and let them know where you are." Omar said in a serious tone. "I would think they'd be worried about you. Seeing as how you gotten yourself shot and all."

"That wasn't my intention." Avarie shot back.

Omar started laughing. "No, your intention was to run away without consequences. Look what happened. You ended up in a strange house in the middle of nowhere with a stranger."

Avarie nodded. He was right. They all warned her over and over that running away only makes things worse. "So what's your intention with me?" Fear started to make her heart thump inside her chest.

Omar crossed his legs and tapped his thumb on the table. "I think that depends on you. It seems right now you're extremely vulnerable and you need protection from whatever is out there. If you want to be safe, I'll keep you safe. But it comes at a cost."

Avarie swallowed a lump in her throat. "What's the cost?" His eyes roamed about her body in silence. "Well?"

"You go back to where you came from." He stood up and stretched. "You eat your food and think about it." With that, he left the room.

ϒϒϒ

Mikhail had teams stretched out all over Moscow. It wasn't just the FSB, it was the Russian Secret Service and the police. There were over 1,200 people combing the area for Avarie. Sweet Jesus, if the others managed to find her they were in serious trouble. If his team found her, he didn't know if he was going to hit her or hug her. He pulled Sasha along and let him know this was the real deal. "This is the shit that you guys were training for. We know that there's Sneakers out here, Sasha." He told him. "You spot them, take them out."

At the FSB he had multiple agents combing over street camera footage looking for any sign of Avarie. A phone call came in informing him that Avarie was last spotted two hours ago at an intersection of the M10 Highway westbound. Footage was sent showing that she took gunfire and a car pulling over to the side of the road letting Avarie in. "*Oi*, Sasha! We need to get a team to that intersection now!" Mikhail knew this was going to be a long night. He loaded the team along with Tori into the vehicle. His head was already started to beat inside his skull. He was extremely upset. If something happened to Avarie and she was taken, they had no chance of winning.

As soon as they arrived, they spread out looking for evidence. Tori found blood splatter at the side of the road and tire tracks. Sasha had a hard time keeping his cool. Avarie could be anywhere by now and it's obvious she's hurt. His head kept spinning on all the scenarios that she could be in. He swung around and saw headlights approaching their team. It was Kirill. He rolled down the window with a shit eating grin. "Well?"

"*Oi*, what are you doing here?" Mikhail spat at him. "This is FSB business not your political bullshit!"

"For shame!" Kirill spat right back. "It just so happens that I found her before you did."

Mikhail's eyes went wide in shock. "What?"

"I'll tell you all about it later. Right now you need to find your shooters. I'll go see to Avarie."

"That isn't protocol!" Mikhail yelled at him. "What's her location?"

Kirill busted up laughing like it was a game. "Mikhail, her location is hidden and she's safe. Now, go clean up this mess."

"*Oi*, You fucking cheated!" Mikhail pointed the Krinkov at him. "I should shoot you in the face you bastard!" Kirill smiled at him and rolled up his window while flipping off Mikhail. He hung his head low and radioed the teams letting them know the mission had changed. Now, they were looking only for the Sneakers and taking them out.

It took three teams and four hours to take out twenty five men. Sasha had three confirmed kills and he was still in training. They left four alive and sent them in for questioning. This was not how Mikhail wanted to spend his weekend. Even after questioning, that meant paperwork. Oh Avarie was going to pay when she got back.

ᛉᛉᛉ

Omar was smoking a cigarette on his porch when the SUV pulled up. Five minutes before he checked on Avarie to make sure she was sleeping. He made sure to give her enough medication to knock her out for quite a while. He needed to have a serious conversation with Kirill and he didn't want her stressing over what was said. This was the second time he was ordered to find her.

The sun was coming up in the horizon and Omar had coffee brewing in the kitchen. He couldn't wait to have a cup. Kirill came out of the passenger side of the car and instructed his security team to surround the perimeter. Once on the porch he greeted Omar and they went inside. "Is she asleep?" Kirill asked. Omar nodded. "It's nice that you can find her faster than the FSB." Omar passed him a cup of coffee.

"It's also nice that you run off your special agents like that." Omar retorted. "I know you tell her not to run away but you're pushing her to it and she feels that she has no options."

"She has options; she just chooses the wrong ones." Kirill said as he sipped on his coffee.

Omar shook his head in disgust while leaning back in his chair. "You didn't give her any other options. So she ran. It's the same reason why she ran from Courtney and I was able to track her down…he didn't give her options. He pushed her away. It's the same shit you're pulling."

Kirill slammed his mug down. "I'm assuming you had this discussion with her?"

"Not really, she tends to talk in her sleep." Omar answered quickly. "The point is, as much as I enjoy finding people for you, she's not one I should always be hunting down."

"What do you want me to do?"

"I want you to understand that she didn't have a choice like we did. We got to decide who we were and our place in this world. She didn't. She's scared shitless of us. Not that I'm a Watcher like you and Mikhail. Courtney and Matthias created her with a purpose and she didn't get to say yes or no. I'm quite sure she's willing to fight for our cause but it's the matter of understanding that she's new to this world. Cut her a damn break. She's seen a side of you two that she wasn't ready for. She's seen more than she's ready for. You're smarter than that!" Omar stood up to refill his mug.

"If anything, it was you two who put her in danger, not the other way around. Sure, she has her elemental but there's so much he can do for her psyche. For Christs Sake, give her hope. The poor thing thinks that she's going to be trained only to die again."

Kirill cocked his eyebrow. "You know?"

"Of course I know. You better let Khalid know sooner than later too." Omar took a sip of his coffee. "You also better find Lukas."

"We'll have to wait until Luscious is off our backs to search for him in earnest." Kirill wanted to change the subject. "So, how badly is she hurt?"

"Gun shot in the right shoulder and in her left thigh. Obviously they want her alive. She's healing quickly." Omar ran a hand through his hair and over his face. "Please tell me Mikhail is clearing the area." Kirill nodded. "Good. She isn't leaving until we get the all clear. Let's just hope they didn't get word back to Dubai that they found her."

Omar and Kirill talked and debated through the morning waiting for the all clear from Mikhail and for Avarie to wake up. Sometime in the early afternoon, they heard gunshots in the distance. One of the security officers shot down a sniper who happened to track Avarie to Omar's cottage. It wasn't until late in the day that Avarie finally woke up. Barely any words were exchanged with Kirill. She ate in silence until the call came in from Mikhail.

Avarie was shoved into the waiting SUV after saying goodbye and thank you to Omar for his help. It was a long silent ride back to Moscow. Avarie was fearful she'd get the belt or a beating worse than death itself. Kirill's face was expressionless as they pulled up to the house. She was still in pain and he helped her out of the SUV. Without any guards, he escorted her upstairs. Instead of walking her into her bedroom, he led her into his and motioned for her to take a seat on the side of the bed. She did as she was told.

"I hope you had a nice adventure." Kirill said softly. Avarie cast her eyes down in shame. Yep, she knew what was coming. She stood up off the bed and went towards the fireplace and started to painfully peel off her clothes. "What are you doing?" he asked as he pulled her shirt back down.

"Taking my beating." Avarie answered curtly and started to pull her shirt back off. Again, Kirill pulled it back down. "What? This is how it usually goes."

Kirill shook his head. "No, *Mishka*. No beatings tonight." Avarie stared at him in a daze. "I wanted to tell you I'm sorry." Avarie couldn't believe her ears. Kirill never apologized, not directly anyway. "I'm serious. I'm sorry for the things that have happened to you. I understand why you run. I know you've told us many times that you didn't ask for this. I don't think we expected you to be so…human I guess."

Kirill made his way back to the side of his bed. "None of us were ready for you. That includes Courtney and Matthias. We all have a big job right now and we put you in situations that you weren't ready for yet. You didn't get a chance to explore this world. If you did do it, it was through electrical signals. That's not the same as actually experiencing life."

Avarie stayed standing where she was. This wasn't Kirill. This wasn't his mentality and this definitely wasn't the man who stole her from Courtney. "So what now?" Avarie dared to ask. "We can't start over."

"No, Mishka, but we can move forward." He stood up and kissed her on the forehead. "I want you to go into your room and go to bed. Just promise me that you won't run away anymore."

"Alright."

"Alright what?"

"I'll go to bed and I won't run away anymore." she answered.

He nodded and walked her to her room. Sasha was already in bed sleeping. Stripping down she crawled in with him. "I'm glad you're back." He whispered. "I have three confirmed kills."

"Congratulations. I took two bullets."

Sasha chuckled. "So we're even huh?"

Avarie wrapped her arms around Sasha and snuggled into his chest. "Yep Sasha, we're even."

CHAPTER NINE

It was two weeks into month three. Courtney's communications picked up chatter from all forces and it kept Jude and Damian busy. Gerhart was still gung ho on protection, warning Courtney that none of this was over. He worked with the FSB and Courtney and the others were introduced to each agent. They had the credentials to back them up in everything they did. He was aware of every situation he was in and followed his gut instincts.

Gerhart and Courtney were in a meeting with the Jr. Executives when the entire building shook with such force, they were all knocked to the ground. Pieces of the ceiling fell on their heads and a fire alarm went off and another explosion hit the building. Gerhart grabbed Courtney and threw him and the others under the table.

Wild screaming and panic reverberated from every direction. His senses were in shock and he didn't know what was happening. Small booms here and there would rock his eardrums. Gerhart was yelling something at him and he couldn't even hear it his ear drums rang so bad.

They had to get out of there. Gerhart took charge and led them out of the office. He yelled at the employees to avoid the elevators and go down the steps. Looking outside, a third of the back half of the building was gone. Car alarms screamed and dust flew everywhere. Hordes of people made their way past him and Gerhart. Courtney's eardrums continued to ring as panic flooded his body. These fuckers were going to kill innocent people because of him.

He ran back to his office and unlocked a drawer. He pulled out two loaded guns and ammo. Gerhart did the same at his desk and they met back on the now empty floor. "Are the explosions done?" Courtney yelled.

"I don't know, but stay low." He yelled back. "You never know what these fuckers have up their sleeves." They ran for the exit and down the stairwell. Shots were fired in their direction and they hung back. The dust cleared somewhat and Gerhart covered Courtney so he could make it to the next floor. More shots fired and Gerhart followed him. His heart beat so hard against his ribs, he could hardly take a breath.

They were at the lobby and it was cleared of people. Gerhart signaled for Courtney to go, as he did, another explosion rocked the entire first floor, spreading dust and debris. The explosion hit so hard, it threw Courtney up against the marble wall knocking the breath out of him. Gerhart skidded up to him and lifted Courtney onto his shoulders and carried him out. Blood ran down the back of Courtney's head. Bullets whizzed by them and Courtney shot in the direction they came from.

Ten more feet to the door, Courtney thought. A bullet caught Gerhart in the leg and he dropped. Pulling him by the arms, Courtney got them both outside in a trail of blood. Paramedics rushed to meet them while firetrucks and a swat team pulled up, clearing the area. Before the firemen could go in, one more explosion threw everybody including Gerhart and himself into the street as it rocked the lobby. Courtney rolled over on his back, ears completely deaf as he watched his entire corporate building fall down into itself, brick by brick.

ϒϒϒ

Matthias heard noises from outside his work area. It sounded like a herd of cattle coming through the front door. At least twenty FSB agents piled into the castle, clearing it of any dangers. Matthias's heart was racing as he stepped into the great room. An agent pulled him to the sitting area. Four agents found Eva and Ivan. Fear spread across their faces and panic was starting to drown Eva. Ivan held her close as they were escorted towards him. Radios were going off and nobody was explaining what was going down.

It was half an hour before the entire castle was cleared. "What the fuck is going on?" Matthias demanded.

A tall male agent answered him in broken German. "Courtney's corporate building was attacked and now you guys are on lockdown."

Eva stood up and started screaming. "Where is he?" Is he alive?" A female agent sat her down, taking her hands into her own.

"He's been escorted to the hospital. He has a nasty concussion and lost a lot of blood. His friend Gerhart was shot in the leg and he's in surgery." She explained. "We're locking you down because they're not playing anymore. We sent agents to the other businesses he owns and have the militia watching out in the States."

Eva sobbed uncontrollably. The danger was real and they weren't ready for it. "How many people dead?" Matthias asked.

"At least 45 dead and over 100 injured. That numbers climbing." The male agent answered honestly. "The entire building is gone."

Matthias had a hard time processing this information. Ivan sat quietly holding Eva. He watched as the fire in the fireplace flickered like crazy. "Can we see him?" He asked.

"Out of the question. We have more than enough men on him and Gerhart. The hospital is on lockdown too. We're working with the police and swat to make sure there's no other terrorist acts going on in the city and more outside sources are on their way." He reassured Matthias.

"Is Avarie safe?" Ivan asked them. Shit, they completely forgot about Avarie.

"Yes. She's at the FSB right now."

"She's gonna freak out if she found out what happened." Matthias told him. "She can't find out."

"Our direktor will be informed."

Matthias sat down in quiet contemplation. Courtney's in the hospital, Gerhart was shot, people were dead and corporate headquarters was gone. *Fuck.*

ϒϒϒ

Mikhail's phone was blowing up as he ran down the long corridors. He screamed into his radio to shut the entire FSB building down. Those fuckers were using Courtney as bait to drag Avarie out and it might work. If she found out, they had one Hell of a fight on their hands.

Avarie and Sasha were eating in the cafeteria when somebody turned up the TV. Everybody stopped as they watched news footage of the devastation in Freiburg. She stood up and came closer to the large flat screen. Sasha joined her. Dust and debris flew everywhere with fire crews, ambulances, police, military and God knows what else. Bright lights flickered red, blue, and orange. The cast was in Russian and she had a hard time understanding what it said. A picture of Courtney came up, being put into an ambulance. Her eyes grew wide with shock and fear. Sasha looked down at her with the same fear. Her body shook with such force that she had to use Sasha to steady herself. There was no point in that because he had the very same reaction.

They played footage over of the one explosion that blew out the first floor from under the building, showing Courtney and Gerhart getting thrown into the street. She tried to open her mouth, but nothing came out. Mikhail was almost to the cafeteria when he heard it. The most God awful high pitched wail he's ever heard in his life vibrated into the corridors. He ran into the cafeteria and found the noise was coming from Avarie. Sasha covered his ears, trying to get her to calm down. It took four Direktor's and Sasha to get her out of there. She clawed and screamed at them. She kicked one so hard, he heard a rib crack.

With the other three, his hands were free to call Tori and meet them in the pool area. It took almost ten minutes to get her down there. Wrestling her that far took the energy out of them. Tori swiped her badge for the ladies locker room and Mikhail had Avarie thrown into the same stall that they had their confrontation in. "Kirill is going to be here soon." She told Mikhail. Finding Sasha she pulled him away.

The other men waited outside the stall while Mikhail stepped in. Avarie was not calm by any means and she was looking for a fight. "Don't fight me, *Mishka*." He said quietly as he locked the door. "I'm tired of fighting you." It was no use, the fire was in her eyes and they glowed a deep green. She tried to throw him away from the door. He knocked her to the ground and pushed her back against the wall. She broke his nose and maybe a rib. He dislocated her shoulder and bashed her head into the tile, leaving a trail of blood that followed down her face and wall. She landed him flat on his back in the tiny shower stall, but he kicked her chest back into the ceramic tile, knocking the breath out of her. She sunk back into the floor of the stall, completely spent.

For good measure, Mikhail turned on the cold water. His white shirt was soaked in blood and so was hers. She leaned back against the wall and let the water pour over her. She lost again. He joined her under the spray, breathing hard and deep. Blood flowed red down into the drain, washing the remnants of the fight away. Broken tile covered the floor and the door was almost off its hinges.

The water felt good on her body as she heaved. The pain in her head was blistering as she paid no attention to it. "I think this stall needs to be remodeled." She said as she looked at him. He gave her a smile and pulled her close to him, letting the water cleanse the blood away. He covered her face in desperate kisses, thankful he shut down the entire building before she could run straight into danger.

They heard sobbing outside and somebody saying, "She's going to run, please don't let her run." It was Sasha she realized. He was scared for her.

"That's the first time I've heard him cry, *Mishka*." Mikhail said as he leaned his wet head against the tile wall. "See what happens when you can't control your emotions?" God she felt terrible. Mikhail signaled for her to hold still. He grabbed her arm and put his boot into her side, putting her shoulder back into place with a scream when it went back in.

A knock came at the door and Mikhail came to unlock it. Kirill stepped in and looked them over. Shaking his head, he cleared a spot for himself on the floor. The ceramic tiles scraped against themselves as he shifted, never leaving her eyes. "Now that you're calm, I can tell you that Courtney is fine. He told me to tell you to stay where you are."

She ran her hands through her wet hair, and stared at him blankly. "I've stayed here, and look what happened." She whispered hoarsely. "Courtney and Gerhart are hurt, people are dead and a building is destroyed because of me. They're going to kill the people I love *again*." Leaning forward, she brought her knees up to her chest and laid her head there. "It's all my fault." She said as tears spilled from her face and her body shook in uncontrollable sobs.

"*Mishka*, none of this is on you." Kirill said calmly. "The Elite did this, not you." He reached over and put his hand on her shoulder. "We're trying to find out how the explosives got into the building right now. We have more FSB agents following Courtney than we have in this building. Believe me when I say, this shatters my confidence. They're trying to drag you out into the open and we won't let that happen."

"Are the others okay at least?" Avarie asked between sobs.

"They are." He scooted closer to her. "Naturally, they're worried about you and Sasha, but I assured them that you're safe." Kirill brought her closer to him as she cried onto his shoulder. "Avarie, as much as you feel like you need too, we can't have you running off into danger. These aren't people who mess around." Kirill was getting wet under the spray, but he didn't care. From the looks of this stall, Mikhail had his hands full. Creatures like Avarie had to rage every now and then. As long as she didn't take off, that was fine. He softly rubbed her back. Looking at Mikhail he asked. "How'd she find out?"

"The damn TV in the cafeteria."

Kirill laid her head in his lap and asked for a wash cloth. She was getting blood everywhere. Somebody threw one over. "She made a scene?" Mikhail nodded. Kirill gently wiped the side of her wet head as she continued to sob on him. Mikhail's shirt turned red from the water and blood mixture. "She beat your ass?"

Mikhail started laughing at him. "She's getting better." He stroked Avarie's back. "She made Sasha cry."

"My God, she is a *demon!*" Kirill declared and chuckled. "She'd make me cry too. Look at her. She looks like a drowned bloody rat."

"Shut up!" Avarie said through a sob. Kirill slapped her ass and told her to behave. A dry hand on a wet ass stung and she rubbed it.

"Pull yourself together young lady. There's more work to be done." Kirill cooed. "Remember, you aren't going anywhere unless you beat my ass."

"I'm tired of fighting." She said as she rolled over on her back. "I'm done."

"No you aren't. You're just getting warmed up." Mikhail said. "You'll always fight, just sometimes the wrong people."

"Let's get her up and home." Kirill said as he shifted Avarie from his lap. Mikhail helped her up and they walked out of the stall. The Direktor's were there waiting in silence. Sasha stood up and joined Avarie.

"Get an escort and meet me at my house. These two are done for the day. Take the lockdown off." Kirill said as he looked Sasha and Avarie up and down. "We need a game changer for these two."

ϓϓϓ

Sasha and Avarie were in the bathroom soaking in the large tub. He was at one end while she was in another. This was their ritual after strenuous training and when they shut off contact to Germany. They remained silent since they came back. There were no words to say to each other. She had an icepack on her shoulder and head. Sasha stared back at her, barely moving. She was given a pain killer and it was putting her to sleep. When she started to nod off, Sasha would nudge her. She wondered if there was even a term for their relationship. Having nothing sexual between them, they couldn't be lovers. Sure, they were affectionate, but not like a brother or sister. It was strange to actually define who they were. Kirill once referred to them as partners in crime. Avarie was the instigator and Sasha only went along for the ride.

She looked him up and down. Today was it; her actions broke inside him like fragile glass. His eyes stared through her. The light swirled around his pupils. She knew his thoughts went deep inside him. "I'm sorry, Sasha." She said gently. "I have to be more mindful of my actions." Guilt ripped through her like a jagged knife.

He reached out his hand and she took it. Pulling her to his side of the tub, he turned her around and leaned her against him. She felt him breathe under her as he stroked her wet hair away from her face. "I don't know where to start with you." His deep voice cooed. "You fight the wrong people. I understand you being upset about what happened today, Avarie. Believe me, I'm upset too. But you scare me sometimes."

She loved feeling the vibrations of his voice through his chest. "I scare myself. I couldn't control it. Something told me to run and save them. Anybody who was in my way is damned." Sasha adjusted her ice packs. "I feel horrible Sasha. My mind is running with guilt, sadness, pain, regret and everything else in between. I don't understand why I can't control how I feel."

"You remember that weekend that we had to spend apart?" He asked and she nodded. "What happened to us?"

"I know what happened to me." Avarie said while stroking his arm. "What happened to you?"

He didn't answer for a while. Finally she looked up at him and his eyes met hers. "I got the honey pot." He said with a shy grin. "You?"

"It went beyond the honey pot." Avarie said with a giggle.

"You know, when they say that the FSB owns you, they mean it." Sasha said smiling.

Even though she was high on pain meds, Avarie understood what he was saying. "Sasha, did you?" He gave her a crooked look and slowly nodded. "Wow." She said with amazement. "How'd that work for you?"

"It worked many times." He busted up laughing.

She turned to look at him in shock. "Now how the hell did this happen? You avoid women like the plague."

He looked up in amazement and said, "All I can say is that she has soft lips, a firm grip, and a warm mouth." He waved his hands in the air. "I don't even know what the hell happened to me."

"You know, Courtney would flip you serious shit if he ever found out."

"Please don't tell him. I don't even know how to process all this." He shook his head in frustration.

"I'll tell you what, you don't tell on me, and I won't tell on you. What happens at the FSB stays at the FSB." She said smiling.

His tone turned serious. "Is it always that good?" He fidgeted his fingers in the hot water, playing with his water skills.

"Courtney told me it gets better every time." Avarie said quietly. "God I miss him."

"I miss them too." Sasha's expression turned somber. "Avarie, you have to pass their tests so we can go back."

"I know Sasha. You don't know how hard I'm trying. I'm going to need your help."

He patted her on the shoulder and wrapped his arms around her. "I'll do everything I can to help you." He whispered. The painkillers overtook Avarie as she closed her eyes. Sasha closed his too. The day wore them down and the warmth filled them up as they slept peacefully.

ϒϒϒ

Avarie heard voices in the background and she stirred a bit forgetting where she was. A large hand shook her awake and did the same with Sasha. They both rubbed sleep out of their eyes and looked over to see Mikhail and Kirill standing before them.

"Did you have a nice nap?" Kirill asked. They both nodded, still heavy with exhaustion. "Good. Someone wants to talk to you both." He hit the speaker phone button and a voice came across. It was a male with a British accent.

"Sasha. Avarie!" It took a minute for the sounds to register. "Hello? It's Courtney." Avarie almost jumped out of the tub. She tried to snatch the phone away from Kirill, but he blocked her.

"She's being very naughty right now, Courtney." Mikhail laughed. Sasha's eyes grew wide with excitement.

"Avarie, are you there?"

"I'm here."

"Good. I'm calling you both to let you know everybody is safe. Are you guys alright?" He asked sincerely.

"We're fine." Avarie said. "Thank God you're alive." Tears started to roll down both Sasha and Avarie's cheeks. It was a sight to behold.

He laughed on the other end. "They can't kill me remember?"

"I know, it's just that I saw the whole thing on TV." Avarie said in a panic.

"Calm down, *Maus*." Courtney said. "I was told you tried to run." Oh his voice went stern. "Did you?"

"Yea." She said softly. "I'm sorry."

"You need to stop that shit right now! They're onto you and they used me as bait." He sighed. "It's becoming very dangerous and you need to finish your training."

"I know." Guilt ripped through her. She wanted to change the subject but Courtney wouldn't let up.

"Avarie, you *have* to stay there. The twins are there to protect you and Sasha. No matter what happens to us, you have to stay. There's a reason why they wouldn't let you take your bike. Just stop running into danger."

God he was making her feel bad and the tears burned hot on her cheeks. She wanted to bring up the other woman, but realized she had no room to talk. She wanted to make him feel as guilty as she felt, but she couldn't do it. "Avarie, I love you so much and if anything happened to you, I'd go bat shit crazy. Please, please, stay where you are. Do everything they tell you."

"*Everything?*" She asked with shock.

He sighed heavily into the phone. "*Maus*, at this point, I don't really care if you have to take it up the ass. You *will* do what they say."

"That's pretty serious, Courtney." Mikhail quipped.

There was silence. "What the bloody hell? Are you still there Mikhail?" He said in frustration. "That was not a *fucking* invitation."

"Sounded like it to me." Kirill chipped in. "I mean, it could be arranged." Avarie covered her mouth with her hands. They were messing with him good, at least she hoped. Even Sasha busted up in laughter.

"Fuck you, Kirill." He said and changed the subject. "Sasha, you don't let her run away."

Sasha moved into the phone and splashed water onto the floor. "Courtney, every time she does, she gets stopped. These guys have her locked down. I don't think you'll have to worry about that." He assured him.

Silence again. "Where the hell are you? At the pool?" He asked confused.

"No, they're in the soaking tub." Kirill answered for him. "Sasha has started a ritual with her and helping us get her into a routine and it's been working. We had to wake them up so you could talk to them. Avarie took pain meds and they've settled into her system."

"Oh, I forgot to mention that pain meds make her loopy." Courtney said. "Why is she on them?"

Kirill sighed and handed the phone to Mikhail. "She tried to run and I beat her ass. The entire FSB was on lockdown after we heard about what happened. It took four men just to restrain her."

"*Jesus...*" He said in shock. "You guys giving her steroids or something?"

"No, that's all her pent up rage." Mikhail answered while eyeballing Avarie. "We have a lot of work to do with her yet. No more fucking around, no more shenanigans." He said angrily. "Now, is there anything else you want to say before we go silent again?"

"Avarie, I love you."

"I love you too."

"Sasha?"

"Yes?" Sasha answered.

"Love you brother. Keep a tight leash on her."

"Love you too, I'll do my best."

Kirill walked out of the room with the phone. Mikhail stood before them again with his arms crossed. "I had to fill my brother in on you, *Mishka*." He didn't look pleased. "When you mentioned that they were killing your family again, he was confused so I had to tell him your entire story. I'm not happy about it, but he is." He paced the tile floor. "The game has changed and so has the battlefield." He looked at them both. "New strategy means new beginnings. There is only you and the FSB. These are going to be the hardest months of your lives and I want you prepared. We're breaking out every fucking piece of our arsenal we possibly can."

"What's that mean?" Avarie gave him a confused look.

He leaned down to look in her eyes. "That means you're going to really fucking hate me." He looked at Sasha. "And this one is really going to love me."

"Can you be more specific?" Avarie had no clue what was going on, but Sasha did.

"It means, I get to spend more time with Tori, and you are spending more time with the twins." Sasha answered for her.

"What the hell? You guys read each other's minds or something?" She said in surprise.

"No, we've been planning this behind your back for some time." Mikhail answered. "We just didn't know when you break it to you."

"I really hate you both." She crossed her arms. "How dare you betray me, Sasha." She gave him the evil eye.

"It's not on purpose, Avarie." Sasha laughed. "It'll be fun."

"Yea, because you'll be screwing Tori." She kicked at him.

"Hey, we promised not to talk about that anymore." He slapped her across the head. "It's not going to be that bad. Do what they say. It should be easy enough right?"

Oh, Avarie raged inside her head. "Sure." She said sarcastically. "Easy enough."

CHAPTER TEN

Month four was a busy one for Courtney. Gerhart was still recovering from his bullet wound and there was a huge mess to clean up. The bombing of Courtney's headquarters was covered internationally. Donations poured in from around the world to help the victims and their families. He had to set up a whole new team just to take care of that and the paperwork for the almost fifty dead employees and the hundreds injured.

November was getting colder and the ruins of his corporate headquarters were almost cleaned up. They set up a makeshift facility outside of Freiburg to keep operations going. All eyes were on Jude and Damian as they were given more responsibilities. They had to hire more people in order to gain back what they lost.

The FSB confirmed that somebody went on the inside and hid bombs inside his building. The records for everybody coming in and out were destroyed so they couldn't see how exactly they did it. The shooters were agents of the Mossad and their primary target was to take out Gerhart.

Matthias had to step in and be an assistant through the chaos. Eva helped where she could and Ivan even stepped up more than he should. He provided counseling and grieving support for families. It was an extremely hard month. Through it all, they were allowed a small respite. Ivan decided to take them out to a pub so they could shake off all the emotions.

Sitting down at a table they ordered their drinks. Courtney wasn't really in a drinking mood, but Ivan was persistent. He told them that if they didn't get out of their environment, it would eat them alive. He made a good argument.

As they drank their beers, Ivan started talking. "I give each and every one of you permission to get shit faced tonight." He raised his glass. "Alcohol is good for two things, forgetting and killing your liver."

He managed to get them to laugh. It was easier getting along without Sasha and Avarie. Courtney was able to get updates from Kirill and Avarie was really struggling.

"So Ivan, why did you get pulled through?" Courtney asked curiously. "I mean, I know how Sasha did, but you guys are like finding a needle in a haystack."

Ivan thought about the question. "I was pulled through by a little boy. He was only five at the time. He kept praying for protection over and over again. His family was dead and he was on his own. An old mystic lady took care of him during the conflict and somehow, they pulled me through the fire."

"Body and all?" Matthias asked.

"Yes, she was a very powerful woman. So like Sasha, I became their guardian."

Eva still had more questions. "So why did Sasha need blood?"

"Ah, that's because he is a water element. Blood is water."

"Interesting." Matthias thought. He looked around and found women checking them out. One was looking Ivan up and down like she was going to take a bite out of him.

"Courtney, has the FSB contacted you at all this week?" Eva asked. The day of the attack never left her and she worried about Avarie and Sasha.

"Kirill said that Avarie is really struggling. She's been raging and they haven't been able to calm her down. The nightmares keep coming and it leaves her tired." He took a drink of his beer. "I'm even told that she has her own time out shower stall in the ladies locker room. They hung a sign on it that says 'Avarie's Rage Locker'." He busted up laughing. "I told them she wasn't an easy one."

"*Jesus*, what are they doing to her?" Matthias asked. "I mean, Avarie never really did that with us, even on her bad days."

Ivan thought this conversation was interesting. "Has he said what her dreams were about?" He asked. "If you can find out about her dreams, then we can see the rage."

"No go, she won't even tell Sasha." Courtney looked down in despair. "I just don't understand. I had a talk with her and she said she'd behave. What's so hard about that?"

"Obviously talking and doing are two different things." Eva said. "Something has to give with her eventually. Has she tried to run again?"

"No, she doesn't even have an opportunity. She's on lockdown." Courtney said as he splayed his hands. "Kirill said that she's the craziest nineteen year old he's ever met. One minute she's an angel, the next she's a fucking demon."

"She has two worlds that live inside her. Maybe they need to bring those different sides out with different situations." Ivan cocked an eyebrow at Courtney. "She is the first of her kind so nobody really knows how she's going to react."

"Point taken." Courtney said finishing off his beer. "I think I have a term we could call her."

"What's that?" Matthias asked.

"A beautiful fucking disaster." Courtney laughed. "There's only so many of us in this world."

Matthias grabbed Eva to dance, leaving Courtney alone with Ivan. A woman was eyeballing Ivan like crazy and she was smoking hot. "You going to ask her to dance?" Courtney asked with enthusiasm. "She looks like she wants to take you home and give you a ride." He nudged him.

"Ah, but I see another one looking your way." He pointed out a hot blond at the bar. "Are you going to ask her to dance?"

"Nope, the only dancing partner I want is in Russia kicking ass. I've had many offers. I may have taken up a few in her absence, but not many." He admitted. He felt guilty but he knew that the FSB had her doing God knows what. They promised him what happens in Russia, stays there and vice versa.

"I thought you loved her." Ivan said.

"Oh God I do. However, I have an issue with alcohol and sex."

"Do the others know of your indiscretions?"

"Pfft, no and I'm not going to tell them." Courtney said in a huff. "They'd just kill me in my sleep."

Ivan laughed. He knew Courtney all too well. If the other two knew, they never mentioned it. Kirill told him that he had to live a life without Avarie and Mikhail warned Eva that it would be hard, but when she came back, things may go back to normal.

"How's Eva's training going?"

"She's getting much better. She can move fire and even make it out of thin air. Pretty soon, she'll be able to summon more elementals."

"Holy shit that's scary!" Courtney exclaimed with wide eyes. "Just don't burn down my castle."

Ivan slapped him on the arm. "She can control the destructive nature of fire and it's amazing."

"Good, maybe she could control Avarie's rage." Courtney joked.

"Avarie can control her own rage. She has to figure out what she's raging against first." Ivan laughed. "But the answer is a simple one."

"Okay, so what is it?" Courtney was smiling at him. This was bound to get interesting.

"She's in a situation she cannot control." Ivan opened his hands. "She has no control over what's going on around her and she needs to trust those who do have control of the situation."

"Ooo, that's good." Courtney agreed. "Every time she ran from us, it was the same thing. She couldn't control what was happening and she decided that leaving would be the best. Or she would fight to gain control of it. Wow, that's insightful." He shook his head in amazement. "That explains a lot about her."

"It does doesn't it?" Ivan winked. "Maybe you should pass that along."

"Well, when I get a call from Kirill I'll do that." Courtney's gaze passed along all the people in the bar. His eyes settled on many women. He couldn't deny that he wasn't horny right now. Shit, he could bang any one of them if he wanted to. The problem was that they weren't Avarie. Ivan watched as Courtney's eyes turned sad.

"You keep looking into the crowd for the person who isn't there." Ivan's voice shut off his thoughts.

"I know." Courtney said solemnly. "There's only one Avarie in this entire universe."

"I've never heard a truer statement." Ivan said, patting Courtney on the back. "However, a man's needs have to be met somehow." He pointed in the direction to a group of girls. "They seem to be looking your way."

"I have to behave myself." Courtney said while ordering another beer. "Besides, Matthias and Eva are here."

"So." Ivan quipped. "They'll be going home soon anyway."

"How can you tell?"

"Look at Matthias, he's getting pretty excited." Ivan laughed at them. "Eva isn't helping him either." Courtney watched as Eva was all up on Matthias and kissing his neck.

"So you're saying you're going to be my wingman?" Courtney asked in jest. "Because I really don't need one."

Ivan was working on his third beer. "I'm saying that it's okay. I've worked with the FSB for many years and I can tell you that they aren't exactly monogamous. I don't mean to bring up a sore subject, but Avarie is probably learning new tricks."

"What if she isn't?"

"Then those fuckers aren't doing a very good job of training her." Ivan laughed. "I'm sure Sasha's learned a few tricks of his own."

"The FSB isn't all about sex are they?" Now Courtney was growing concerned about what they're really about.

"No, but it's a very big part. Humans are very sexual in nature. You're a prime example." Ivan pointed at him. "Sex makes humans very vulnerable."

"Please tell me she's learning other things." Courtney said downing a shot.

"Of course she is. When you get all these reports about her, it's from being in combat or situational awareness training. She has the power to control sex, but not those situations."

"That makes me feel a little better." Courtney admitted. "But not by much."

"Well, let's take your mind off of it." He put a shot in front of Courtney.

"My God, you're an enabler." Courtney joked. "You're going to get me in serious trouble."

Ivan laughed as he stood up. "You're already in trouble Courtney, might as well enjoy tonight."

He took the shot and followed Ivan over to the ladies. Matthias let Courtney know they were headed home. Eva shot him a dirty look and Courtney pointed at Ivan. She shook her head and followed Matthias out. Yep, Courtney was going to be in trouble and Ivan was an instigator. Damn red heads.

ϒϒϒ

Kirill was extremely pissed off with Avarie. Mikhail tried to handle her as best he could, but she was stubborn. Twice this month, she was thrown into the shower stall. She was starting to get a reputation in the FSB as a renegade. They never took in agents so young for a reason. Everybody knew she was good at what she did. Shit, she was a natural with weapons so there were no problems there. She worked well most times in a team and that was awesome. It was the things she avoided and should avoid that was the problem. She'd run into danger without regard to herself or others, but when it came to situations she was uncomfortable with, she ran away from it. Her fight or flight was off.

She avoided the deep end of the pool, however, she'd run straight into gun fire. What the fuck was the difference? On top of that, Sasha was worn out with her. Most nights, he'd sleep fine and others, he'd be up all night. She was wearing down her partner and he was tired of that shit. Two days ago, Kirill had to give her the belt for telling him to go fuck himself and to eat a dick. Inside his head, he really thought that was funny coming from her. While he beat her ass, he tried to hide his smile just thinking about how she said it. Then while he was hitting her, she called him a pussy. Damn she was feisty. Where the Hell was all this rage coming from? At this rate, she'd go home in about thirty years.

Lately, she's been doing the strangest things just to piss him off. In front of company, she slapped his ass and walked on by like nothing happened. At dinner, she unscrewed the lid of the salt shaker and he dumped salt all over his favorite meal. Wednesday, he had to come into their room and yell at her about not following orders. He got in her face and she licked his cheek. Friday, she stole his favorite vodka and downed it like nobody's business. She was so drunk she danced around the hallway singing *Louie Louie*. How the fuck did she even get into his liquor? Sasha had no clue what she was doing. He said that it was rebellion inside her head and she was the only one drawing swords.

When he told Mikhail, he thought that was funny as Hell. Jesus Christ, her shenanigans were crazy. Out of desperation, he called Courtney. What a help he was. He told Kirill he needed to get the upper hand on her and that stress does crazy things to people. The bottom line was, she was becoming scary. He debated in his head over and over again how to tame this wench.

It was supper time and they were waiting for him. Sasha looked like he was ready to kill her. She watched as he sat down and she gave him the sweetest smile. *Fuck, what did she do now?*

"Sasha, why is Avarie looking at me like that?" Kirill asked. He shook his head. The look in his eyes said that he didn't even know who she was anymore.

"Avarie, did you behave yourself today?" He asked with suspicion. She nodded excitedly. "Are you being honest?" Again she nodded with excitement.

Sasha looked at her like he was ready to cry. He didn't sleep last night and she had a crazy look in her eyes. Either she really was going nuts, or she was fucking with him. It could be both. His eyes never left her as they brought out the food. She was good the entire meal and Sasha just watched her. This wasn't good. She announced she was done and started to walk up to her room. Kirill stood up, but the fucking seat came with him. That crazy bitch super glued the seat to his ass. He screamed her name and she ran out of the room, cackling like a crazed killer. He ran into her at the hallway and she fell and started rolling in laughter. What a sight he was. Running around with a dining room chair stuck to his ass.

Sasha came up into the hallway and saw her. He shook his head and went to his room. Avarie was laughing so hard, she couldn't breathe. Since the chair was handy, he sat down on it in the hallway and watched the insanity take over. When she calmed down, she walked up to him and sat on his lap. He was ready to smack her. Total calm overtook her as she sat there and looked into his eyes. She did something strange. Wrapping her arms around his neck, she laid her head on his shoulder and started crying. Those cries turned into uncontrollable sobs. All he could do was hold her and rock her back and forth. He had no clue what was going on in her head. She fell asleep in his arms, completely worn out from her breakdown. Instead of sending her back to the room with Sasha, he had his men take her to his. Right now, she was dangerous and he didn't want Sasha becoming collateral damage.

He had to take his pants off in order to get out of the chair. He checked on Sasha and let him know that Avarie was with him and that she was already asleep. When he went into his room Avarie was laying on his bed in sweet slumber. He called Mikhail to let him know what was going on. She wasn't going to training tomorrow, not like this. Mikhail thought that was a good call and said that Sasha needed rest and wanted to send him over to Tori's. If they didn't figure out what was wrong with Avarie soon, they'd have to lock her up or worse, kill her. Maybe that's what she wanted.

Kirill got undressed and laid down next to her. He swept her hair away from her face. She was so angelic when she slept and she wasn't shit talking. He realized that she must have removed her clothes when he was in with Sasha. She wore a t-shirt and black lace panties. With her arms over her head, she looked completely worn out. What a waste, he thought. She was so damn beautiful but she was a fucking disaster. More demon than angel at this point was more like it. He pulled the covers over them and fell asleep.

He awoke to her stirring. He opened his eyes and saw that hers were wide open and staring at the ceiling. The clock said it was almost 3am. It looked like her eyes were glowing green. "Go to sleep, *Mishka*."

"I am asleep." She said without her eyes moving.

"But your eyes are open." He said sleepily. "How can you sleep with your eyes open?"

"Because they never close." She said in the most honest response he's ever had from her.

He propped himself up on his elbow, this was getting interesting. "Why don't they close?"

"Because I can't make them close." She answered. "They always stay open, even in the dark."

God, this conversation is strange, he thought. *Well, let's roll with it.* "What do they see?

There was a bit of silence. "Strange and wonderful things."

He had an idea and grabbed his cell phone. He needed to record this conversation. "Like what?"

"Like things that scare me and things I can't control. Other things I can control, but I don't know how."

"What are the things that scare you?" He asked.

"You scare me, Mikhail scares me. But I love what you do to me." She whispered.

"What do I do to you that scares you?" Maybe he was actually getting somewhere.

"You're anger scares me."

Well no shit, he thought, *I'm supposed to scare you.* "What do you mean you love what I do to you?"

She smiled, her eyes never blinking. "I love how you touch me. When you talked to me in the bedroom the weekend I went with Mikhail, I wanted more of you." Her voice was starting to wane a bit, but he wanted her to keep talking.

"*Mishka*, I was just talking to you. That's all."

"You did, and I loved it." She started to roll over and he grabbed her to face the ceiling again.

"What else?"

"I love it when you hit me with the belt." Another smile rolled on her lips. "It feels really good."

Okay, now she was fucking with him. Nobody loves the belt, well, accept him but that's because he was the one holding it. "Now you're messing with me, *Mishka*."

"It doesn't matter, because this isn't real." Her eyes changed color on him. "It's just a dream, and you don't care anyway."

Woah, she thinks she's still dreaming. "Tell me about why you like the belt."

"It hurts, but it feels good at the same time."

He started to giggle. Maybe she liked the kinky shit or something. He shook his head at her. Her right hand moved to his chest as she still stared up at the ceiling. She felt every muscle under her fingertips and worked her way down to the band of his boxers. "I think you hate me."

"I don't hate you, *Mishka*. You just manage to piss me off. *A lot.*" He smiled at her.

Her hand reached for his and she brought it over and placed it on her abdomen. "I'm sorry."

"Sorry for what?"

"Existing."

Now that broke his heart. Nothing that was going on in the world had anything to do with her. Tears rolled down her cheeks. He scooted closer to her. It was almost 4am. It wasn't like he was going to let her go to the FSB anyway. "This isn't the world against you."

"No, it really is. They're after me and you're all in danger just because I exist." How true that was, he thought.

"That may be true, but I'm not going to let anybody hurt you." He meant that. If anybody was going to get her, it was Courtney. Fuck.

He held his cell phone and was grateful that it was still plugged in. "I know I'm just dreaming, but can we just be here…like this." She asked.

"For how long?" he asked.

"Until the alarm goes off like always. That's when my dreams end and the nightmares start."

She was starting to shuffle into him. She rolled on her side and put her body against his. Her eyes were closing. "Alright, *Mishka*. We'll stay like this until the alarm goes off." She nodded. Her talking stopped and eyes were closed. He shut the alarm off on his phone. They weren't going anywhere in the morning. Putting the phone back, he wrapped both his arms around her and held her tight. He'd have to show Mikhail the video sometime tomorrow. This shit was just incredible.

ϒϒϒ

Kirill woke up in time to hear Sasha leave. He quickly pulled on pants and met him in the hallway. Sasha looked refreshed from a good night's sleep. Kirill explained that he was going to spend time with Avarie today and that he wanted Sasha to relax and not worry about her.

"Are you going to hurt her?" Sasha asked with sad eyes.

Shaking his head no, Kirill answered. "I think she's hurt herself enough don't you?"

"She's losing the war inside her head." He heaved a deep sigh. "I've never seen her like this."

Kirill put a hand on his shoulder. "We'll help her win some battles, okay?" Sasha nodded and Kirill motioned him off.

Back in his room, Avarie was still sound asleep. He picked up his phone and dialed the office letting them know to clear his schedule. He dialed another number and went into his bathroom.

"President's office?" The Russian woman answered.

"It's Kirill, is Konstantin in?"

"Hold on." It took a few moments for him to pick up.

"Kirill, is something wrong?" Konstantin asked sleepily.

"Please tell me you're awake." He said in annoyance.

"Of course I'm awake, I'm an old man. I've been awake since 5AM." He chuckled. "Are you coming to the office today?"

"No, I have a problem with the new recruit."

"The girl? I thought she was doing well." He yawned. "I hear good and bad things, but mostly good."

Jesus, what shit is Mikhail feeding him? Kirill thought. "She's hit a barrier and I thought maybe you could give me some insight."

"It's been years since I've been in the FSB, but I can try to help." He answered thoughtfully. "What issue are you having with her?"

"You remember Pandora?"

Silence on the other line. "Of course I remember her. We worked together for almost ten years."

"Well, she's kind of like her." Kirill didn't want to give too much away. "She's stubborn, hot headed, and feisty."

Konstantin started laughing softly. "Those are usually the best, especially in bed."

Kirill shook his head in shame. That is not where he was going with this. "*Oi*, for shame! Seriously, how do I get through to her? She's struggling badly and rebelling like a fucking teenager."

"But she is a teenager. Isn't she only 19?"

"Yes."

"Well then, that's part of the problem. I've raised children and know how they act."

Oh for fucks sake. "Konstantin, she's a mature adult. Now, how did you get through to Pandora?"

He could hear clicking on the other line like he was clacking his teeth. "I had to earn her trust and that was no easy feat. That is, until we actually talked. We'd sit there for hours, just talking."

It couldn't be that simple, Kirill thought. "Are you *fucking* serious?" He shook his head. "I didn't think she was the talking type."

"Oh God Kirill, that woman could talk, and…she sang. She loved music and when she drank, she was hilarious." Konstantin sighed. "Most of all, she loved her family and she missed them dearly. She used her rage against them you know. She channeled it like summoning a demon from the pits of Hell, hence the name, Pandora."

More like Satan, he thought. Kirill had to ask. "Did you sleep with this woman?"

Konstantin laughed so hard, Kirill thought he would choke to death. "God yes! She was very talented."

Kirill busted up laughing. This was the most enthusiastic conversation he's ever had with him. "So I just talk to her, that's it?"

"That's it. Let her do most of the speaking though. It sounds like this one has a lot on her mind." They finished their conversation and he went back to bed. Thankful that he didn't wake her up, he laid there for a while. He almost forgot to send Mikhail the video from last night. He'd wait for a response. Damn she was beautiful when she slept. She shifted over towards him and started to run her hands in his hair softly. He thought she'd wake up, but she stayed asleep. A text came in from Mikhail. He said that was some deep shit and he was amazed that she actually talked to him.

Avarie still ran her hand through his hair. Her touch was soft and gentle. She'd find an extra soft spot and linger there, taking a lock of his hair and swirl it through her fingers. He looked at the clock, it was almost 8am and the weather outside threatened snow.

Finally, Avarie stirred. Her eyes opened a bit and she looked straight at Kirill. Looking around the room, she almost forgot where she was. Letting go of his hair, she shot up. "I'm sorry, I didn't hear the alarm. I'm late for training."

He propped her back down. "No training for you today, *Mishka*. I shut off the alarm. You and I are spending time together today."

Fear spread across her face then it turned to defeat. "I'm getting the belt aren't I?"

"No. You're going to stay here with me and we're going to talk."

Relief flooded her face. She didn't know if talking was worse or getting the belt. No doubt he was angry with her. It was easier to give her the belt and send her away. "Why would you want to talk to me?" She asked defensively. "You don't give two shits about me."

"Oh, I care more than you know." He pulled her closer to him. "Did you know you talk in your sleep?"

"I do not." Avarie waved him off. "I sleep like a baby." She teased.

"Yes, a baby who wakes up every night at 3am." He said, brushing her nose with his finger. "Now tell me, why are you going crazy on us?"

"I'm not the crazy one." She smiled. "I'm sane, the rest of you are fucked up."

Oh, this was not where he wanted to be with her right now. She was avoiding and he didn't like that one bit. He pulled out his phone and played the video for her. As she watched in shock she tried to get him to shut it off, but he slapped her away.

"Now, let's break down this conversation you had with me in your sleep. You said your eyes never close when you sleep. Explain that to me."

She hesitated but with deep thought. "My mind never shuts off. It's always going and I have a hard time telling it to leave me alone."

"Fair enough." He said. "Your body is tired, and your mind is always on. You aren't the only one who struggles with this, *Mishka*. I too have restless nights." He moved onto the next topic. "You also said that you see things that you cannot control and scare you, what are those things specifically?"

"It's stupid." She said trying to roll over, but he wouldn't let her.

"Tell me."

"My mind goes to dark places during the day. One minute, I'm on the firing range then the scenery shifts, then I'm in the middle of some strange battlefield. I go to places that this body has never been before and it's scary." She really didn't want to talk to him about this. She was afraid he'd use it against her. He coaxed her on though. "When I dream, I go to awesome places if my mind lets me. I'm back at the castle or riding my bike. Shit, sometimes I even go places with Sasha."

"Interesting." He said as a knock on the door distracted him. He opened it and a tray of food rolled in. He brought it over and they ate on his bed as they spoke. "You also said that Mikhail and I scare you."

"You're like him…" She said as her voice trailed off.

"Who's him?" He asked as he sat up. She went back inside herself. He cupped her face in his hands. "Tell me who he is." His tone was stern and he needed the name.

"Luscious." She said as tears threatened to break the barriers of her lashes. "He killed them and left me alive with that memory to forever burn in the back of my head."

Oh shit, she did remember him. Nice. "I'm not him. He's a vicious fucking demon who likes to play childish games. Always has, always will." He sighed. "We aren't like him. If we were, this world would be the proverbial Hell on earth. Is that all that scares you about us?"

"You're always angry." She looked away. "For once, I'd like to see you smile."

"I wear anger like an Armani suit. It looks good on me." He joked. "If I promise to be nicer, you need to promise to stop pissing me off so much. If you want my attention, pranks are not the way to do it."

"It made me feel better." She giggled. "You should've seen your face last night stuck to that fucking chair."

Oh now that pissed him off. He slapped her ass hard. She hissed as her hand rubbed her left cheek. "Dammit! That hurt."

"I thought you liked getting whipped." He said seductively. "You said so last night, remember." Her face flushed with embarrassment. Warmth flooded through her body and even in her panties. Kirill gave her a look of knowing. "You love pain. You think you deserve it…and I love giving it to you." He growled in her ear as he smacked her ass again and she winced. Her face turned beet red. He didn't slap her again, but she got the point. "I think you're a little pervert." He said naughtily. "Believe me; I know when a woman enjoys kinky play." He rubbed her left cheek and felt the heat of his slap.

Her eyes went wide. Chills worked its way up her spine as pleasure pooled around her. If he kept going, she was going to lose it. "You trust me when I hold the strap, don't you."

"I trust you to beat the shit out of me." She said sarcastically. The look on his face said he was getting ideas and she wasn't prepared for that right now.

"No, you like that I can control you when I hold it. You gave it away to me. Think about that."

Damn, he was right. She had to give him control; it wasn't the fact that there was pleasure in her pain. She was forced to escape herself and that was really nice. She shed her identity whenever he had her alone.

"Alright, I'll give you that." She admitted with a heavy heart.

"Good. Can you admit that it's nice to give up control every now and then?"

Shit, he was pushing it. "Sometimes."

"You can't control every situation and you need to trust others within that situation." He kept rubbing her ass. "Let them take over for once. You'll find that it eases your conscience."

"That would be fine, but I don't know when to let them take that control" She said honestly.

"That's because you have trust issues. Trust that others know what they're doing." He pulled her as close to him as possible. Heat from his body melted into her with his member pressed into her belly. "Do you trust me right now?"

"I don't have a choice right now." She let her left arm go back to his hair. The green of his eyes started to move around and she was losing herself in them.

"You do. You just assume you don't. You could run out that door, it's not locked."

Pandora Rising

"I know if I do, you'll just come running after me and I'll be punished." The thought made her head swoon. What is this guy doing to her?

"So this brings me to my second point about control. It's just an illusion. It's never been there to begin with." He chuckled. "You stay here, you have no control. You run, you still have no control. You understand?"

"That's confusing." She said giving him a strange look. "So no matter what I do, I'm not in control." She thought about it. "So, does that mean you're in control now?"

He laughed at her and shook his head. "I've never really been in control of you unless you give it to me. The only thing that we can control is our reactions to situations. This is what they teach you in situational awareness."

She could feel his soft breathing on her face. He didn't shave for the last few days, and it only made him that much more handsome. Her finger ran across the tattoo that threaded from the upper part of his chest, to each wrist. "So, what should I be aware of in this situation?" She asked softly.

He grabbed her hand and brought it to his lips. "Just me." He smiled at her and her heart melted. Now this was the man she could hang in bed with all day. "What are you thinking?" He asked.

"I'm thinking this is the man that I like." She slowly nodded. "Are you saying that it's okay to lose control right now and it won't make me look weak?"

"No. If there's anything that you're not, it's weak." He wanted to make her feel better. When she was Pandora, she controlled everything even when she couldn't control it. She wasn't that person anymore and weakness was a thing of the past. They talked for the rest of the day, just as they were. He watched as Avarie grew more comfortable with him. He discovered things about her that he had no clue. Her fears, the nightmares, how it killed her that she couldn't define the relationship between her and Sasha and the guilt she carried with her. She feared that Courtney would forget about her and that he was with other women but she didn't have room to talk because she was here. He explained that even if he was with another woman, they only satisfied one desire. It didn't mean that he didn't love her still; it just meant that he had needs and they should be fulfilled in her absence.

The more he held her, the more she opened up. Konstantin was right, if you let them talk, they'll say just about anything. Truthfully, he actually liked it. She was becoming normal and the more she released, the better she felt. Her pent up tension just flowed out of her like a lake into a river. It was a beautiful transition for them both. She realized that the asshole part of him was a front. It shielded him from the demons of his kind and hers.

It was twilight, but only around 6pm. She looked outside and saw white flakes falling softly from the sky. "What's that?" she asked pointing to the window.

"It's just snow." He waved his hand. "Russia gets really cold in winter, so we need to bundle you up when you leave for training."

"I've never seen snow." She said as her eyes grew wide. "Can I see it?"

He laughed. That's right; she's never seen snow before. "Knock yourself out." He walked her over to the patio door and opened it up for her. She was barefoot as she stepped out into the soft cotton. The cold pierced through her and burned at the same time. There was no wind and she held out her hands to catch snowflakes. Only in her t-shirt and thin panties, she stood outside breathing in the cold. He watched as her nipples grew hard from the frigid air and goosebumps ran up and down her body. Bringing her in from the cold, he wrapped her back under the covers.

Her hands were freezing and she put them on his chest. He almost jumped out of his skin. "*Mishka*! Your hands are cold." With a shit eating grin, she put her feet on his legs. "*Oi!*" He yelled and jumped out of the bed. He started laughing at her. "You're a mean one."

Grabbing a pillow, she threw it at him. She laughed hysterically as he threw it back at her. They wrestled for a good fifteen minutes before she wore out. He covered her body with his and said, "*Mishka*, I don't know what you're doing to me, but I must admit, I'm having fun."

"Good, you need to let loose every now and then." Avarie laughed at him and he cracked up. This girl was contagious. "See, doesn't that feel good?"

Her eyes were turning blue as he stared into them. She wrapped her arms around his neck and played with his hair again. He found a lock of hers and twirled it in his fingers. Damn she was soft, he thought. She was going to make him lose control. He moved in and kissed her neck. She giggled like a schoolgirl. Dammit, she was going to make him laugh again. With a bit of control, he held it in and moved to her ear. She giggled harder as he licked and tugged at her earlobe. "What's so funny, *Mishka*?" He whispered in her ear. He looked at her and she tried so hard to hold back a smile. "Tell me what the joke is." He demanded and kissed her nose.

Her face turned red. "I think you and your brother are the same person." She whispered and busted up laughing again.

He gave her a stupid smile. "Well, we could be if you want?' He cocked his eyebrows at her. "You know what they say about twins?" She shook her head. "If you've had one, you should definitely try the other." He said seductively and went to work on her neck and ear. A knock on the door disturbed him. A man said that supper was ready and Sasha was home. Damn, the games were over. He made her get dressed and they went downstairs to join him.

ϒϒϒ

Sasha sat at the table while he waited for Kirill. He came down with Avarie behind him. Sasha couldn't believe what he saw. Avarie looked normal again, her eyes were brighter and the calm has taken over her body. He glanced at Kirill and he winked at Sasha. He was happy that he didn't lay a hand on her. He knew Avarie was out of control, but that didn't mean he had to scare her back into herself.

Relief flooded him when she sat and ate normally. Sasha watched her for any signs of stress and so did Kirill. Her eyes were thoughtful and any questions that were asked of her were answered mindfully. *What the Hell did he do to her?* Sasha thought to himself. Maybe he was taking the wrong approach with her.

When Avarie was done, she excused herself. Kirill informed her that she wasn't going back to training tomorrow and she was sleeping in his room again. She almost rolled her eyes; instead she caught herself and nodded. Sasha watched in wonder as she just shut her mouth and went upstairs with her escorts.

Giving Kirill a suspicious look he asked, "Alright, what did you do to her?"

Kirill swirled his wine around and answered. "I made her talk."

Sasha let that sink in a bit. "You made her talk." Kirill nodded. "Let me guess, you honey potted her?"

Kirill busted up laughing. The honey pot was now their inside joke. "No. I took a different approach. It turns out she spills secrets in her sleep."

"She's never talked in her sleep with me. Usually, she just gets up around 3am and goes back to bed."

Kirill pulled out the cell phone and let Sasha watch as Avarie talked about strange things in her sleep. He never thought to talk to her when her eyes were open. She's a strange creature indeed and some of the things she said made him blush.

"Sasha, it turns out that Avarie has fears that well up inside her head and she carries guilt with her. Because she exists, everybody she loves is in danger. She tries to take control and when she realizes she can't, she rages. I've talked to her all day today. We haven't left my bedroom until supper."

"I can't believe you two just talked." Sasha said laughing. "Really, what did you guys do?"

"I'm serious. I just let her talk." Kirill smiled as he finished his wine. "It turns out just talking is extremely sexy."

Sasha's eyes turned to worry. "Is she still dangerous you think?"

"Sasha, one talk doesn't take that danger away; it just opens it up to possibilities." Kirill nodded his head in contemplation. "We've all talked *to* her over and over and she's reverted back. So, this time, I made her talk. I think the more we make her talk, the better she'll get. Keeping the lines of communication open with her will help take that danger away bit by bit." He stood up. "I want you to go to training tomorrow and know that she's in good hands."

What choice did he have? "Alright." Sasha said and walked out of the dining room. When he plopped in bed, it was strange not having Avarie there to steal the covers or snuggle into him at night. The plus side was he'd be getting sleep.

ϒϒϒ

She slept without incident. Her iPod was in and sweet music played in her ears. When Kirill woke her up, he said she slept peacefully through the night. When she asked what they were doing today, he answered that they were talking. Avarie was tired of talking. She already spilled as much as she felt comfortable with, but he pressed her on.

Earlier that morning, Kirill sent Mikhail another video. This one she wasn't talking and it was extremely naughty. By far, this was the best video he had of her and it made him hot. Mikhail responded back and the response made him laugh. *Oh my brother*, he thought. As much as Kirill wanted her, he knew not to touch yet.

Later, Avarie was allowed to sleep in her room again. In the morning, Sasha reported that she slept much better and seemed at ease. After breakfast, Sasha asked if they could go outside and check out the snow. Kirill reluctantly gave them permission. He watched from his balcony as Avarie and Sasha threw snowballs at each other and she screamed happily. He got her good a few times, knocking her over on her ass. He turned away to grab his cell phone in the room, when he came back out, he lost sight of them. He almost panicked until a snowball hit him square in the chest. His eyes roamed the garden and he looked for them. Another hit him on the shoulder. Hearing giggling in the distance, he saw Avarie and Sasha working together to pummel him with snowballs. If Avarie would shut up, they'd be a damn good sniper team.

Kirill brushed off the snow like nothing happened. He acted like he was going to turn around and watched from the corner of his eye as Sasha made to aim another. Quickly, he grabbed the snow that collected on the balcony and got a shot off before Sasha, hitting him in the shoulder. Now the fire fight was on. All three were whipping snow balls at each other until Kirill ran out of ammo. When he did, he went back inside and shut the doors. He flipped them off from the window and busted up laughing. Those two act like children sometimes, he thought. What a pairing the universe has brought together.

CHAPTER ELEVEN

Avarie was in for a surprise on Sunday. He arranged for a meeting with her training group at the FSB. That afternoon, Avarie had to face two other Direktors', Karl, Tori, Valentin, and Mikhail with Sasha joining. She knew even before she stepped in the room that she was in serious trouble. Her heart pounded in fear.

With Kirill opening the discussion, he informed them of the breakthrough he had with Avarie. God she was embarrassed. She knew he was going to use it against her and she kicked herself up and down for it. Instead of judging her though, they understood. Valentin and Karl asked questions and she answered truthfully. Her body language said that she felt awkward about this confrontation, but Sasha tried to comfort her as much as he could.

Both Karl and Valentin were grateful that this barrier was broken. It wasn't that she raged often, the problem was when she did, it was violent. They warned her that if she regressed again, they couldn't keep doing this over and over. The consequences were dire if she didn't follow orders.

Kirill sent Avarie back to training on Monday with that warning all through her head. She behaved herself. When she started to feel loss of control, she tried to shake it out. Karl watched her closely as they put her in situation after situation. When she struggled with something, he pulled her aside and made her talk. If a team member did something wrong or said the wrong thing, he watched Avarie's reaction. She took serious deep breaths and tried to shake it off.

"Avarie, when you start getting mad, what do you say to yourself?" he asked when the training was done.

She met his eyes and said, "I just tell myself that I don't want Mikhail to throw me in the shower again."

He laughed and said that was a good answer. The week went so much better for her. She let things go that normally she wouldn't. Sasha saw a change in her demeanor and felt like he had his Avarie back. Things were going good until Wednesday. She hit a brick wall in situational awareness. Karl and Mikhail were watching her closely and it seemed she was going to rage. Calmly, she stood up and left the room. They watched her as she walked down the hall. Mikhail wasn't sure what she was doing, so he followed behind her. She stopped and turned around. "I'm alright, Mikhail. It was just a flashback." She said. He nodded and walked her back into the room. That was the end of it.

ϒϒϒ

Mikhail decided that he wanted to push her buttons a bit on Friday. At the pool, Mikhail tried to talk Avarie into staying at the deep end for longer than ten seconds. She refused and told him that she was afraid of it. He acted like he was going to let it go. When he saw her at the deep end side of the pool he quickly grabbed her and jumped in.

She wasn't prepared and struggled against him. He pulled her completely under and held her there. Panic filled her body and she struggled against him. Opening her eyes, the scenery changed. She was looking into muddy water and a current was pulling her farther under.

Hearing loud voices above the water's surface she looked up and saw nothing. Below her, tail lights of an SUV sunk lower into the abyss. A hand broke through the surface reaching for her, but it was too late. Her lungs took in water and everything went black.

When she woke up, Sasha was pushing water out of her and she expelled it in a coughing fit. Gasping for breath she reached for him. Her ribs hurt and she felt light headed.

"*Jesus*, I'm sorry Avarie." Mikhail said with sorrow.

Tori pushed him out of the way and slapped him hard across the face. "I told you! She doesn't like the deep end because of a past life experience! Why don't you ever fucking listen to me?" She screamed at him. "You could've killed her!"

Tori hit him so hard, she bloodied his lip. The red stream oozed down his face as he held his mouth. *Wow, don't fuck with Tori,* Avarie thought. Pushing through the cloud of confusion, Sasha helped her sit up. "What did you see, Avarie?" He asked as he pulled a towel around her.

"I was in a muddy river and a car was sinking and pulling me with it." She said in exhaustion. "Somebody reached in for me, but it was too late." She was shaking with fear.

Tori started screaming at Mikhail again. "This is how you get her to regress with your fucking stupidity! We're done for the day." She spit on him and helped Avarie stand up to take her to the locker room.

Sasha shook his head at Mikhail and walked away. Avarie was taken to have x-rays to make sure she didn't dry drown. Her lungs were clear of fluid and she was able to go home. Once in their room, Avarie asked what exactly happened.

"When Mikhail jumped with you in the water, he held you under for a bit and then let go so you could break the surface. There was a strange vibration that sounded like a thump and a small wave came out of the water. He looked under and saw your eyes open but not moving. He reached for you and pulled you out. He laid you down and I helped get the water out of you." He said sadly. "Tori and I told him not too even drag you over there. I don't know what he was thinking."

Avarie didn't either. She thought they were getting along well. There was a knock at the door and Kirill stepped in. "I heard that Mikhail was an asshole today." He said as he crossed his arms. Sasha nodded while Avarie looked at the ground. "He's very sorry for what happened."

Avarie thought about it. "I'm not really mad at him." She said quietly. "I'm mad because I couldn't control what happened to me and I panicked."

Ah, Kirill, thought. She's being honest with him now. "You've been very good this week, *Mishka*. I'm very proud of you." He opened the door wider and said. "I got you both a surprise." It was Tori and she had an overnight bag. Sasha stood there with wide eyes and a nervous look on his face. "What Sasha? I give you another girl and you freak out."

"Sasha, we've been through this before." Tori purred. "You don't have to be nervous around me."

Kirill smiled at him. Giving Sasha a wink he threw the door closed and locked it.

"Alright, how'd you talk him into letting you stay the night?" Avarie asked Tori. "Where are you supposed to sleep?" She hopped on the bed and patted the mattress.

"Where's Sasha gonna sleep?'

With a sly grin, Tori patted the other side of the bed. Sasha slowly shook his head no and she nodded with a smirk. Avarie looked at them both with amazement. She could tell he was getting excited, but he was skittish. "Maybe I should leave you two alone?" Avarie said in jest.

"That would be fine." Tori said as she tried to coax Sasha over to her. "I told Kirill that I wanted to watch over you to make sure you were okay after Mikhail went full retard."

"Well, I'm going to soak in the tub. I'll leave you two alone." Avarie said as she grabbed her iPod. Shit, Sasha was in for it. Tori had the look of pure sex in her eyes and there was no way in Hell he was going to get away from her.

Avarie rushed into the bathroom and turned on the water for the soaking tub. When it was full enough, she hopped in and put in her earbuds. After a while, curiosity gotten to her and she peeked through the keyhole and gasped. She couldn't see them, but the mirror above the mantle told her all she needed to know. Tori was riding the living Hell out of him and he went to town on her. *Fuck, Sasha*, she thought. Avarie saw more than she needed to see from those two. Yep, she lied to Kirill so she could get into Sasha's pants. Nice move. Shit, now she'd have to sleep in the same bed. Going back to the tub, she turned up her iPod. There was no denying she was tired. Sasha always told her that when she felt tired in the tub, to get out. Well, she didn't exactly have a place to go right now so she stayed there. When they were done, they could wake her up. She closed her eyes and let the warmth of the water take her over.

ϓϓϓ

Kirill and Mikhail were out on the four seasons porch, drinking vodka and smoking cigars. Kirill wasn't happy with Mikhail at all. "Now why the Hell would you do that to her?" He asked taking a puff of his cigar. "We just had a great week until you did that."

"I wanted her to face her fears. She'll have to someday soon. Luscious wants her badly, I see his men snooping around. I've gotten reports that he's been personally watching Courtney from a distance." He waved his hand around. "We still haven't told him we have the girl."

"And we won't ." Kirill said defensively. "He's a rule breaker and he'll try and steal her somehow."

"No, it's not a good idea to dangle her in front of him." Mikhail breathed deeply. "At the same time, he might leave Courtney alone."

"He's not going to leave anybody alone." Kirill huffed. "We keep her safe here until the time's right."

Mikhail looked him over with suspicion. "You don't want to give her back do you?"

Kirill thought about it. "I do, but I want to know more of her. She's complicated and she intrigues me." He said rubbing his chin. He pulled out his cell phone and they watched the video of the naughty behavior in her sleep.

"She's a pervert!" Mikhail joked. "Next time, she'll let you join her." He said as he winked.

"You never told me what happened that weekend she spent with you." He relit his cigar. "Are you going to at least tell me she was a good girl?"

"Avarie was a very good girl. She only tried to run once." Mikhail busted up laughing. Kirill shook his head at him and poured another glass of vodka.

"Is she good?" Kirill asked seriously. "I know her weapons training and classroom skills are getting good, but is she really as good as Valentin and Karl tell me?"

"*Oi*, Kirill, she's got this." Mikhail took a deep swallow of his liquor. "For a minute there, I thought you were going to ask if she was good in bed."

"I can figure that out for myself." Kirill busted up laughing. "I almost had her too."

"So what's holding you back?"

"The fact that she isn't so sure about me. I don't want her falling in love with me you know."

"Dear God, you're a sick man, talking about love." Mikhail thought this was the funniest conversation they've had to date. The liquor was starting to swoon in his head. "She enjoys the belt, and you're all over her." He busted up laughing. "That woman is something else."

"She told me she swears that you and I are the same person!" Kirill declared. "Imagine that." Mikhail was laughing so hard, he almost fell over in his chair. When he calmed down Kirill said. "I have Tori over tonight. She said she wanted to watch over Avarie."

Mikhail slapped him. "No, so she could molest Sasha!" He busted up laughing again. Kirill was chuckling. The booze was getting to them both. This was their third bottle and everything was funny to them at this point. "Maybe we should grab Avarie and get her out of there?"

Kirill rubbed his chin and thought about it hard. "You think they're really going at it?"

Mikhail nodded his head. "Tori is an even bigger pervert than Avarie. I don't want her learning things that I can't teach her myself." He joked.

"You know, I can look and see if they're really fucking." Kirill nudged him. He pulled out his cell phone.

"What? You put cameras in their room?" Mikhail said in shock. "That's not right, brother."

"When you have a runner, you make sure they stay put. I didn't think she'd bring her partner in crime with her." He winked. "I don't look at it unless I have too. I had to watch the night she shattered the windows in her room. She didn't move one inch from her bed."

"Interesting." Mikhail said in almost a drunken slur. "Was that the only time?"

"Pretty much. They don't have a sex life in there. Honestly, it's pretty boring." Kirill gave him a wink. "Here we go." He showed the screen to Mikhail and he almost spit out his vodka. "It looks like Sasha has his hands full. Our niece is very persistent."

"My God, she's a tiger and he can't get away. Look at that poor bastard, he's just taking it!" Mikhail started laughing so hard he went into a coughing fit. "Look at the expression on his face, he really likes this."

"For the record, I didn't raise her that way." Kirill said with the biggest grin on his face. "I blame you."

"I blame the Internet." Mikhail quipped. Sasha flipped her over and took her doggy style. "Sweet Jesus, Joseph, and Mary. We need to save Avarie. I bet she's been hiding in the bathroom."

"I don't have cameras there, so I'm going to assume that's where she is." Kirill put out his cigar and grabbed his vodka bottle. "I'm agreeing; let's get her out of there."

Both stood up and stumbled a bit. They had to support each other all the way to Avarie's room. Busting open the door, Sasha dropped down on the bed and threw the covers over him and Tori. Mikhail and Kirill started laughing so hard, they tripped over Tori's duffel bag. "We're here to save Avarie!" Mikhail announced. Kirill walked up to the bed and slapped Sasha's ass through the covers. "Get her tiger!" Mikhail yelled.

"You two are bastards!" Tori yelled from under the covers. "Don't you knock?"

Their laughing never stopped as they busted into the bathroom only to find Avarie asleep in the tub with her music still going in her ears.

"Shh, Kirill, she's sleeping." Mikhail said and tried to quiet his drunken laughter. "Maybe we should leave her alone?"

Kirill took a slug of his bottle and handed it to Mikhail. "Look, her damn nose is only millimeters above the water, she's going to drown."

"Her water sprite won't let her drown." Mikhail said as he took a drink. "But we should get her out of here."

"How can she not hear us right now?" Kirill asked. His voice was starting to slur a bit. "We're loud as Hell and she isn't even stirring."

Sasha came into the bathroom with sweatpants on. "She can't hear you because she has her headphones in!" He was going to wake her up but Kirill slapped him away.

"You get your ass back in bed and take care of our niece. We got her." He handed the bottle to Sasha and Mikhail motioned for him to take a drink. Tori came in and stole the bottle from him and took a swig. She had on pants and a t-shirt.

"Leave her alone! We'll wake her up when we're done." She slapped at them.

"How the *fuck* is she not waking up!" Kirill yelled at the top of his lungs.

Mikhail took the earphones out and she started to stir a bit. "Avarie, wake up." Her eyes shot open and she saw all four hovering over her. The twins looked drunk and the other two looked like they were busy destroying the bed. They were quiet as they watched her reaction.

"What's wrong?" She asked in panic.

"*Mishka*, you're sleeping in a tub that's what's wrong." Kirill said and took a gulp of vodka. She looked them both over.

"Are you guys drunk?" She asked puzzled about what was going on. They nodded and Sasha shook his head.

"We're wondering why you aren't joining in on the action that's going on in your bed." Mikhail busted up laughing. "He's a big man and he could handle two of you."

Avarie was not happy. Tori slapped them both hard and Sasha walked back into the bedroom. She wiped the water from her face as she stared at them. "Are you boys jealous of him?"

"*Oi*, she just challenged us." Kirill said slurring. "Don't tempt us *Mishka*." He gave her a devious glare. "We are very naughty boys."

"Get the *fuck* out of here!" Avarie pointed to the door. "I've had enough of your shit for the night." Sasha looked so embarrassed when she turned to see him in their room. She could tell he was caught balls deep in Tori and he wore his shame.

"No, you get out!" Mikhail demanded stumbling a bit. "You can hang with us so Tori can finish her sexcapades with Sasha." Tori slapped him again.

Nope, Avarie wasn't going to win between these two assholes. "Fine, get out so I can get dressed." she said in defeat. Tori ushered them towards the door. She handed Avarie a towel and slammed the door shut.

"God their such assholes when they're drunk." Tori said shaking her head. "I'm sorry Avarie."

"It's alright Tori. You aren't the first person to get busted while in the buff." Avarie joked and whispered. "How is he anyway?"

"*Mishka*, he fucks like a dream." She said waving her hand in front of her face. "I'm surprised you haven't done anything with him." She whispered back.

Avarie dried off and pulled on her pants. "We don't have that kind of relationship." She patted Tori's shoulder. "More for you." She winked.

Avarie was dressed and headed out the bathroom door. The twins were waiting for her with anticipation. "Come little one! We're waiting impatiently. Never keep Russian men waiting!" Mikhail yelled. Sasha sat in the chair and looked down. He wanted them out.

She bent over to Sasha and whispered, "I'll take one for the team tonight and you have fun." She kissed his cheek and was escorted out of the bedroom.

"Those two fuckers." Tori exclaimed. "Busting in here like they own the place."

"So, what are they going to do with her?" Sasha asked in shock.

"They're so drunk, who knows. As long as she stays sober, she's fine." Tori took her clothes back off and looked at Sasha. "So my water demon, are you ready for another round."

His head popped up. God he was torn between worrying about Avarie and fucking the shit out of Tori again. He looked her up and down seductively. Needless to say, Tori won.

ϒϒϒ

The twins gained composure for a bit as they walked her to the back door. "Get your coat on *Mishka*; we're going out on the town." They pulled on their coats and handed Avarie hers.

"You guys can't drive like this!" Avarie was exasperated. "You're so fucked, we won't even make it out of the garage."

"Ah, Mishka, you're driving." Kirill said as he handed her the keys to Mikhail's SUV.

"Are you joking?" She took them and zipped up her coat. "I've hardly driven, let alone on snow." Damn, these guys were scaring her.

"You'll learn." Mikhail said walking her out into the parking ramp. They got into his vehicle. Avarie was in the driver's seat while the other two sat in back. She started it up and backed out.

"Where we going and how do I get there?" She asked annoyed. They were both laughing and told her to turn right.

"It's called 'Red October'." Mikhail said.

"I don't have my ID on me."

"You don't but we do." Kirill pulled a card out of his pocket. "It says you're of legal age and you can drive." They shared the bottle of vodka back and forth. Twice, she had to tell them to settle down or else she'd turn the car around.

They arrived at their destination. Bass throbbed outside the massive building. They each took an arm and escorted her in. She didn't like this at all. There were too many people and the noise did nothing for her senses. "This isn't a good idea boys!" Avarie yelled over the music.

"Sure it is!" Kirill said. "You're going to have fun, we promise." He kissed her nose as they entered the building. A huge guy checked ID's and allowed her to pass. She wore only her jeans, t-shirt and ball cap that Mikhail gave her a while back that said FSB. The twins wore jeans and button up black t-shirts. Handing their coats to a person in the coat room they walked her to the bar and ordered her a drink.

"You get maybe only one…maybe." Kirill said. "We'll see how you handle your liquor."

She didn't like this place one bit. Music thumped inside her head, the damn twins were drunk, and the place was packed. Mikhail led her to VIP seating in the corner. A few ladies joined them. They sat in their laps and flirted with the ladies. *Fuck, this wasn't going to end well*, she thought.

"*Mishka*, let loose, have fun." Kirill said as he did a titty shot off a blonde lady.

"This isn't a good idea, boys." Avarie shouted. "I'm completely lost here. What if I lose you?" She was feeling rage build up.

Mikhail handed her a shot and motioned for her to take it. "*Mishka*, if you lose us, it's for a reason." Oh My God, this is on purpose. They're testing her. *Fuck me*, she thought. She reached into her pants pocket; she still had Mikhail's car keys. She debated on just leaving them there. The shot worked its way through her system and she started to feel warm and fuzzy. Damn, now they're getting her drunk. *Assholes*. She felt like crying. This was not her element and they were going to get her snatched or killed.

She asked where the bathroom was and a lady escorted her there. When she came back out, the lady was gone. Avarie went back to the VIP area and they were gone. Panic rose up in her body and she felt like she needed to flee. Pulling her cap down, she bumped through the crowd, trying to find the twins.

Thinking she saw them on the dance floor, she made her way to them. The place smelled of sweat, sex, and booze. She stopped and tried to gain control of her senses. She knew their vibration so she tried to follow it. People were dancing all around her and the strobe lights messed with her eyes. *Concentrate.* She looked around again, turning slowly. She was in the middle of the dance floor. Her white shirt glowed blue. She realized the she wasn't wearing a bra. Looking down she could see her nipples poking through her shirt. Great, just what I needed, unwanted attention. She pulled down her hat further and continued on her way.

This wasn't cool, not by any means. At least she still had the car keys. She could go wait out in the car and turn the heater on until they came out. She didn't know her way home and she had no cell phone. They also left her without an ID or money. *Those two stupid fuckers.* A man was eyeing her from the bar as she came out of the crowd. He wasn't bad looking, but he could be a threat. She broke eye contact and walked around the crowd. She searched along the bar and there was no trace of them. Looking up, there was a second floor that had a balcony. She made her way up the steps carefully. The music felt louder up here. Finding a perch, she looked down at the crowd.

She closed her eyes to reign in her senses again and breathed deep. She felt something or someone behind her and she turned. A brunette man stood behind her with a drink in his hand. He was the guy who was checking her out at the bar. "Are you lost, *Mishka*?" He said in Russian. She didn't know how to respond. He didn't feel like a threat. She looked at him with blank eyes. "Do you speak English?" He asked in his think Russian accent. She said nothing, but turned around to stare at the crowd. He was damn good looking, but she wanted nothing of him. Finding the twins was the only thing on her mind right now.

She knew he was still there looking at her. He came up behind her and said in her ear. "I can get you a drink?" She shook her head no. She just wanted him to go away. God, she was ready to cry. Her eyes scanned the large area furiously. She tried to fight down her panic. "Who are you looking for?" The guy asked her.

Taking a deep breath, she turned around to face him. She was having a debate with herself to actually tell him. This place was so big, he wouldn't know who or where they were anyway. Crossing her arms she said. "My brothers. They were in the VIP room and left me here." She said in

Russian. Damn it was getting good too. It rolled right off her tongue. He asked what they looked like and described them to him.

"Have you checked the powder room?" He raised an eyebrow at her.

"What the hell is that?" She really wanted to know. He plugged one nostril and sniffed really loud. She rolled her eyes and put her head in her hands. "Where is it?"

He took her hand and led the way back downstairs. In a back room, it opened up to another area of the building off the dance floor. "Are you really FSB or is that just a hat?" He asked.

"It's just a hat." She lied.

They were at a door and he knocked until somebody opened it. He asked for her ID and she explained that Kirill had it. He let her in with the guy following her. She walked up to a table with white powder in lines and women sniffing it through straws along with other men. Not finding them there, she looked in the corner. They were each getting a blowjob from some coked up whores.

She stood in front of them and they looked up. "*Mishka*!" Mikhail shouted, he was either really drunk or drugged up. "Look, she found us!" God, she was going to lose her shit. She stood there and shook with rage. "Why don't you sit down? Maybe you could learn a thing or two from these ladies."

"You stupid mother fuckers! You left me out there so you can get blowjobs and ride the white lightening?" She shouted, but it was in German. They both laughed at her. The women never looked up as they bobbed up and down on them. She backed up and pulled the keys out of her pocket and waved it in front of them. "Go *fuck* yourselves. Sasha and I are out of here." She turned away and left the room. The guy was following her and he grabbed her elbow.

"If you're going to leave, at least let me walk you to your car." He said in Russian. "I don't want you by yourself." Wow this guy was sweet. "Or, you can stay with me until they come to their senses." Now that offer was just as tempting as leaving. Stay or go....*shit*.

ϒϒϒ

Sasha woke up. It was almost 1am, Avarie wasn't back yet and neither were the twins. Tori lay naked at his side. Something didn't feel right. He woke up Tori.

"She's not back." He was panicked. "I knew we shouldn't have let her go!" He stood up and threw on his pants.

"Sasha, we don't even know where she is."

He paced the room. "Call them, find out." God damn, if something happened to her, Courtney was going to kill him. She picked up her phone and dialed each of their numbers without an answer. "Sasha, they aren't answering." She said. "Calm down okay?" She rubbed his shoulders. The room was locked from the outside so they couldn't get out if they wanted to. "Sasha." She said stopping him in his tracks. "Avarie is very smart and her abilities are very strong. Trust that she knows what she's doing."

He nodded. He hoped that she would be okay. Those God Damn twins.

ϒϒϒ

"What's your name?" She asked the guy.

"Viktor." He said. "Yours's?"

"Nikita." She said. It was the first name that popped into her head besides her own. Technically speaking, she was Nikita.

"Well Nikita, do you want to leave or go?" He asked honestly. "Either way, I'll stay by your side."

"Let's go." She said and pulled him towards the door. She was almost at the exit when something happened. She felt the presence of something evil. It wasn't the twins, no, this one was different. She pulled him back in.

"What's wrong?" He asked.

"We can't go that way. Is there another way out?" She asked almost in a panic.

He thought about it. "If we go out the front, we can grab our coats. There's another exit, but it's not safe." He said thoughtfully.

"Do you have a cell phone?" She asked. He pulled it out, but it was dead.

"Are you in danger?" He asked concerned. The presence was coming closer. Shit, they had to get out of there. She wondered if she could feel them, could they feel her.

"Yes and no." She said quickly and pulled him to the dance floor to lose themselves in the crowd.

"We can grab your brothers." He yelled in her ear. "They'll get you out of here."

"They're too fucked up to do much right now." Avarie said in earnest. "They aren't of any use."

Viktor pulled her further into the dancefloor. "Just dance. Trust me." He started to dance with her and she followed along. It took a bit, but she let loose. She felt the presence go away, but that didn't mean she wasn't still looking around. She relaxed a little more and let this guy lead her. The music became louder and the crowd started cheering.

She was getting hot and he led her back to the bar. She asked for water and watched the bartender pour it for her. She gulped it down while Viktor scanned the club. He tapped her shoulder. "*Mishka*, there's a man over there who is trying to catch your eye." He stayed casual with her.

She stared into the bar. "Describe him to me."

It took him a bit. "He's very tall, blonde and has brown eyes it looks like."

Courtney? She thought. "How blonde is his hair?"

"It's very blonde."

"How much taller than you and how far away?"

"I'm six foot; he has to be four inches taller than me. He's at least fifty feet away."

Wow, this guy was good. He spotted this guy checking her out, gave a description, and could tell how far away he was. "Are you a cop or something?" He nodded. Shit, that's why he's never left her side. He's very focused.

"He's coming closer. Stay or go?"

"Go."

They headed back to the powder room trying not to act suspicious. The same man answered the door and let them in. The twins were still sitting in the corner. The whores were gone and so was the coke. They sat there drinking their vodka straight.

"Boys, we have to go." She said in a panic.

"We thought you left us, *Mishka*." Kirill sat his glass down and crossed his arms. "Where we going?" he asked.

"He's *fucking* here, boys." She leaned her hands on the table in front of them. "Viktor spotted him checking me out." She pointed at him.

"Viktor! We're glad you found our girl!" Mikhail sat up and shook his hand. These guys were fucked up.

"Mikhail, if she's in danger, you need to get her out of here." He shook his head at them. "You know better than that." Avarie looked him up and down.

"You know these two fucks?" She asked.

"All cops and security in Moscow know the FSB." He said impatiently. "What's the game plan?" He asked them tapping his foot.

"Is it Luscious?" Kirill asked, downing his vodka and setting the glass back on the table. Viktor described him. "Fuck, its Luscious. Game up." Kirill said throwing his hands in the air. "*Mishka*, stay here. We'll find him in a hurry and get him out of here."

She wasn't so sure by the way they were moving. "You guys are blitzed! How the hell are you going to deal with him?" She was seething. "This isn't a god damn game you assholes!"

Mikhail stood up and stretched out. "Viktor, make sure she stays in here. She's not to run into danger. If you have your gun on you, shoot her in the leg if she tries to run."

Great, fucking great. Viktor grabbed her hand and sat down in the corner with her. She sat there and tried not to let the panic take over her. "Deep breaths, Nikita. Drunk, drugged up, or sober, they know what they're doing." God she hoped so.

He talked to the security guard and asked to see the footage. He pulled out a tablet and let them watch the encounter. It looked like they were just leaning back against the wall and talking shit to each other. She wished she could hear what they were saying. They found him easy enough it looks like. Mikhail gestured for him to sit at a table. Drinks were brought out and they had a few beers between the three.

ϒϒϒ

Mikhail and Kirill searched until they found him. Luscious gave them a shit eating grin. Confidently, they strutted up to him. "Now, Luscious, I didn't think you would be in town. Why didn't you call us?" Kirill said. Mikhail gave him a smile and winked at him.

"I did, but nobody answered." He chuckled. "God, there's some beautiful women here tonight. I had my eye on one, but she was with another man. Shame." He clucked his tongue.

"Don't you have women in Dubai?" Kirill asked. "These are ours."

Luscious looked him up and down in disgust. "You know I'm a traveling man. I love foreign women."

Mikhail motioned him to sit at an empty table. A waitress brought them beers within a few minutes. "What are you doing back here,

Luscious? We don't have the girl, you know that." Mikhail said with a smile.

"Since we don't have the girl, maybe he wants something else?" Kirill said to Mikhail.

Luscious took a drink of his beer and glanced around the club. "Well, since you don't have the girl, maybe you have something for me."

"For shame Luscious." Mikhail said with a laugh. "We aren't in the business of throwing bones. You know that."

"Oh, I know." His eyes turned deadly. Kirill watched him closely. This place was packed and Luscious was a stone cold killer. If he blew the shit out of Courtney's corporate headquarters, he had no problem killing innocent people in a club.

"What is it Luscious?" Mikhail leaned into him like he was ready to strike.

"I want you two to go *fuck* yourselves." He broke into a maniacal laugh.

"*Oi*, Luscious that broke my heart." Kirill said with his hand covering his chest. "I thought we were friends." He said sarcastically.

"Oh we are, we keep our friends close, but our enemies' closer right?" He gave them a devious glare.

Mikhail shook his head. "Luscious, your forces out number ours and you're sitting here broken hearted. You should go into the back and get a blowjob. There's white powder back there too." He said pointing towards the powder room.

"Get drunk, get high, *fuck*, and get laid." Kirill encouraged him. "The women here are more than willing. When they feel the power off of you, they'll gladly suck your fat cock." He said slapping his back. "We're not in full blown war yet." Kirill said raising his hands in the air. "Have some fun tonight."

Luscious finished his beer and set the bottle back down. "Like old times?"

"Oh my God yes!" Mikhail said loudly. "Remember Pompeii before that volcano ripped the shit out of it? That was the best damn island in the world."

"And the sex was amazing." Kirill added. "You could bang two women at once and nobody batted an eye!"

That made Luscious laugh. These two cracked him up when they were drunk and high. They were so fucked right now; it wouldn't be a fair fight. "Well, lead the way." He started to stand up.

Mikhail finished his beer. "Hey, go with Kirill and get the vodka and girls, I'll make sure there's enough coke for us." Mikhail clapped his hands with excitement. Luscious looked at him suspiciously and nodded.

Quickly, he made his way into the powder room. "Alright, we have him distracted. *Mishka*, keys." She handed them to him. "We hide in plain sight. They'll be in here soon."

His eyes were really dilated. Yep, she was screwed. He looked around the room. "Viktor, trade shirts with her." He was about to protest but he motioned him on.

Avarie's breasts were bared and Mikhail stared at them. Viktor traded his gray shirt for her tight white one. He looked at the bouncer. "Boris, hand me a rubber band." He handed one over while watching the monitor. "Are they coming?" He shook his head no. "Put your hair in a ponytail like the other ladies." She did so quickly. Her heart was pounding like crazy and she told it to be calm. He grabbed her hat and threw it into the trash. "You see that corner there?" They nodded. "Go sit over there and start going at each other." Avarie said no. "You will do as I say!" His voice boomed. "Now go!"

"They're coming." Boris said. "The powder is under the seat."

"*Mishka*, you leave with Viktor five minutes after he gets here. Stay calm and show no fear. Don't even look at him." She had no choice. "Listen carefully. Don't look over at all. Concentrate on Viktor. When you leave, look for others. Get her back to the Prime Ministers house." He hissed.

She sat on his lap straddling him. She whispered in his ear. "Don't say my name." He nodded. A knock came at the door and Boris gave Mikhail the signal. He motioned for them to start making out. Viktor did so immediately.

She closed her eyes and tried to lose herself in him. They walked in and she could hear them talking. She faced a corner so she couldn't turn around. Running her fingers through Viktor's hair, she let him run his tongue on her neck. The laugher of ladies almost had her attention, but she focused on him. If this is what an FSB agent was all about, it was scary and awesome at the same time. She was right in the danger zone and it was turning her on for some reason. She kissed Viktor harder and deeper. Digging her hips into his groin, he moaned. She let him dry hump her.

"They're putting on a show for us." She heard Luscious' voice. She almost cringed and remembered to face the wall and pay no attention to him. They couldn't stop now that they had his attention. Like the damn whores weren't enough. Jesus she wanted out of there. She heard the twins laughing with him while they snorted more coke. She kept kissing Viktor and she could tell he was really getting into it. When he came up for air, he tried to breathe her in. His hands found her breasts and started caressing them. He pulled and tugged at her nipples through the gray shirt while he kissed her neck. He felt damn good. Sensations of pleasure rolled through her as he continued to dry hump her right there in front of everybody.

Mikhail and Kirill watched the whole thing as they drank their vodka and let the ladies work them and Luscious. Yep, just like old times. They clanked glasses and cheered each other. They both noticed that Luscious was getting turned on by watching Avarie and Viktor in the corner. There were other people in there to watch, why them? He licked his lips as the dark haired lady started to go down on him. Mikhail caught Viktor's eye and motioned for them not to leave yet. He whispered the message in Avarie's ear.

"Luscious, it's not nice to stare." Kirill said, trying to break his gaze from them in the corner. "You're getting a nice blowjob. You should watch her use her tongue." He said with zeal as he stared down in amazement. Shit, he got a hot one too.

"This one is wonderful." He said slowly moving his hips into her as he bent over to snort a line. "But that one, I wanna see her tits." He pointed at Avarie and licked his lips.

"That's not polite." Mikhail said breathlessly as his lady worked him up and down. "That's her boyfriend and they're having a good time." He waved his hand. "Besides, she looks underage."

Luscious looked at them with his devious glare. "It would make me very *happy* to see her tits."

"We don't own her. You have your own woman, play with hers." Kirill said as he put his hands on the woman's head. "*Oi*, woman, you're working me too fast." He said to her as he leaned his head back.

"*No*, I want a show. I love the smaller women and he's working her good." He said breathlessly. "It'll make my night boys. Since I can't touch her, I wanna see her naked."

"What exactly do you want from her?" Mikhail said taking a swig of his vodka.

"I want to watch him fuck her." His eyes were wide with excitement. "I want to see everything."

The twins looked at each other in disgust. This has gone too far already. They needed to get Viktor and Avarie out of here now. No agent of theirs was going to get naked in front of a crowd of strangers, especially Avarie. This was too much. "*Oi*, that's too bad, Luscious." Kirill answered sternly. "She's too young and she's not here to give you a damn show."

Luscious glared at Kirill. Without hesitation Mikhail yelled at Boris. "*Oi*, get the underage girl out of here! We don't want the cops to bust in here because management is serving under the legal limit!" Boris nodded and came up to Avarie and Viktor.

"Time to go you two." Boris ordered. Avarie heaved a sigh of relief as Boris slipped Viktor the keys to the SUV. In a whisper he told them, "I have a guard waiting outside the door for you." Viktor nodded and escorted Avarie out.

ϒϒϒ

They sat in silence with the heat running and the radio softly humming. Her eardrums rang. Half an hour later, they came out and got in the backseat. The damn car smelled like sex and sweat. They were both laughing so hard, they could hardly be understood.

"*Mishka*, good show!" Mikhail said as he patted her shoulder. She said nothing as she stared straight forward. "Viktor, my God you're a blessed man." The twins erupted in laughter again as Viktor shook his head at them. They went silent when they realized that Avarie wasn't speaking to them.

"*Mishka*! You did good." Kirill said with pride. "My God, you're going to make a great agent."

Slowly, she turned around in the driver's seat to stare at them. Rage filled her eyes. Suddenly, she bitch slapped them both with one strike. She managed to give them both bloody noses. She looked like she was done, but she bashed their skulls together with one fell swoop of her hands. They fell back laughing and chuckling. "It's nice to know that you assholes think this is funny." She said quietly. "You drag me out of the house, bring me to some strange sex club, lose me on purpose, then I run into danger and you bring that danger to me. Very smart boys."

"We didn't know Luscious was in town, Avarie." Kirill said. "The last reports we got was that he was in Germany. He showed up to mess with us." He started laughing. "We turned the tables on him."

"Viktor, we'll have Avarie drop you off at home." Mikhail said. "Please don't tell your dad what happened, he'd kill us."

Viktor looked her over and asked. "So you're Avarie?" She nodded. "My father told me about you. He said that Courtney sent you over to Russia to help win over the Elite and stay with the twins."

"Who's your dad?" She asked.

"He's the President of Russia. You heard of Konstantin?" he asked curiously.

"She's never met your father. He's been a busy man and she's been busy." Kirill said waving him off.

"For the record, I hate you both right now." Avarie said in a huff. She shifted the car and they drove out of the parking lot. Viktor directed her how to get to his place and she dropped him off. The twins were asleep in the back seat of the car. She debated on going back to the river and driving the car into it.

Once she was back at home, she shut off the SUV. Slapping the boys awake, they rubbed their faces.

"That wasn't very nice." Mikhail slurred. "Could've just told us to wake up."

She was turned around in her seat, facing them. "I don't know what game you're playing with me, but it's not funny anymore."

"No, like its not funny how you pulled pranks on me, or went into rages at the FSB, or how you always tried to run." Kirill said glaring at her. "No, it's not funny at all."

"I think you assholes set this up." She accused. "You made your point."

The twins looked at each other. "I'm glad the point is made, but we didn't set this up." Mikhail said sitting up in his seat. "How did it feel?" Mikhail cleared his throat. "I mean the situation."

"I was truly scared boys. Had it not been for Viktor, we'd all be screwed by now." She said seriously. "Does Luscious know who I am?"

"No. He just checked you out because he likes the smaller females." Kirill answered. "You felt him near didn't you?" She nodded. "Good, keep that sense in you and you'll be fine."

She wanted to smack him again. "You enjoyed it didn't you?" Mikhail asked.

She rolled her eyes. "There were parts that were good, others not so much."

"We enjoyed watching the show." Mikhail winked at her. "So did Luscious. He's perverted!" His eyes went wide with revulsion.

"How did you guys get out of there without him following?"

They both laughed. "We had one of the ladies spike his vodka. He'll wake up thinking he had too much coke and booze." Mikhail answered.

"Why didn't you do that beforehand?" She was starting to lose it.

"Because, he was aware of his surroundings. With your distraction, we were able to catch him off guard."

"Is he that stupid?" She asked. "If you guys could catch him off guard, what's that say about you?" They went silent. She made a good point. "He picked me for a reason remember?"

"That's because you were the most beautiful woman there." Kirill said. "You're young, cute, and have a great body for being so small."

"There were other women much better looking than me." She could bring up more points, but it was almost 5am and she was tired. "You know what? Fuck you both." She got out of the car and went inside.

Avarie went to her room as the escort unlocked her door for her. Sasha and Tori were asleep on the bed wrapped up in the covers. Turning on the shower, she stepped in and washed off her shame. Coming back into the bedroom, she slipped into Sasha's side of the bed and snuggled into him. He was naked and so was Tori. At this point, she didn't care; she wanted to go to bed. As she lay on him, he wrapped his arm around her. He was about to talk but she told him to go to bed. She fell asleep as the sun was coming up.

CHAPTER TWELVE

Two weeks after the incident at Red October, Avarie has said little or nothing to the twins. Hell, she didn't even tell Tori and Sasha the full story. It was more like she left out as much as possible so Sasha wouldn't freak. He already felt guilty for not being there. However, if he was, it would've been worse.

Mikhail left this week to go back to Germany. Hopefully, he wouldn't say anything to Courtney about what's been happening in Moscow. Avarie cringed at the thought. Guilt ripped her apart and she had a hard time coping. It wasn't just that, she saw a side of the twins that she really didn't want to see or know existed. She was confused, were they good or bad? Were they toying with her emotions just to get her to do what they wanted? This shit was complicated.

Sasha and Avarie were in combat training with Tori and a stand in instructor. He was impressed with their skills and progression. It was nice to hear a compliment for once. Mikhail always yelled and shamed her if she didn't move or knock him down. They sat back against the wall so they could take a break. The two sucked down water and wiped the nasty sweat off themselves.

"Avarie." Sasha whispered quietly. "I know something happened that night and you didn't tell me the truth." He scooted closer. "Please tell me what happened."

She swallowed hard. She didn't want to tell him as it would only make him angrier. He's developed a relationship with the twins since then. Somehow, Sasha earned their respect and she didn't want that to regress. "Sasha, when I'm ready, I'll tell you."

"*Maus*, it's eating you up." He patted her shoulder. "We're a team remember? You need to tell me so I can protect you."

She fought back the tears that were starting to form in her eyes. "Please don't make me tell you." She pleaded. "I don't want to remember it."

Sasha's electric blue eyes looked her over solemnly. He put his arm around her and kissed her head. "Avarie." He whispered. "I felt your fear and panic that night. It's been eating me up." Jesus, now he looked like he was ready to cry. "I can't tell you how guilty I feel right now."

As soon as he said it, the instructor came over. He was about to tell them that break was over, but his gaze lingered on them. Taking a place in front of the duo his face became thoughtful. Ling Chu was from China and had mastered all forms of martial arts including samurai skills. He had to be in his 60s but his eyes were much older.

"Why do you despair?" He asked in broken English. "You two have wandered into a black corner of your minds and have sat there in the darkness I see. Why don't you get up and leave that place?"

Avarie had serious respect for this man. Whenever they worked with him, he brought a sense of calm over them both. She thought about how she would reply, but Sasha answered for her. "It's not a corner, it's a room and the doors are locked from the outside." He looked at Avarie.

"But who locked the door trapping you in?" Ling asked thoughtfully. "Did you lock yourselves in or was it somebody else?" Tori saw them sitting and placed herself by Avarie.

"They've locked each other out." Tori answered with a soft smile. "They each have their own room where they hide from themselves."

Avarie and Sasha both looked down in shame. "You two are blood bound. What happens to you," he pointed at Avarie. "Happens to him and so on." He continued. "You cannot lock each other out for too long." He leaned in. "However, the only one who's door is unlocked is Sasha's it seems. His door is open for you Avarie." He waved at him. "Step inside. His room isn't so dark. In fact, it may not be dark at all."

She couldn't take it and bolted out of the room. Tears spilled everywhere and she ran for the locker rooms at the pool. In her shower stall, she shut the door and turned on the cold water. Laying down and placing her legs up against the wall, she let the water spill onto her body. Sobs escaped her mouth before she could trap them inside. When exhaustion came over her, she closed her eyes, shivering from the cold.

ϒϒϒ

Matthais worked for months on his pulse wave machine for Eva and it was finally ready for a test drive. Jude and Damian stopped by to help program and sequence it. All three were excited when they pulled Eva into the room. When she walked in, she was in shock. "Damn Matthias, it looks like something out of a science fiction movie." Her heart raced as she walked around the giant pod. "How's this supposed to work?"

"The same way it worked for Avarie." He answered. "It's called suspended automation. You're going to be kept in a place between life and death." He rubbed his hands together like a villain. "This is going to be awesome!"

Jude shook his head at him and Damian laughed. "You do realize that unless she's drugged, the process of sleep training will be painful right?" Jude asked.

"Of course, I have all kinds of drugs."

"Oh my God! What did I sign up for?" She slapped Matthias and he flinched.

"You signed up for SCIENCE!" Matthias cackled evilly. "You will be my red headed warrior!"

Damian put his hand on Matthias' forehead. "Yep, he has Frankenstein fever." He laughed as he walked away.

"Well, are you ready?" Matthias asked with wide excited eyes.

She huffed a deep sigh. "I guess so." They prepared Eva for the test round of pulses. Putting in an IV line, electrodes, and a strange skull cap, they set her in. Little did she know, she was in for one wild ride.

ϒϒϒ

Mikhail was in the kitchen with Courtney and Ivan. He drank strong coffee as he sat at the island. Mikhail has been in Freiburg for almost a week now, making sure that the FSB and other factions were doing their job. His focus was too much on Avarie and he could tell she wasn't happy with him. Deciding that it was a good time to give her space, he decided to come here.

"It's a good thing I came." He said sipping his hot coffee. "I see you're making strides with Eva. She'll be a powerful force when her training is done."

"She's a quick learner." Ivan responded. Pulling out a cigarette, he lit it. "The fire burns inside her and she controls it." He blew out smoke. "I feel the universe coming together for once."

Courtney looked at them impatiently. "So, are you going to give me an update on Avarie?" He asked. "You've been here a week and haven't mentioned one word."

"That's because I've been avoiding it!" Mikhail said in an annoyed tone. "You don't need to know what she's doing. Besides, if she found out what you've been doing, she might not want to come back." He smiled sheepishly at him. Courtney wanted to punch him straight in the kisser. "Don't be angry with me Courtney. You know how all this works." He waved his hand around. "You fell in love with her and now look at you. You're a hot mess and so is she." He picked up his mug. "You should've contacted us first so you could've avoided all this shit."

Courtney rubbed his temples. "That's not the point."

"It is the point!" Mikhail slammed his mug down. "She's so emotionally conflicted, she regresses. If you hadn't touched her, she'd be putty in our hands."

Ivan looked at Mikhail. "Really Mikhail? I think that's bullshit you're spewing."

"And what bullshit is that, Ivan?" Mikhail became defensive.

Ivan cracked up. "She wouldn't be putty in your hands. I think she's got you boys wrapped around her pinky." He wiggled it in front of him. "I think you purposely push her buttons because you like her."

Courtney cocked an eyebrow at Ivan. "Is that true Mikhail? Are you boys falling in love with her?" Courtney said in a shameful tone. "She's been there for almost five months and you still can't tame her. Is that because of her, or you?"

Mikhail didn't like where this was going. "Courtney, what if I told you I slept with her?" He said with a sly grin.

Courtney shook his head. "I'd say it wouldn't surprise me one bit." He laughed. "You two are perverted. Also you've been part of the KGB before it turned into the FSB. We all know you guys have a history with using seduction to get your way." Ivan busted up laughing again, almost choking on his cigarette smoke.

"Would it bother you if I slept with her?" Mikhail said in jest.

Courtney knew he wasn't really joking. "She belongs to the FSB now remember? Even if it did bother me, there's not a damn thing I could do about it."

"Not to change the subject boys." Ivan said putting out his smoke in the sink and throwing the butt away. "We know Luscious' been snooping around here. Has he been in Moscow?"

"How'd you know he's been snooping?" Mikhail looked at him with wide eyes.

"Shut up and answer the question." Ivan said, pouring another cup. "I've felt the presence of evil and it's not just you."

Mikhail sighed. "He's still looking for the girl. We ran into him at Red October a couple of weeks ago and he paid a visit a while back to Kirill."

"So, we can't throw him off her trail?" Ivan asked seriously. "He knows you have her; he just hasn't seen her yet." Mikhail started laughing so hard, he almost fell over. "What's the joke?"

"The joke is that he has seen her!" He continued laughing. "He was just so distracted from snorting coke and getting a blowjob, he didn't even know it."

"Good God!" Courtney yelled. "How in the living hell did that happen?"

Mikhail calmed down enough to tell them about Red October and how they were able to distract Luscious from grabbing Avarie. He left out the intimate parts for all their sakes.

"*Jesus*, he hasn't changed has he?" Courtney asked in shock. "That man loved his orgies." He just shook his head in wonder. "You two aren't any better. I can't believe you exposed her to that."

"This is what being an agent is all about!" Mikhail was getting flustered. "The more she knows, sometimes the less she understands. It is a dark world and she isn't going to be sheltered from it." He paced the floor. "She has to know evil in order to fight it."

"Then why don't you tell her that?" Ivan asked slamming his cup down in frustration. "Maybe she wouldn't fight you so much if she actually understood what you were and why she's fighting these battles." Wow, Courtney thought. Ivan stood up to Mikhail and that was astonishing.

"I'm not here to discuss her!" Mikhail boomed. "I'm here to make sure everybody stays safe!" His eyes glowed and the points on his eye teeth grew. He curled his lips back at Ivan in a cruel grin. "No more discussion of Avarie." Mikhail stormed off and Ivan busted up laughing.

"He needs anger management." Ivan looked at Courtney. "She's a sore subject with him."

"So I noticed." Courtney answered in wonder. "What's going on with him anyway?"

Ivan looked into his mug thoughtfully. "He's scared of her."

Courtney was confused. "What?"

"Look at him." Ivan lowered his voice. "He's scared of her. Something about her threatens him and he doesn't like it one bit."

Courtney looked at him dumbfounded. "Ivan, these are the original Watchers. What the hell do they have to be scared of? She's only five foot and a little over a hundred pounds soaking wet. It isn't like she can do much damage to them."

"Courtney, it isn't the physical damage she's doing to them, it's the emotional damage." Ivan said pointing to his head. "She feels things deeply and she forces them to feel it too." He snapped his head at Courtney. "I think you know exactly what I'm talking about."

"Right now, I'm thinking about how those two have survived this long. I swear they're crazy. I never worked with them back in the States, but I heard whispers of them."

"I thought that the first time I met them." Ivan chuckled. "I always wondered how in the hell the universe could make two of one man?"

Courtney almost spit out his coffee. "Hell, they're the same person?"

Ivan busted up laughing. "No. I mean they made two of the same people I guess. I don't know how to explain it. It'd be like two of you, only slightly differing personalities."

"My God." Courtney shook his head. "That's scary."

ϒϒϒ

Avarie was finally pulled out of the shower by Valentin and Karl. They covered her with a large towel and dried her off while she slept.

"Nobody was here to put her in the stall. How'd she get here?" Karl asked.

Valentin shook his head. "Ling said she broke down in combat training and ran out."

"So she just put herself in here?"

"I guess. I think it's become her safety net for when things get too real."

Tori found them in the locker room and talked to them about what happened. She told them about Avarie's outing with the twins and that she didn't really talk about it and how she's closed up into herself again. Then the conversation with Ling and Sasha.

"Poor *Mishka* is emotionally exhausted." Karl said somberly. "She's seen too much before she's ready."

They woke her up and had her and Sasha taken home. Kirill took one look at her and sent her to her room without supper. That was fine because she wasn't in an eating mood anyway. Sasha came back upstairs and started to run water in the tub. He coaxed her in without much fuss. They went to each of their ends and laid back for a while in silence. Finally, he reached for her hand and pulled her over to him. He leaned her back against him.

"Tell me now." Sasha said in a hoarse whisper. "If you don't tell me, I'll drag it out of you and you won't like that."

She turned to look at him. "Wow Sasha, are you threatening me?" Her eyes grew wide.

"Yes I am. If you don't tell me what's going on I'll have to use the alternative."

"And what's the alternative?" She asked defensively.

He stared into her and his eyes turned pale blue. He parted his lips a bit, flashing her the sharp points of eye teeth. *Holy shit*, she'd never seen him like this before. "Don't make me be like *them*, Avarie." His voice changed. "It's easier on you if you just tell me." Damn, she lost this battle. Hesitantly, she leaned back on him.

"Sasha, the reason why I don't tell you things is because I don't want you to carry my guilt and emotions. I'm not your burden." Tears of frustration rolled down her cheeks. "It's not fair of me to ask of you."

"You let me decide what's fair." He whispered in her ear. He held her hand in his while stroking her neck. She sighed deep and let it all spill out about what really happened at the club. Telling him how she met Viktor and the shit they had to do just to get out of there. She was disgusted.

"*Maus*, you didn't look once to confirm if it was really Luscious?" Sasha asked with confusion. "How did you know without even looking?"

"I felt his presence. It wasn't anything like the twins. This guy was pure evil."

"He sounds perverted." Sasha shook his head in wonder.

"Are you kidding me? The twins were all about it too!" Avarie's mind flashed back to how they were egging him on. "It's like they all enjoyed it. Afterwards, they were telling me that it was a good show." Oh she was disgusted.

Sasha went silent for a second. "I just don't get those two. They're insane!" He put his hand to his head. "Good thing you were smart though."

"If I was smart, I would've left them there."

Sasha busted out laughing. "Now I see why you've been so upset. Not only have you seen a side of them you shouldn't have, they put you in danger and you literally had to lay with a stranger to get out of it."

"Now I can't shake that guilt, Sasha! I feel horrible." God, she was going to cry again.

"Easy, *Maus*." He said pulling her into a hug. "I can take care of that for you."

She looked at him like he was crazy. "What the hell are you talking about?"

He gave her a strange look. "Don't you know anything about water?"

"Yea, we swim, drink, and bathe in it."

He busted up laughing. "No, it's the first element to life. All life thrives on water."

"So, how's that help me?" Avarie asked confused.

"Water is used for purification. I can use water to help you with your emotions."

Avarie thought this over. "Alright. Do your thing."

He gave her a serious look and said, "I need you to relax and close your eyes." She started to giggle. "Stop it. I'm serious." She wouldn't stop giggling. He grasped her hand and a strange sensation ran up her arm. It felt like small needles attached themselves to her nerves and she couldn't feel her arm. Her giggling stopped. She remembered this! As she was about to say something, the words wouldn't come out. A ball of darkness enveloped her and when she thought she was gone, a huge burst of bright light flooded her vision.

She didn't even feel her body. When she looked down, there was no body to be found. Extreme sadness filled her system and she felt like she was going to break apart. As hard as she tried to keep herself together she had to finally give in after the pressure built up. When she did burst the sadness went with it. Pleasure rolled through her and transported her to sounds of water.

Her feet hit the ground. Soft grass tucked between her toes as she walked. Looking in the distance she was at a lake and it's waves gently lapped at the shore. Running her hands across her body, she wore a white two piece swimsuit. Hearing splashing, she headed in that direction.

Pandora Rising

Coming along the sandbar, two children were splashing around. She had to smile, they were so cute.

"Mommy! Come in the water with us!" They yelled. She looked around for their mom. A little blond haired girl about eight years old came out of the water all soaking wet. "Mom! Get in!" Avarie was stunned as this little thing dragged her into the water and started to splash her getting Avarie all wet.

A little boy about four or five came up to her and motioned for a hug. She picked him up. He had blond hair too. "Mommy, can we get ice cream after this." He asked in a funny voice. Giving him a strange look, she nodded. She wondered why they were calling her mommy. A slow realization creeped in; these were her *children*. She looked around for the third. Was she here? Avarie wondered.

"Niki!" A man shouted. She wandered out onto the sandbar. To her left she found the man. He was sitting in swim trunks with a toddler in his lap playing in the water. He was tall with thick black hair, he turned and looked at her. "Look, Trina loves the water." He said smiling. He had blue eyes and facial hair, *just like Sasha*. The little girl squealed with delight as he was playing with her. His voice didn't sound like Sasha's. How strange? Was Sasha her husband? He motioned for her to sit with them and she took a seat.

"What's that look for?" He asked in confusion as he lifted the girl into his lap.

"Sasha?" She asked him. Then he gave her a stranger look.

"Niki, are you alright?" He laughed. She shook it off as the other two kids came closer.

"Mommy, Lissa found a shell!" The little guy said excitedly and she showed her.

"Wow, that's awesome." She responded with a laugh. Her heart was filling with joy at the sight of them.

"Mommy, sing us a song." The little girl begged. "Tosh wants to hear a song." They made their way and sat down next to her.

The man nudged her in the rib and said, "You can't deny our children a song can you?"

She gave in. "Alright, what song?" She asked the children.

Tosh came up with one. "Mommy, the song that you sing to us at bedtime." Avarie had to think about that one.

Lissa said, "Mom, he's talking about the song called *Heaven*." Oh, Avarie had that on her iPod and it was one of her favorites. She started to sing for them as the children looked at her in wonder. The man put his arm around her and looked deep in her eyes. Tosh looked like he was ready to cry as she sang and snuggled up to her. Lissa followed suit. When she was done, the children climbed onto her lap and she held them. The man turned to her and gave her a deep kiss. It was like electricity running through her. She felt amazing and didn't want this to end. Trina fought the other two for her attention and she held her with her blue eyes and brown hair. They all chatted a bit as they watched the sky turn to twilight. Each child fell asleep on her and she felt them breathe softly against her skin.

The man turned to her and said, "Why don't you go in the water?" Avarie was confused. "You better leave while they're asleep." He moved each child from her body and laid them on the soft ground. Grabbing her hand he led her to the edge of the lake. She turned to look at him and asked, "Who are you?"

He smiled at her and kissed her forehead. "I'm the man who's supposed to protect you. Now go. It'll be harder to leave once they're awake."

"Can I come back?" She asked.

"Niki, one day, you'll come back, but not anytime soon." He whispered in her ear. "I love you, now go."

"I love you, too" She said as the tears spilled over. He kissed her again and wiped the tears away. She turned to look one last time at the children and stepped into the warm water of the lake. When she was waist deep, he motioned her on further until she was completely under. Her feet touched nothing and she breathed nothing. *Avarie, wake up.*

ϒϒϒ

Kirill watched over her as she lay on the bed. The electricity in the house kept flickering and he flew upstairs to warn them of a possible attack since this wasn't a regular thing. He found Avarie asleep on Sasha in the soaking tub. The lights were out of control in the bathroom and Sasha paid no mind.

Sasha used him to help get Avarie out of the tub. Putting her in her bed clothes, they both stood watch over her. "What's wrong with her?" Kirill asked Sasha in confusion.

"She's dreaming is all." He shrugged. "She's had a rough few weeks and she passed out in the tub."

"What did you do to her?"

"Not much." Sasha turned out the lights and covered her up. "I just compartmentalized her emotions so she could handle them better."

"Purification?" Kirill asked. Sasha nodded. "Should we watch over her?"

"If you want, but she'll wake up in the morning refreshed."

Kirill passed out on the chair and woke up to her singing a song he hadn't heard for years. She wasn't awake but her angelic voice filled the room. *What is she?* He asked himself. When she was done, he went back to sleep.

The alarm gave its annoying buzz at 6am. Avarie's eyes flew open only to see Kirill looking at her from the chair. He stood up and gave her a strange look. Remembering where she was, she shook Sasha awake. He sat up in bed.

"Why's he here?" Avarie asked.

"Because he thought we were in danger. The electrical grid went nuts last night. When you passed out in the tub, he thought there was something wrong with you." Sasha explained. Kirill stepped out so they could get ready. When he was gone, Avarie quickly explained what happened and how he was her husband in her vision.

"That's not possible, *Maus*." He shook his head as he got in the shower. "I've never met you before all this and I've never had children."

"Then why don't I know what my husband looked like?" She asked in frustration.

"I can't answer that." He said as the room filled up with water vapor and he washed his body. "Maybe somebody else has the answer."

Avarie brushed her teeth with vigor. She felt refreshed but that one part of her vision really threw her off. "Well, why would it use you as a stand in for the person who's supposed to be my husband?" She spat in the sink.

"Avarie, did you have a good vision?" He asked annoyed as he stepped out and pushed her in the shower.

She answered as she got under the spray. "Yes, but it leaves me with that one problem." Now she was frustrated.

"*Maus* just let it be for right now." Sasha coaxed and laughed at her. "By the way, Eva says hello."

She about dropped her shampoo bottle on her foot. "Did you talk to her on the phone?" Avarie asked.

"Nope." He said as he finished brushing his teeth. "Hurry up, I'll explain to you on the way to the FSB."

ϒϒϒ

When Eva was strapped into the bedlike pod Matthias put the drugs into her body and she melted away. Any thoughts of going back were lost and she disappeared into the darkness. She whooshed into a bright light and felt a current run painfully through her body, but then it dissipated. Her own body vanished as she went sailing in between life and death.

Atoms crashed into others as she went spinning into the universe and it was amazing. The scenery changed and she found herself outside the castle, but it was different. The gazebo by the little pond had more flowers and there was no graveyard behind her. A man skipping rocks caught her attention and she walked up to him. He turned around and asked, "Eva?" It was Sasha! She threw her arms around him and he hugged her back.

"Am I dead?" She asked him.

"No, this is just a place where you land sometimes I guess." He laughed. "This is where I took Avarie when she came over."

"This is beautiful. No wonder why you hesitated coming back." She looked around and laughed. "How are you guys?"

"Avarie's having a tough time, so I worked some magic." He said flexing his fingers and flinging another rock across the pond. "She's homesick and the twins are crazy."

"So I've heard." Eva shook her head. "Where's she now?"

"Hopefully having good dreams." He handed her a flat rock. "I see Matthias got that machine running he warned us about."

"How did you know?" She asked in amazement, flinging rocks with him.

"Because you're here, silly."

"Sasha, tell me everything." He didn't hesitate and filled her in practically everything. From the very beginning to the end and didn't hold back.

"Woah, so you got laid..." She said with marvel. "How was it?"

He thought about it and said, "It was amazing. That woman knows what she's doing." He laughed.

"How about Avarie?"

"What about her?" Sashed winked.

"You know what I'm asking." Eva put her hands on her hips.

"She's handling her own with help." Sasha avoided her glare. "Fine, she has good and bad days. The twins pester her a lot. They're sexed up drug demons or something." He shook his head. "I get along with them fine, but that night in the club, they scared her bad."

"Courtney would freak." Eva said. "I can't believe this shit."

Sasha shook his head. "How's he doing?"

Now that was a question Eva didn't want to answer.

"Eva?" Sasha said accusingly. "Has he been bad?" She nodded in shame. "She doesn't need to know." He said and shrugged it off. Eva filled him on from the time Ivan arrived to the present.

"Ivan sounds like a nice guy." Sasha said. "It seems the elements are coming together."

"These are crazy times we live in." Eva said in amazement. "Until I met the boys, I thought I saw everything."

"You haven't seen anything yet."

"What's that mean?"

"It means it's going to get crazier and you better hold on." Sasha took her hand and sat her down. "The twins have a feeling that this world is going to open up soon. I haven't told Avarie yet, but we're in for a battle this world hasn't seen since the beginning."

"Oh my God." She exclaimed. "Should I warn the others?"

"Nope, let it be for now." He looked around. "I have to get back to Avarie." He hugged and gave her a kiss. "I'll see you next time." He winked. Like that he was gone. Eva stayed there for a while longer exploring this new wilderness. In a whoosh, she was transported back to the pod. Matthias opened up the lid and helped her out. "How was it?" He asked concerned.

"*It. Was. Awesome!*"

ϓϓϓ

Sasha filled in Avarie about what happened while she was out. Matthias had his machine going, Courtney was just being himself, and the new guy Ivan was teaching Eva how to cast some fire magic. All of this was enthralling. They could meet Eva in between worlds and communicate with her!

At the FSB, Sasha noticed that things went smoother for her. Ling thought the talk he had yesterday with them helped her out. Sasha smiled as she took on every challenge and killed it. Maybe he should do that more often. Then again, not too much. If she actually knew what he did to her, she'd freak out. Best to let it be for now.

CHAPTER THIRTEEN

Mikhail returned to Moscow on Monday. Kirill told him that Avarie better be ready to fight him. He took the day off to see if she had work to do or not. Neither told her their plans so she was caught off guard when he showed up in the training room looking like he was ready to kill.

"What's he doing here?" Avarie asked Mikhail.

"*Mishka*, he's here to fight you." Mikhail said laughing at her. "We told you this day would come. You need to fight him off or subdue him."

"I do that and we go home?" She asked with confidence.

"No, it's not that easy." He crooned at her. "You think that just because you take him down you're ready? That's not the way to think."

Kirill stood on the mat in his fighting pants, barefoot, clean shaven, and without a shirt. Damn he looked good. Avarie hesitated. He motioned to her that he was ready, but she could only stand there and stare at him. "*Mishka*, you have to fight me."

"Why can't I fight Mikhail?" She said pointing towards him. "He's my trainer."

Now Kirill was becoming annoyed. "Avarie! That isn't the point. You fight *me*." Mikhail motioned her over to meet him on the mat. Her heart raced and it beat inside her chest so hard, she thought her ribs would explode. He noticed her fear and snickered deviously at her. He stopped to cross his arms around his chest. "*Mishka*! What's the problem? The first time we met, you had no problems facing me head on. What's changed?"

Avarie contemplated deeply about what was really holding her back. He strutted up to her and lifted her chin. "Are you scared?" She bobbed her head. "How about I give you an incentive?"

"Like what?" She asked suspiciously.

"If you win, I bring your lover boy to you." He wagged his finger.

"If I lose?"

He put his fingers to his chin and squinted his eyes. "Let's not think about losing." He went back into position. Sasha, Tori, and Mikhail all leaned against the wall and out of the way. Fear crossed Sasha's eyes.

Building up courage she went up to him. He looked down at her to size her up. This shouldn't be that hard, he already knows how strong I am. Without a flinch, he went for a jab and she blocked it at the last possible second. He was going after her with too much force and she wasn't ready. Every punch he threw she blocked. "Stop blocking and start punching!" He shouted. She kicked for him but he moved out of the way. She made contact with his face, but it wasn't enough. She knew he gave her that one. He circled her and laughed. "Come Avarie. I know you can do better than that." He mocked.

Quickly she gave him the round house, just grazing his cheek. He struck her with the front of his elbow to the nose, sending blood gushing. Almost losing consciousness she shook it off. He didn't give her a chance to fully regain herself as he hammered on her. She tried to block where she could, but he was too strong. It was over with a massive kick to the chest and she went flying into the air only to land on the mat with a thud. She stopped breathing, her eyes were open, but she saw nothing.

Tori ran over to her and checked her pulse, she was still alive. "Dammit, Uncle Kirill! You weren't supposed to kill her!" Tori screamed while she checked for a breath where there was none. Sasha skidded up to her and started to gently smack her face. Taking a huge painful breath in, she tried to sit up but couldn't. They let her lie there for a moment as the twins watched in disgust.

Avarie could barely move. That son of a bitch broke one of her ribs or maybe more. She shook with incredible pain. Sasha grabbed a water bottle and poured it over her chest. Putting his hands over her, he whispered something and the pain started to reside. They lifted her up onto her feet. "She's not done!" Kirill yelled.

"She's hurt, you made your point!" Sasha shouted back. "What more can she do?"

He walked up to him and threw Avarie back down on the ground. "As long as she has a breath in her body, she can still fight." He shoved Sasha back from her. Oh that pissed Avarie off. While he was off his guard, she swung her body around and knocked his legs out from under him. Not giving him a chance to get up, she straddled him and kept swinging until her fists were bloody. He blocked some punches, but not many. He threw her off him and kicked her hard in the stomach. She tried to get up, but a foot cracked down on her back, holding her there. He dropped down beside her and started to bash her head into the mat, sending blood everywhere. When he was done, he stood up, brushed his bloody hands on his pants and walked out.

Mikhail walked up to her as Sasha grabbed another bottle of water and brought it to her limp body. Her head felt like somebody chiseled away at her brain and her hands stung. Every nerve of her body screamed in pain that it has never felt before. Shit, she lost and badly. Kirill was too strong for her. Mikhail said something to her, but she couldn't hear it. Her world went black.

ϒϒϒ

Avarie's eyes blinked until they focused on the confines of her bedroom. Her body raged in agony as it shook in small convulsions. Mikhail hovered above her like a saint. "*Oi*, Mishka. I see you're awake."

He crooned at her softly. He had a needle and a vial in his hand. Avarie looked at her own hands and saw that they were bandaged. She went to touch her head and Mikhail smacked her hands away. "Don't touch! You have a nasty gash." He filled the syringe with a clear fluid. She tried to protest but he motioned for her to be quiet. "This is a pain killer." He was about to inject it, but he stopped.

"Before I give it to you, I should tell you that you fought like a weakling. I'm very disappointed in your hand to hand combat." She tried to move her lips but he shook his head at her in anger. "You're faster than him, *Mishka*. For shame." He tisked at her. "You held back and that I cannot stand. Next time, you're going to land him flat on his fucking back and keep him there. We have work to do with you."

"He's stronger than me." She managed through clenched teeth. He chewed his gum at her and rolled his eyes. He slapped her stomach and she tried to ball up, but the pain soared through her body.

"I want you to think about this; if that were Luscious or the others, they would've killed you without a second thought. You saw how he was the other night. He's pure *evil*." Mikhail's eyes widened as he came closer to face her. "Right now, you disgust me." He spat on her. "I don't even know why I'm kind enough to give you this." He looked at the syringe. She really didn't want it and said so. "*Mishka*, I want to give it to you. Whether you want it or not isn't up to you right now. You can't even move you're in so much pain."

Without warning, he pulled on her right arm and she let out a small scream. He didn't care as he easily found a vein and stuck the needle in. The warmth from the insertion point slithered through her body like a snake on sand. She felt the pain still, but almost didn't care about it enough. As it spread into the rest of her body, the pain started to subside to the point where she felt completely numb. He watched thoughtfully as her body relaxed on its own. He gently saddled up next to her, careful not to disturb her position. "It feels good right?" She tried to nod as her eyes grew heavy. The pain meds hit her brain too hard she was having a hard time concentrating. She could feel her stomach bite into itself as the pain killer washed over her. Nausea threatened and she tried to coax it back down into her pit. "Feeling sick?" She blinked. He laughed at her. "You're not going to throw up. It'll go away soon." He assured her.

She felt vulnerable. He was lying next to her in bed and there was nobody else in the room. The look in his eye said he was thinking naughty things. *Pervert*, she thought to herself. He ran a finger from her tender head down to her neck. His lips were close to her ear and the smacking of the gum in his mouth was annoying her. If she could move, she'd slap him. His breathe held the sweet scent of peppermint this time as he breathed on her. Avarie wanted to move or scoot out of his way, but she couldn't. *Jesus*, he was lying there annoying the hell out of her. She'd take a night with Kirill over this any day of the week.

"You want to know what I'm thinking, *Mishka?*" He giggled in her ear. "I'm thinking I could do anything I want to you right now." *Oh Gawd! Go Away*, she thought. "I'm thinking that I want to pull up your shirt and feel your soft nipples under my fingertips." He stretched his arm across her chest while he was still talking into her ear. It tickled and she wanted to giggle. *Damn him!* "Oh Avarie, the things I could do to you in this bed." She rolled her eyes at him. *Would you go the fuck away?* For being disgusted with her he sure wasn't acting like it.

"Fuck you." She managed to whisper as she fought against her drooping eye lids.

"*Oi*, that hurt." He said softly. "Now why would you say that?" He kissed her ear and neck. It sent shivers down her body. The fight over sleep was a losing battle. She let one eyelid drop in the hopes that the other would stay open. The door swung free and Kirill came into view. He looked pretty banged up. She was happy that she at least did a number on him. The other eye was closing slowly as he slapped Mikhail's hand away from her chest.

"I told you, no pain meds." He hissed at Mikhail.

"She was suffering. Have some humanity." He went to touch her again and Kirill slapped his hand away. "What?"

"She doesn't deserve to be touched." He didn't even give her pity as he spoke. "I hope you can hear me. I'm not very happy with you." She struggled to keep that one eye open. "You're very lucky I stopped when I did. Normal humans would be dead." Sleep was starting to take her and she didn't want to hear any more of his shit. He grabbed her chin and slapped her. "You're fucking weak and pathetic. I should take you and drop you off my balcony!"

"Do it." She softly whispered. "Do it and just leave me the fuck alone." Kirill gave Mikhail a strange look and they gazed down at her in wonder. Her eyes closed and she was asleep.

"Well, she told you." Mikhail said as he climbed out of the bed. "That mouth of hers, too." Sasha came in the room. He eyeballed both of them intensely.

"It's time for both of you to go." He motioned them out of the room. "You don't need to antagonize her, she's had enough."

Kirill walked up to him but said nothing. He stalked out the door in anger. Mikhail patted Sasha on the shoulder as he followed Kirill. "These fucking twins." He knew she was asleep and he was only talking out loud. "It's hard to know where anybody stands with them." He pulled the covers over her and shut off the light. "*Maus*, you'll sleep good tonight. I'll be right here with you." Carefully, he snugged her close. By the morning, she'd be mostly healed. Through the night, he worked his magic on her. In the morning, the twins would be in shock.

ϒϒϒ

During breakfast, Kirill joined them at the table. He took a double take when he observed that she was almost completely healed. "*Mishka*! You heal quickly." He exclaimed with delight. "Does that mean you're ready to try again?" He asked playfully.

She glanced up from her plate. "We can wait till you heal up." She said as she patted his hand gently and smiled up at him. He softly chuckled at her. She stood up when she was done and gently swept her fingers along his neck as she passed by him. Chills ran down his back from the heat of her fingertips. He walked them to the door. When Avarie went out first, Kirill mouthed a 'thank you' to Sasha. He nodded in response and followed behind her. He glanced in the hallway mirror at his reflection. Both his eyes were blackened and swollen and a cut graced his lower lip. He smiled to himself as he thought about every blow she handed him. God she was a beautifully complicated creature.

ϒϒϒ

Mikhail used this week wisely to train Avarie even harder in her hand to hand combat. There was no doubt she was fast with her jabs, but it was putting everything they learned together. At break, Avarie looked frustrated. "What's wrong?" Mikhail asked her.

Avarie hung her head low and heaved a deep sigh. "I guess I just don't understand why I have to beat Kirill is all." She sipped on her water bottle and looked away from him.

"Maybe I should've explained this before so here it is; you have to beat Kirill because you can always be disarmed. Even though he's a politician, there was a point where he too was a great warrior."

"How so?"

Mikhail busted up laughing. "I'm not going to tell you the full story. I'll save that for him. What I will tell you is that not a single Watcher will fight him hand to hand. Not even me."

Avarie threw up her hands. "Now wait a minute! If they won't fight him bare handed, why the hell am I required to do it?"

Mikhail smiled at her and pulled her back to the mat. "Because beings like you and Sasha can beat him. If you cannot beat him, you can subdue him. If you can subdue your victim long enough to get out of danger or others out of danger, you've won that battle." Avarie had her stance at the ready but brought down her arms.

"Alright. So what happens if I get others out of danger but can't do that for myself?"

"*Oi, Mishka*, this is the first time I'm hearing of you caring about being in danger. Usually you care more about others than yourself." Mikhail put his hands on his hips. "But since you asked I'll tell you; you kill your attacker."

"That's it?"

"That's it." Mikhail answered back in a matter of fact tone. "However, I don't want you to kill Kirill; I want you to subdue him. He'll know when he's down and out." He started to circle Avarie on the mat. "Watch your opponent. You'll always find weaknesses in their stance. Notice how their eyes watch you. You'll know their intentions because their eyes are the windows to their soul."

Mikhail stood in front of her and crossed his arms. "Your size is a great under-estimator. For being so small, there's the strength of two Watchers in you. You're also faster than us. I need you to remember that." He backed up from her and went back into battle stance. "So, at this point I need you to give me all you got. If you mess up remember, I'll help you through it. Don't worry about hurting me and don't hold back. Channel all your anger towards me."

He motioned for her to come at him. Quickly Avarie came at him with a blunt kick to his upper knee and used her other leg to swing into his neck. She got his knee but not his neck. Mikhail dodged her foot and grabbed it midair and flung her to the ground. She rolled back around and went for quick jabs to his face and ribs. Mikhail had a hard time holding her back. He swooped down and knocked her feet out from under her. Jumping back up, she managed to flip kick him in his chest and knock him flat on his back. She was on him so quickly; she spun around and slammed her left foot into his chest.

"*Oi, Mishka!*" Mikhail yelled as he started coughing and tapped on her foot. "That's good. Oh, that's so good." She lifted her foot off him as he struggled for air. Avarie looked spent. Her face was beet red and she dripped sweat from her forehead and body. She laid down on the mat next to him on her stomach with her head in her hands. "My god you're fast." He looked up and started smiling while holding his ribs.

Mikhail turned his head to look at her and rubbed her shoulder. Poor Avarie was panting hard and battled for some form of composure. "Just so you know that was the shortest fight of my life. That was less than a minute. You're getting better." Avarie nodded from between her hands but never looked at him. "Now the bad part is you're getting winded. Let's use some Judo in order to give you a break from moving so fast."

Avarie rolled over on her back as Mikhail stood up. "You know, I remember Valentin telling me that I'd fight other agents. Why haven't we done that yet?"

Mikhail grabbed her hand to stand her back up. "We haven't done it because you'd kill them." Avarie shot him a confused look. "Avarie, you may not realize it, but your hits come hard. If I was an ordinary man, my ribs would be broken and I wouldn't be able to stand up."

"I guess they wouldn't want me killing them." Mikhail shook his head no. "So, instead of Krav Maga, you want me to use Judo?"

"Avarie, in case you haven't noticed by now many Judo moves use throwing. It's easier to throw your opponent away from you so you get a break from jabbing, kicking, and blocking."

Mikhail readied himself again. The next three hours were spent using only Judo moves. Both Avarie and Mikhail dripped with sweat to the point they couldn't get a grip on each other anymore. By the time it was ready to call it quits, Mikhail knew Avarie would come very close to subduing Kirill.

ϓϓϓ

All week long, Kirill noticed that Avarie would flirt with him. At the table, she'd feel up his leg with her toes and act like nothing was happening. Later that day, she stood before him looked him up and down with sex in her eyes, then walked away. His cock stirred and he mentally told himself to calm down. He passed her in the hallway and she'd let a finger graze along his abdomen on her way to her room. It drove him crazy. What was her game? Did she need attention from him? He shook it off. She was getting into his head.

On the four seasons porch, he drank vodka and smoked cigars with Mikhail. "She's very flirty lately." Kirill said waving his hand in the air. "I don't understand this."

"It's complicated." Mikhail said with frustration. "I'm surprised you haven't given into her. She's very beautiful." He gulped down a swig of the vodka. "Maybe you should use your hands to feel her silky body other than to hit it." He suggested.

"You don't know how much I'd like that." Kirill chuckled. "Those green eyes stare at me in the dark." He said wistfully.

"Ah, but those eyes turn blue." Mikhail responded thoughtfully. "They change with her mood. When she's sad, they're blue, when she's angry, they glow green."

"I've never seen such eyes before." Kirill said lighting his cigar. "They can't be human, but somehow they are."

"It doesn't help that she has such thick lashes. *Mishka* doesn't need make-up at all." Mikhail exclaimed. "My God, those little breasts! So firm but so soft. Her nipples are like bright red cherries."

"You're working yourself up!" Kirill laughed at him. "*Damn you*, now you have me going." He slapped his brother's arm.

"Have you ever asked yourself why Avarie and Sasha don't have sex?" Mikhail said in wonder. "It's extremely odd to me that he hasn't ravished her yet."

Kirill was still laughing. "That's not their relationship, brother. No, theirs goes deeper than what sex can bring. They're in love with each other's souls, not the body itself."

"Sasha does love her very much doesn't he?" Mikhail relit his cigar and blew a puff in the frigid air. "She loves him too. If anything happened to one another, we're in big trouble." He cocked an eyebrow at Kirill. "We need to keep them both as safe as possible and together." He crossed his fingers. "We must be careful not to break that bond."

"I've deliberated over that myself." Kirill said leaning his head back. "They give each other strength and power. She's hurt, he heals her. His heart hurts, she opens up to him. It's very much give and take between them and they share almost everything."

"Yes, their affections run deep as the ocean." Mikhail rubbed his chin in quiet contemplation. "Love is the highest vibration in this universe and it rings deep within them both."

"We need to be more thoughtful towards Sasha. He's one of the most benevolent creatures we've ever met." He smiled to himself. "He isn't going to like us tomorrow, though."

"No he isn't." Mikhail shook his head in grief. "I've prepared her enough this week for you. She's ready to *fight*." He rubbed his hands together deviously. "I've been telling her that if she loses against you the next time, I'd take her back to Red October."

"You're so *mean*!" Kirill busted up laughing. "She holds that against us all the time."

"Oh, but she's fired up now. All she has to do this time is subdue you." They continued to drink and laugh until Mikhail left. Kirill opened her bedroom door to find both Sasha and Avarie sleeping. Poor Sasha had no covers again because Avarie kicked them off. This was a massive bed and she's so small, how the hell does she keep doing that? He thought to himself.

He went into his room, grabbed an extra comforter and put it on Sasha. He stirred awake. "Shh, go back to sleep, water sprite. She's stolen your covers again. You can keep this one." He nodded and fell back asleep. Damn women always stealing the blankets. Or they put their cold feet, hands, and asses on you. He shivered just thinking about it.

♈♈♈

Sasha was in the training room with the others. His head snapped to attention when Kirill stalked in, looking for a fight. Putting his head in his hands he kept thinking, *not again*. Avarie turned to face him and she rolled her eyes. "So soon?" She asked him.

"Of course, why you ask this?" He cocked an eyebrow at her. "You're ready aren't you?"

"I'm ready; I just thought you needed time to heal." Her hand waved up and down his body. "You do look better."

"I always look good, *Mishka*." He quipped.

"You won't today!" Mikhail yelled at him. "She's going to fuck you up!" Sasha hung his head not wanting to watch this battle. Tori stood against the wall with her arms crossed and a blank look on her face. Kirill walked up to her and got into fighting stance. Avarie gave him a sly smile and walked right up to his chest. He wondered what the hell she was doing. Mikhail and the others were wondering the same thing as her finger grazed across Kirill's chest to his belly in a slow circular motion. He shuttered and a stupid smile crossed his face.

Her finger wandered into the waistband of his pants while she kept her eyes locked on his. Those eyes spoke a thousand words. "What are you doing, *Mishka*?" He crooned. "We're supposed to be fighting."

"I have a different battle in mind." she whispered back hoarsely. Avarie jumped up and straddled him, kissing him furiously. Arms wrapped tight around his body. He grabbed her ass and took her down to the mat, flat on her back. His lips nipped her ear and neck as he panted heavily on top of her. "This isn't a fair fight!" Mikhail yelled. Kirill felt strong arms drag him off of Avarie and back into a corner.

He stood up while Mikhail was cussing and yelling at him in fast Russian. Sasha threw up his arms with wide eyes and mouthed 'what are you doing'? She mouthed back 'distraction' and gave him a wink. Tori giggled as she watched the twins argue back and forth. Kirill still had a goofy look on his face every time he pointed and glanced in Avarie's direction. Tori became excited and clapped her hands together in delight.

Mikhail walked away from Kirill and stood before Avarie. "*Mishka*, your game isn't fair to him. This is hand to hand combat, not lip to lip. Please take him out the way I trained you." He scolded her in frustration.

"You told me that I could use everything in my arsenal. This happens to be his weakness." She said moving her hands up and down her body. "He likes this." She said and slapped her own ass with a loud crack.

Mikhail's eyes were wide as he shook his head. "He can have that later if he wants. *Please*, just fight him." Kirill was rubbing his face in his hands trying to regain his composure. "Are you ready now?" He yelled at Kirill.

Strutting back over to meet Avarie on the mat, he went back into fighting stance.

"What is she doing to him?" Sasha whispered to Tori.

"She's using the art of seduction to weaken his defenses." She whispered back. "She knows that Kirill wants her and she's using it against him."

"Will she subdue him?" Sasha asked with concern.

"Maybe not, but she could at least get a few good hits in at this point." Tori said with confidence. "He's stronger than her so we'll see."

This time, the fight began in earnest. Avarie blocked many of his blows, keeping eye contact with him the entire time. She felt the sting of his hands on her ribcage, but kept going. The fight shifted between their feet and hands. He was able to grab her and throw her down on the mat in a half nelson. She got out of it by pinching the sensitive flesh inside his thigh. He yelled in pain. They rolled around on the mat, punching, kicking, and even slapping each other. Avarie was able to throw him off her several times. The fight finally ended when he pinned her down and held her there.

Mikhail clapped his hands. "Good, there was no blood this time either." Kirill lingered there staring down at her. She smiled up at him. "Get off the mat, the fights over!" Mikhail yelled. Kirill panted on top of her, debating on whether he should follow his brother's orders. She ran her fingers through his thick black hair, still smiling. She too panted hoarsely under him. The rise and fall of her chest almost drove him mad. The heat coming off her body went into his. Cupping her face, he dove in for a deep kiss. He licked her neck up and down and he felt her tremble under him.

A swift kick to his ribs brought him back to reality. "Kirill! Stop thinking with your cock!" He pointed a finger at Avarie. "You! You're a naughty little one. I'm disappointed in you." He spat as Kirill stood up and placed his hands on his ribs.

"She is naughty!" Kirill exclaimed. "But you still lost." He busted up laughing at her and headed for the locker room.

In pain, she managed to stand up. Tori and Sasha met her on the mat. "What the hell was that?" Sasha asked with scorn. "You're supposed to fight him, not fuck him."

"I tried my best." She giggled.

"Those were some beautiful moves, Avarie." Tori said with excitement. "You had him flustered and he *liked* it."

Mikhail walked up to them with purpose. "That's all good and well fighting with Kirill, but when you have to face the others, they won't be won over by *seduction*." He hissed. "You will genuinely have to fight them." He shoved her back in anger. "You lost either way." He turned on his heel and walked out.

"Wow, he's pissed." Sasha said. "You need to watch out for him today."

"He'll get over it." Avarie said as she wiped herself down with a towel. Tori was still laughing as she escorted Avarie into the locker room.

ϒϒϒ

Mikhail didn't take her back to Red October, instead he announced Saturday morning that Kirill was having a dinner party and they all had to be there instead of hiding in their rooms. Kirill joined them in the room and had boxes put down on the bed.

"What are those?" Sasha asked pointing at the boxes. "I didn't think we deserved presents." He laughed at the twins.

Mikhail patted him on the back and asked him, "Have you ever worn a tux?" He shook his head no.

"Well, today is your lucky day. You'll look stunning when we clean you up!" Mikhail busted up in laughter. "You." He said pointing at Avarie. "Tori will be here to help you dress. Yours is a little more complicated."

She opened the box and pulled out a white flowing gown. It was strapless and the fabric was silky soft. The back had laces on it like a corset. She looked it up and down with disgust and threw it back on the box. "*Mishka!*" Kirill said with discontent. "What's wrong with you? You'll be the most glamorous woman at the dinner party."

"I'm not wearing that!" She pointed down to it. "I don't do dresses." Sasha laughed at her and showed her the high heels to go with the dress. "I don't do those either!" She huffed.

Mikhail stared at her like she lost her mind. "You're a young woman! How is it that you don't wear dresses or high heels?"

She crossed her arms. "I'm just not comfortable in it." She turned her head away from them but not without an icy glare. "I'm more of a combat boots and hoodie kind of girl."

Sasha cracked a smile. "*Maus*, if I have to wear a tux, you have to wear a dress." They argued with her for over half an hour. She finally gave in just so they would leave her alone.

"What's the occasion for the dinner party?" Avarie asked haughtily.

Kirill took her hand in his. "It's for you and Sasha. It's tradition for new agents to have a coming out party for the politicians. Especially if the agents are damn good."

"Can't we just hide in the shadows like vampires or something? I thought FSB agents were supposed to be a secret." Avarie said.

"No! You're not a vampire and you thrive on daylight. And you're your status with the FSB is supposed to be secret. However, there are certain politicians who do know about you and want to meet you in person. Now Tori will be here within the hour. Sasha, we'll help you get ready. I don't want Tori alone with you for too long." Mikhail said with laughter in his voice. "You wouldn't have a chance to put it on."

"I'm curious, how is it that she's your niece?" Avarie asked them.

"Well, if you must know, her parents were FSB agents who died in action while in the States. We adopted her and raised her ourselves." Mikhail answered. "We sent her to the best boarding schools. She wasn't the only one, she had a brother too. But he died in a car accident. He drank too much vodka."

"That's sad."

"It is, he was her twin and she's felt his loss deeply." Mikhail shrugged. "He was a womanizer and he loved his booze."

Sasha shook his head. "I'm sure he learned that from you both."

"*Oi*, Sasha." Kirill shook his head. "That hurt." Laughter erupted from all of them. Tori did show up within the hour. She asked why she couldn't help Sasha get ready. Mikhail told her because she couldn't behave herself when she was around Sasha and she pouted at him.

"Tori, you're staying the night anyway. You need to wait until after the dinner party to molest your water demon." Kirill laughed so hard, he almost fell over.

"Hold up!" Avarie threw her hands in the air. "Where the *hell* am I sleeping then?"

"*Mishka*, we didn't forget about you." Kirill answered. "I have a nice warm bed across the hall." He gestured towards the door. "You'll sleep soundly there."

"Wonderful." She said sarcastically and folded her arms over her chest. "I don't think you have sleeping on your mind."

"Maybe not. We'll see how much I drink." He threatened with mischief in his eyes. Leading Sasha out of the room with his stuff they closed the door.

"Wow, I've never seen him like this. That fight really turned him on yesterday!" Tori said as she pulled the stuff from her bag. "He's really into you." Avarie busted up laughing. It was strange the thought of being with two brothers...especially twins.

"I hope you like the dress I picked out for you."

"I'm not a dress kind of girl." Avarie said.

Tori looked her up and down. "You wait till you put it on; you'll change your mind. When all the men stare at you, it'll get your heart pumping." She said with excitement and a growl in her voice.

"My God, you thrive on sex don't you?" Avarie joked.

"Oh Avarie, your Sasha is one that I could thrive on for the rest of my life." A fiery hunger rang in her voice. "I don't understand how you don't touch him."

"It's easy." She said as Tori started to work on her hair. "We don't have that kind of relationship."

Tori tisked her with a finger. "For shame. You're missing out."

Tons of girl talk ensued. They heard laughter coming from Kirill's room. "I think they're messing with Sasha." Avarie said.

"They have deep respect for him you know. Don't be surprised when they start treating him like one of their own."

An hour later, a knock came at the door. Tori answered and allowed the men in. Sasha was a whole different man in a tux. It was all black for the exception of his button down shirt under the blazer. All it did was accentuate his handsome features. Tori looked him up and down with desire. "My God. Leave him here with me for a few minutes."

"Tori, we just got his tie straightened." Mikhail laughed. "You keep your hands off him." He slapped her away. "Where's Avarie?" He asked while looking around the room.

"I'm not going!" She yelled from the bathroom.

"You come out here now!" Kirill yelled impatiently. "We're going to be late."

The room was blanketed in silence. Tori smiled over at them. "She's embarrassed." Tori tried to coax her out.

"Avarie, if you don't come out, I'll break down the door!" Kirill yelled again.

"Promise not to laugh?"

"*Mishka*, there is nothing funny about you. Come out."

The door opened and she stepped out. Hearts stopped beating around the room. Tori had to close their mouths for them as she giggled. The dress hugged her curves and exposed her toned shoulders. It reached to the floor and the fabric was light and soft. Both girls looked exquisite. The twins and Sasha wore the dumbest looks on their faces.

"What?" Avarie asked self-consciously. "Do I look that bad?"

"*Oi, Mishka*, you look radiant." Mikhail said in shock. "You're going to turn heads tonight."

"She's already turned mine." Kirill rubbed his hands together with delight.

"Stop it!" Tori grabbed Avarie's shawl. "Perverts!" They laughed and walked out the door.

ϒϒϒ

The limo arrived at their destination. It was a large building with old Russian architecture. A man took their belongings and ushered them in. They already discussed what was going to happen in the limo to put Avarie at ease. Tori would stay by Avarie to keep her comfortable. She helped her mingle and introduced her to new people. The twins never let her far out of their sight.

A warm hand touched her arm. It was Mikhail. "There's somebody here who would like to meet you, *Mishka*." He led her away from Tori. He walked her gingerly towards an elderly gentleman. "Avarie, this is our Russian President Konstantin." She took his hand and he held firm.

"I've heard much about you, Miss Avarie." He kissed it tenderly. "Have the twins been good to you?"

She cracked a smile. "Not really. They're kind of mean." She joked.

He laughed heartily. "That they are. It's all for a purpose." She liked this guy. He felt kind hearted and his voice was light. "I heard you had Kirill all flustered in training the other day." He winked at her.

"I fluster him all the time. It's nothing new between us." She smiled slyly at him. Damn, he looked so familiar. "Have we met before?" She asked curiously. "I feel like I know you."

"I feel the same." His eyes twinkled. "Dinner will be served soon, but before we go, I'd like to introduce you to my family." He waved a man and two women over. "This is my mistress, Abigail." She shook her hand. "This is my daughter in law, Maria and this is my son Viktor." Avarie looked up and took his hand. Her eyes went from him to his wife. *Oh shit.*

"Nice to meet you." She said trying to hide her surprise. Mikhail chuckled and saved her by leading the way to the dining room. It didn't make her feel much better knowing that she was sitting at the same table as Viktor and his wife. The twins broke up her awkwardness by telling stories about her and Sasha's training while sipping a sweet and dry white wine. Avarie looked around the massive room. Tori was right, Avarie was turning heads. Some people spoke and looked in her direction. She quickly turned around to avoid their gazes.

Dinner was served and she ate in silence, only answering questions that were asked of her. Thank God the twins sat on either side. Tori's eyes continually swept across Sasha as if she'd devour him at any minute. Avarie could tell she couldn't wait to get him alone. The look on his face told the same story.

Avarie found out that Maria was a nurse and Viktor worked security for his dad and Kirill. The twins coaxed stories from Konstantin about fighting in the States. Avarie listened as he told tall tales from a war many ages ago.

"What was Pandora like?" Maria asked.

Konstantin glanced at Avarie. "She was a fiery bitch from Hell and I loved it!" He said in voluptuous excitement. "Wherever she went, Hell came with her. That bike of hers warned everybody of her coming. Oh the stunts she'd pull on it." He wiped his brow. The twins were chuckling and Mikhail was nudging her in the ribs. "She was a force to be reckoned with."

"So you slept with her then?" Mikhail asked with wide eyes. Remembering where he was, he looked at his mistress and she waved him on with enthusiasm.

"Boys, let me tell you, I learned a few tricks from her. She was as limber as an acrobat and devious as a cougar." He almost stood up from his chair and yelled. "I could bend her legs behind her head she was so flexible." The booze must be getting to him.

Avarie lost it and busted up laughing. She almost fell back on her chair but Kirill caught her. She couldn't imagine this old man in the sack with a woman like that. "What's so funny Avarie?" Kirill asked in a giggle.

"You're working this old man up! He's going to have a heart attack if you don't stop." Avarie couldn't control her laughter.

Konstantin sipped on his wine. "You remind me of her you know. You even look like her."

"Don't get any ideas old man, I'd wreck you." She gave him a sly grin. The entire table erupted in even more laughter. Now she was starting to see why he was so familiar. She knew him but couldn't remember him.

"I'd die a happy man." He exclaimed. Abigail slapped his arm and giggled.

"Well, I know who Avarie is going home with tonight." Mikhail joked and looked over at Kirill. "We'll see you at your funeral, Konstantin." He held up his glass. Avarie shook her head at him with disgust.

After dessert the band played. Tori pulled Sasha out on the floor. She led him in a slow dance as Avarie watched on from her seat. Everybody was dancing but her. Her system flooded with sadness. This reminded her of the night with Courtney when he took her out. He wasn't here to dance with her. It didn't matter, she didn't dance well anyway and she didn't want to step on toes. She'd be too embarrassed.

There was a tap on her shoulder. She turned to see Viktor. Damn this boy was handsome. "Would you like to dance?" He asked. She hesitated. Maybe it was alright. It wasn't like they were at Red October and had to perform again.

He took her hand as she stood up and eyes followed her to the floor. He put her hands behind his head while resting his on her hips. Viktor swayed her tenderly to the sounds of the soft stringed instruments. She looked over at his wife and found her dancing with Mikhail.

"I'm sorry about the other night." Avarie said with shame. "I had no clue."

"Don't worry about it." He waved her off. "It was very exciting for me."

"I didn't know you were married."

"I've been married for a little over a year now." He said without concern.

Avarie's voice dropped to a whisper. "Does she know what happened?"

"No, she was at work that night and I never told her." He smiled and winked. "Besides, she doesn't need to know. It'll be our secret." Wonderful, in her past life, she screwed his dad, and in this one, she did his son. Oh God how she hated karma right now.

The song was done. Konstantin wanted a dance and she obliged. He looked her up and down excitedly. "My God, you really are beautiful." He said with the twinkle in his eye.

"Easy old man." She said smiling up at him. "Your excitement gives you away." She said as she pressed herself into him. His eyes grew wide. Man she was good, she thought.

He danced her around the entire floor. Her curiosity got to her. "Konstantin, I know that Pandora had three children and a husband. Did something happen to him?"

His eyes changed to sadness and he hesitated to answer. She implored him with her eyes. "Avarie, her husband was killed along with the rest of her family. He was her second husband. The first two children weren't his, but the youngest was. The elite blackmailed him and he turned on her. He tried to take off with the youngest, but it was too late. They came and killed them all." Her heart shattered into tiny little pieces that pierced inside her ribcage. She couldn't breathe. Quickly, he escorted her to the open air balcony. "Breathe child." He coaxed. "Maybe I should've left that sad tale alone." He rubbed her back.

The cold air lifted up her dress and snowflakes melted on her skin. When it turned to water from the heat of her body, the droplets ran down her bare arms. "I'm sorry." She whispered. "I shouldn't have asked."

He turned her to face him. "Avarie that was another life." He winked at her. "There's no need to carry the past around with you now." *Oh shit, he knew. That sly bastard.*

"How'd you know?" She whispered.

He let out a hearty laugh. "The twins showed me a picture of you. You were all over the internet on your bike you know? I knew instantly you were back." He rubbed his hands. "Kirill described you to me a few times not knowing any better thinking that I lost my memory." He shook his head. "Are you alright now?"

"Yea, but I have one more question." He nodded. "Did we really sleep together?"

His smile grew wide. "Oh yes. You were a passionate one and I'll leave it at that."

"Wow, we must've had some good times together."

"Oh we did." He chuckled to himself. He motioned for them to go back inside. As she turned she stopped. An evil crept up on her and her eyes swept the landscape. Konstantin snapped her out of it, asking if she was okay.

"He's here." She said to him with panic. "He wasn't supposed to get in." He waved Kirill over to see Avarie.

Kirill hushed her. Konstantin asked who he was and Kirill explained. "That evil son of a bitch." Konstantin shook with rage. "He has the balls to disturb our night."

"Calm yourself, he isn't in the building." Kirill assured him. Avarie looked for him in the shadows. Her eyes moved up and saw him. He was on top of a building looking down.

"He's up there." Avarie said without looking at Kirill. "He's watching us."

Kirill looked up and waved with a smile and then flipped him off. The man turned and left. "Did he see me?" She asked.

"No, he's spying on us, not you. He was too drugged up to remember you anyway."

"Ah, was that at the Red October?" Konstantin asked.

"How the hell does he know about that?" Avarie snapped her head at Kirill.

"What did Viktor tell you?" He asked Konstantin.

"Just that he met Avarie." He winked at her and whispered, "He said you were a wonderful kisser."

With a heavy sigh, she walked away from them both as they laughed. Mikhail caught her, pulling them to the dance floor. She updated him on what she saw. "Fuck him." Was all he said. She looked around for Tori and Sasha but didn't see them. "Easy *Mishka*. They're still here. He better have his bow tie on straight when we see him." He was in a good mood.

They were spotted ten minutes later sitting at their table. Sasha's face was flushed and Tori had her hands all over him. *God, they're like teenagers*, she thought. Mikhail introduced her to more people and he helped her mingle. She met so many politicians and FSB people; she had no clue how to remember them all.

The night ended and they headed back. Viktor and Konstantin joined them in the limo after they bid good night to their ladies. Tori smiled at her with a knowing look. They all sat in the four season's porch, smoking cigars and drinking vodka. Mikhail was messing with Avarie. "So, *Mishka* you ready to go back to Red October?" He busted up laughing as she gave him an icy glare.

The boys were getting drunk along with Sasha. Tori sat on his lap, drinking from their vodka bottle. She was becoming feisty with him and he seemed to enjoy it. Avarie flushed at the thought of them getting it on. She lost her high heel shoes a long time ago, thrown in the foyer along with her combat boots because her feet hurt. A fire burned in the old pot belly stove as the men told stories and laughed.

Avarie grew tired. She had enough to drink and wanted to go to bed. The twins told her she wasn't allowed yet. "You guys are assholes." She exclaimed. "Why don't you both go fuck yourselves."

"Wow, she's got a mouth on her." Konstantin blurted out. "I can only imagine the things you say to these two."

"*Oi*, you should hear her rage. Right now, it's just the exhaustion talking." Kirill laughed. "Tori and Sasha can go upstairs if they want. She's itching for him. Look at that display." Tori flipped him off and continued to kiss on Sasha's ear. "Tori, if we wanted a show, we'd be at Red October right now."

"What the hell, is that your running gag now?" Avarie stood up laughing.

The twins motioned for her to sit back down as Tori and Sasha left. "Language little one." Kirill said. "You want the belt again, all you need to do is ask." She slapped his shoulder.

Konstantin swirled his vodka around in his mouth. "What's this with a belt?" He asked Mikhail

"She likes getting slapped with it. She loves the pain." He said with wide eyes. "It gets her excited."

My God, these guys aren't holding anything back tonight. "I'm going to bed." She stood up and passed by Mikhail. He grabbed her arm and escorted her back to her seat. "Fine, can I at least go to the bathroom?" He thought about it with a devious grin on his face.

"Fine, but Viktor takes you and escorts you back." He waved her off and she went. Viktor waited outside the door for her. When she opened it he busted in. Picking her up he set her on the sink and she knew what was about to happen and she stopped him cold.

"Viktor, you're married. We can't do this." Her hand was on his chest, holding him back. Oh this man was handsome. She wanted to kiss him so bad, but it was wrong.

"*Mishka*, just one kiss and I'll leave you alone." He whispered. She shook her head no. "Why not? You had no problems the other night at the club."

"Viktor, I was doing what I was told so we stayed out of danger. I didn't know it would go that far." She tried to explain. "Your dad is out there right now."

"But I loved it. You were fantastic." He leaned in and kissed her hard. He pulled back. "He doesn't care really. He won't tell anybody." She gave in and kissed him gently while brushing her hands through his hair. "Now see, that's all I wanted. If you want more you know where to find me." He winked.

He escorted her back to the porch. Snow was softly falling outside. The flakes reflected the light of the room. "What took so long?" Kirill asked.

"I had to poop!" Avarie said loudly. They busted up laughing, almost falling out of their chairs. Viktor told his dad that it was time to go. When they left Kirill said good night to Mikhail and took Avarie to his room.

"I want to see you take off that dress." He said slurring in his Russian accent. "I want to watch it fall to the floor."

"Really Kirill, you're too drunk for me right now." She shook a finger at him. "Besides, I can't undo the back." He turned on the gas fireplace. It wasn't long before the room warmed up a bit. His stance said that he wasn't going to let up. "Fine, but you have to undo the back."

He turned her around and undid the strings. She turned and let the dress sink to the floor. "*Mishka*, you have me so excited, I don't know what to do with myself." Her chest was bared and the only thing under the dress was her white lace panties.

"It's called sleep. You know what that is right?" She joked with him.

"You've been flirting with me all week. I think you've been a very bad girl." He started to pull off his bow tie and take off his blazer. "You deserve to be ravished for your teasing."

Oh he isn't joking, she thought. She was going to get it tonight. "Wait a minute. Maybe I want to take your clothes off for you?" She said with a sly grin. He dropped his hands and let her slowly remove all his clothes. His bow tie was thrown in a corner while the rest of his clothes were thrown over a chair.

She looked him over in the fire light. His now hazel eyes smiled at her seductively. The light from the fire accentuated every feature of his body. He had thick eye lashes and soft lips. He grew somewhat of a beard for her. His hand reached behind her head and let the clips holding up her hair fall unto the floor, releasing her mane on her shoulders. Running his hands through it, he pulled her slowly into himself. "*Mishka*, you have no clue what you do to me." He whispered hoarsely to her.

He gently picked her up and laid her on his bed. He slid her panties off and threw them to the floor. *Oh this was really happening*, she thought. Even if she didn't want it this would be forced upon her sooner or later. She took deep breaths to calm herself. He covered her body with his and shrouded her with slow lingering lips. He started from her head and very carefully, worked his way down to her feet. He held her right foot against his chest and chuckled. "Look at these long toes! My goodness, you could scale a tree."

She smiled. "Matthias said I could choke a small child with those toes."

"He wasn't wrong." He played with them and it tickled.

"Would you stop, you're tickling me." He did and worked his way back up to her. Whatever he was doing was working. Sensations of pleasure bathed inside her core and she became extremely aware of her body. The heat from him melted its way into her. She moaned when he came back to her neck. His cock laid on her belly and he pressed it into her, teasing her with its presence. Her arms moved along his back, feeling every curve of his muscles. She opened her legs beckoning him in. His lips met hers once again as he laid tiny kisses along her bottom lip. He was driving her crazy. When he wanted to be he was soft. He cupped her left breast in his hand and kneaded it gently. Avarie leaned her head back and his lips caught her chin. It was becoming harder to remain in control; her breaths were shallow as he touched her slippery nether lips. "You're so ready for me."

She found his member and it throbbed in her hand. He moaned while biting down on her lip. "I think you're ready for me too." She whispered hoarsely. She stroked him gently and he responded by moving with her hand. "Tell me you want me." She whispered in his ear as she suckled on it. "Tell me you'll be gentle." She kissed the side of his face, letting her lips linger in his sensitive areas. His breaths became shallower and he pinched and pulled softly at her nipple with his fingers.

"*Mishka*, I'll tell you anything you want." His eyes met hers. "I'll tell you things that could only be whispered in the dark. I'll tell you how your presence stirs the shadows within my soul." She watched as his eyes started to turn green and he whispered softly. "Avarie, I'd fight off every force that would come after you with my entire being. I'll shield you from every storm that threatens to rain upon your soul. If I had wings, I'd carry you back up to the heavens and place you where you belong."

Avarie was blown away. He said the most beautiful things to ever come out of his mouth and it stirred within her soul. "So the short answer; yes I want you and yes, I'll be gentle." That's it he won a piece of her heart.

She softly sucked on his bottom lip, running her tongue back and forth across it. He gathered her body in his arms to hold her close. Avarie felt his heart racing against her chest. He lingered on her neck and worked his way down to her breasts. He tugged and nipped at hard peaks of her nipples with his teeth. She brought her hips up, letting him know she was ready. Her pants came faster as he grabbed a condom and put it on. "I don't mean to be unromantic, but you have me very worked up and I plan on lasting a bit." He whispered in her ear.

Within seconds, he slowly worked his way inside her. His strokes were long and he buried himself to the hilt. She shuddered under him as he held her. Moaning in her ear he let his lips linger upon her. He was so big she felt every inch stretch her walls. She was very wet and it only enthralled him more. He covered her with more kisses and stayed at one pace. Giving her a sly grin, he found her hard clit and rubbed gently in circular motions. Intense pleasure spread like a wave over her body. She felt every inch of his body with her fingertips. He sucked on one of her fingers as she rubbed them across his lips. His warm wet tongue rolled over it and passed up and down.

Rising up, she sucked on his right nipple while playing with the other. "Oh *Mishka*, if you keep doing that, you're going to make me come. Give me time to enjoy you." He pleaded. She let up but ran her lips across his chest. His strokes were still long and slow but he worked her clit faster. She couldn't hold on anymore. She grabbed the back of his head and brought him to her chest. Moans escaped her lips as her core exploded. Wetness leaked from her and ran down her thighs and bed. He kept going and so did her orgasm. She tried to buck against him, but he held his ground. He felt her contract against his member. "Oh *Mishka*." He moaned into her neck. "You feel so good." He started to buck into her harder and she held on for dear life as shock waves rocked over her body. He buried his head into her neck. Sweat from his skin poured down onto her. It wasn't just sweat it was tears. He moaned loudly as he came into her. She shuttered underneath him, still panting from being so sensitive. He let out a desperate moan and collapsed onto her body.

She turned her head to him. She was right, he was crying. Tenderly, she wiped his tears away as he still shook on top of her. His face remained buried into her neck and she stroked his hair. It was a while before she caught her breath. He inhaled and exhaled softly into her and she realized he was asleep. She smiled to herself and shifted to pull him out of her. As strange as it was, she pulled the condom off gently and whipped it into the trash. He stirred and kissed her neck softly. Using her feet, she pulled up the covers. He was so warm and soft it was like he melted into her. Kissing his forehead, she fell asleep with him covering her body.

ϒϒϒ

Kirill woke up from a groggy sleep. He almost didn't remember where he was until the fog cleared from his mind. He laid a kiss on Avarie's cheek and quietly removed himself from the bed. She was still out somewhere in dreamland. He stared down at her from beside the bed and studied every inch of her body while he picked up the phone to have the chef bring them something to eat.

In the bathroom, he cleaned himself up and splashed water on his face. As he was brushing the film of liquor and cigar residue off his teeth, he gazed in the mirror and stopped. Leaning closer, he looked at his eyes. They were almost the color of gold. *What the fuck*? He thought. He shook it off throwing the toothbrush back in its holder.

He wondered if the other two were awake. He threw on boxers and went to their door. He could hear the headboard banging against the wall and Tori moaning. "Perverts!" he said to himself. He knocked on the door. "If you guys want food you better tell me now." Silence. "I'll have it sent to your room."

"That's fine. Now go away!" Tori yelled. "I'm busy."

He stalked into his room and called the chef back. Sometime in his departure, Avarie shifted to her belly. Running a hand across one of her ass cheeks he was tempted to slap it. He smiled to himself and decided better of it. He busied himself with his work tablet until the food arrived.

He woke her up so she could eat. She stirred like a sleepy child. "Morning *Mishka*, you need to eat." He crooned softly. "I think I wore you out last night."

She sat up slowly against the headboard, pulling the covers to her body. "I think you wore yourself out last night."

"What do you expect after four rounds of sex?" He teased.

She squinted her eyes at him and started laughing. "It was only one round and you passed out."

"Don't lie to me, *Mishka*. I know I'm a ferocious lover." He growled at her.

Going to the trash, she picked up the spent condom with a bit of disgust. "Does this answer your question?"

He busted up laughing. "Fine, I won't argue with you. I see you have the proof in your hand."

Setting up the food, she went to the bathroom to wash up. They ate on in silence. Avarie looked like she contemplated something deeply. "What's on your mind?" he asked.

She popped a morsel of fruit in her mouth and chewed. "I think you have an angel inside you."

Kirill gave her a quizzical look. "An angel you say?" She nodded. "How so?"

"You were the sweetest man last night." She said smiling as she drank her juice. "You said things to me that nobody has ever said. Oh, and your eyes changed colors." He shifted uncomfortably in his spot. Avarie decided not to push it. "I should go shower." She pushed her empty plate towards him and jumped off the bed. In his bathroom, she turned on the shower. Maybe it was just a farce, she thought. The notion upset her as she let the sprays of water run down her body. His bathroom was set up just like hers. A huge glass shower stall, a seven foot soaking tub, toilet, and pedestal sink.

Avarie washed her hair. Leaning back she closed her eyes. Opening them back up, she saw Kirill in the shower with her. It startled her. "I don't need you stealing all the hot water." Playfully, he scooted her to the side. He was so tall and well built; she shivered when the tiny droplets hit her body since he was blocking the water.

He smiled as he soaped up his thick black hair. "Maybe you should wash my back for me?" He suggested chuckling.

She busted up laughing. "You're so tall; I'd only get to your ass."

"Oh *Mishka*, I'd let you touch my ass." He winked at her. "It's a very nice ass."

Avarie sighed deep and shivered. "I can see that." She reached behind him, placing both hands on each cheek and squeezed. Then she slapped it, hard.

"*Oi* that hurt." He proclaimed. "You're a naughty girl. Don't get me excited." He wiggled his finger at her. "It would be hard to take you in the shower."

"You're right. I'm already cleaned up and that would just mean that I'd have to shower again." She turned to walk out. He grabbed her elbow to pull her back in. Avarie really didn't want to do this. Kirill released her as she backed herself up against the shower glass. Her eyes followed every line of his body. The tattoo that stretched from wrist to wrist was identical to Mikhail's.

"Kirill, if I ask you a question will you answer me honestly?" Avarie crossed her arms around her chest and slunk down to the bottom of the shower. He nodded as he washed his hair. "Mikhail said that no Watcher would ever take you on in hand to hand combat. Why?"

Both hands were in his hair as he washed the shampoo out. Kirill chewed on the inside of his cheeks deep in thought. "Mishka, what we are is complicated to most humans. It should be no secret to you by now that there are different ranks of us." Avarie nodded in agreement. "The short answer is that Mikhail and I are what some religions would call Arch angels. We are warriors and the original Watchers are exactly what they are....Watchers. They weren't trained as deftly as we were. No matter what, your body is your weapon. This is why it's so important you fight hand to hand. You understand?" Avarie nodded. "Do you have more questions?"

Avarie pulled her knees to her chest and looked away. Gently he coaxed her on. "I guess this doesn't really pertain to Watchers but, why is this place so intact when the States are a total disaster?"

Kirill washed the soap off his body and sat down next to her. "I know Courtney made you study history. However, I think we took you before you really gotten into what happened to the States. How far did you get?"

"The 2016 election." She answered.

"*Oi*! That's when a lot of things have really changed for the States. So, you didn't read about a man named Donald Trump then?" She shook her head no. "Alright, well, the Americans were very pissed off at their government and had enough. The cost of living was high and wages weren't enough for people to have a decent living. This man named Donald Trump ran for president and won against Hilary Clinton. Ah, 2016 was a shitty year for all involved."

"So what happened?"

"What happened was revolution! It wasn't to the point of armed revolution, but the divide and conquer was so bad Americans fought against each other. Now, Donald Trump wasn't the perfect man, but he made great relations with us Russians. He wasn't stupid by any means. When the Elite figured out that he was fighting them tooth and nail, that's when the shit hit the fan."

"It all started there?"

"It sure did. It's the reason why you were targeted. You were a writer and I'm surprised you haven't searched for yourself on the internet yet." Kirill chuckled. "The Elites started turning the people against themselves and when people like you figured it out, that's when they came for you."

Avarie pulled into herself tighter. Kirill knew from her body language that this was turning uncomfortable for her. "Enough about you." He patted her leg. "The UN brought in their blue hats and Russia armed the militia *and* the Natives. Believe me when I say we had a good hand. However, the Elite fire bombed the living hell out of the US. Food ran low and it was a literal apocalypse. It still is from what you seen I guess. There are only select cities that are running full force. With the help of technology the Elite were able to create humans that wouldn't fight back."

Avarie stood up to shut off the shower. "Should I finish the story before we get out?" She nodded hesitantly. "Anyway, this part of the world managed to stay intact because it's easier to fight your enemy in your territory than theirs. Technically speaking, the Elite don't belong anywhere. Do you understand?"

"Im not sure what you mean by that." Avarie admitted as she stepped out and grabbed a towel.

Kirill followed suit and grabbed his towel. "What I mean is the Elite are interlopers. We are creatures not of this world, Avarie. None of us belong here. The original Watchers have no real home so they invade others and bend them to their will. However, they didn't win here, nor in Europe."

"Because of you?"

Kirill shook his head as dried off. "Not just because of Mikhail and I. It's mainly because of the mentality of the people. When the Muslims started to invade in the 2010's, the people fought back and won their culture and heritage back. Russia included. We helped change the way things were run. Have you noticed that there's no homeless people here? How about murders? As many times as you've been out and about, think about how many times you've seen actual violence. You won't find it here because Russia and the rest of Europe have changed its tune. No one goes without. We are all stronger together than separate."

Avarie pulled on yoga pants and a hoodie when she came out of the bathroom. Kirill watched her as she laid back down on the bed. "Fair enough."

As Kirill slipped on a t-shirt and sweatpants he added, "The rabbit hole goes much deeper, *Mishka*. However, it would take many lifetimes to know all this information." He joined her on the bed. "None of this happened over night. The Elite are very patient and have been doing this for thousands of years. Their protocol is passed down from generation to generation."

The next question from Avarie came completely out of left field for Kirill. "So is this your true form?" she asked waving her hand across his body.

"*Oi, Mishka!*" Kirill became extremely flustered. "Why would you ask such a question?"

"Because you said you aren't from this world!" Avarie answered defensively. "So if you aren't from here what are you?"

Kirill flipped to his back and rubbed his hands against his face in frustration. He pursed his lips together in a desperate attempt to either dodge the question or answer it truthfully. "Kirill!"

"Alright. The answer is no this isn't our true form."

"Then what is it?"

"Let's just say if you saw our true form you'd be running out of the room." Avarie slapped his chest hard. "Okay! I guess you could say we're like lizard people."

Avarie cocked an eyebrow at him in confusion. "Care to elaborate?"

"No I don't."

It was Avarie's turn to be frustrated. "Seriously Kirill! How am I to understand the enemy if you can't tell me what the hell I'm dealing with?"

"Because we come in different forms, Avarie!" Kirill yelled. "Now can we please drop it?" Avarie could tell Kirill was angry. It was the last thing she wanted but she needed answers. "You want to really know?" Avarie nodded. "Fine." Kirill stood up from the bed and took off his shirt. "Just remember you asked for this and you don't get to look away."

He backed up to the fireplace and took off his sweatpants. Avarie watched as he transformed before her eyes. His feet grew bigger and longer with black talons at the ends. His already sculpted body doubled up to reveal massive muscles and scales appeared all over his body that seemed to glow grey. His hands grew sharp talons just like his feet. However the biggest change wasn't in his actual body, it was his face. Kirill's brown eyes turned red and his tongue forked out with scales all over.

He started to scrunch up his body as if he was in pain. Suddenly he let out a sharp yell as strange leathery wings grew from his shoulder blades, taking up the entire expanse of the room. From his black hair emerged two stubby black horns and spikes emerged from his shoulders. Just when Avarie thought the transformation was done, she was wrong. She couldn't turn away as he grew another two feet and his facial features changed to a more lizard like appearance. His ears disappeared into his head and his hair was completely gone.

Avarie's heart thumbed so hard inside her chest she believed it was possible to break a rib. Kirill stood before her a completely different being. She started to shake as he slowly stepped closer to her. She willed herself to calm down. He stared down at her in the bed and she noticed his eyes blink. Once up and down and once sideways. "I see you're not looking away." He hissed. Avarie shook her head no. "Do I scare you?" Avarie nodded as she tried to build up her courage. A smile crossed his thin lips. "Just so you know the ladies of our kind find me very attractive."

She couldn't help it, Avarie busted up laughing. She laughed even harder and he folded in his wings to reveal a lizard like tail when he turned around. "*Oi*, why are you laughing at me?" Avarie stood up from the edge of the bed and ran her fingers across his body and found his tail. She pulled on it and swung it around in her hands. "*Mishka*! You never touch a man's tale!" His tongue darted in and out of his mouth as he snatched his tail from her hands and Avarie lost it. She was laughing so hard she had to hold onto a chair for support.

Between breathes she asked, "Can you fly?"

"Yes I can fly!"

"Can you take me?"

"No!" Kirill yelled. "Here I'm thinking I'd scare the shit out of you. Look at you laughing at me and asking me to take you flying!" He shook his head. "You're full of surprises!"

Avarie stumbled around furniture trying to get at his wings. Kirill stood impatiently as she ran her hands along the leathery surface. They were soft, warm, and strong. She rubbed her face against his wing to feel the smooth velvet against her skin. Where ever she could touch, she did. Grabbing a chair she stood on it to feel the sharp spikes on his shoulders. "Are you done?" Avarie shook her head no. Kirill smiled at her to reveal fangs.

"Are you poisonous?" She reached towards his face but he turned away.

"I'm not a damn serpent."

"You look like one." She stuck out her tongue to mimic a snake. He turned his head back towards her and licked her ear. "Eww!" She scrunched up her face and continued to laugh. "Wow, I think I like you like this!" Avarie's eyes were wide with excitement. Kirill shook his head no. "Why not?"

"Because we'd scare ordinary people."

"So how is it you're able to look human?"

"When you're what we are, we're able to adapt to our environments. Think of our kind like chameleons." Being careful of his spikes, Avarie wrapped her arms around his neck. With his left hand he lifted her off the chair and placed her back on the bed. "Can I change back now?"

Avarie crossed her arms in defeat. "Fine."

"Just so you know, this takes a lot out of me. If Mikhail were here, this would be different."

"Whys that?"

Carefully turning around he answered, "As my twin he makes the process easier. Technically speaking, you're only seeing half of me." Avarie decided to leave it alone. Now she understood why they were so much alike. It wasn't the fact that they were twins, but they were conjoined in some way. "*Oi*, before I change back, would you like to see a trick?" Avarie nodded enthusiastically. He coughed and cleared his throat. All of a sudden he opened his mouth and flames shot out. "You like that?"

"That is so freaking *cool*." Avarie clapped with glee. "Okay, you can change back now."

"Well, with your permission…" Within minutes he was back to his human form. He didn't bother putting on his shirt or sweatpants as he crawled back into bed. "Now I'm worn out."

Avarie pulled the covers over him and kissed his shoulder. "Thank you." She whispered.

"That's the only show you get for a long time." He wrapped an arm around her and pulled her close. "Nothing scares you does it?"

Avarie snuggled closer into him. "Oh you have no clue what scares me." she answered. She wasn't sure he heard her as Kirill was already asleep.

CHAPTER FOURTEEN

Matthias spent hours on the pod. Within a month Eva had every training available to her. Dear God she was turning into a badass. No way would she be at the level of Avarie but she came damn close. He could only imagine what the twins were doing with her. He shuddered at the thought. In the training room, Ivan was working with Eva on her combat skills. The FSB trained him to be an expert fighter. Matthias decided to join them today and have a break from his workshop.

In his workout gear he sat at the mat as Ivan sparred with Eva. What a sight they were; two red heads going at it. He laughed to himself. He never thought he'd see the day.

"What's so funny?" Eva turned to him.

He grinned at her. "It's just that I'd never seen two ginger's fight against each other."

Ivan busted up. *Man this guy is cool*, Matthias thought. "Why don't you get yourself some then?" Eva said, motioning for him to come join them on the mat.

"Oh honey, I had some last night remember?" He joked. Ivan had to walk away and laugh somewhere in a corner. She beckoned him forward. "Alright, let's see what you got."

He stood next to her and without warning, she threw a punch and it landed square in his jaw. Wow, he couldn't remember the last time he saw stars. He regained his balance as the pain radiated into his temple. She was in fighting stance this time. Her eyes burned ready for the fight. Matthias threw a punch and she blocked. He jabbed, only making contact once. Ivan watched as their fight seemed to dance around. Eva swung her arms and rotated on her heals. She was getting much better and it showed. Matthias was able to eventually throw her off of him. He called an end to the fight.

Matthias was drenched in sweat. He pulled off his shirt and toweled off. His jaw and ribs hurt like crazy. Ivan looked him up and down in curiosity. "Matthias, have you ever fought two people at the same time?" He asked. *Oh shit*, Matthias thought. The look in Ivan's face was a tad bit devious.

"Are you asking me if I want to fight you and Eva?"

"Why not? It would be fun." Matthias put his hands on his head. "Well?"

"Fine. Just don't kill me." Ivan allowed him and Eva a rest. When they were ready they met on the mat. Ivan came at him first and he had to block. Eva got him in the jaw and ribs. Both pushed him back, trying to subdue him. Courtney stood at the doorway watching as the most epic kung Fu fight in history was taking place in his cellar. With a few moves, Matthias was able to push them back. This was getting gritty with Ivan throwing in some dirty Judo. Matthias had blood streaming from his face and chest. There was a point where it was all elbows and knees with these three. Ivan blew Matthias in the chest with an elbow and knee at the same time. He got Ivan back with a spin kick to the face. Eva became collateral damage with a backhand under her knee, taking her feet out from under her. She took herself out of the fight after that.

It was between Matthias and Ivan now. Matthias got in a few good strikes, but he was worn down. This was getting brutal, Courtney thought as he shook his head. Ivan was shaking blood off his body with a cool ease. There were so many spin kicks Courtney was becoming dizzy just watching. Eventually, Ivan won by an upper kick into Matthias' chin. He flew back, landing with a loud thud into the mat.

The sound of clapping snapped their attention to Courtney. "That was vicious." He grabbed towels and water, handing it to each of them. "Amazing skills, Eva."

"Thanks, Courtney." She said as she wiped the gooey blood from her nose and body. "Matthias is still stronger than me." She took a swig from her bottle and dampened her towel. "You know, you guys should really put showers down here."

Courtney laughed. "We could, but the building is old and the plumbers would have issues with that. But we can try." He studied all three. "My God, you guys really beat the shit out of each other." He exclaimed. His eyes wondered over Eva. Her body was extremely toned. This was a huge change from a month ago.

"I thought you were staying in town tonight." Ivan stated. "Otherwise, we could've waited for you to join the battle."

Courtney cracked up laughing. "Oh no, you guys are too much for me right now. I haven't been practicing." No, he's been drinking himself stupid and smoking weed like nobody's business. Not to mention a few ladies here and there. "Those were some sweet moves Ivan. Where'd you learn that?"

"The FSB. Mikhail trained me personally."

"Woah, so Avarie will move like that?" Eva asked.

"Oh no, she'll be even faster." Ivan said taking a large gulp of his water. "Knowing him, he's pushing her to her limits, same with Sasha."

Courtney thought about this, pretty soon, she'd be able to kick his ass. He didn't know if that was good or bad. "So, maybe she'll be done soon?"

Ivan wiped his brow and blew blood into his towel. "No. It doesn't happen like that. The challenge is always the same. She has to beat back Kirill. He's dangerous." Ivan said somberly.

"We knew that the moment he busted into my home." Courtney said with disgust. "Shit, I like his brother more than him."

"Kirill does have a soft side. You won't see it that often though." He sighed. "It's not that he's always the demon, it's that the demon tends to rule him."

"Jesus, that doesn't make us feel any better about Sasha and Avarie being with him." Matthias said.

"So what you're confirming is that Mikhail is the good twin?" Eva asked. "He was really cool with us when we all met the first time."

"Oh yea, Mikhail is cool as hell. He's a funny guy. Take heart and know that he's the one who spends more time with them than Kirill."

Their conversations always fell to Avarie and Sasha somehow. Mikhail dropped off contact the last time he was in Germany. Any questions about Avarie, he avoided. Sasha, he'd gladly talk about, but not her. She was off limits to them all.

"Who's this girl named Tori?" Matthias asked. "I've heard she has a thing for Sasha." He winked.

Courtney gave him a sideways glance. "Now where would you hear this shit at? You know there hasn't been any contact with the FSB in Moscow."

Oh shit. He said too much. He tried to change the subject but Courtney wasn't having it. "Spit it out, Matty!" Matthias nudged Eva and urged her to tell the story about meeting Sasha on the other side. She rolled her eyes and only held back certain things about Avarie.

"Okay, so Sasha isn't a virgin anymore?" They nodded. "He's getting it on with the twin's niece?" He asked in shock. They nodded. "Other than that, he's keeping Avarie on the straight and narrow."

"As much as he could. The twins drive her mad." Eva said in frustration. "I guess they took her to a club called Red October and things got dangerous. She wasn't happy with them."

"Holy hell!" Courtney shouted. "I've been there before. That's not a place for someone like her." Oh, those guys were going to get it. "Do you know what they do there?"

Ivan answered him. "Raves, sex, drugs, the occasional blow job..." He shrugged. "That's the twins for you." That didn't make him feel any better.

"I'm going to kill them both." Courtney's heart rate spiked. "Those dirty assholes." He sighed. "What else Eva?"

"I know she completely freaked and tried to run to us when your building was bombed. The twins stopped her." Eva said softly. "Sasha says that she asks about us all the time. She's somewhat home sick. They stick to a routine and it keeps her grounded for the most part."

"The part about the bombing I know since I was able to talk to them to calm her down. Is there anything else?"

"That's about it."

Courtney's face turned serious. "No it isn't." He gave her a sideways glance. "Just tell me, I'm a big boy. I can handle it."

Eva looked down. "Courtney, would you want Avarie to know what you've been doing in her absence?" She chewed on her lower lip. "Sometimes, it's better to not know these things."

Matthias shook his head. He didn't want this conversation to get this far. "Courtney, she's with the FSB. Those guys will do what they want with her. I heard that conversation you had with her. You literally told her that you didn't care what she did as long as she was safe and listened to the twins."

He was right. He did tell them that. *"Touché."* Courtney said as he stood up. "I haven't exactly been an angel either." Guilt ripped his gut almost in half as he walked out of the training room. It wasn't just guilt, it was really knowing that Avarie was more than likely forced to into the art of seduction. He made it to the staircase when Eva caught him.

"Don't you go to your room and drink yourself stupid!" She screamed at him. "Sasha told me that she still loves you! The reason why she's never revealed her nightmares to the twins is because they're about you! Sasha told me that she screams your name in the dark and when she thinks he's sleeping, she cries holding your picture to her chest." Eva's face turned red. "Do you remember when Mikhail told you about her nightmare that shattered the windows in her bedroom?" He nodded. "It was because she saw you dying! She screamed so loud every *fucking* window shattered into little pieces. Her nightmares aren't always about anything from her past life. They're about the possible things that could happen to you!"

She started to storm off and he ran down the stairs after her. "What happened in those dreams?" He was holding her by the elbows. "Did he tell you?" He didn't realize he was shaking her until Ivan and Matthias came up from the cellar staring at him.

She shoved him off. "He said that Luscious is always in her worst dreams. Somehow, he meets up with you and threatens you to give her up. Eventually you do, but he kills you anyway. The dreams you don't give her up, he kills somebody close to make you talk."

That shook him to the core. Dammit, Luscious was coming and she saw it. He knows through Mikhail that he's been watching all of them. "Did she say who?"

Eva shook her head. "She can't see who the person is."

"She told Sasha all of this?" His voice shook as he spoke.

Eva swallowed hard. "No. He performed a purification ritual on her and he saw everything she hid in the back of her mind." Courtney almost broke down in tears. Jesus, no wonder she raged so hard. She feared for him. Eva touched his shoulder. "We have to trust the twins in what they do with her." She said softly. "I know this isn't easy for any of us. You do what you need to and she'll do the same. Forgive her for what she does and I know she'll forgive you too. She still loves you Courtney. Sasha made that clear."

He nodded and walked to the seating area by the fireplace. Knowing that she still loved him made him feel better. Yes, he's done other women, but he still loved her. Hopefully when she comes back, she'll still feel the same about him.

It was neat that Eva was able to travel to the other side and meet with Sasha. If they met again, they could deliver messages to him without the twins knowing. A phone call disrupted his chain of thought. It was Mikhail. Speak of the devil.

"Mikhail?' Courtney asked.

"Courtney, are you sitting down with something strong to drink?" He asked

"I'm sitting down, but I don't have any booze on me. Why?"

Silence on the other line. "Courtney, there's been an accident..."

ϒϒϒ

It was Friday. Avarie and Sasha were excited because Kirill told them that the FSB would be closed for the next two weeks for the Christmas holiday. They didn't know what Christmas was and he had to explain it to them. He asked Avarie what she wanted. She told her that she wanted to see Courtney and the others. "*Mishka*, it's too dangerous to bring them here or you to them. Think of something else." There really wasn't anything else she wanted. When she told him, he laughed. "We'll find you something nice."

He asked the same of Sasha. Oh the grin on Sasha when he said he wanted Tori. Kirill busted up laughing. "Oh Sasha, you could have her anytime you want." Kirill told them about his plans for having two weeks off. "There's many parties that you're expected to go to. Politicians have to show off their guests and security will be extra tight. Things have been quiet for now but you never know what those fucking Elite have up their sleeves."

"What are we doing besides parties?" Avarie asked. "I mean, is that all anybody does?

"*Mishka*! For shame!" Kirill said tisking at her. "We sleep in! We let our bodies rest. We drink ourselves into the gutter. Maybe I should take Sasha to Red October!" He laughed. Sasha told him hell no. "Why not? I have no doubt you could handle your booze. The women give excellent head too. However, we'd hold off on the white lightening."

"Kirill, I don't even want to know what the hell that is." He shook his head at him. "If you ever drag me to that place, I'll wreck you." He threatened. "If you take me somewhere a little tamer, I'd actually take you up on your offer." Man his Russian was good, Avarie thought. The more Sasha spoke, the sexier he became. No wonder Tori was all over him.

"I know a little place. We can go there and leave Avarie with Tori." Kirill answered. "Besides, you need to experience more than one woman. Maybe Tori could teach Avarie a thing or two about that." He winked at her.

"Oh hell no!" Avarie yelled. "Sasha, it's time to go." She jumped up from the table as Kirill laughed at her.

"What did I say?"

She grabbed him and rushed him out the door before Kirill could get more ideas in his perverted head. Avarie already did enough for the FSB. Sleeping with another woman was not an option. They laughed at Kirill on the car ride to the FSB. The atmosphere was light and airy due to the break the facility would have. It was a good day for them all. Even Mikhail was in a good mood. "It's the last day before we close down. My God, I'm going to get so fucked you won't know who I am!" He announced to Tori and Avarie.

When they were alone, Mikhail asked Avarie what she wanted for Christmas. She said that there wasn't anything she really wanted. Everything that she did want was out of reach for her. "You've both been doing very well. Maybe we'll find something special." He assured her. Avarie still didn't really understand how Christmas worked. It was a strange holiday.

Tori explained to her about the legend of Babushka ever seeking Jesus. They celebrated Christmas on January 7th each year and New Years on the last day of the calendar year. Grandfather Frost visits the children on New Year's bringing them presents. This concept was somewhat complicated to Sasha and Avarie. On their way home they stared at all the Christmas lights and decorations lining the streets. The shops were still busy and there were merchants selling their wares on the street.

The car was stopped at a red light. Sasha pointed to the right of him as something would catch his eye. "*Maus*, look, those people are singing." He said in wonder. To Avarie's left, the vehicles zoomed by on the snow plastered streets. The driver pointed out more lights and decorations for them.

The light turned green and they started to roll through. Out of nowhere, an impact on Sasha's side threw him into Avarie. It was so violent it knocked him unconscious. The SUV rolled on its side and Avarie tried to hold on to Sasha and herself for dear life. She slammed into the roof, the second roll; she slammed into the driver's seat. The third, she slammed into Sasha. The fourth blew her out the rear window. Sailing her along with shattered glass across the air for what felt like slow motion, she saw the SUV roll to a stop on the driver's side. Without thinking, she tucked and rolled, miraculously landing on her feet in a snow bank.

Adrenaline pumped through her veins. Any pain or soreness she felt wasn't even there. She sprinted towards the SUV. It came to rest on the left side near the busy sidewalk. A crowd gathered around the scene and Avarie shoved her way through. Gas filled the air and when people realized that the situation could be dangerous, they backed a safe distance away. Avarie got to the vehicle and jumped on the passenger side. Everything else disappeared. With all her might, she ripped the right side passenger door open and threw it to the ground.

Through blurry eyes, she reached for Sasha. Avarie realized that she was too short. She looked over at the driver and found him dead. Brain splatter on the windshield and steering wheel told the entire story. Sirens shouted in the distance. The smell of gas was almost overbearing as she reached in further. "Sasha!" She screamed. "Wake up!" It was no use, blood poured from his head as his body lay limp against the spot she once sat. She climbed in just as a spark from the still warm engine ignited the pool of gas.

The sirens came closer screaming inside her head. Brushing away the shattered glass, she pulled him to a sitting position. The flames reached the driver's side and it was getting hot. Beads of sweat formed on her brow and she prayed to get him out in time. "Please, please." She pleaded to whoever or whatever would listen. Heaving him up in the confined space of the backseat, she inched his body up. The sleeve on her coat caught on fire and she quickly put it out. Smoke filled the passenger area of the SUV and she choked in ragged breaths. With one big shove, she was able to get his body out of the vehicle. Her head came up for air, but it was still smoky. Coughing to clear her lungs she checked for a place to safely land Sasha. Flames started to engulf the vehicle now. "Shit!" She yelled.

Where was everybody? She wondered. No bystander would be stupid enough to try and pull him out around these flames. Gaining her balance on top, she picked up Sasha in a fireman carry and counted to three before she made a giant leap to the sidewalk below. She landed hard on her feet but she still held him on her shoulders. That was a relief. With the rest of her strength she ran towards anywhere that looked like it would have cover. Half a block away into an alley, she threw him into a snowbank and covered his body with her tiny frame. An explosion rocked the buildings and the earth beneath her feet, sending debris and fiery ashes. The flash was so bright, it temporarily blinded her.

The sirens were there. Men rushed towards the SUV with firehoses. An ambulance skidded to a halt in front of the scene. Avarie looked down at Sasha. His eyes were swollen shut, blood dripped from his mouth; his left arm was bent in an inhuman position. Dark red blood pooled in the white snow behind him. She leaned in to make sure he was still breathing. It was there, but shallow. Utter exhaustion took over her body. She had a pounding headache and her body started to tremble violently and she couldn't control it. "Sasha, stay with me. You promised you'd stay with me." She sobbed into him as paramedics arrived. It took four men to pull her off of Sasha. Everything after that was a blur. She heard screaming and panic, the lights overwhelmed her. She was thrown into an ambulance and a stretcher with Sasha's body joining her. They pulled away, screaming into their radios. She had no control over what she was doing. Big men held her down on the long seat as she tried to tear out of their grasp. Then everything went white.

ϒϒϒ

"Courtney, they were t-boned by a semi who ran a red light. The SUV rolled several times ejecting Avarie out the back window." Mikhail took a long ragged breath. "The bystanders said she landed on her feet like some mystical ninja and came running back for the vehicle. The driver was dead on impact and Sasha…Sasha was unconscious. While they rolled, his seat belt broke off and it flung him everywhere."

"Dear God, tell me they're alive." Courtney said interrupting him. His voice shook with panic. "Tell me they're alive."

"Courtney…let me finish." Mikhail said softly. "When Avarie reached the SUV, she ripped off the door and pulled Sasha out. However, not before it started on fire. She managed to get them both to safety."

"Is Sasha dead?" He asked quietly.

"Sasha is in intensive care. He suffered broken ribs, broken arm and a concussion, possibly a fractured skull. He's going to be there for a bit. Thank God he was knocked out; otherwise his injuries would've been worse. Avarie is under sedation right now. She went into what we call at the agency 'white rage'. Her panic button triggered its defense mechanisms and fought off everybody who tried to help Sasha and her. It took four huge men just to get her in the ambulance and another four to hold her down to sedate her."

"What are her injuries?" Courtney's body was now shaking. He put the conversation on speakerphone so the others could hear. Everybody turned pale.

"Well, she dislocated her shoulder, broke two ribs, a minor concussion…and she has internal bleeding. She's going into surgery now."

"That wasn't a staged accident was it?" Matthias asked with concern. "They don't know who they are right?" Tears spilled down his cheeks while he held Eva in his arms. She sobbed quietly into his chest.

"No, the semi driver lost control on the ice and snow. He was going too fast to slow down and just pummeled the SUV. This has nothing to do with the others and we already checked into that. If it was, Avarie and Sasha would be gone by now." Mikhail answered. *Jesus*, even he sounded like he was ready to cry.

"Are they going to make it?" Ivan asked. His face was bright red and he trembled in his seat. "If Sasha's body dies…"

"Right now, Avarie is in worse shape than he is. There's no worry with Sasha. It's Avarie we need to think about." Mikhail continued. "So, we have two dead drivers and two critically injured. Their rooms are being watched by the FSB and we have two guards stationed outside the operating room for Avarie." He assured them. "Right now Tori's with Sasha."

"Where's Kirill?" Courtney asked. There was nothing but silence on the other end for what seemed an eternity.

"He's in the process of becoming extremely drunk as we speak. He took one look at Avarie and Sasha then freaked out." They heard Mikhail sniffle. "Leaving me to deal with this mess."

"Shit, so you wouldn't be calling us if this wasn't serious." Ivan said.

"Exactly, this is very serious business we're dealing with here. How Avarie managed to do what she did is beyond me. Sasha would've been burned alive had she not pulled him out in time. She was in deep blood loss by the time they got her to the hospital. Everybody is wondering how the hell she's still alive."

"Including you?" Ivan asked.

"Including me." He answered. "This girl cannot be human. She's hard to kill. Same thing could be said of Sasha, but we all know where he comes from." He breathed deep. "Alright, I'm going to let you go. I'll update you when Avarie comes out of surgery and Sasha wakes up."

"Thank you for letting us know." Eva cried. "You know you didn't have too."

"I know, but you're their family and you deserve to know if something's happened to them. I'll call after a while." The phone went dead.

"Jesus, Avarie pulled Sasha out of there after being *ejected* from the SUV? How the hell does that happen?" Matthias asked. "Most people don't even live through that." He shook his head.

Courtney was still shaking. "You said you made her hard to kill. Her cells regenerate 85% faster than normal."

"That's true. I'm guessing she's already healing, but Courtney that impact knocked Sasha out! He's a big dude! If that semi hit them that hard to where it killed the driver on impact and he was on the same side as Avarie, statistics say she would've been toast." Matthias tried to run the numbers in his head and all the possibilities. "Think about it. Sasha can heal himself, all he needs is water or blood. Avarie's body can withstand a lot, but not an impact like that. Sasha would've been the only one walking away if the vehicle didn't catch on fire."

A message beeped on Courtney's phone. He looked down, it was from Mikhail. It was titled "Footage from Traffic Camera". "You guys, he sent a video of the accident from a bystander, there's multiple videos…damn."

They watched as the street camera caught the impact. It was a good thing it was Christmas time and there were lights everywhere. The semi just plowed the shit out of the SUV. It almost tore it in half. Courtney fought back nausea as he watched the SUV roll over and over again. It chucked Avarie out of the window like a burnt out cigarette. She flew over the double lane tucked and rolled with the force, landing on her feet. As soon as she had her ground, she tore over to the vehicle. They turned white as they watched her pull off the door with almost zero effort and go inside. A fire started in the undercarriage. They held their breath and watched Sasha's body slowly come forth. She was able to heave him up on her shoulders and navigate her way to safe ground, jumping far from the fire landing on her feet. She then ran out of sight with Sasha in a fireman carry as the flames consumed the vehicle for it to finally explode.

Courtney puked all over himself. Matthias snagged the phone from him. "Jesus, get him some water." Matthias yelled. He continued to puke until he was on his hands and knees in front of the fire. His body trembled violently. When he thought he was done, he heaved out more. Eva ran over with a bucket and covered her nose. Ivan pulled him to his side and wrapped him in a blanket. Courtney sobbed into the carpet.

The boys pulled him up and shouldered him upstairs with Eva behind them. All three put him in his bathroom. Eva helped them peel off his clothes. She started up the shower, making sure it was warm and not too hot. Ivan had a hard time getting a grip on him since he convulsed so hard. They laid him down naked in the shower. "Shh, Courtney, she's not dead." Eva cooed to him, trying to settle his body down. "She's alive and she saved Sasha."

It took almost half an hour for him to calm down enough to sit up. The others were wet from the spray of the shower. They sat in silence as Courtney got a grip on himself. "I'm sorry." He whispered. "I didn't mean to freak out." Eva stroked his arm while Ivan patted his back. "You're right Matty, she would've been dead. There's no doubt." He shook his head in wonder. "I realized then how she made it out alive." Courtney said softly.

"How?"

"The twins." Courtney answered. Ivan plopped his head back against the tile. Eva shut off the water and grabbed Courtney a towel so he could dry off.

"The twins weren't there." Eva said accusingly. "They didn't even know the accident happened until they got them to the hospital more than likely."

"No, Eva. Courtney isn't talking about that. He's saying the twins gave her abilities." Ivan splayed his hands. "She's alive because one or both of them did a ritual on her."

Eva looked confused. "What kind of ritual?"

"One that involves sex." Courtney blurted out. "One of them fucked her." He put his head in his hands with his knees pulled up to his chest. "I don't know if I should be pissed or thankful."

"You could be both." Matthias said without a doubt. "Pissed because they fucked her and thankful because it worked."

Courtney's stomach felt queasy just thinking about it. He stood up and wrapped the towel around him. His cell phone rang. Quickly he answered it.

"Courtney, she's out of surgery and doing fine. They were able to stop the bleeding. Sasha woke up a few minutes ago. They both have to stay for a while."

"I understand." Courtney said with a clear voice. "We're glad they're okay now."

"I am too. I swear that girl isn't human…" His voice trailed off.

"Mikhail, did you watch the video?"

"I watched it while she was in surgery. The police sent them all to us."

Courtney hesitated to ask but he needed to know the answer. "Mikhail did you or your brother perform a ritual on her?"

"By God No!" Mikhail said defensively. "We haven't performed rituals in centuries."

"Then how the *fuck* did she survive that accident?" Courtney yelled into the phone.

"I'm as dumbfounded as you are! I told you I don't think she's human!" Mikhail yelled back. "Maybe we should all be thankful they're still alive!"

"I am thankful!" Courtney shouted again. "But none of this shit makes sense!" Eva grabbed the phone from him before it became a full-fledged pissing contest.

"Mikhail, he's just upset. If you say you don't know I believe you." She assured him. "Will you keep updating us on them?"

"Of course I will my little fire spark. You tell Courtney to settle down. When we get to the bottom of this maybe we'll find out exactly what she is."

"Thank you." They said their goodbyes and hung up the phone. "He swears they didn't do it Courtney. I know he avoids questions, but when he does answer he tells the truth." She slapped it back in his hand.

"I hope you're right." He said. "I hope you're right."

ϒϒϒ

Avarie was released Monday morning. The doctors were stumped that she recovered so quickly. She stayed a total of three nights. Sasha remained in the hospital but he was out of ICU. Mikhail was still running Friday night's events in his head as he drove the slumbering Avarie home.

After her surgery, the doctor updated him on her condition telling him that her baby didn't survive. He was stunned. Asking how far along she was, the doctors answered somewhere between a month and a month and a half. He debated on telling her, but she had no clue and mentioned nothing of being pregnant. He decided that it would only upset her more.

As he drove he chewed his gum vigorously. He counted how many sexual partners Avarie had. It was just him and Kirill. He had sex with her months ago and that was only once. Kirill always used protection. This was driving him mad. He ruled out Sasha. Theirs was not a sexual relationship. Maybe he should've had it DNA tested just to ease his mind.

Fuck, should he tell Kirill? No. He'd be extremely pissed. They'd fight and he'd accuse him of foul play. Great, now he had to hide this fact from everybody and it would burn inside him forever. He decided he could handle it. Unless Avarie gave mention he wouldn't say anything.

He finally arrived at Kirill's place. Gently, he carried Avarie inside with the escorts bringing her things in. He had to buy her a new winter jacket. The old one was bloodstained and burnt. He had the hospital throw it away for him like they did with the dead baby. He shuddered at that morbid thought. He laid her down upon her bed and took her boots off. The escorts carried her things into the room and left.

This was the worst weekend of his life. Kirill went to the scene on Friday while Mikhail rushed to the hospital. He gazed at Avarie on the bed. She was bruised from head to toe. He was told that she needs to be awakened every two hours. He set the alarm on his watch and left to find Kirill. He wasn't hard to find, the cigar smoke on the porch led him there. He found him staring blankly at the falling snow while holding a bottle of vodka in one hand, cigar in the other.

"She's upstairs asleep." Mikhail told him and took a chair. "We need to wake her up every two hours."

"Why?" He asked slurring. "She's supposed to be fine if she's home now."

"Because she's bleeding from her lady parts." Mikhail said without hesitation. "That accident almost tore her womb up. We need to make sure she doesn't bleed out."

"How horrible. They get in an accident and her internal bleeding isn't just from her intestines, but her baby maker." Oh man, Kirill was drunk off his ass. "I was hoping one day to have little ones with her." Mikhail gazed at him awkwardly. The mention of babies wasn't something he talked about drunk or sober.

Gently, Mikhail took the bottle away from him and set it down on the floor. "Kirill, you're very drunk and you're not supposed to drink when you're sad. You know this." He said wagging his finger at him. "You know how the booze affects your brain. You did this when we lost Tori's brother." He picked the bottle back up and took a swig. "You were drunk for days after the funeral."

"You bring up the dead." Kirill said as he swooned around in his chair and waved Mikhail off. "Avarie and Sasha are alive so I drink for joy. It was that American shit that had me hammered for days. What do they call it? Moonshine?" Mikhail nodded. "It was like liquid fire running down my throat. My cock hung limp for days!" Kirill proclaimed.

"*Oi*, it wasn't like you were using it!" Mikhail busted up laughing. Damn his brother was drunk. He wondered how many bottles he went through this weekend.

"It wasn't like I didn't try!" Kirill said with wide eyes. "I would jerk off in the shower and he didn't respond. I tried everything I could think of. I talked to him. I told him that he has other uses than just hanging there like a limp sausage. But noooooo, he just hung out, resting on my nut sack using them as two soft pillows while he went into a cock coma." Okay, Mikhail had to shut him down. This was too funny and they had serious business but Kirill kept going. "It was like he was completely spent. Remember the Roman orgies? My God it was like the old times when we went to three in one night. By the time the weekend was over, we'd be shooting dust and it burned when you took a piss."

"Okay! For shame, Kirill." Mikhail was trying to breathe through his laughter. "So you're drinking for joy that their lives were spared. Wonderful."

Kirill's tone turned solemn. "How the fuck did she survive?" He shook his head. "Normal humans would've been dead brother." He shook his head in drunken wonder. "Sasha can't be killed, only seriously injured. Avarie is another story. I swear she's not human." He tried to relight his cigar. "I watched the footage over and over again. I can't comprehend how the hell she was able to do that."

Mikhail took the cigar out of his hand and lit it for him. Handing it back he said, "Courtney thinks we performed a strength ritual on her. I told him that we hadn't done that for centuries. Eva was the only one who believed me."

The pitter patter of bare feet distracted them. Avarie strolled in high on pain meds. Her eyes looked blankly at them. "*Mishka*! You're supposed to be in bed resting." Mikhail rolled his eyes and remembered that he forgotten to lock the damn bedroom door.

"There's no rest for the wicked." She said pointing a crooked finger at Mikhail. "We have to bust Sasha out of the hospital!" She raised her hand in the air.

"Avarie, you're just as fucked as Kirill. You speak madness." He sat her on his lap. "The pain meds run strong in you." She wrapped her arm around him and stroked his hair. Her eyes were dilated and half closed. He gently rocked her back and forth in his chair. "I'm going to ask you something and I want you to tell me the truth okay?" She nodded. "Did you have a ritual performed on you?"

Her eyes told him that she was trying to process the question. "I've never seen a ritual. The only thing ever performed on me was *sex*." She spit it out like it was nothing. Kirill busted up laughing again.

"She's funny this one." He looked her over. "Good thing she didn't try the cocaine at Red October."

"*Mishka*! Pay attention." Mikhail said grabbing her chin and pulling her face to his. "The strongest rituals are usually performed with sex. Now, did you have sex with anybody else besides the usual suspects?" She shook her head no.

"We don't perform rituals. Not anymore." Kirill said as an ash fell on his shirt. He brushed it away. "Her and Sasha don't have sex."

"Avarie, have you had sex with Sasha?" He asked seriously. She started laughing hysterically.

Waving him off she said, "Sasha's Tori's boyfriend." Dammit, this was going nowhere.

He carried her off and put her back in bed. He decided to rule out Sasha too. This situation was very strange. Somehow, she ended up pregnant and she gained more strength. He decided to ask Sasha when he came home. Maybe he had some ideas on what's going on.

ϒϒϒ

Sasha came home on Wednesday and Avarie pestered the twins so much they had him released with home care. "Avarie, you need to leave him alone." Kirill scolded her. "Even though he's back it doesn't mean that he's in any shape for your shenanigans." Avarie was beyond elated. "You cannot sleep in the bed with him. The nurses need access to him during the night. Do you understand?" She nodded in agreement.

"So where will I sleep then?"

Kirill gave her a sly smile. "You can sleep in my room next to me." He cackled. "I'll be nice. You're still bruised up. I want you all healed up before you have to go back to the FSB."

Avarie hesitated. Kirill was a persistent one and what he wanted he got. "I don't know if I trust you."

"*Mishka*, it's in our best interest for you to get better. I can behave myself as long as you do." He winked at her. She gave in as it was no use fighting. She was ordered to grab her things and put them in his room. Sasha would have strict visiting hours and Tori wouldn't be allowed in there alone with him either. He needed his rest.

When he did arrive, the staff brought him in on a stretcher. He could walk, but his head would swoon. His ribs have healed but his arm was in a sling. He looked strange with his head all bandaged up. Mikhail met him in the room with the nurses. He asked them to give him some privacy and they left. "Sasha, I'm glad you're home." He said meaningfully. "We were so worried about you and Avarie." Sasha smiled at him. "You're a tough one. Anybody who could screw Tori into a daze can handle being hit by a semi." He joked. Sasha tried to laugh but it hurt. "Sasha, I have a very serious question to ask you."

"Alright." He said trying to sit up. Mikhail pushed him back down. "I can sit up." He declared. "I only lay down for the nurses."

"Sasha, you're perverted! Look what Tori's done to you! For shame." Mikhail jokingly scolded. "Now this is serious. No matter what the answer is I promise I will not be mad. We have a deep respect for you." Sasha looked nervous. "Sasha, did you perform a ritual on Avarie?"

"What kind of ritual?" Sasha asked back. "You need to be specific."

"A strengthening ritual?"

"No, I did a purification ritual while you were in Germany."

"Okay, so how is it performed?" Mikhail cocked an eye at him.

Sasha rolled his eyes. "She's immersed in water. I baptized her using my blood."

Mikhail deliberated on telling him about the baby. Before he came to that he had to bring up what happened to Avarie during the accident. "You saw the videos of your accident, correct?"

"Of course."

"How did Avarie survive you think?" He chewed viciously on his gum. "You and I both know that under those circumstances, nobody would have survived."

Sasha's eyes roamed the room. This fact wasn't lost upon him. Even Tori brought up that there was no way in hell she could've survived being thrown like that from a vehicle. "As much as I want to say she isn't human I know that wouldn't be true. Maybe the universe is just looking out for her, that's all."

Mikhail felt that statement went deep. Sometimes they forgot that the universe is mysterious and to question it is like questioning why the wind blows or the sun shines. "You know, I think that explains a lot. It wouldn't make sense to lose either of you now, would it?" Sasha shook his head no and smiled.

"One more question before I leave you to your hot nurses." Oh man, the grin on this guy's face, Mikhail thought. "Have you and Avarie had sex?"

"No." He said almost defensively. "That's not how we work."

"Alright." Mikhail said patting his shoulder. "I believe you. You get enough action from Tori." He laughed at himself. "Just so you know you have visiting hours until you get better. Avarie will sleep across the hall. I'll send for her after the nurses settle you in." He left the room feeling more stumped than ever.

Later, he sent Avarie in to see Sasha. She only got an hour to visit with him. Poor girl missed him so much she bawled like a baby. The twins could hear her sobs through the thick oak door. They were all happy to have Sasha home. The doctor would arrive in the morning to check on both of them.

That night, Avarie slept next to Kirill. As promised he left her alone so she could sleep. The most he did was kiss her tenderly every now and then. Her pain meds helped her slumber. The bruising was uncomfortable and she shifted throughout the night. Around 3am, he had to give her morphine.

In the morning, Dr. Alex checked her over first. She was still asleep as he pressed on her belly and looked her over. She winced only once or twice when he got to her lower abdomen. The bleeding stopped, but she was still tender. They spoke about the accident and how courageous she was saving Sasha's life. Kirill asked the doctor how it was even possible for her to pull Sasha out like that.

"Adrenaline is a powerful hormone. It gives people super strength when they need it the most. The lungs tend to dilate sending oxygen to muscles that need it at the moment. It also triggers blood vessels to contract, shutting down blood supply to areas of the body that don't need it. With that, her body's ability to feel pain diminished. That's the only medical explanation I can come up with." Kirill decided to drop the topic. She was alive and so was Sasha. He couldn't ask for more.

Sasha wasn't asleep when the doctor arrived. He checked his IV and vitals. The gash on his head was clearing up faster than he imagined. The arm still needed time to heal. Later in the day, Sasha would go in for one last CT scan so he could be cleared. That made the twins happy. Sasha gotten the worst of the damage and they needed him on his feet as soon as possible.

Mikhail kept in touch with Courtney, updating him on their conditions. Avarie begged him not to tell them about the accident. She didn't want them to worry about them. He explained that he already did and she was angry with him. "*Mishka*, they're your family. They deserve to know that you're fine. The videos of this accident are all over the place. Eventually, they'd know and Courtney would come beat the shit out of us." She had to except it. She was in no condition to fight him about this topic.

By the weekend, Sasha and Avarie were both in the clear. Sunday night, they would celebrate Christmas. The twins took them both shopping on Saturday. Avarie wasn't interested in anything but Sasha was. Having been starved for most of his downtime, he ate the living hell out of all the Christmas meats and anything sweet. The twins flipped him shit about how much he could put down.

"*Oi*, Sasha. You act like we starved you the entire week." Mikhail joked. "You don't want presents; you want to eat the hell out of Moscow."

"Well no shit!" Sasha quipped. "I was on a damn liquid diet for a week!" He held Avarie's hand throughout the square and she hardly let him go. Tori was on his other hand. He had to free himself every time he went to a food vendor stand. The twins thought he was the luckiest man on earth.

"*Mishka,* is there something you want for Christmas. This is killing us! You're the hardest person on earth to buy for. You don't like dresses, you hate jewelry, you're too old for toys and any weapons we get you would have to stay locked up. It's never fair to know you have weapons and not play with them." Mikhail exclaimed with goofy wide eyes.

"You know what I want for Christmas." She said. "Can't have that either. So why ask for things you can't have?" For the first time, she let go of Sasha's hand and walked away.

"She's so somber. It's like that accident took the light out of her soul." Tori said sadly. "I noticed she's really changed. When I ask her about it she avoids the question."

They watched as Avarie blankly stared through shop windows. Many were clothing or shoe stores. She lingered by an electronics store, but not for long. It was the next window she lingered over the most. Mikhail studied her as she peered into the glass window of a baby store. She watched as women came out with babies in strollers all bundled up. Packages of clothes or toys filled their hands as they walked by. She stood there for a good ten minutes never going in. Mikhail saw her face go melancholy as she touched her stomach, head hung down. Strutting over to her he asked, "Avarie, would you like to go in?" She shook her head no. "Why not?"

"Because it's just another thing that I can't have." She said wistfully and walked back towards the group; taking Sasha's hand, they walked around some more. That right there just broke Mikhail's heart. For the first time in ages, he felt like crying. He hated keeping secrets from her and this was a big one.

It was Sunday and they feasted with Konstantin and his family. It was informal so Avarie wore her hoodie and stocking caps with bare feet. Viktor would throw a wink in her direction every now and then. The wine flowed freely along with other hard liquors. Konstantin passed around a jar of moonshine from the States while they were in the large sitting parlor. Sasha almost puked when he took a small swig. "What's wrong Sasha? You're such a bad ass you can't handle American booze?" Kirill joked. Sasha was still choking on the ethanol flavored drink when they started to make fun of him. He managed to flip them off before chasing it down with a beer.

"Avarie, this comes from your people, take a drink." Konstantin smiled coyly.

"I've already managed to escape death once this month; I don't think I need to tempt fate." She responded. "Besides, that shit's just nasty. Damn redneck brews." She shook her head in disgust. "Back in the old days, they used that to power their tractors on the farms. Why you'd drink that is beyond my scope of reasoning."

Presents were finally passed out. Sasha was spoiled rotten by the twins. They got him a watch, manly shower stuff, new workout gear, a gift certificate for a new tattoo, two bottles of vodka, and God knows what else. Tori got a new holster, hair things, jewelry, make-up and some other girly things. The twins bought each other new guns and mostly booze they wanted to try from local distillers.

Konstantin's family traded presents among themselves. Viktor and Maria announced that she was pregnant with their first child. Good lord did the booze flow then. Avarie felt a tinge of jealousy. It wasn't because she had a thing for Viktor, which she didn't. Mainly because she felt like she was missing out on having a family of her own.

She never mentioned that she didn't receive presents yet, but at the same time, she didn't care. "*Mishka*! We almost forgot about you!" Mikhail said with a shit eating grin on his face. "We didn't give you your presents. Shame on us." He slurred as he drank from his vodka bottle.

"I didn't want anything." She shrugged and sipped her wine. God, what the hell did they get her? Hopefully not something that would embarrass her.

"You need to come with us!" Kirill slurred. "You'll love it!" She followed the twins to the back of the house. The others followed with smiles plastered on their lips. Damn, she thought, the jokes on me. They made her throw boots on and escorted her to the enclosed parking garage. This is where everybody parked and the twins kept their nice vehicles. Mikhail covered her eyes as they all walked out. When Mikhail uncovered her eyes, there was a massive wooden shipping crate standing before her.

"What's this?" she giggled.

"Open it *Mishka*!" Mikhail urged her on handing her a crow bar. It took her about five minutes to get the door off. Once it fell to the floor, she almost died and went to heaven.

"Black Betty!" She screamed at the top of her lungs. There was also a military foot locker. It had all her riding gear, the short swords, German chocolate, pictures of everybody from home, hoodies galore and so on.

"Can I ride her in the garage?" She begged the twins. They looked at each other with sly grins.

"Sure. We wouldn't have let him send it without the intention of you riding it now would we?" Kirill smiled. "Just be careful and don't run us over."

She hopped on and turned the key. The bike was so loud they had to cover their ears. She did a burn out. The garage was wide enough for her to pull her tricks. Konstantin stood with eyes wide open. He couldn't believe what he was seeing. Everybody cheered her on as she rode her back wheel and did spins around them. Eventually the garage filled up with fumes and they had to shut her down. The guys carried her footlocker inside.

Konstantin was really worked up. He stood up to shout things and the twins would sit him back down. He'd talk about the old days in the States. Avarie didn't even remember a third of it. Kirill made Avarie show off her sword skills. They sparred together. She won easily because he was drunk off his ass. They partied until they couldn't party anymore. Seeing her bike sparked her spirit.

That night, Kirill made love to her just as passionately as the first time. He told her watching her ride the bike really turned him on and he couldn't wait until the snow melted to watch her ride the streets of Moscow in her riding gear. She fell asleep that night soundly in his arms.

CHAPTER FIFTEEN

Courtney stayed at work late. He had to finish up the days business and Gerhart was out patrolling the city for any signs of the Mossad. It looked as if they almost completely backed off. The FSB still held their ground with other factions in Freiburg. The twins were good to their word when they said that Courtney had their protection.

It was late and time to leave. He already missed supper with Matthias and Eva and Ivan went to the pub to have some time out. Grabbing his stuff, he pulled on his coat. He was completely alone in the makeshift corporate building. After the bombing, he still had work to catch up on. It kept him occupied most nights, others were miserable. Security roamed the perimeter and he bid them all a safe night walking out the door.

Keys in hand, Courtney shuffled through the fresh snow. He parked too far away from the door since he arrived at work late. He unlocked the door but froze. A shutter went up his spine, not from the cold, but an evil presence lingered. He swallowed hard against the cold night. This was it, this was the eerie feeling that Avarie felt around Kirill.

He turned to face the parking lot. In the distance, headlights seemed to come closer. He thought about driving off, but he had a feeling he better stay. The car passed by without incident. Focusing his attention once again to getting into his SUV, he heard feet crunching in the snow.

He turned around and watched a ghostly figure approach. Good thing he had his gun tucked in his pants. *Where the fuck was security?* Courtney thought. The evil feeling creeped closer as the man approached. He wore a stocking cap and a black coat. Courtney looked down and saw combat boots. Shit, this wasn't good. When the man was about ten feet away, he stopped. The shadows played on the features of this man. In his heart, he knew exactly who he was.

"Hello Aldric." Luscious said.

"Luscious." Courtney said trying to keep his calm.

"Ah, so you aren't surprised to see me? How long have you known that I left my tomb?" He asked with a venomous smile.

"Long enough." Seeing this man again after almost 2,000 years still gave him the chills. "I see you've been busy."

"Oh yes, I've been very busy." Luscious said, peeling off one glove at a time. "I see you've been busy yourself." Courtney nodded. "So Aldric, I'm going to make this visit short and sweet for us both."

"Alright." Courtney agreed quietly. "What do you want?"

Luscious laughed. "I think you already know what I want." Courtney shook his head no. "Aldric, I want the girl."

"I don't know what girl you're talking about."

Luscious signaled somebody behind Courtney. The same car that passed him earlier came driving back. "I think you know exactly what girl I'm talking about. You created her in the States and brought her back here. She's run away from you a couple of times. Smart girl if you ask me. Suddenly, she disappeared into thin air."

"I have nothing for you Luscious." Courtney spread his hands before him. He kept his tone quiet and calm. The car pulled up behind Courtney's SUV. *What fucking game is this now*? he thought.

"Aldric, I've given you immortality, the castle, the riches, everything that I had. All I ask in return is the girl. That's it."

"Luscious, even if she was here, she wouldn't go with you. I don't know where she is. I stopped looking a long time ago." Courtney turned to get into his car, but Luscious kept talking.

"You know, I might have a bargaining chip for you." He signaled two men and they stepped out of the car. The trunk opened and they pulled a man out. It was Jude Vargas. He was bound with duct tape around his mouth, wrists, and ankles. Blood crusted on the top of his head and he struggled against his bonds. "I'm going to ask you nicely one more time. Where is the girl?"

"I don't know."

A man pulled out a gun and pointed it at Jude's head. "You know, he already told us everything we needed to know."

"Then why the fuck are you asking me?" Now Courtney was pissed. "If he told you everything, why come to me?"

"Aldric! We're old friends." Luscious walked around him and ran a finger down Courtney's cheek. "Maybe I wanted an excuse to see you. We made great memories together. Remember the things I've done for you? I've thrown women your way and let you have at them. Hell, I've even thrown a man or two in your direction just to satisfy your curiosity. I've fed and clothed you. You wouldn't be here today if it wasn't for me." he said wistfully.

Courtney shook his head at him. "Luscious, you're still a sick fucker. You've always gotten off on death and sex. Just the thought of blowing this guy's brains out is making you hard." Luscious stood in front of him and Courtney jutted his hand out and grabbed his crotch. "See, I'm not wrong." He let go.

"I'll really kill him, you know that." Luscious chuckled deviously. "I'll splatter this guy's brain all over the place." He licked his lips. "You know I love the smell of blood."

Courtney looked down at Jude. He moved his eyes left to right, giving Courtney the signal that he said nothing. Jude was covered in sweat even though it was freezing cold outside. His eyes wore anger. They didn't plead with Courtney as his body trembled.

"Come on Aldric." Luscious tone changed to anger. "Where is she?" Courtney said nothing. He stared straight into Luscious' evil eyes. "Alright, just so you know, we found other things in his apartment too." Jude shook his head back and forth. "It turns out your friend has had information on your girl all along." He whispered in Courtney's ear. "We know enough about her to find her with or without your help."

Fuck, Courtney thought. Jude hid information on her and now it's in their hands. He struggled to remain cool. Obviously, Jude didn't tell them where Avarie went. He looked at Jude. His head snapped forward and back from the gunshot to the head. The Mossad agent shot him without warning. Blood splattered on Courtney's clothes and car. Jude's body lay in a pool of his own blood at Courtney's feet.

"I knew you'd be stubborn." Luscious' eyes grew wide. "Now he's dead because of you." Courtney was now losing his shit and Luscious saw it. "What's the matter?" He cooed. "You've always seen this side of me."

"I really don't give a *fuck*." He said. "Why don't you get the hell out of here?" Courtney was trying to stand his ground. "Go disappear for another two thousand years you worthless piece of shit." He said with conviction.

"Oh Aldric. Now you know that's not nice." He started chucking again. "I'll tell you what. You tell me where the girl is and I'll leave you to your own."

"I don't know where she is."

"Bullshit!" Luscious screamed. "I'll kill you where you stand!"

"Go ahead!" Courtney screamed back. "You should've killed me when you had the chance you dirty bastard! Everywhere you go, you leave death and devastation. The seas run red with the blood you spilled. It's nothing for you to tear apart a newborn child and drink its blood. So what's one more death on your disgusting hands you goddamn prick?" Courtney was thrown back into the SUV by a hard smack to the face.

"Don't you preach to me about being a prick!" Spit escaped his lips in fury. "You stupid little shit! Everything I have given you, you've almost thrown away!"

"And how did you gain all that? Through death and destruction." Courtney's eyes filled with rage. "No you sonofabitch! I'm trying to make things right."

Luscious started cackling. "You're so fucking stupid. You think you can make things right? You're as dumb as the twins."

Courtney held fast. His eyes never left Luscious'. It was getting colder outside and he fought back the chills. "So, are you going to kill me or not?" Courtney opened his arms wide. "I'm ready whenever you are."

Luscious shook his head no. "Killing you would be like killing my own child. But I will tell you this, I'll tear your friends apart if we don't find her." Luscious turned and signaled the men to pack it up. Opening the passenger side of the vehicle he left one last message. "Don't you worry; I'll pay a visit to the twins soon." The car started and drove away.

ϒϒϒ

Mikhail gotten the call after Courtney had the mess cleaned up. He knew Luscious was getting desperate if he paid a visit to Courtney. Killing a cohort in front of his eyes was meant to shake him up. It only made Courtney livid and willing to leave Avarie where she was. He was finally getting the point that Avarie was safer with them than she was with Courtney.

Mikhail forwarded the information to Kirill. His only response was, "Fuck him." The twins knew that they could easily step toe to toe with Luscious. His devious nature was easy to outwit. However, he wasn't the only one they would have to make a stand against. No, there were others. Those others were almost ten times as dangerous as Luscious. Their ring leader was an absolute prick and he would be at their doorstep soon to confront them on the girl. He didn't like that thought.

Today, Avarie's combat training was made harder. Mikhail didn't let up on her for one bit. Every time she fell, he yelled. When she wasn't able to back him off, he told her he was disgusted by her performance. There was a point when Tori started screaming at him to back off. She was enraged at the way he was beating Avarie down. "Where is that woman who saved Sasha from a burning car?" He screamed. "Where did she go? She sure as shit isn't here!" He threw a punch that landed in her ribs. Another jab went to her lower abdomen.

Avarie fell back on the mat, holding her stomach. The pain burned inside her with a fury of a thousand infernos. She could hardly breathe as she tried to sit up. He kicked her in the face, knocking her out for a bit. When she was finally able to get up without help, Mikhail stopped. She looked like she was involved in a dirty bar fight. Her hair was a mess, blood ran down her nose and lips, and she walked with a limp off to the locker room. He wouldn't even stop berating her when she went there to clean up.

"*Mishka*! You get blood on that floor I'll use your hair to wipe it up!" He screamed down the hall. She didn't even turn around to flip him off or cop him attitude.

Tori helped clean her up in the shower. Avarie stayed silent while Tori went to work washing the blood off her naked body. "Mikhail is in a foul mood and he took it out on you. He shouldn't have said those horrible things. I swear sometimes I don't know the difference between him and Kirill." She stated as she checked on Avarie's appearance. "He better be nicer to you tomorrow or else I'll take the firing pins out of his guns."

That almost made Avarie smile. When she and Sasha came back that evening, Kirill looked her up and down in revulsion. His only comment was, "I'm glad you're sleeping in your own bed tonight." Sasha was trying to process what the hell was wrong with the twins that they looked upon Avarie with such disgust. It was easy enough for Kirill to take Avarie to his room any night he wanted, but when she didn't do or couldn't do what they wanted, they tried to shame her. It was a putrid practice and he hated it. Those two assholes played dirty with her. They fed off her vulnerability. He came to the conclusion that they were only using them to get what they want or something stirred them up.

Sasha lay in bed next to Avarie and held her close. "Avarie, I need you to start doing me a favor." He said softly. "When you don't give them what they want, even when you try, I need you to hold your ground."

Her eyes stared blankly at the ceiling. She did this when she was deep in contemplation. He could tell her thoughts were in turmoil. "Those assholes always make me lose my footing you know." She swallowed hard. "Sometimes I wonder if I really am stronger than them. Most times they prove me wrong. They've had millions of lifetimes to play this game, Sasha. Sometimes I wonder who the bad guys really are." She turned towards him, propping her head on her elbow. "Sometimes, I wonder if I just shouldn't run to the others and let them have me. Maybe that way, everybody would be left alone. They would destroy me and that'll be the end of it."

"Avarie, you know the nature of the others. They thirst for power. Whatever it is that you have, they want it badly enough to resort to any means necessary. I haven't even really decided if these two are on the side of good or evil yet myself. However, they seem to care when it counts. I don't think you'll get that from the others."

"Sasha, we're just pawns in their game. They move us around strategically to thwart off the others just long enough until they're prepared for whatever it is that's coming. They may respect you, but that's because they don't have a choice. They're idiots to think that they've fully won me over. The stupidest part, they almost had me too." Avarie lay back down on her bed. "I feel like the biggest fucking shit tard in this world. I've tried to tell myself that they actually like me. Truth is they don't. Honestly, I was surprised that they even felt something when we were in that car accident last month. The twins acted like they really cared about our feelings and how hurt we were and everything in between. But hey, once they knew we were healed, it was back to their normal shit without a care in the world."

Wow, he thought. He was glad they were on the same page about the twins. "But you know what I don't get?" She asked through tears. "I don't get the fact that they can't win without us. What the fuck do we have that others don't? Aren't there others who are willing to fight the Elite?" She sniffed and wiped her nose with her hand. "We need to run Sasha. We have to get out of here."

"Avarie, I'd love to run away with you. You know as well as I do it's more dangerous to run than it is to stay put. Learn to play their games. Have some fun fucking with them. God knows I do." He chuckled.

"I'm going to bed." She flicked off her light and fluffed the covers around her. It was easy to see why Sasha gotten along with the twins so well. All three were powerful in their own way. These guys were way out of her league and they expected her to kick Kirill's ass? *Really*? She didn't know when Kirill was coming to fight her again. She didn't even know how she was going to pull it off.

There was another dilemma that had her stumped. Avarie was struggling with really liking the twins. Their way of doing things was foreign to her. It's like they enjoy sharing her body. Last week, Mikhail acted like he was mad at her and pulled her into a custodial closet just to fuck her. He said the dirtiest things and it was maddening. Kirill on the other hand pulled her into his room whenever he felt like it. There were times when he had sex with her and others where he only wanted to cuddle her in his arms. There was one time he let her beat him with his belt. Now that was interesting to say the least. Damn these two were hard to read. The reality is that she didn't know if the things they did were acceptable or not. Either way, she was told to do what they said so she just went with it.

ϓϓϓ

"Why do I always have to wear these slinky princess type dresses?" Avarie asked on their way to another dinner party. She shifted in a beautiful chocolate formal gown that hugged every curve of her body. When Tori helped her put it on, Avarie felt almost scandalous. The neckline was a thick spider web of straps that lifted up her breasts. Tori helped Avarie throw her dark brown hair up into a glamorously messy updo that framed her cat like eyes.

"*Mishka* that dress isn't even close to *slinky*." Mikhail beamed. "You look ravishing. Maybe if Kirill is nice tonight, I'll get to take you home and help you take it off." Avarie rolled her eyes and Kirill nudged him in the ribs.

"It depends on how the booze treats me." He flashed his brother a grin. "Maybe we'll let her pick which one she wants when the evening is done."

Dear God, she thought. Might as well have them both at the same time the way these two are going tonight. They already had two bottles getting ready. Shit, even Sasha joined them for a few swigs. Tori was all over Sasha as she made out with him on his lap in the limo. Avarie heard every naughty thing she whispered in his ear. Kirill had to break off the party by telling Tori to behave herself. Were Russians always horny? It seemed like it to Avarie.

They arrived and were escorted inside. Kirill handed the standing guard his invitations for all of them. There were butlers to take coats in the lobby. Servers ran around with silver platers of wine and horderve's. Mikhail whispered instructions in Avarie's ear. "If you sense anything you find us. Kirill and I need to mingle before we find our tables. Practice your situational awareness here. Avoid fighting at all costs. Go mingle, make allies, and be gracious. I'll explain why we're here later."

He kissed her hand and broke off from her. Kirill gave her a wink and sent a kiss her way. Grabbing a wine glass she went to find familiar faces. "I hope to God this works Kirill." Mikhail said to him. "This is very dangerous bringing her and Sasha here."

"Mikhail, this fuck has been sitting on the sidelines too long. We need them to convince him to get off the goddamn fence. I don't give a shit anymore if the others come. They're in our territory and if they even think of fucking with us, I'll fuck them all up." Kirill said seriously. "If they even think of trying to take our beautiful *Mishka*, all hell will break loose." Mikhail was in agreement. Avarie was theirs and theirs alone. If the others even touched her in the wrong way, they were going to see serious rage.

They spotted their target. He was the leader of the House of Saud. Khalid was a man of great stature and wealth. His family has had ahold of Saudi Arabia through hundreds of wars. He's fought with and against the illuminati for thousands of years. In every shape and form, he looked like a Sheik from the olden days. He was a handsome man. Black wavy hair, golden eyes, thick eyebrows and eyelashes. His facial structure held obvious indications that he was from the Middle East. He wore a black tux that gave off his olive skin tone.

As he walked by, the twins bowed their heads in a respectful manner with Khalid doing the same. "Gentlemen." He stated with a thick Arabian dialect. "How wonderful of you to help host this event in my honor." He took their hands and shook them. "I'm thankful that they aren't serving pork." Khalid shot them a devious smile. "After dinner, we shall discuss your proposition. Until then, let us feast."

Avarie walked around with her wine glass. Her eyes wondered the dining area looking for anything out of the ordinary. She wondered why Mikhail would warn her to use her training here. She spotted Tori and Sasha in the corner. He caught her eye and nodded. It was his signal letting her know that his eyes were following her, waiting to step in if danger arose. Tori gave Avarie hand signals of all clear on their end. She stalked the room, only speaking to those who approached her.

Within thirty minutes dinner was ready to be served and the patrons took their seats at the extremely long tables. Avarie was seated between the twins with Sasha and Tori across from them. This allowed a better vantage point. She didn't ask questions of the twins during the entire meal. Guests would speak and a conversation would arise. Avarie made sure her facial expressions didn't give her away. Tonight, she had the cool collected confidence of a cougar. "*Mishka*, you're doing wonderful. Keep up the smiles and small talk. You're swooning the males around you." Mikhail patted her hand.

"You and Tori are also making the females jealous. I see them eyeballing you both." Kirill growled deep in his chest. "I knew your dresses would turn heads." He cocked an eyeball at her. "If you're a good girl, I promise to give you something special later."

"I thought you said I would get to choose who I wanted tonight?" Avarie teased him seductively. "I haven't had Mikhail in a while, you know that."

Kirill's eyes went wide with fervor. Mikhail looked down at her sheepishly. "Avarie, you better settle down. You're getting us excited and this is serious business we're dealing with tonight. We both better be the best Russian assholes we can be. We can't do that when you make us giddy like little school girls."

Sasha cackled at them. "It sounds like you both need to settle down." He said leaning in towards the twins. "It seems no matter what she's doing, she's always running around naked in each of your heads. *Perverts.*" He shook his head at them.

"*Oi*, Sasha." Kirill said teasingly. "That hurt." Tori giggled. These guys were distracting Avarie from sensing danger. She closed her eyes for a few seconds to clear her senses. She looked around the room. So far no threats for the exception of Mikhail who put his hand on her thigh. He was stroking it gently. Mikhail's hand felt warm and soft against the thin silky fabric. He needed to stop distracting her, so she gently tapped his hand away. He looked like he was offended and she brushed him off without guilt.

Within the hour desserts were served. Kirill was chatting up Sasha and Tori. Mikhail had most of his attention scanning the room. "You feel off about anything?" He whispered in Avarie's ear. She shook her head no. "Don't let me distract you tonight." His hand ensnared with hers under the table. "Go dance when dessert is over and always keep Tori and Sasha within your sights. We will be out of range for a while."

"Are you going to tell me what's going on?" Avarie whispered. "I don't like it when you two leave me in the dark." Her eyes implored him to speak up.

He held her hand tighter and his face turned somewhat morose. "I can't tell you yet. Just work your natural charms tonight. Be beautiful and seductive towards your threats, they'll break down easily. If you ever need saved from a situation, Tori will be there." Even at formal events, he still chewed his gum.

"Now you're scaring me." She fought back tears that threatened to spill.

"*Mishka*, don't get upset. If the others are here, they can sense your fears. That gives you up. Mask yourself in the same confidence you do with us." He pulled her hand closer to his body. She could tell he was nervous. He's never really held her hand before and the expression on his face told her that something big was up and she better do her part.

ΥΥΥ

The twins were in another chamber with Khalid. They drank expensive vodka and smoked imported Cuban cigars. Normally, this was botchery for the Saudi's but Khalid was different. He didn't care for customs or dogmas of the country he helped run.

"Let's get to business boys." Khalid said clapping his hands together. "I understand I was invited because things are ramping up."

"It's more than ramping up. This is it, Khalid. This is the war to end all wars." Kirill said solemnly. "If you don't pick a side, you'll be destroyed by both."

"And how many of our kind are on your side may I ask?" He sat back with his hands splayed on his temple. "It seems to me it's just you both. Now I'm not saying you're not intimidating. All I'm saying is that there are more of us."

Mikhail let Kirill do most of the talking on this one as politics was his thing. "What does it matter how many are on our side? My brother and I will wage war against them regardless. Their blood lust has become uncontrollable and will not rest until the entire world is under their thumb." Kirill leaned in closer. "Khalid, we have no qualm with you. We've helped you beat them back during the Saudi uprising in 2016. Shimon and the others have fucked with you for too long. You've sat neutral since then like Switzerland in WWII. Your silence is consent and I will not have you silent."

"You know, Shimon and Luscious gave me this same visit a while back." Khalid said thoughtfully. "However, their visit wasn't so welcome. Luscious threatened to rape my offspring and drink their blood in front of me. He's the reason why the humans talk of Satan." He hissed. "I fear for my human family and my countrymen. Every day they pray to Allah that the peace stays within our boundaries. There are many rumors of war and I know there are still wars raging in the States.'

"We were once watchers, gentlemen." Khalid looked off in the distance. "Our job was to observe this plane of existence and not meddle in their affairs. Now look what happened." His voice started to falter. "We laid with the daughters of man and tainted their DNA. We fought with each other over our own existence. "

Khalid's eyes trailed over the twins but rested sorrowfully on Mikhail. "You were the Arch of us all. What happened?'

Mikhail had the simplest answer for him. "When we entered here, the universe gave us free will, Khalid. With free will comes responsibility. The ones who broke off from that responsibility decided to break every rule given to them as a Watcher. Friends turned into enemies and we waged war. The rivers turned to blood and bodies to ash. Innocent lives taken across the many centuries only to have them taken again and again."

"So we wage war again?" Khalid asked refilling his glass. "Wars never end, Mikhail."

"What if I were to tell you that wars can end?" Mikhail smiled slyly at him. "What if I were to tell you that all we need is one more key and we got this?"

"I'd think you're full of shit!" Khalid spat at him.

"*Oi*, Khalid." Kirill said defiantly. "That's my brother you're disrespecting. You watch yourself."

Khalid sat back staring at them both with caution. These two had something up their sleeve and he wanted assurance that all this bullshit would end. He was just as tired as them with the others playing their games with the human race. He made a life here after falling from grace and he loved mankind with all his heart. "Give me something." Khalid crossed his arms. "Give me something that shows that you two aren't full of shit." The twins went immediately to discussing amongst each other about this request. Khalid didn't even bother to try and eavesdrop. It was less than two minutes before their decision was made.

"Alright, we have something for you so you'd believe us. Once you see it, you're completely with us." Kirill said without regard to Khalid's feelings. "You breathe no word to the others even if you are confronted. This is serious Khalid, they're already snooping and we're lucky they haven't found it yet."

He heaved a deep sigh. "Alright. Is it here?" They nodded, smiling sheepishly at him. "This better be damn good."

"Believe me, its mind blowing." Kirill said.

ϒϒϒ

Avarie was leaning against the balcony. She danced with strangers and drank wine. Nothing was off so far about this party. She looked across the vast expanse of Moscow. The weather was warming up, but not enough to take the chill out of the air. Her breathe came out in vapor when she exhaled. Holding her wine glass to her lips, she let her senses take over. The last time she saw Luscious was when he was spying from the last dinner party she was at.

She was going over why the twins would be worried about danger without informing her of the implications of coming here. It was obvious they let Tori and Sasha in on it. She let her mind wonder about home and Courtney. She missed him, but was scared that when she came back, he might not want her anymore. The thought almost made her cry where she stood.

Her body perked up. Feeling somebody coming, Avarie mentally prepared herself to sense them out. It wasn't evil but it wasn't human either. It had to be one of the others. She calmed herself as they approached. "You have to be the most beautiful woman here tonight." The man whispered in an Arabic accent. His hand went softly to the small of her back. Slowly she turned to face him.

A handsome Arabic man stood before her. His eyes burned gold and was only offset by the fact he wore a black tux. *Damn, were all these guys good looking?* Avarie thought to herself. "I can see the universe in your eyes. Do they always glow green in the dark?" The man asked thoughtfully.

"I wouldn't know." Avarie answered back smiling at him kindly. This one wasn't going to hurt her. He was curious about what she was and it showed in his body language. His eyes roamed her body. She still held the wine glass in her hand and sipped on it. She let him take his time.

He smiled back. Wow, this one had soft kissable lips. His goatee was shaped into an upside down triangle on his immaculate chin. "Are you done looking yet?" Avarie asked gently.

"What's your name?" The question was light and wistful.

"It's Avarie." She held out her hand. He took it and planted a soft kiss on the top, leaving her with a soft chill that ran up her spine.

"I am Khalid. I'm old friends of the twins. They told me about you."

"What did they say?" God, it better not be anything sexual. *Perverts*.

"It wasn't what they said; it's what they didn't say." He still held her hand as he continued to look her over in strange wonder. Avarie took this time to look back inside. The twins were standing a distance away and they nodded at her letting her know she was okay in this man's presence. Sasha and Tori were with them, sipping on white wine watching Avarie's interaction with this man. *Behave*.

"Is there something you need to ask me, Khalid?" She kept her tone quiet as not to startle him from his train of thought as he looked over her body. His face wore disbelief.

Holding on to her one hand, he gently placed his hand again at the small of her back and brought her closer to him. "What are you? Where did you come from?" His eyes bore down into hers. "I feel a strange power within you and it threatens to pull me through the vail." He whispered softly. His face came closer to hers. "You can't be human." Avarie wanted to look back at the twins, but she kept her eyes locked in place.

Pandora Rising

"I'm very human." She placed her hands on his chest. "I came from the same place every human has." Heat radiated from his body. He almost trembled at her touch. This man was elated in her presence and she felt it through her finger tips.

His lips were inches from hers. His breath smelled of wine and vodka mixed with cigar smoke. "Avarie, may I kiss you?" His voice was but a hoarse whisper. The pace of his heart picked up under her hand and his breaths were shallow. "I need to know if you're truly real." His eyes implored hers.

Without moving her head, her eyes found the twins and she raised her eyebrows. The twins were waving their hands for her to go on with an excitement that she'd never seen. Sasha stood between them with wide eyes shaking his head no. Mikhail looked over at him. Grabbing the back of Sasha's head, he bobbed it up and down. Tori laughed at the trio.

"Alright, but make it good." Avarie challenged him. Obviously this person was important enough for the twins to give her the go-ahead for something this intimate. He leaned further into her while cupping her left cheek. His eyes half closed and he cleared the distance between them with his lips on hers. He pressed gently, opening his lips only a little. He stole the breath from her and softly used his tongue to reach for hers. A gentle roll of pleasure built up inside her. He pressed his body harder into hers. She was already against the rail and he pushed her further into it. Avarie felt his member press into her belly. He ran his tongue along her lower lip and nipped at it gently. She pulled away, letting her lower lip slip from his enthralled grasp.

"Are you satisfied?" She asked running her hand through his thick black hair.

"Very." He answered breathlessly. He smiled sweetly. "We should go back in." Avarie nodded in agreement. He tugged her hand to follow him and he held his grip firm. He walked up to the group with Avarie in tow. He smiled again at Avarie. "Gentlemen, your friend here has managed to convince me to join you in your endeavor."

Mikhail put his arm around Khalid's shoulder and announced with a maniacal grin. "We're going to *win!*"

ϒϒϒ

Avarie went home with Mikhail that night. Kirill was staying behind to party with Khalid. Tori took Sasha back to her place. Mikhail grew virtually too excited when Avarie removed her dress. By 4am, he already had her five times and she was tired. They lay side by side in bed with their hands entangled. Mikhail kissed each of her digits and sucked on her index finger, nipping it with his teeth. "Are you ready for another round?" he said mischievously.

"I'm tired." She said with eyes half closed. "You need to give me a break." Her eyes stared up at the ceiling and Mikhail could tell she was deep in thought.

"What are you thinking?" He leaned in and kissed her cheek. "You only stare up when you think so hard."

It took a while for Avarie to answer. She wasn't happy about the fact they didn't warn her about this other man. Nor was she happy about being shared between the twins like some whore. She felt she didn't have a choice either. It wasn't that she didn't enjoy them; it was how they could so casually trade her off. Something deeper bothered her though. "Mikhail, why are Khalid's eyes the color of gold?"

He ran his fingers up and down her side, letting them linger in tender spots. "I think it's because he's fathered children. Or it could be because Arabian men have almost orange eyes. I'm not truly sure." He answered softly. "Why you ask?"

She took a deep breath. "Because Kirill's looked like that for a while too. They weren't that golden, but his eyes changed." She propped herself up on her elbow. "It doesn't make sense. I know you guys never had children, so why would his eyes be like that? After the accident, it went away like something died that night."

Now that he thought about it, he did notice Kirill's eyes changed a bit. The entire month after he was with Avarie the first time, Kirill seemed light hearted. Granted Mikhail didn't see him much between then and the accident. "It could be something else you know?" he said assuring her. "I myself don't have answers to everything." Avarie fell asleep mid conversation. He was glad he didn't have to answer any more questions. He knew his culprit now.

ϒϒϒ

Kirill came into the flat still dressed in his tux sometime around 11am with a bag for Avarie. Walking into the bedroom he sat at the edge of the bed. Avarie was sound asleep and so was Mikhail. He threw off his shoes and made himself comfortable next to her. He smiled down at

Avarie. This girl worked miracles, he thought. Through her, they gained another ally. He ran his fingers through her dark brown hair.

Mikhail slowly lifted his head. "Did you work out the details?" he asked sleepily. Kirill nodded. "Good. I hope he assured you he'd keep quiet about her."

"He did. He's very elated to say the least. He has renewed hope." Kirill scooted closer to Avarie. "Did she sleep well?"

"I wore her out." Mikhail growled. "She begged me to let her sleep." Avarie stirred only a little moving her hand under her cheek facing Kirill. "Kirill, we need to speak the old language now." Mikhail said seriously. Kirill nodded in agreement. *"Avarie told me that your eyes were gold for a time like Khalid's. You and I both know that gold tones in our eyes only mean one thing."* Kirill didn't answer him. In fact his expression turned to sadness and he avoided Mikhail's gaze. *"Did you know?"*

Kirill rolled to his back. *"The next morning, I looked in the mirror and my eyes changed. I joked with Avarie that we did it four times and she had to prove to me we didn't. She pulled the condom from the trash and there was a tear in it. I just assumed it ripped when it was pulled off. It wasn't until maybe a week after that I noticed a change in her and me. Mostly, I've left her alone up until the accident."* Tears started to form in his eyes as he spoke in ragged breaths. *"When we received the call about their accident, I went to the scene and you went to the hospital. After I was done there I joined you. I looked at both of them all bloodied and beaten up. I knew they had to sedate Avarie. I grew fearful and I left you there. I went home and looked in the mirror. I knew then that she lost the baby."* Kirill sniffled. *"I would've told you, but I myself wasn't sure. We never had children and this was a new experience for me. I was so angry with myself. I felt relief and anger at the same time. Relief that a child wouldn't be in danger and anger that something that belonged to me died recklessly."* He shook his head. *"Do you think she knew?"*

Mikhail stroked Avarie's arm as she breathed deeply. *"I think she knew something, but I don't think she knew exactly what it was. She was extremely depressed after the accident. Sasha told us that she confided in him that she felt empty inside. I don't think he even knew she was pregnant."*

"Should we tell her?" Kirill asked. *"She didn't mention anything."*

"I think we should leave it alone. Unless she brings it up she doesn't need to know anything."

Avarie's eyes fluttered awake. Her vision fixed on Kirill. The fog cleared in her mind. "I know I'm in trouble when you both are in the same bed with me." She smiled sleepily. "I'm too tired." She pulled the covers over her head.

The twins laughed. "*Mishka*, he's here to take you home. This bed isn't big enough for all three to have fun in. Maybe some other time." He joked with her under the covers. "If you're awake now, you need to get dressed. I have work to do later and I can't do it from my bed."

"Do I get to go back to sleep?" She peeked her head out at Kirill. "I'm really tired."

"I'll let you sleep. I haven't been to bed myself. You and I could cuddle." He kissed her cheek. "We can sleep the day away. Besides, it's only Saturday."

"Do you promise to leave me alone?" She asked as she stretched. "I had to beg him to get off me." Mikhail pulled the covers off and let his right hand wonder over her breasts. He gave her a hicky around her left nipple sometime during the night. She slapped him away and rolled onto her stomach and out of bed. "See what I mean?"

"Avarie, I didn't even get to do half the things I wanted." He slapped her ass. She almost fell over but Kirill caught her while laughing. "You better get dressed before I drag you back under the covers." He threatened. Kirill handed her the bag and she threw on her street clothes while the twins watched with devious grins. She could tell they were getting ideas. What was wrong with these two?

Avarie was silent on the ride home. She buzzed in and out of sleep. When they arrived and entered Kirill's bedroom, she passed out quickly. He crawled in next to her and held her close. He breathed in her soft skin. Sadness threatened to overwhelm him as he placed his hand on her lower abdomen. Now wasn't the time for children. His mind was in turmoil because he knew that he'd have to give her back to Courtney for a while at least. He and his brother shared the same woman without guilt and he knew that Mikhail loved her just as much as he did. They never said it to each other or her.

This was quite a situation they put themselves in. He could only imagine how Avarie felt. She hardly mentioned Courtney anymore. It's been seven months since she's been in Russia. What month was it? February? Two more months and they'd celebrate her birthday. He debated on letting her call Courtney before then. Hopefully it would encourage her to work harder. He was getting drowsy and couldn't hold onto his thoughts. He cradled Avarie closer and closed his eyes.

ϓϓϓ

Avarie awoke in the middle of the night to an empty bed. She searched the dark room for Kirill. She went into the bathroom to clean up and while coming out, she flicked on the light. On the nightstand was a note.

Avarie,
I went to Red October with Tori and Sasha. I'll be home before 3am.

Kirill

She set it down. Throwing on her pants and hoodie, she walked out of the room and noticed there were no guards around. That was extremely odd. Usually there was somebody standing guard. Her stomach growled. She went to the elevator and wondered around the darkened mansion. There was nobody in the kitchen and she was desperately hungry. The clock on the wall said 1:30. There wouldn't be anybody to make her food. Opening the fridge door, all she found was ingredients. Damn her luck!

She went back into Kirill's room. Opening the balcony door scents of food wafted through the air. Oh My God! Now she wanted whatever they were making down there. The air was cool but not too cold. She had no money so she rummaged through Kirill's nightstand drawers. There was enough there to at least get her something and a drink. If they found out she left, she knew she'd be in trouble.

Heading back downstairs, she found the security office. There was only one man on duty tonight. She talked to him about where to get food. He directed her to a kebab café that was only a five minute walk. He would only let her go if she promised to grab food and come back to the front door so he could ring her in.

Heading out with cash in her pocket the square was filled with people, most leaving the bars. She kept her hands in her pockets as she observed the area for any danger. A few men made cat calls her way, but that was about it. At the kebab station she ordered a doner kebab and a soft drink. The scent made her stomach claw at her insides. She paid and shoved the meaty sandwich into her hoodie pocket and rushed back to the mansion. Once there, she tore into it with the grace of a pig eating slop back in Kirill's bedroom.

She watched out the window as the lights cast eerie shadows against the snow swept streets. She ate in the muted light next to the balcony windows. Having her iPod in her ears, she listened to music as she devoured almost half of the large kebab. She was on a Nirvana song when Kirill busted in. She didn't even look in his direction when he sat next to her. Shit, she couldn't even get rid of the evidence. It was splattered all over the foil wrapper under her kebab. Guilt spread over her face.

Kirill was dressed in a black shirt and baseball cap. Jesus, was there anything this man couldn't pull off? Avarie thought. He pulled the earbud out and looked her over with disbelief. "*Mishka*, where did you find food?"

She dropped it on the wrapper and sipped her soft drink. "I walked down to the kebab station." Shit, she knew she was getting the belt. "I know, I'm in trouble."

"Where did you get the cash?" He slanted his head at her with cocked eyebrows. "I know the guard didn't give it to you."

"I stole it from your nightstand. I'll pay you back." She said defeatedly. "Look, the only reason why I left is because I don't know how to cook. I was hungry. I mean *really* hungry." She dropped her eyes. "You're mad aren't you?"

"No *Mishka*, I was wondering why you didn't get two. I'm starving myself. Makes me wish I left more money in the nightstand." He busted up laughing. She offered her other half by pushing it in front of him on the table. "You're really going to share this beautiful meaty sandwich with me?" He smiled at her and she nodded. "Thank you."

She watched as he ate intently by the light of the street lamps that filtered in the room. She let him sip on her soft drink. Somewhere along the lines, the kebab got messy and the white sauce spilled on the exposed skin of his chest. Without thinking, Avarie licked it up for him. Excitement grew in his eyes. She observed him as he ate. The black t-shirt was tight around his muscles. The biceps of his huge arms flexed as he held the sandwich with both hands, elbows on the table. His blue jeans were also tight and revealing every thigh muscle could be seen as he shifted his legs back and forth, enjoying the rest of her sandwich. He trimmed his beard, but not too much. The ball cap cast shadows along his eyes and made him all the more irresistible.

"Why are you watching me like that?" He asked coyly. "You've seen me eat before." Avarie gave him a sheepish grin and she blushed.

"How was your outing?" Avarie asked not really wanting to know the answer.

"Sasha and Tori had a good time. We drank, we danced and most importantly, we stayed away from the white powder." He winked at her.

"Now why was that?" She asked quizzically. "That's what you do when you go there, dance, get blowjobs and snort coke. What's different about tonight?"

He wiped off his hands on the napkin and took another sip of her drink. "The difference was that my girlfriend was waiting at home sleeping. I don't like coming home to her all fucked up." He pulled her towards him, sitting her on his lap so she straddled him on the chair facing him. He placed her hands behind his head wrapping them around his neck. She stroked the soft hair at his nape that wasn't covered by the ball cap.

"So I'm your girlfriend now?" She asked confused.

"Well I think we're beyond dating at this point don't you think?" He rubbed his warm hands up and down her sides. A smile formed on his face as he gazed wistfully upon her.

"Wait a minute." Avarie gasped. "What does that make Mikhail?"

"Oh, he's your boyfriend too." Kirill laughed. "But when you're here, you're mine. When you're with Mikhail, you're his."

This was getting humorous. "Alright, what about when I'm with you both?"

"*Mishka*! We share." He chuckled as he gripped her tighter. Leaning in he kissed her lips softly. He moved towards her chin, then her neck. He smelled of booze and kebab. She giggled when he licked her delicate earlobe. "Oh, I know you like that." He whispered in her ear. It tickled and made it worse. She felt the heat of his arousal between her thighs. Gently, she pulled back from him, letting her eyes wonder from his head to his chest. Her finger traced the paths of his muscled features through his tight shirt. He smelled of cologne and male musk. She breathed him in. Sometimes when he left her alone in the room, she'd find one of his shirts and breathe in his scent.

"What are you thinking, Avarie?" He asked sweetly. "I see there's something on your mind."

Her eyes wondered the room. She knew exactly what she was thinking. It was words that should remain unsaid. How it got this far? She didn't know. Sadly, she was starting to forget Courtney. She had to live and breathe the training they gave her but she didn't think it would end up like this. Jaded and confused she felt like running from the room. His hands stayed on her hips and he watched her patiently, waiting for an answer that she didn't want to give him.

"I want to get out of here. Is there something we can do this late at night?" She asked with coaxing eyes. He let out a deep breath. The smile never left his face.

"Of course we can. Would you like to drive around or walk?"

"Can we do both?"

He chuckled. "We can do both. I see I've been keeping you cooped up too much." He lifted her off his lap. Within minutes, she was driving the SUV out of the garage. They parked somewhere away from his home and walked hand in hand in the cold. They were in an extremely busy square and Avarie kept watch of her surroundings. Every now and then he pulled her in for a kiss. They talked and laughed. She was having a good time in the cold with Kirill walking the old cobblestones. People were busy coming out from pubs. Some cat called Avarie now and then. Kirill would yell at them and tell them that she was his girl.

He stopped in the middle of the square and turned to her with lustful eyes. "I want you to sing to me." He requested.

"Here?" She asked. He nodded. "I wouldn't know what to sing and there's tons of people here." Heat grew in her body making her feverish.

"I've heard you sing in your sleep you know." He confided. "It was a beautiful song that I hadn't heard in years. I'd like to hear you sing it."

Avarie thought about what he was asking. She didn't know she sang in her sleep. That was odd. She shook off the thought. "Do you remember how it went?"

"Something about laying in your arms and heaven." He answered back. That was a tough one for Avarie. Grabbing her iPod, she flipped through the songs thinking about which one he was talking about. She found it.

Pandora Rising

"Alright." She said to him. "It's called *Heaven* by Bryan Adams. Maybe we can find a piano and I can play it for you."

"Good idea Mishka." He grinned. "It just so happens that there's a street piano outside a pub here. They keep it warm in winter." He led the way. It was an upright and kept very well protected from the elements. He kicked the drunks off of it with playful laughter. "My woman is going to sing to me. You go away!"

"What if a crowd gathers?" She asked him with a hint of fear.

"So what? Let them listen to your beautiful voice." She awkwardly ran her hands across the keyboard finding her notes. Within seconds she started to play the beginning of the song. She sang softly and with his coaxing eyes, her voice grew louder. The noises of the people outside wondering around started to fade as her voice floated into the distance. Kirill kept his eyes on her and leaned against the back of the piano. She focused on him as she sang. When the song was done, the entire square stood together. Many yelled for her to sing another and Kirill laughed. "Go ahead, *Mishka*."

She thought of another song. Something that the crowd would know. Seeing a guitar player from the corner of her eye, she asked if he knew a certain song. He nodded and she pounded out the chords on the piano. They started playing Journey's *Don't Stop Believing*. Holy shit if she didn't get the crowd going. It seemed everybody was just a small town girl when this song played. The voices of the crowd rose up on the chorus. Before the end of the first verse, somebody hooked her up with a microphone and amp. Same with the guitar player. Avarie had never seen so many party animals in her life.

"It seems you riled them up, *Mishka*!" Kirill was laughing. "I believe you have your own concert going." She blushed. "Play more; they want more and so do I." Somehow, a street drummer moved his kit towards her and a guy brought his bass guitar.

"Do you sing Kirill?" Avarie asked smartly. "Because I think you can sing, you just don't do it enough."

"Oh *Mishka*, I'm drunk enough to sing a few songs." He smiled. She thought about something that he could possibly sing. She talked to the other band players and they decided on a song for him.

"Honey, I have a feeling you know Seven Mary Three." She said sweetly. "I bet you can pull it off."

"Oh." He said rubbing his hands together. "I have an even better one." He pulled the guys in. This was too funny. "Default *Wasting My Time*."

The guitar player went to work on the intro and he snagged the microphone from her. When he pulled out the first words, Avarie was blown away. *He could sing*! He climbed on top of the piano towards the crowd and sang for them. They were chanting something but she didn't understand what it was. When his song finished, Avarie had the band go into *Mony Mony*. Hundreds gathered in the square and started dancing. Avarie was having too much fun playing for them she forgot about her fears. Cell phones recorded Kirill singing and the band playing. He danced on top of the piano like a stripper. Man he was fucked. She didn't realize he had that much to drink before they came.

Before the party got too far out of hand, the police arrived to break up their shindig. It was almost 5am and the police scattered the crowd. They spoke to Kirill and many 'fucks' were thrown around from him. Russians are so angry, Avarie thought. When they got back to the car Avarie asked him. "What were they chanting when you sang the first song?"

"Oh, they were saying "Prime Minister'." He said without a care.

"Wait a minute; those people knew who you were under that ball cap?" Avarie laughed as she drove home.

"Of course, I'm famous. Konstantin can't hold a tune so I have to do it every now and then. They know I party." He shrugged it off like it was nothing.

"So nobody cares?" Avarie said confused.

"No, *Mishka*, I go to Red October. Why would they care what I do? We live in different times than when you lived in your past life. Certain things are widely accepted." He waved her off.

"No wonder why you're so messed up." Avarie blurted out giggling. Avarie laughed at him all the way home. They crawled in bed and slept for hours. She had an incredible day. She giggled in her sleep thinking about Kirill up on the piano dancing like a Chippendale.

CHAPTER SIXTEEN

It was the beginning of April. Sasha and Avarie could barely believe that they've been in Russia for this long. The snow started to melt and droplets of water trickled from the gutters. Avarie stared outside the windows of the FSB. Today, she wasn't feeling centered. It's been a few months since Kirill has shown up to fight her and it left Avarie wondering why. Sasha slipped beside her and leaned his massive arm against the window. He looked just as lost as she was.

"Sasha, do you remember what home looks like?" She asked him sadly. "Sometimes I try to remember what my room looked like or Eva's red hair. There's times when I can't even remember Courtney's face or Matthias' smile." She leaned into the window further. "I'm scared that maybe there isn't a home to return to."

He wrapped his arm around her and pulled her close. "*Maus*, if anything happened to them the twins would've said something. I see you're torn up about here and home. There are many times I have the same thoughts. We need to take it one day at a time right now. None of us know what the future holds. It seems things become more unpredictable as the days go by." His tone was wistful and his eyes turned sad. "At the end of our training we just need to see where everybody stands and what the plan is."

"I've never meant for any of this to happen, Sasha." Her fingers played with the vapor that rolled up on the window pane. "I don't know what to do."

Sasha turned to her in confusion. "What do you mean when you say 'you didn't mean for any of this to happen'?" He asked peering into her eyes. "I don't understand what you're trying to say. Can you explain for me?" Avarie spotted Mikhail down the hallway walking towards them. He was a good distance away and her eyes caught his. Sasha turned to see what Avarie was looking at and he understood.

"I see." He whispered softly. "You've fallen in love with them haven't you?" She gave him a guilty nod. "I guess we have ourselves a dangerous love triangle don't we?" Avarie looked down at the floor and fidgeted with her fingers. "Well, you aren't the only one. Tori has me wrapped around her damn pinky." He confessed. "You're right, Russians are messed up." Avarie gave him a small chuckle.

"Well, I see you two are done with your break. Shall we proceed to the training room?" Mikhail asked seriously. He smiled at Avarie. Lately Mikhail has started to take extra time with her after combat and weapons trainings. Most of the time he only snuggled her close. One day they had a conversation about watching the news. He told her he wanted her to start ignoring the news reports from around the world. When she asked why, he only told her that things are getting bad and she needed to focus on the good things in life.

Later that night Avarie and Sasha were on the bed staring at the ceiling. "Sasha, what if we can't go home?"

"Then we stay here." He rested the back of his head on his hand. "I don't think the twins would be hurt if it came to that."

"You aren't doing anything to reassure me at this point." Avarie huffed. "We haven't gotten an update in weeks and when I ask, they just avoid the question. I tried to drag it out of Mikhail the other day and he was all pissed off."

"That's because he's an asshole." Sasha laughed. "I think they're avoiding questions about home because the thought makes them uncomfortable. My thoughts on it are they don't want us to leave. Maybe we shouldn't. It seems to be safer here than in Germany right now."

"I still think of running away." She said wistfully. "You and me escape all this and go somewhere safe."

"You always go back to that don't you?" Sasha asked credulously. "There is nowhere safe from them. You can't hide for the rest of your life. Avarie, you know I'd go wherever you want, but that's no life for us." He continued. "You need to push that stupid thought from your head. Its fear that makes you run from yourself and when you're confronted with something uncomfortable, your answer is always running. So tell me, what are you running from and be specific."

She heaved a deep shaky sigh. She didn't want to say it out loud because in her heart, she knew it was true. "I'm afraid Courtney's moved on. I'm afraid that when we get home, things will be different. I don't want to be in a house that has no love for me. We've been gone too long, Sasha. They've kept us segregated from them. I'm over here wondering if his feelings for me are fading because sometimes mine do." She propped her head on her elbow facing him. "It seems like he doesn't really exist and I'm holding onto a fantasy of a man who never was and never will be. I can't even remember his face anymore. Sasha, I have to look at his picture and close my eyes to try and hold that image in my head, then it fades away which brings me to another topic. Have you seen Eva lately?"

Sasha gave her an 'oh shit' look. He decided he'd skim this topic a bit. "I have. She said they saw multiple videos of you and Kirill rocking the square the night he took me to Red October." A shit eating grin crossed his face. "They said it was so funny knowing that the man on top of the piano drunk was Kirill and you were just going with it. Matthias said he didn't know what the hell you did to the twins, but obviously you won them over. How much so, he doesn't really know and that will remain between us. Courtney thought it was funny until he realized that Kirill was stupid enough to drag you out without protection of the FSB. Needless to say he wasn't happy with the stunt. However, he was happy that you weren't a prisoner either."

"Does he still love me Sasha?" Avarie asked seriously.

He reached for her hand and held it tight. "All I can say is that Eva said he's becoming more and more distant. Whenever you're brought up, he leaves the room. It isn't fully expressed whether he does it out of sadness, anger, or guilt." Avarie knew those emotions well. Truth is, she felt the same way. It was eating at her system and she didn't know how to deal with any of this. Mikhail tried to explain over and over again that a man cannot remain celibate when the person he loves is gone.

Their conversation was put on hold when Kirill opened the door. "Sasha, there's a new bottle of vodka that just came in. Mikhail is getting *fucked.*" He laughed with delight. "You need to try it!" He rubbed his hands together. "*Mishka*! This is a men only deal. You stay here." Sasha got off the bed still in his pj's.

"Alright, a couple of drinks then I'm back to bed. I'm serious Kirill." He shot him a warning glance. "If I'm gone too long Avarie tends to steal the covers and it's a losing battle." They both busted up laughing and walked out the door.

Avarie snatched her cell phone from her bag. She flipped through the photos of Courtney and the others. She missed everything about them. Ten minutes later she clicked out of the gallery. She stared at her phone blankly. In the corner of the screen something odd was happening. The damn phone had service! How the hell was that possible? Courtney had it shut off in the deal with the twins. She could keep the phone, but service had to be off.

Without thinking, she dialed his number. He had to be awake this late at night. The phone rang and excitement grew in her. Four rings and her heart raced. The fifth somebody picked up. It was a woman. "Hello?" Avarie was stunned. Maybe he had a new secretary?

"Hi, is Courtney around?" She asked timidly. There was silence on the line.

"Courtney is not available." The woman's velvet voice answered. "May I ask who's calling this late?"

Avarie didn't know what to say? It was unusual for him not to answer his own cell phone. "It's Avarie. I'm his girlfriend." She said almost as a question. The lady chuckled confidently on the other line.

"I'm sorry dear, but that isn't possible." The woman caught her breath. "You see, Courtney is actually my boyfriend. We've been together for almost three months now." Oh God, Avarie's heart raced and her breaths became ragged. She didn't know what to say but the lady kept going. "Look, I can send you proof." She said manically.

"That's alright. I don't need it." Avarie hung up shaking like leaf in a severe thunderstorm. Nausea rolled up in her stomach threatening to spew all over her bed. A text came through; hesitantly she opened it up. It was a picture of a beautiful raven haired woman lying under the covers with a beautiful blonde man sleeping in her arms. There was no doubt in her mind that man was Courtney. The nausea won and she went to the bathroom to throw up. Dear God she couldn't stop the shaking and the fear that pinned her nervous system in one place over the porcelain throne. She reached desperately for her calm place. Taking almost thirty minutes to control her body, she brushed her teeth and went to bed. She threw the phone back in her bag, powering it down before she did. Her fears were realized. Now she knew she didn't have a home to go too.

ϓϓϓ

Avarie managed to hold it in for two weeks, never telling the twins or Sasha what happened. Instead, she busied herself with drills at the FSB. Mikhail wondered how she was so into them this week. Her demeanor has changed quite a bit. It was like she immersed herself into the life of an FSB agent. She shouted out orders, ran up into danger but also letting others lead. Her mind was completely focused on the tasks at hand.

He studied her movements, covering Sasha when he needed to be covered. He was so impressed; Mikhail decided to run them both through seventeen drills this week with different situations. She was speaking like an FSB agent and so was Sasha. During combat training she was ferocious. Not once did she let up on any of her partners. One day, she flung Sasha against the wall and kicked Tori in the head, almost knocking her out. There was a point in the middle of the week Sasha had to pull her off Mikhail.

Friday Avarie was surprised to see Kirill in the training room waiting for her. He already warmed up and was bouncing around on the mat. Her heart rate rose and she felt the pounding in her chest. She knew that if she beat him she was closer to going back to Germany. She debated in her head if she should fight him or not. She had to come up with a game plan quickly. Kirill started mocking her. "Come on, *Mishka*. You can't go back home if you don't beat me up." He walked around her and he wouldn't shut up. "Maybe you don't deserve to go home." His eyes met hers. "Maybe there's nothing to go home to."

Avarie shook with rage. He didn't know how right his words were and they echoed off the walls in her brain. *"Maybe there's nothing to go home to." "You don't deserve to go home."* Avarie understood he only said it because it worked her up. She looked over at Sasha and Tori. Concern crossed their eyes. They hated fighting days with Kirill and today was no exception. She breathed deep. Her game plan was just to play along and fight but not actually try and knock him down. That would buy her more time until she figured out what to do. "Maybe Courtney doesn't want you anymore." Kirill hissed in her ear.

Her vision filled with a bright white light. She violently threw down Kirill and stomped on him over and over again. Screams filled her ears as she straddled him and punched him over and over in the face, chest, and neck and there wasn't a damn thing he could do to defend himself. He was yelling something but she couldn't understand. Her fists were bloody and her mouth moved. Whatever it said, she had no clue. She wanted to see him dead and didn't even care. Four arms wrapped around her pulling her off of Kirill as he tried to slither away from her deadly grasp. A hand was free and she snatched his ankle and pulled him towards her. He managed to kick her off quickly and find a place to lay down as she fought off whoever was trying to hold her back.

They drug her back towards the other wall. There was a mirror and when she managed a glance, she found herself covered in blood from head to toe. The sticky fluid bound itself to her hair and hands. Her once white workout shirt was covered in crimson ooze and it stuck to her body like some sort of sloppy glue. She looked up to find Sasha trying his hardest to keep her pinned while Mikhail gripped her feet. "Avarie!" Her name was screamed over and over again. A black haze filled her vision. She closed her eyes as she struggled against the men, trying to clear her vision. Her world stopped when she didn't open her eyes again.

ϒϒϒ

She woke up when water was splashed on her face. She wasn't in the training room, but her rage locker. Mikhail turned the cold water on her and watched her like a hunter stalking his prey. He pointed a gun at her and threatened. "*Mishka*, I don't know what happened to you, but if you make any moves to hurt me, I'll shoot you."

He was covered in blood too. Avarie had no clue what happened between the training room and the showers. She wondered why he pointed a gun at her. Did she bruise up his face also? What the hell was happening? "Mikhail." She pleaded but her throat was scratchy and parched. The blood was running down the drain in a strange whirlpool between her legs. She wanted to ask so many questions, but they were stuck somewhere in her throat. He threw a water bottle at her and she drank greedily. It felt like hours that Mikhail stood like that until she got her bearings.

"Mikhail, what happened to me?" She asked through the lifting haze. "Where's Kirill? Did I kill him?" Tears ran down her cheeks, mixed with the droplets of water falling on her head. Her body trembled with fear and remorse.

"Avarie, you didn't kill him. He's badly injured though. I thought I told you to just subdue him, not try and kill him." His voice was stern and eyes were wide. She covered herself with her hands and sobbed uncontrollably. "He's in the infirmary getting his injuries taken care of. However, on the bright side, you won." He nodded his head in anger. "We can probably send you home for your birthday." The gun was still pointed at her.

"Mikhail, kill me." she pleaded as she ripped off her shirt. "Please, just shoot me in the heart and we can wash our hands of all of this." She sobbed harder. "I don't want to live anymore just let me go!"

"You mean to tell me you'd rather die than go home?" He hissed.

"I don't want to go back." She bellowed. "Kirill was right, I have nothing to go home to and if you do send me back, I'll just run anyway."

He wondered what game she was playing. Shutting off the water, he handed her the gun. "I'm not going to kill you, but you can kill yourself." She popped out the magazine and made sure it was really loaded. 9mm hollow point rounds were ready to go. Chambering a round, she put it to her head and looked up at him. "Thank you." She whispered and pulled the trigger. There was just a click. Mikhail's eyes were wide with shock and fear. That gun should've fired. He grabbed it back from her and pointed it at her head and pulled the trigger. Another click. He tried to fire five more times with the same result and Avarie didn't flinch once. In a rage, he flung it over the shower stall. When it hit the floor, a round went off, vibrating their eardrums while the echo bounced off every wall.

"*Oi*! You're not supposed to be shooting off weapons in here!" It was Kirill and Avarie's eyes went wide. Now he was really going to beat the living hell out of her. The door of the shower stall ripped open. "Mikhail! Get out!" He screamed.

"Fuck you! She almost killed you!" Mikhail screamed back.

"That's what she was supposed to do!"

Kirill grabbed him from the shower stall and pulled him out. "She didn't mean it! I set her off! Why are you trying to kill her?"

Avarie lost sight of them. She hunched over and tried to cover her ears to mute their yelling. She debated on running, but knew they would stop her and she'd feel Mikhail's absolute rage. Their language went from Russian to one she couldn't understand. Avarie didn't know how long it took for them to stop screaming at each other. The door opened silently and she was scared to look up.

"*Mishka*, look at me." Her eyes only allowed her to see the bare feet and bloodied pants. "*Mishka*, it's alright." Kirill said again softly. Slowly, he met her at the back of the stall, sitting on his haunches. He wrapped an arm around her and tried to bring her as close to him as possible. He winced from the pain in his chest. "It's alright." He cooed again softly. "Let it out."

She closed her eyes against him and held onto whatever it was that her hands happened to grasp. She really didn't mean to almost kill him. She started to babble and Kirill couldn't understand her. He told her to take her time. He laid her head down into his lap and stroked her back. He still dripped blood from his nose and Mikhail angrily handed him a washcloth. Sasha handed Mikhail more towels. He heard everything she said when she came to. It broke his heart. Mikhail actually handed her the gun to end her life and that made him angry.

Tori stood with him, hands on his biceps as they watched Avarie completely break down on Kirill. The top of her workout shirt was thrown in the corner of the stall and she was bare chested on his lap. Blood still ran down the drain. It was an ominous sight. Kirill was patient as a saint because he's been through this before with her. Not quite this bad, but close enough. Mikhail sat down in the stall and put his head between his knees in defeat. Kirill continued to coo to her, telling her things are alright and she was fine and she did a good job. He also mentioned that Mikhail was an asshole and he needed to fuck off. Mikhail lifted his head up and rolled his eyes at Kirill. Kirill responded by flipping him off.

Sasha spoke first. "Avarie, what happened?" He spoke gently to her. "Remember, we can't help if you can't explain what happened."

She lifted her head up a bit and opened her eyes. They've never seen her eyes so blue. "I don't know." She whispered.

"Avarie, you know something happened. Maybe you can't explain it." Tori was trying to help her find her words. "What did you see?" Avarie closed her eyes. Exhaustion took over her body. Kirill waited but realized that she went to sleep. They wrapped her in towels and took her home. Tori and Sasha put her in the soaking tub and washed her up. Kirill came in later and told them that Avarie was to be in his room tonight despite the warnings from Mikhail.

He put her headphones in for her and covered her up. Sometime in the night, she started crying in her sleep again. She held onto his arms for dear life as he observed nothing less than a night terror spreading through her. His body hurt, but he held her firm. He made sure before he brought her in that he had sedation medicine just in case she got wild. He didn't need it after all. She tried crawling into him as much as possible. He kissed her head over and over. Kirill fought back tears. This girl was truly scary and he loved her. Every flaw, every heartbeat, every word that escaped her lips. His brother almost killed her in rage. It was an unforgivable act.

As the morning light filtered in through the room, Avarie still breathed softly against his skin. He went to get up, but she pulled him back. "Don't leave me." She whispered hoarsely.

"I'm going to the bathroom. I'll be right back." He assured her. She let go sleepily. When he came back, her eyes were half open and still blue. He crawled back under the covers and entangled himself around her. "I'm back, *Mishka*."

"I'm so sorry." She said solemnly. "I didn't mean to try and kill you."

He grabbed her hand and kissed her palm. "I know you didn't. You went into white rage. I set you off and I have only myself to blame." His lips trailed down her soft arms. "Last night, my brother said you begged him to kill you. Now why would you make such a request?" He moved her hand to the back of his neck. "It hurts me to know that's how you feel and that you actually pulled the trigger. It hurts even more knowing that he tried to fire the gun on you too."

She let her fingers carefully graze the back of his neck. He looked like he was hit by a truck. Kirill's left eye was swollen and black. Actually, his entire face and neck were pretty messed up. It was then that Avarie realized her fingers and hands were bruised.

"I wanted him to kill me because I almost killed you. I don't want to kill you." Her voice was but a whisper. "It seems that my entire existence has brought nothing but hell for anybody who gets to know me. I'm forever cursed." Tears burned her cheeks. "Konstantin said that wherever I went, I brought hell with me, I'll be damned if that man wasn't right." Kirill kissed her nose and chuckled.

"I have to make a confession." He smiled at her. "I love the Hell you bring." His hand stroked her hair. Kirill probed her more for answers. "He said that you could go home before your birthday. That's when you told him to go ahead and kill you. Why would you choose death over going home, Mishka?" His eyes implored hers.

"Because I know there's nothing for me there anymore." Her eyes dropped to his cut lips.

Kirill became confused. "Now how would you know if there wasn't anything there? You have a crystal ball that shows you images from home that I don't know about?"

"If I'm honest with you will you be mad at me?" Her eyes still avoided his. She looked for other things to focus her gaze upon. He shook his head no. Taking a shuttering breath in, she told him about the cell phone and the lady she spoke to and the picture that was sent to Avarie's phone. "There's nothing to go home to Kirill." She was defeated. Even though he said he wouldn't be mad, she knew on the inside he was fuming. He asked where her phone was and she told him.

Gently placing her on the bed, he went out and came back within minutes. He held her phone in front of her and switched it on. His eyes went wide when he found she spoke the truth. He searched her text messages and saw the picture with his own eyes. He gave her the 'what the fuck' look and switched it off. Setting it on his night stand he asked her, "*Mishka*, would you like to stay here?" He stroked her back. She loved the feel of his soft warm hands. "You can stay you know. Fuck him." He waved his hand in the air.

"If you'll have me." She cupped his face in her hands. "I don't have a place to go and if I run I won't get far anyway."

A smile formed at the corners of his mouth. "I'd love nothing more than to keep you here with me. Tori would be elated to know that you're staying. She's in love with Sasha." He chuckled. "I need to formulate a game plan alright? You don't have to go back to Germany anytime soon." He shook his head. "Let me talk to Mikhail when he's done being a prick. We can figure something out." She nodded. "Go back to sleep, Avarie. I'll have food sent up when you awaken."

Her lids grew heavy and he waited until her focus was off his and she drifted off. "I love you, Avarie." He dared to whisper to her. She was limp and he grabbed his phone. He needed to tell Mikhail about Avarie's phone being on. He texted quickly. Her position was compromised and they needed to protect her. Mikhail said he'd be there within the hour. He laid it back down. Kissing her head, he got off the bed. This was going to be a long day for all of them.

ϓϓϓ

Sasha paced the bedroom and talked to Tori. He wanted to understand what happened to Avarie. She seemed fine for the last two weeks and now she snaps. He stopped pacing with a rancid thought. He went through her bag and found her notebook. He hovered over it and flipped through pages and pages of writing. Pausing at a strange page, he sat next to Tori and read it out loud.

'I am stranded here. No one will come ashore. Tell me I'm dreaming because I don't want to be here anymore. There are no boats to rescue me and pull me from the sand. I sit here and wait patiently upon this hollow land.'

"Is there another one?" Tori asked impatiently. Sasha flipped through the notebook and handed it to her. "Is this her journal?" She asked. He nodded.

"She keeps it with her always." He leaned back on the bed. "Normally, I can take care of the demons in her head, but most times, she writes them down. The pages are filled with just her thoughts. Some of them are scattered, some morose. I swear some nights she could set her pillow on fire with her tears."

"Why is she so sad? We're so excited about her presence. She brings us all hope and joy. Why can't she see that?"

"It's because she's on the inside looking out. So far, she's had a rough existence. There are many phantoms that move in the shadows of her mind, Tori. Her vessel is haunted." Sasha said sadly. "Sometimes I wonder who steers the ship."

"She's very cryptic isn't she?" Tori asked. "Her nightmares, her visions, and the turmoil that she fights every day is beyond reasoning." She

Pandora Rising

shook her head in wonder. "It's like there's a constant thunderstorm in her head and when the lightning flashes it strikes her soul."

Sasha clasped his hands in his lap. "Now you understand what I go through with her on a daily basis. Her mind is beautiful but it rages." He bit his lower lip. "Right now, I'm angry that Mikhail handed her a gun to kill herself. Then that asshole takes it away from her and pulls the trigger himself."

"Why didn't it go off?" Tori asked in amazement. "It went off when he threw it on the ground."

Sasha laughed. "Because the universe is a bitch sometimes."

ϒϒϒ

Mikhail met Kirill in the study. "You have her phone?" He threw it at him. Mikhail caught it and switched it on. "Yep, this has service. Now who would do such a thing?"

"I don't think it was Courtney. His judgement may be clouded sometimes, but he's not that stupid." Kirill responded. "So, what's the plan?"

"You said she called him right? Did he answer?" Mikhail asked. He shook his head no. "Did anyone answer?"

"A woman did." Kirill poured himself a drink. "The woman mocked Avarie and told her that she was his girlfriend and sent Avarie a picture to rub it into her face." Mikhail gave him a worried look and went through the text messages. "Said they've been together around three months." He found the picture and almost threw the phone against the wall in frustration. "*Easy!*" Kirill said.

"Now why the fuck did this woman answer the phone?" Mikhail asked in a huffed tone. "She could've acted like his secretary or something instead of pissing Avarie off to the point of killing you." He shut off the phone and put it on the desk.

"Women! They're scary sometimes. I noticed that most are threatened of Avarie." Kirill sipped on his brandy. He put the glass down. "But, now we know she's been compromised and soon the others will be at our doorstep. We need to choose which battle we fight first."

"Let's find out who turned the phone on first. I have no doubt it was the others, but we need to speak with Herr Cambridge first. Are we agreed?" Kirill nodded. "Good. I'll call him now." Mikhail dialed his number. It was picked up within three rings.

"Hello." Courtney answered.

"Courtney! How are you?" Mikhail asked nicely.

"Oh fuck, what now?" He huffed at him. "Let me guess, another accident or did she run away?"

Mikhail busted up laughing. "No my friend. Two weeks ago Avarie tried calling you from her cell phone. Did you know that the service was turned on?" He put it on speaker phone so Kirill could hear the conversation.

There was silence on the other line. "I didn't turn it on. Remember, I made you guys a deal that I'd shut off her cell phone. The only reason she was allowed to take it was because of that." He paused. "I don't remember getting a call from Avarie."

Kirill grabbed the phone. "That's because you were asleep in another woman's arms. Have you checked your call logs and texts?" He asked.

"Yea, I didn't send her a text nor did I get her call. When was this?" he asked confused.

"Two weeks ago yesterday around 11pm at night." Kirill answered.

"There's nothing showing up." Courtney said. "What's going on?"

Kirill and Mikhail looked at each other in dismay. They didn't know how this conversation would go. "Courtney, were you with a raven haired woman in your hotel suite?" Mikhail asked

"Yes." He answered softly

"That night?"

"I can't remember."

"Courtney, it's easy to remember these things. You must've been drunk off your ass if you can't remember. This woman said that she's been your girlfriend for three months."

"Shit!" He yelled into the phone.

"Shit is right my friend. This woman sent Avarie a picture of you two together and now you're fucked. She begged us not to take her home. Actually, she told me to kill her and believe me, I tried." Mikhail spit into the phone. "Her heart is torn into pieces and now we have to figure out what the hell to do with her." He paused. "We have two major problems at the moment; a broken heart and her position has been compromised. Do you understand the gravity of this situation?"

"Yep." Courtney answered shortly.

"Good, now what do you recommend we do?" Mikhail asked.

"You know what? If she wants to stay there let her." Courtney hissed into the phone. "Fucking keep her." He hung up on them.

"Shit, he's pissed." Mikhail laughed and hung up. "He fucked up!" He announced. "Well, she's ours then. We can keep her here until the time comes for us to go to full blown war."

"If you don't try and kill her first! For shame!" Kirill slapped Mikhail across the face.

"*Oi*, that's my money maker you just hit you bastard!" Mikhail rubbed his cheek. "You're lucky she messed you up yesterday."

Avarie stood outside the door while they talked. That was it, Courtney didn't want her back. Her fears were realized. Before they could catch her eavesdropping, she hurried back to Kirill's room. On his bed, she cried into the pillow and wished the room would turn into a blaze.

ϒϒϒ

Courtney came home from work utterly depressed. He was defeated, the twins won. Matthias and Ivan met him in the kitchen. "How was work?" Matthias asked pleasantly. Courtney stood there with sad eyes. "What happened to you?"

Courtney hesitated but answered calmly, "I messed up and now Avarie isn't coming home. She's staying in Russia. We're done." He rushed passed them not wanting to face Eva. She was in the pod right now and he wanted to be left alone with his liquor. He slammed the door shut with wild rage and locked it. Grabbing all his hard liquor he slammed as much of the fiery drinks he could down his throat.

He reached for every reasonable explanation as to why this woman would call him her boyfriend or even answer his phone for that matter. He'd only seen Celeste every now and then for a few months. She wasn't his girlfriend. She understood the rules, don't answer his phone and don't tell people she was with him.

He grabbed his cell phone and called her. She picked up.

"Courtney, why are you calling?" She asked.

"Celeste, two Friday's ago, did I get a phone call while I was asleep in the hotel room?" He asked angrily.

"No!" She huffed. "I was asleep too. I don't remember your phone ringing that's not my business. What happened?"

"Are you being honest with me?" He yelled.

"Yes! I don't answer your phone and I don't look into it!" She yelled back. "Are you going to explain to me what happened?"

"A girl called two Friday's ago. Said a woman answered and told her that they were my girlfriend and sent her a picture of us in bed together. Was that you?" He demanded.

"Courtney! Your phone didn't ring! I wasn't awake! Now stop accusing me of stupid shit! I'm not that evil of a person to tell another woman things to make her go mad." She paused. "If that really happened, believe me, it wasn't me."

"Alright. I gotta go." He hung up. She sounded sincere but it couldn't be trusted. This is why he loved and hated females. He searched his mind as he took another swig of whiskey. He had an idea. He got back to his phone and dialed up Matthias.

"Matty! Do me a favor. Run Avarie's phone number through our records and tell me what you come up with." He demanded.

"Are you going to tell me what the hell's going on before I do? Besides, we shut off the phone remember?" Matthias said angrily.

"I'll explain to you later, now go!" He hung up. Panic surged through his body. Right now, it didn't matter if Avarie wanted to stay in Russia and she was angry with him. He needed to keep her safe. Half an hour later the phone rang.

"Not good, Courtney." Matthias said almost panting. "Her phone's been compromised. The last call she made was to your phone two weeks ago and your phone was bypassed to a ghost phone."

"How?" Courtney demanded.

"The only two people who would have access to her lines are Damian and Jude. Damian's records show no foul play, however Jude's does."

"Holy shit!" Courtney yelled into the phone. "Luscious stole his equipment. He said that he had more than enough information on Avarie. Fuck!" He screamed. *Touché*, thought Courtney. Game well played.

ϓϓϓ

Kirill returned to his room only to find Avarie crying again. She made herself into a blanket burrito with all his covers. "Oh *Mishka*." He cooed. "There you go stealing the blankets again. I swear this is a war we men will never win." He tried to unroll her but she held fast. "Avarie, those are my blankets!" He said playfully. "You are a thief! For shame."

She giggled a bit. The sound of his tenor Russian voice made her giddy. She loved cuddling on his chest while the vibrations of his voice filtered through her. She sniffled a bit. "Go away." She stuck her hand out and waved him off. "These are my blankets now!" she said defiantly. "I put all my tears into them. They're claimed." He rubbed his hands together and chuckled. Finding a lump under the covers, he landed a slap on her ass with a hard crack. "Damn you!" She screamed rubbing her cheeks under the covers.

Kirill covered her body with his and tried to smother her. She found a pillow and started beating him with it. "*Oi*! Be careful of my face!" he growled into her ear. "You fucked me up yesterday and I need time to heal." They wrestled playfully until Mikhail busted through the door.

"Avarie!" He yelled. "Why are you attacking my brother? You beat the shit out of him yesterday. For shame!"

"What is it, Mikhail?" Kirill looked at him frustrated. "I almost won the wrestling match and you bust in here breaking it up."

"It's Courtney. He's on the line and he found out what happened to *Mishka's* phone." He held out his cell phone. "You need to hear this shit." He pushed the speaker phone button. "Alright, Kirill is here."

"Matthias ran her phone number through the database. When Jude was killed, Luscious raided his apartment. He grabbed everything!" Courtney said in a rushed tone. "Boys, he's coming for her."

Avarie shook in fear. Mikhail asked the question that was on her mind. "So, the woman who answered the phone?"

"Definitely not a girlfriend. The call was re-routed to a ghost phone."

"What about the picture?" Kirill asked. "That was you my friend."

"I don't know what the picture looks like. Before Avarie, there were many women." Courtney confessed. Her stomach churned and she felt nauseated. "Can I talk to Avarie?" He pleaded. Kirill looked over at her and she was violently shaking her head no.

"I'm sorry Courtney. Avarie isn't exactly in the mood to speak to you right now." Kirill answered. "She's extremely upset about everything that's happened."

There was a quiet reserve at the other end of the phone line. "I can handle that right now. I'm sure she's livid with me." Shit, livid wasn't even the word, Avarie thought. "Regardless, you guys have a shit ton of trouble heading your way. I haven't seen Luscious since that night so he could be in Moscow right now." Courtney warned.

"Fuck him!" Kirill said as he climbed back into bed with Avarie. "I'll rip that assholes throat out if he steps one direction near the little *Mishka*!" He declared throwing his hands up. "Bring that bitch on." Wow, Avarie thought. Kirill looked sexy when he was worked up.

Mikhail was still holding the phone. "Kirill! Avarie almost killed you yesterday. You're in no shape to take on the others."

"Wait a minute!" Courtney said through the phone. "Avarie beat the hell out of you, Kirill?" He asked.

"She's vicious, Courtney!" Kirill's tone turned stern. "She has more work to do but yes." Courtney busted up laughing at him. "Shut up! It's not funny. She hits hard." Kirill put his arm around her and kissed her head. "She's a fighter."

"Well no shit! She either fights or runs away!" He was still laughing.

"Alright Courtney. I'm getting off the line. We have work to do." Mikhail said their goodbyes and hung up. "So, Luscious is coming little lady." He pointed at her and she tried to smother herself into Kirill. "Nobody is safe right now. You need to be on your guard." He turned to walk out.

"Don't you have anything to say to our *Mishka*?" Kirill prodded him.

Mikhail huffed as he turned around. He squinted his eyes at her. "I'm sorry about trying to kill you yesterday." He turned and shut the door behind him.

"Well, he's still pissed. Fuck him!" Kirill waved him off. "He'll get over it." He nuzzled into Avarie. "So, you ready to eat?"

"Not yet." She said. "My stomach doesn't feel good." Her eyes were still swollen from crying.

"*Mishka*, you need to eat." She shook her head no. "Well, what would you like to do?"

Avarie thought about it. She looked around the room and an insidious smile spread across her face. "Let's make a fort!" Kirill busted up laughing. That response did not match her facial expression.

"How old are you?" He said in astonishment. "You want to make a fort?" She explained her game plan and he thought it was funny. "Alright. Let's get Sasha and Tori in here. If it makes you feel better, I'll play along.

I'm still ordering food!" She nodded in agreement. "Avarie, the shit I do for you."

ϒϒϒ

Sasha and Tori had their fort set up in Sasha's room. They drug the blankets off of the bed and used the table area to set up their joint operation. Across the hall, Avarie and Kirill did the same thing. They gathered anything that could be used as a weapon. The goal was to capture the other person's fort and/or flag. Sasha and Tori had their game plan together and so did Kirill and Avarie. Armed with large rubber bands from Kirill's night stand, they used change and anything else that could be a projectile.

Once the game started strange items started to be flung across the hallway. Paperclips, change, dirty socks, and even panties weren't off limits. Sasha had the grand idea to use Tori's bra as a sling shot. The game went on for hours. Since Kirill was still hurt, their fort was taken twice and Sasha's only once. Everybody was laughing so hard the game had to be put on hold for a break. Once they continued, Tori and Sasha were able to take Avarie as prisoner and demand Kirill give up his post.

"I don't negotiate with terrorists!" He declared laughing.

Sasha responded back, "That's because you are a terrorist!"

Mikhail walked into the hallway and couldn't believe his eyes at all the debris between the two rooms. All he could hear was laughing with giggling. Slowly he approached Kirill's room. Something bounced off of him. Turning around he could see it was Sasha flinging strange shit at him and laughing.

"Mikhail! Get in here. They took *Mishka* hostage and they're making shit demands." Kirill waved him into a strange blanket fort from in between two small tables and chairs.

"Kirill? What the fuck is going on?" Mikhail said confused. Kirill kept waving him in. Oh God, Mikhail thought. Quickly, he made his way into the small fort. Watching his brother act like a child was truly too much and he cracked up laughing. "What are you guys doing?"

"We're playing capture the fort and those other two are vicious. They have Avarie hostage and they want me to give up the fort for her return." Kirill said seriously. "I don't negotiate with terrorists but I need my Avarie back."

"You're drunk?" Mikhail said with a confused face.

"No, just pain killers." Kirill said as a matter of fact. "You're the negotiator, you get her back."

Mikhail rolled his eyes. He heard Avarie laughing inside the fort across the hall. Sasha yelled his demand again. "Fuck you Sasha!" Mikhail yelled. He looked around for anything he could use to sling it at him. "Water Sprite!" Mikhail yelled. "Quit hiding behind your pillows and come fight me like a man!" High pitched laughter could be heard from Tori.

Sasha came out with Avarie. He had her arms behind her head. Somehow he managed to make some sort of makeshift rubber band gun. "Fort or she gets it!" Sasha demanded. Mikhail had him where he wanted him. A huge pillow slapped Sasha in the face. While he was stunned, Avarie scampered back into Kirill's room. All five were enthralled in the game. Kirill was laughing so hard he had to take a break.

Eventually the game was over when Kirill passed out in the fort snoring and the other two lost interest. Avarie looked over at Kirill in disappointment. Whatever pain killer he took knocked him out cold. Mikhail smirked while poking his brother in the ribs. "He's succumbed to the opiate devil, *Mishka*. She has him in her evil clutches." Mikhail said rubbing his hands together maliciously. "Let's get out of here. I'm hungry for a donner kebab." Avarie wasn't going to disagree on that. Kirill hadn't even ordered their food from the chef because they were playing so hard.

Throwing on her hoodie and shoes, they told the other two that they were going out. Before she entered the car she asked him, "Are you sure it's okay if we go out? Aren't they looking for me?"

"Avarie, they already know where you are for sure." He said shaking his head. "If they're going to make a move, they would've done it by now. Or they have something else planned." He waged his finger at her. "Better you're with me than Kirill right now."

He started up the engine while she popped into her passenger seat. He rolled down a block and they ordered food. "We're taking this back to my place. I have a chore for you when we get there."

Within minutes, they were in Mikhail's flat eating their food on his coffee table. Avarie wondered what his chore was. The flat was a mess. Clothes were strewn everywhere along with dirty dishes in the sink. His bedroom wasn't much better. She felt like she was walking through a land mine when she first came in. Secretly Avarie prayed that she wouldn't step on a Lego as this place was a casualty waiting to happen. After scarfing down her dinner Mikhail announced what her chore was. "Avarie, you're going to help me clean up!" She gave him an odd look. "Seriously. This place is a disaster." She shook her head no with wide eyes. "*Mishka*! Remember, you're supposed to follow orders and this is one of them." A playful smile ran across his lips.

"I don't know where to start." Avarie said throwing her hands up in the air. "Do you at least have a washer and dryer?" He pointed towards a closet. "Alright, how about cleaning supplies?" He pointed towards a closet.

"Everything we need to clean is here." He laughed at her. "I've been busy so I haven't been able to clean up. I'm to the point where I ran out of clean dishes." Avarie rubbed her face with her hand in frustration.

"Fine, let's start with your dirty clothes and put them in a pile." She said. They each went around the small flat and collected the dirty clothes and dishes he had strewn everywhere. He showed Avarie how to use the washer and dryer. It was a good thing he was helping her. By herself, this would take an entire weekend. They made small talk as they worked room to room. To Avarie, it seemed his anger with her diminished. Every now and then he'd give her small kisses on the cheek as he walked by. When she scrubbed his tub he slapped her ass. Somewhere along the lines, he turned on the stereo so they could listen to music while they cleaned.

Something occurred to Avarie. "Mikhail, why don't you live with Kirill?"

"I did." He exclaimed as he started the dish water.

"Why don't you still?" She asked as she switched out laundry. He laughed at her like it was common knowledge. "What's so funny?"

He piled dishes into the sink. "What's funny is the fact that you took my room. I moved out two weeks before you came." That made her feel horrible. He had a nice cushy lifestyle before she came and her appearance turned his life upside down. Not once did he complain that he had to move out and that just made her feel worse. Mikhail noticed her changed expression. "*Oi*, it's not a big deal. I travel a lot. These flats are reserved for government workers anyway. I get more privacy here." He smiled slyly at her. He went on to scrubbing the dishes.

"I'm sorry." Her eyes hung low. He wiped off his hands and went over to her. Lifting her chin with one finger, he kissed her deeply. His tongue trailed her lower lip and he pulled her tightly into his chest.

"Avarie, don't feel bad. I like it here." He laughed into her. "I just don't clean up after myself very well." He slapped her ass and went back to his chores. Three hours later things were cleaned up. The floor was swept and mopped. All carpets were vacuumed and even Mikhail's bedding had been washed.

Avarie was pooped. This man made her into his personal maid. Both were covered in sweat and Avarie didn't have a change of clothes with her. She desperately wanted to take a shower. Reading her mind he grabbed himself clean clothes and a towel. "*Mishka*, I have something you can wear." He winked at her. "Come into the shower with me. It's almost bedtime anyway." He motioned her to the bathroom. She snagged a clean towel and followed him. "We can put your clothes in the washer so they're fresh for tomorrow."

As the shower warmed up she threw her dirty clothes in the hamper and he did the same. Gently, he eased her into the hot spray. They showered in silence mostly due to exhaustion. After they toweled off, Mikhail threw her a tank top and boxers. Slipping under the covers Avarie fell asleep almost instantly.

ϒϒϒ

The information crossed the screen quickly in binary. Shimon hated technology. For all his time on Earth he never took the time to study computer programming. Having hired the best encryptionists, he figured they could do the job for him. The Mossad intelligence had great minds and they could figure out almost anything. However, this job was proving to be the hardest. Courtney did a good job hiring people to cover up his tracks.

Growing frustrated he headed back for his office. Things were heating up in the States and Russia keeps providing them ammunition. They managed only to push back the militia in certain segments. The damn twins continue to fight even though they're outnumbered. Those bastards are too stubborn to stop. Shimon blamed pride.

Earlier in the week Luscious came to him to let him know the whereabouts of the girl were tracked. It turns out the twins had her the whole time. Luscious was questioned on how he never spotted the girl in the first place. His excuse was plain and simple; any pictures of her never showed her face and therefore he had a hard time picking her out of the crowd.

It wasn't until multiple videos of an accident involving an SUV in Moscow shattered the Internet that their attention was caught unawares. Granted it was night time when the accident happened and the face of the woman wasn't able to be seen, but she had superior strength in order to pull a much bigger man from the overturned SUV. It was then that Luscious had the most devious idea; go straight to Courtney.

Over the years Courtney has been a great source of information, especially when probed correctly. With many agents researching Courtney's employees a target was found; Jude Vargas. This man had years of IT experience and they were able to find records of his previous employment at a research facility in Illinois. It was the very same facility the girl was from. It could be nothing more than pure luck that he was found or stupidity. Shimon couldn't decide which.

Jude had encrypted the information so well it took an entire team of engineers to just decrypt one file. They looked for anything that could be used to track the girl. A ghost phone number came up with no name. They turned on the number weeks ago with no luck. Luscious had members of the Mossad track Courtney and figure out personal habits. They noticed the last few months, he'd take a certain woman to bed with him. An agent on the inside had access to her phone and raided any pictures she may have of her and Courtney together. They hoped that eventually somebody would notice the phone service was active and curiosity would take over. With infinite patience, it worked.

They were able to track the phone to Kirill's residence. They heard her voice and had her name; Avarie. What a beautiful heart breaking show she made. Shimon almost felt sorry for her. She hasn't been spiritually aware for a very long time. Courtney was a notorious playboy and she fell for him. Then as if her luck would have it, she was sent to Russia with the twins. They weren't any better. Those two were full of danger, drugs, and sex. Shimon felt that this girl would've fared better on their side. There's still time.

The new problem was that Luscious made a deal with the twins. If the twins found her first, they get to keep her and vice versa. Shimon almost beat the living hell out of him. The twins were smart enough to hold them off; for a while at least. Since the deal wasn't made with Shimon it had to be broken. Too bad. Soon, they would pay the twins a visit on their own territory for the girl. If they refused, she'd be taken.

She was very important to their cause. Courtney had the balls to create such a human under their noses. Her survival was miraculous indeed. Her existence could only mean two things; destruction of the New World Order or its survival.

CHAPTER SEVENTEEN

Mikhail seemed better after the weekend and Kirill's injuries were healing up. The entire weekend he spent with Avarie left him with many questions and most of all; fear. That was something he would never admit out loud. Mikhail tried to distance himself from her, but his curiosity got the best of him. It only took less than five minutes for Avarie to almost tear Kirill limb from limb. Yes, Kirill angered her, however, her job was to only subdue, not kill. If she was capable of taking him down like that, what would she do to him?

Irony is that she is a little thing. Barely five foot and a hundred fifteen pounds soaking wet. Her size is a great under estimator. If the others came for her, they would have one hell of a fight on their hands. How did she gain so much strength? Most of all, what was she? She was something that thrived in light and darkness; happiness and pain. She could speak the most beautiful words and with the same tongue, spew complete vile.

Mikhail spoke with Sasha alone and asked him what his thoughts were on Avarie. His only response was that she was a completely new type of being and first of her kind. Needless to say that didn't help him much. Mikhail spoke with Kirill over this issue after he brought Avarie back on Sunday afternoon.

"Well, did you kiss and make up?" Kirill asked laughing.

Mikhail didn't find that amusing. "Fuck you." He stated sternly. "We didn't do anything. I made her help me clean my apartment."

"*Oi*, you're an asshole!" Kirill tried to smile, but he winced from the pain that lingered over his cheek.

"Seriously though, she beat the living hell out of you and you aren't the least bit angry?" Mikhail cocked his eyebrow at him. Kirill shook his head no. "Care to explain?"

"Look, she did what we asked her to do. Yes, she was supposed to subdue me. However, I hit a very sore spot with her." He wagged his finger at Mikhail. "You know as well as I do that women are very emotional beings. Their strength comes from their emotions. You asked how she became so strong, well, there's your answer."

Mikhail wasn't buying it. "Are you saying the more emotional she is, the stronger she is?" Kirill nodded his head. "So, that means what for us?"

"That means you don't fuck with her emotions." Kirill slapped Mikhail on the back of his head. "We have nothing to fear from her if we don't rile up the rage inside of her. Now, we teach her how to channel it."

"You aren't telling me shit I don't already know." Mikhail was growing frustrated with this conversation. They've dealt with Avarie's rage before but never on this level.

Kirill huffed in exasperation. "This is *love* we're dealing with. Remember what I said to her? I told her that she may not have a place to go home to. I vocalized her worst fear and look..." He said waving his hand in the air. "It came true. Love and Fear go hand in hand. She feared the worst, I vocalized that fear and Courtney told us to just keep her." He shook his head. "The man that she loved rejected her and I don't even think she knows it yet." He shrugged his shoulders. "Maybe she does, but it doesn't matter anymore."

Mikhail walked over to the liquor cabinet and helped himself to a bottle of vodka. Kirill leaned his body against the door frame as Mikhail poured a glass for himself and Kirill. Now Mikhail was still baffled. "So, where do we go from here?" Mikhail asked taking a drink of the fiery liquor. "Do we start over again? I'm confused."

Kirill swirled his vodka around in the glass. He gazed upon the clear liquid as if it possessed the answer. "We keep going." He said with a sigh. "Learn from our mistakes. This girl has untapped power and now we know how to tap into it. I think now we know why she tries to run away and why she runs into danger. Her emotions guide her." He rubbed his chin in thought. "Have you noticed that she never initiates sex?"

Mikhail paused as his glass was halfway to his lips. "I have." He set down the glass on the mahogany parlor table. "What are you getting at?"

"I'm getting at the fact that she takes orders from us. If I pull her into my room, it's because that's an order. If you or I tell her that she's going with you then she goes without question. She's never asked to go to your place. She's never asked to come into my room." He said finishing off his drink. "If she goes out, she goes with us." Kirill strutted over towards Mikhail and took a seat on a chair. "She has respect for us now. In case you haven't noticed, Avarie is a tough girl to earn anything from. Tori even noticed a change in her."

"Is that good or bad?" Mikhail asked seriously. "Because I see a lot of bad things and I also see a lot of good."

"She's not perfect Mikhail. Shit, we're worse beings than she ever could be. Does she have the power to rip us apart? Sure. But she can do more harm to you and I emotionally than she could physically. Since her time here in Russia she's grown and she's faced many of her fears. The biggest is about to come to our doorstep." He said tapping on the table. "Sooner or later, she will have to face Luscious and I for one am not going to hold her back from tearing him limb to limb." Kirill sat back in his chair gazing at Mikhail. "Keep going with her training. You have nothing to fear from her and neither do I."

"You talk to me about fear?" Mikhail said pouring himself another glass. "I watched as she almost beat you into a bloody mess on the mat. She's like a rabid dog!" He declared.

Kirill stood up in anger. "That is exactly what I'm talking about!" He slammed both hands on the table. "She does more harm emotionally than physically. She scared you by beating the shit out of me. She'd done more harm to you at this point than me." He rolled his eyes. "Monday, just have a little talk with her. I know she's more than sorry for what happened. For fucks sake, you tried to kill her and obviously you didn't get any closure this weekend. Please be an adult and deal with this."

Kirill walked out of the parlor ending their conversation. Mikhail was ever more frustrated. In the end, he knew Kirill was right. He didn't get closure on the weekend and fear still gripped his heart. He had to talk to Avarie sooner than later.

ϒϒϒ

It was almost 7:30am and Mikhail waited at the front entrance for Avarie and Sasha. He spotted them as they had their bags in tow. What an odd coupling, he thought. Sasha was over six foot and built like a brick shithouse and Avarie was only five foot. He observed them as they walked side by side in silence, intent on their destination. Quickly, he raced over to them. Grabbing Avarie by the elbow he told Sasha that he needed her and would escort her to class once he was done. He already told Valentin that he was going to talk to Avarie so he expected her absence.

Avarie gave him a strange look. Never letting go of her, he walked her down the expansive hallway. The only sound that could be heard was footsteps on the gleaming tiles. They took a left into a little office. Shutting the door behind them, he motioned for her to take a seat. She dropped her bag by a small table and sat down. He took the other seat. Clasping his hands together he tried to think of what he really wanted to say to her.

"Is this your office?" Avarie said looking around. "I figured it'd be bigger for being a director."

He nodded. "This is my office, Avarie. I don't spend much time in here. I'm one of the only Direktors who go out into the field. That being said my office is small and I don't require much room."

"So, why am I here? You're not going to pull another broom closet stunt again are you?" Avarie's eyebrows were raised in questioning.

"No Avarie. I'm not really horny right now." He gave her a small smile. "The truth is you're in here because we need to talk about what happened on Friday."

"I said I was sorry. I didn't mean to hurt Kirill that bad." Tears were starting to form in her eyes. She tried to blink them away but Mikhail moved in closer to her. She could feel the heat of his body from a short distance away. Maybe it wasn't really heat, maybe it was anger. She couldn't tell.

"Avarie, what happened on Friday was extremely unexpected. Yes, he mocked you and he even said he deserved what he got. However, it scared me. I've come to the realization that there's more power within you than we've ever regarded. Somewhere, there's a hidden strength and we need to tame it." Mikhail leaned back in his chair and looked her over. Avarie's eyes stared out into the distance somewhere. There were no windows in here, just blank walls.

"*Mishka*, I know you didn't come here willingly, but here we are. I'm not quite sure what you are and if I'm not sure, I know you aren't either. I'm sorry that all this had to happen under dire circumstances." Her eyes still wondered everywhere but on him. "Look at me." he demanded softly. Slowly her eyes met his. "I need you to understand that if you destroy my brother, you destroy me and vice versa. Just having the knowledge that you can tear us up terrifies me. But what terrifies me more is the fact that I can do nothing to stop it."

She knew exactly what he was talking about. The gun was loaded at her head and no bullets came out. After her first try there was nothing. After his five times, there was nothing until it landed with a loud thud on the floor it fired. "So you're saying I can't die and you're scared of me?"

she said in a whisper. He nodded. "You know, the last thing that I want to do is hurt either you or Kirill. Do I need to go?"

"No, you aren't going anywhere. We made a deal with Courtney. You stay here." He pointed his finger on the table. "I need you to stop thinking you're burdening other people with your problems. Stop pushing us away." He pulled something out of a drawer and threw it on the table. It was a notebook. "You know what this is?" She opened it. *How the hell did he get her notebook?* "It seems there's a lot of shit going on in your head." He said tapping his finger on his temple. "You see, this isn't just about Courtney, this is about everything that's going on inside of you."

Avarie could hear her heart pounding in her ears. She licked her lips since they were becoming dry. "How did you get it?" she asked hoarsely. She always left it in her bag.

He slammed his hands on the table. "It doesn't matter how I got it." He said angrily. "What matters is that you understand that you have people here. We can give you advice. We can help you fight your demons, Avarie. You sit here and think you're all in this alone and the truth is you aren't. You think that hiding your burdens from others makes you unselfish. That couldn't be farther from the truth." He leaned in further to her.

Avarie leaned in to meet him. "Because of my existence all of you are in danger. Anybody who even looks at me is a target. Look what happened to Courtney. Luscious stalks you guys like a madman just to get his hands on me." She squinted her eyes. "The others are pissed! What am I to do when they come for you guys, huh? You have something they want and they out number you! There is no army on the face of this earth that can take these guys on! That's why we've been fighting a losing battle."

"Avarie, what the fuck do you care about what happens to us?" Mikhail said pointing at himself. "You don't even really like us. You're only following orders anyway. You know if you don't follow them there are only consequences. It's easier for you to follow orders and go with the flow."

"It doesn't work like that!" She screamed at him. "I care what happens to you guys!"

"Really? Because sometimes it doesn't feel like it!" He screamed back. "When you first came you hated us! You played pranks on Kirill and pissed him off to no end. You only dealt with me because you felt you didn't have an option and even then you raged." Good God, he was about to lose his gum.

"Well I don't do it anymore do I?"

"No, now why is that?" He folded his arms across his chest. "So what's changed?" Avarie shifted in her seat and fidgeted with her hands. She looked away in the distance again. "You don't get to hide inside yourself this time, *Mishka*. Answer the question, what's changed?" He calmed himself down. Her breaths were ragged. She opened her mouth to speak but nothing came out. The expression on her face changed from anger to sadness. "Say it Avarie." He coaxed. "You can say it."

"I…" She started to lose the capacity to breathe. He looked at her and waved her on. "I care about you guys and I don't want anything to happen to you."

"Avarie, I care for my agents but you don't see them getting overly emotional."

"They don't have the weight of the world on their shoulders either now do they?" she whispered.

"They go into dangerous situations and some don't come out alive. I've lost agents already in Germany protecting Courtney. They didn't run away or hide like you do towards us. So answer me and don't give me a *bullshit* reason." His gum chewing became furious. Avarie could hear the gum crackling between his teeth.

"I already gave you the reason."

"No Avarie that was pretty watered down. When I drink my vodka I don't add ice or water. I like my shit straight." Jesus he was holding her hostage with this conversation. "The sooner you spit it out the sooner you can continue with your day."

Nope, he wasn't going to give up. Avarie knew he read the notebook and he already knew the answer but he wanted to hear it from her mouth. "If I tell you, will you leave it alone and not bother me with this subject again?" She said giving him a sideways look. He nodded. "Oh shit." She exhaled a deep sigh. Here it comes. "Even though you two are complete douche nozzle's you've grown on me."

"And…" He waved her on.

"And…that's it?" she said hesitantly.

Pandora Rising

"I believe you have more." He leaned in again. "You see that door?" He pointed to the office door to her left. "You say the rest and you get to leave this uncomfortable conversation."

Her heart was still racing and her body was flushed. She really wanted out of this room. He's a consistent asshole when it comes to wanting things. "Alright, you win." She raised her hands in the air in defeat. "I love you guys alright? May I please go?" She begged.

Mikhail sat back with wide eyes and surprise on his face. Avarie thought that maybe that wasn't the answer he was looking for. Suddenly she felt embarrassed. "*Mishka* is the love you describe like…" he waved his hand in the air. "Brotherly love or the 'I wanna wake up next to you every day for the rest of my life' love?" Oh shit he had to go there.

"Fuck Mikhail! Maybe a bit of both. I don't know." She said in frustration. "Can I *please* go now?"

"Alright, you can go." He waved her towards the door. Quickly, she stood up and grabbed her bag. She was about to swing the door open when Mikhail caught her arm. He turned her towards him. "Avarie." Her eyes met his. "I love you too." He tilted her chin up and met her lips with his. Slowly, he probed her lips apart and his tongue found hers. At this point he was regretting telling her she could leave. He lifted her up by the waist pressed himself against her. He trailed his lips from hers to her neck. It seemed she breathed into him. Slowly, she pulled herself away.

"Mikhail, I have to go to class." Her fingers lingered in his soft black hair. "You need to put me down now." He smiled sweetly at her and lowered her feet back to the floor. He backed away from the door so she could open it. She smiled back at him and walked down the corridor.

"By the way *Mishka*. We are not douche nozzles. We are dickheads!" he yelled at her. Without turning around she flipped him off. He chuckled to himself and went back into his office. He looked at the table where her notebook was. He shoved it into his bag so he could give it to Sasha later. Mikhail knew from this point on, he was going to wear the stupidest grin on his face today. He felt like skipping the halls like a little school girl. He debated on calling Kirill. Grabbing his cell phone he dialed the Prime Minister's office. He was rung through to Kirill.

"What is it?" Kirill said annoyed. "I have a shit ton of meetings today so this better be good."

"Fuck you!" Mikhail laughed. "I have some good news."

"Alright, what is it?"

"She said the L-word."

There was silence on the line for a bit. "She said 'lick'?" Kirill asked confused.

"No dumbass. She said she loved us."

"*Oi*, no way!" Kirill replied with astonishment. "What did you do to her? Was she drugged or something?"

"No, I just talked to her." Mikhail said as a matter of fact. "She opened up a bit and it was a surprise even to me."

There was silence again. "Okay, so you should've saved this for the end of the day. Now I'm going to wear the most fucked up expression going into my meetings and I need to be a serious prick today." Kirill busted up laughing. "You've killed my poker face. Thanks asshole."

"You're welcome." He hung up the phone. Mikhail decided that he wasn't going to come out of the office for a while. Maybe he'll wait until lunch time. He needed time to get over the shock of Avarie's admission.

ϓϓϓ

When Avarie and Sasha arrived home, Kirill was waiting for them. He announced that supper was ready and had a huge smile on his face. Avarie whispered to Sasha when they were alone at the table. "You think he's high on something?"

Sasha started to chuckle. "If he is we'll fuck with him." He rubbed his hands together. "I wonder why he's in such a good mood."

The meal went fine with no incidents. It was the usual conversation about how training went and how his day was. When they were finished they headed upstairs. Kirill went with them this time. He wished them good night and kissed Avarie on the cheek as he usually did. Sasha decided to be a smart ass.

"Where's my kiss?" Sasha asked winking his eyebrows.

Kirill snickered. "Well big boy if you really want a kiss I'm man enough to give you one."

"Never mind, I'm afraid you'll slip the tongue. I know how perverted you are."

"*Oi*, Sasha! That hurt." Kirill said putting his hand on his heart. He motioned them in the room. They plopped their stuff down on the ground and jumped onto the bed. Avarie finally had time to tell Sasha about the conversation between her and Mikhail.

"No wonder he was in such a good mood." His eyes widened.

"Which brings me to how he got a hold of my notebook?" She poked Sasha in the ribs. "You're the only one who knows it exists."

He threw his hands up in the air. "Mikhail asked for my help with you and I couldn't deny him. He gave me the pouty face and I felt sorry for him." He pulled her notebook out of his bag and handed it to her. "I'm sorry. I was going to warn you but he made me promise to secrecy."

She flipped it open and noticed a page missing. It was the page with the admission that she was falling in love with the twins. "Um, I believe I'm missing a page."

Sasha opened up a drawer and pulled out a folded piece of paper. "I couldn't let him have everything you know." She unfolded it and there it was.

"You know, I think we're shitty agents. I thought he already knew because he said he read my notebook and here you pulled out that page. I could've taken that knowledge to my grave."

Sasha smirked. "There's no doubt that we're shitty agents. I think we're going to be here for a while longer."

Avarie leaned back on the bed. "Sasha, we're fucked. I mean truly fucked. I told you we should've ran away."

Sasha met her on the bed. "No, we're not that fucked and we can't run away now." He gave her a deep throaty chuckle. "Now this is getting interesting. You know your birthday is coming up?" He changed the subject quickly.

"Please don't remind me." Avarie waved him off. "There isn't anything I want." In reality there was. She imagined herself sandwiched between Kirill and Mikhail. Secretly she wondered what that would feel like and how it would actually work. A shit eating grin crossed her face. This didn't go unnoticed to Sasha.

"Alright, what dirty thought did you have just now?" He asked mockingly.

Avarie brushed her hair away from her face. "Sasha, just know that it was completely perverted."

He propped himself up on his elbow. "I think you better tell me." He poked her ribs hard. "If you don't, I'll tickle you till you pee the bed."

"Alright!" She yelled. She covered her mouth in shame. "I thought about doing them both at the same time." She giggled. "Isn't that horrible?"

His eyes were wide in shock. "My god you *are* perverted." He shifted to his back. "And I thought Tori had a dirty mind. They're turning you into a Russian."

"You never talk about what you do with her." Avarie poked him in the ribs this time. "So, I think you better tell me!"

"*Maus*, it isn't any different then what you do with either one of the twins when they feel like stealing you."

"So she throws a condom on you and you go to town?" Avarie asked giggling.

"Pretty much." He admitted. "Now can we go to sleep? I'm tired." He wanted out of this conversation and Avarie couldn't blame him. The way the twins talked about Tori it sounded like she was some sort of mystic deviant contortionist. Within 15 minutes they were both snoozing.

ϓϓϓ

Courtney sat at the table with the other three. They stared at him while eating the Chinese Courtney picked up. Matthias obviously wasn't happy with him. This is why Courtney hardly ever stayed home. Eva sort of glared at him every time she looked up. *Damn red haired harpy*, he thought. Ivan on the other hand wasn't so judgmental. He managed to make small talk with Courtney and that was nice.

"So, Avarie's birthday is coming up." Matthias said with a full mouth. "Do we get to send her anything?"

Courtney sighed. "I don't know. I haven't heard anything from the twins since we last talked." He stabbed at his rice with his chop stick.

"Is she going to come back?" Eva asked with forlorn eyes. "I know you guys had somewhat of a falling out, but we really miss her."

Courtney threw down his chop sticks. "Look you guys, if I could change what happened I would. I know I'm an asshole." He shook his head. "If she comes back it's the twins who make that decision not Avarie. She's still in danger and Moscow is the best place for her." He picked up the chop sticks again. "Those two could keep her better protected than we ever can at this point."

"Are you just saying that or is it the truth?" Matthias asked as he picked up his Lo Mein.

"It's the truth. She's under their watchful eyes. She hasn't run away or put herself in danger while there. Plus, she has Sasha for extra protection." Courtney was trying hard to convince himself that she was okay. "We lost Jude. He was part of our plan to keep us safe and look what happened to him. They have all the equipment needed to track her and they found her. We screwed up there."

"You know it took months for them to even find Jude." Ivan chipped in. "Your plans weren't as ill-conceived as you think they were. They have no clue that neither Sasha nor I for that matter exist. For not being a part of a security agency, you've done pretty well."

"Not well enough." Courtney stated solemnly. "I let all of you guys down. I've said things in anger to the twins and now they think they can keep Avarie indefinitely. My corporate headquarters was blown up with people dead and injured and I have a dead IT engineer."

"Courtney, you can't blame yourself for all those things. You've done everything you could." Eva said soothingly. "None of us are angry with you. Avarie is still young and she can make her own decisions. Yes you could've done better hiding your affairs, but in the end it's better that she find out sooner than later."

"And whys that?" Courtney's frustrations grew.

"So she has time to process what *she* wants. This poor girl has the weight of the world on her shoulders and things are happening at break neck speed." Eva chewed on a piece of chicken. "There's many things she needs to experience too before she actually decides to settle down with you. Give her that opportunity to stay away for a while. I'm sure living with Kirill has become interesting over the past few months."

Courtney flung a fortune cookie at her. "Oh yea. Those guys are a hoot aren't they?" He said sarcastically. "I'm sure they're tormenting the hell out of her or leading her into danger." Ivan busted up laughing. "What's so funny fire crotch?"

"I keep picturing Kirill showing off his sexy moves on top of the piano with Avarie wondering what the hell was wrong with him!" Ivan almost died laughing. "Every time I go to those videos she's just staring up at him wondering if she should keep playing or watch him fall!" This had the entire group going. Courtney almost choked on his food and so did Matthias. Eva was laughing so hard her face turned red.

"Who knew that Kirill could dance like that? Was he a stripper you think?" Eva started coughing.

Ivan had to breathe between words. "We call that the cocaine dance!" He pounded his fists on the table. "I'll bet he was riding the white lightening!"

"Oh thank god I only smoke weed." Courtney raised his glass.

"I'll salute to that!" Matthias raised his. When the laughter calmed down they cleaned up after themselves. Eva spent most of the day in the pod and she was worn out. She and Matthias went to bed early. Ivan stayed up in the library going through the tomes. Courtney went upstairs and stopped at Avarie's bedroom door. He opened it and stepped in. Georg started sleeping in the room with Eva and Matthias. He turned out to be a great mouser. The only exception was when he was caught playing with the mice in the bathtub.

Looking around he could almost smell her on the bed. He grabbed a pillow and breathed it in. She was a mixture of roses and fruit. Some of her things were still on the night stand. She took the picture of her three children with her along with pictures of him. He walked back out into the hallway and went to his room.

He hated being alone. It was different when he was traveling. He was never alone when he traveled because it had a purpose of being around people. No, this was utter loneliness. He knew he screwed up when he hung up on Mikhail and Kirill that day. Courtney was tired of his own bullshit. Eva was right, Avarie needed to explore the world before she could decide if she really wanted Courtney. Under normal circumstances, he protected his heart. He went to his walk-in closet and sat down next to Nikita's trunk. Opening it up, he sifted through all her pictures.

He laughed at all her goofy ones with her children. By God he could tell she loved them. There were pictures of them all at a lake. Granted she was in her late 30's, but she still looked good in a bikini. Courtney wished he could someday give her those memories again. Instead of her husband standing next to her, he pictured himself. Throwing the pictures back in the box, he made his way to bed. Peeling off his clothes he climbed under the covers. Laying alone in the darkness he uttered one wish. "Please bring her back to me."

ϒϒϒ

Pandora Rising

It was Thursday going into Friday. Mikhail worked the hell out of them again today and Tori wasn't any better. They did forty laps in the pool after combat practice and Mikhail held Avarie in the deep end again. This time without dire consequences. She hated the shit he put her through. She woke up around 2:47am with a dull thud in her head. Lying on her back, she shifted towards Sasha. The moon was bright through their windows and his body shimmered in the beams. She laid her head on his shoulder hoping that the sound of his heart would ease the ache in her head. Most times it worked like a charm.

She stared out the window and put her hand on his chest. He was breathing softly and watched her hand rise and fall with each inhale and exhale. He didn't stir once as her fingers traced the trenches between his muscles. She loved how soft he was. She could compare his skin to either silk or velvet. Avarie kissed his shoulder and tried to pay attention to his heartbeat. She was still somewhat half asleep as her fingers wondered aimlessly lower onto his abdomen. She traced his belly button with light fingers.

Listening to the thump of his heart it seemed to gain a faster pace. He shifted his left arm around her and caressed her shoulder. Sometimes he complained that she made his arm numb because she lingered there too long. Concentrating once again on his heartbeat she let her fingers once again trace his belly button. By the light of the moon, she could tell he wore boxer briefs. She didn't know when she fell asleep, but it was earlier than him. Hell, she didn't even feel him steal the covers back from her.

He left the fireplace on low and the room was too warm to justify covers. He kicked them off himself sometime in the night. Sweat formed on his brow and also his stomach. The light allowed her to see a little more of him from the band of his boxers. He had an epic V-shape from his pelvis and those muscles were stretched taunt. She traced the line gingerly. He hated when she tickled him on his hips because that was where he was the most sensitive. Suddenly his heart rate picked up again. She decided that she'd quit playing with his stomach. She waited until it calmed down again. She studied his lower abdomen as her fingers danced around it and watched in amazement as his muscles shifted under her touch.

A strange thought grew in her head. Avarie wondered what his true form was. She never told him about Kirill showing her what he looked like and she didn't confide this to Mikhail either. Where did they all come from? How were they able to pass from their world into hers? Avarie's fingers danced around his abdomen as she lost herself in thought.

"*Maus*, are you awake?" Sasha asked drowsily. Avarie nodded against his shoulder. "Are you alright?"

"My head hurts and it won't shut down for the night."

"What are you thinking about?"

Avarie rolled over to her back and stared up at the ceiling. "I'm wondering what your world is like. How you really got here. You know... things like that."

"I told you how I came here."

"But you didn't tell me about your world."

Sasha started to chuckle. "My world is just like yours. We have males and females. We live very long lives and hold a special kind of magic."

"So you only came over to our world because you were called over?"

"Avarie, I came over to your world because I died in mine." Sasha answered softly. She bolted upright and stared down at him. She didn't expect that answer at all. "Easy." Sasha cooed. "It's alright."

Avarie shook her head in disbelief. "No Sasha it isn't alright." She threw back the covers and paced the room in the dark. Sasha got out of the bed and held her still.

"Listen Avarie, it isn't what you think."

"So what is it?"

Sasha smiled at her warmly. "Death is an adventure. We never know where our souls go when we die. I didn't expect to cross over into your world. We go where we're needed. I didn't die just to come here. I died because my time was done. That's it and nothing more."

"Jesus Sasha!" Avarie exclaimed. "That makes me feel horrible."

"Why? You died and here you are. We all go where we're needed. It just turns out the Universe needed you right now."

Tears streamed down Avarie's face. This was more than she wanted to deal with right now. "Oh, *Maus*." Sasha pulled her into him. "Don't cry."

"I'm so sorry, Sasha. I didn't know."

"Hush now, we're alright." He pulled her away to look into her eyes. "Do you wanna know a secret?" Avarie brushed away her tears and nodded. "It's much better this time around."

"How so?" she managed to ask as he pulled her back into bed and wrapped the covers around her. He pulled her into him as tight as possible.

When they were settled he answered in a hushed tone, "Because I have you."

ᵧᵧᵧ

The next morning at breakfast Kirill looked over at Sasha with concern. "*Oi* Sasha, are you not getting sleep?"

Sasha rubbed his eyes. "It isn't a normal night if I don't get woken up at least once, Kirill." He dug into his eggs. "For one night a week, I'd love to not share a bed with her." He pointed a fork at Avarie.

"Hey!" She said offensively.

"How about I make her sleep with me on Wednesday and the weekends?" Kirill lifted his eyebrows at him. "This way you can sleep with covers and not have her leach off your shoulder."

Sasha smiled at him drowsily. "That would be fucking epic." He looked at Avarie. "No offense Avarie, but you do steal covers and make my arm numb."

"Asshole." She mumbled taking a bite of her roll. "You're such a traitor."

Kirill couldn't help but laugh. "*Mishka*, you act like sleeping with me is a burden."

"You snore when you've drank too much!" Avarie almost yelled. "You're the reason why I sleep with my earbuds in."

"I don't drink so much on the weekdays. It's only the weekends that I get lit!" Kirill shot her a wink. "Besides, you do strange things in your sleep too. You fidget like crazy…among other things."

"Of for fucks sake is it time to go yet!" Avarie yelled pushing her plate away. Sasha and Kirill busted up laughing.

Kirill wiped a tear away. "I forgot to tell you. Your driver is out sick today so I'm letting Sasha drive you guys to the FSB." He pulled the SUV keys from his pocket and handed them to Sasha. "Just beware of people following you and you need to park in the garage in the back. Use your badges to swipe in and out okay?" Sasha nodded and took the keys.

"Why can't I drive?" Avarie asked.

"Because Sasha drives all the time." Kirill said waving his hand above his plate.

"When?"

"Whenever we tell him!" Kirill threw his napkin at her. "Now stop throwing a fit and finish up."

Wow, now Avarie felt like they were up to something. Once they got into the SUV she started to flip Sasha shit. "What the hell was that about?"

He started the car and backed out. After they were on the main road he answered. "Whenever I'm with Tori, she makes me drive. I got to learn all kinds of car stunts and how to outrun enemies."

Man she was jealous. She didn't ask any more questions and turned her attention to their mirrors until they pulled into the FSB. Grabbing their stuff from the car they scooted inside. Mikhail was there to meet them.

"Change of plans today." He pulled them off to the side. "There are no classes because the agents were pulled for an operation here in Moscow."

"What does that mean for us?" Sasha asked.

"It means that we can either go join them which I'm not comfortable with or we plan on something else today."

"This doesn't have to do anything with me does it?" Avarie asked with fear in her eyes.

"No *Mishka*. It's some crazy Muslim who's threatening to blow up a city square. It has nothing to do with you." Mikhail answered. "So I guess today is a free day." He said clapping his hands together. "You guys have anything you want to do?"

"Sasha was complaining that he didn't get enough sleep. Maybe you should let him lay down on the training mat or something." She said with a smirk.

"*Oi*, she woke you up in the middle of the night again?"

"That's the norm isn't it?" Sasha said giving him a wink. Mikhail shook his head. He motioned for them to follow him downstairs. They were in the training room and he handed Sasha a soft mat.

"Go to sleep. I'll handle this one." Sasha thanked him and was out almost instantly. "Good thing Tori is gone or else he'd be molested by her." Avarie didn't even want to think about that. Mikhail led her back to his office. He threw their stuff on the small table.

"I guess I don't know what to do with you today, *Mishka*." Mikhail told her honestly. "Truth is, I don't want you wondering around here by yourself and Kirill is in meetings all day."

"Can we just hang out?"

Mikhail smiled at her. "Of course we can." Sometimes Avarie enjoyed being alone with Mikhail, especially when he was in a good mood. She wasn't sure that today was a good mood kind of day. "My office is a bit small. Is there something in particular that you'd like to do while we hang out?"

Avarie looked around the room. It was nice for her body to have a break, but at the same time, she was antsy when she wasn't doing anything. Mikhail could tell she was becoming anxious. "So, your birthday is coming up. Is there anything you want?" She shook her head no. "Ah, just like Christmas. There's nothing you're interested in."

"Actually there is..." Avarie said wistfully.

"Really?" For the first time this week excitement crossed Mikhail's face. "Well, go on." Avarie hesitated and sat back in her seat. "Don't leave me in suspense, *Mishka*."

"Kirill showed me what your true form is." She said as she heaved a deep sigh. "Is that what they all look like?"

Mikhail's eyes went wide with shock. He wasn't expecting that at all. It took a moment for him to gain some form of composure. "Oh, shit Kirill." He mumbled and looked away. "Mostly yes." He answered quickly. "That is what you're up against if that is what you're getting at." Avarie nodded. "I'm surprised he didn't scare you."

"At first he did." She admitted. "He said that it would be easier for him to shift if you were there. He said I only saw half of him."

"That's true. I'm the other half."

"How does that work?"

Mikhail started to chuckle and leaned into her. "You understand the phenomena of conjoined twins?" She nodded in response. "That somewhat explains what we are."

"But he shifted into one being."

"I'm sure he did. What he performed was an illusion. If you touched him, he may have felt real, but the truth is your senses can trick you."

Avarie sat back and tried to process what he was telling her. Mikhail could tell the wheels in her head were spinning but they weren't getting anywhere. "Do I need to fill in the blanks for you?" She looked at him unsure if he should. He smiled sweetly at her. "Are the pieces of the puzzle coming together at least?" Avarie zipped her lips closed, afraid if she said it out loud, it would confirm her suspicions. It was clicking now. Their mannerisms, their tastes, their likes, dislikes, everything....

"You're the same person..." Avarie said softly. "Two heads....same person." Mikhail started clapping in excitement. "Oh my god..."

"Easy." Mikhail said as he put a hand on her shoulder. "It's a strange realization. But yes, that is what we are."

"How?"

"Three things little lady; adaptability, environment, and survival."

"My god this is messed up." Avarie said as she shook her head. "This this some strange shit for sure." She rubbed her hands over her face. It explained everything. This is why the twins both like her and have no problems 'sharing' her. This is why Kirill is the politician and Mikhail the warrior. "Sweet Jesus!" Avarie exclaimed as she looked up from her hands. "You train me to fight Kirill because he's you!"

"That's right! If you can take out Kirill, you can take me out!" Mikhail was wearing an ear to ear grin. "If you kill Kirill…"

"I take away the half that makes you whole!" Avarie stood up in shock. Suddenly she smacked him across the head. "You son of a bitch! Why didn't you tell me all this stuff beforehand?" She yelled at the top of her lungs. "All of this shit would make more sense if you told me upfront!"

Mikhail covered his head waiting for more blows from her, but the smile never left his face. "We didn't tell you because you're still new to this world." Avarie grabbed a chair and flung it against the wall. "Easy!" Mikhail yelled. "Don't go busting up my tiny office!"

Avarie was close to tears. "Why are there always so many damn secrets? Just tell me so I understand!"

"*Oi, Mishka*!" Mikhail yelled. "Because you act like this! Now settle down." He stood up and sat her back in her seat. Avarie sat shaking in her chair from anger. He waited until she settled down before he started speaking again. "Not many people understand what we are. Now you do."

"Is that why they're scared of you?" Mikhail nodded. "You're a force to be reckoned with."

"So are you." Mikhail said assuring her. He tucked a strand of hair back behind her ear. "We know that there's untapped power in you yet. I'm sure in the coming months we'll find out what they are." He started laughing to himself. "I don't think Courtney and Matthias realize what they created."

"A hot mess?"

"Oh, there's no doubt that's what you are. However, I feel that you're an equalizer to the world's current situation." He was about to continue when they heard a knock at the door. "Come in."

Valentin and Karl stepped in. "Direktor, the situation was diffused."

Mikhail looked at his watch, it was almost lunch time. "Wow that was quick." They filled him in on the situation without giving too much away. The look in their eyes said they didn't want to frighten Avarie. Mikhail stepped out of the room leaving Avarie alone. Within minutes he was back. "Alright, let's go get Sasha and get you two home. There wont be any training today."

Mikhail and Avarie woke Sasha up. "Let's go big guy." Sasha stood up and stretched out. They filled him in on what was going on and he was more than ready to go back home.

ɣɣɣ

When they arrived back home lunch was ready. Kirill left a message for them to stay indoors today due to more possible terrorist threats. He would be home early with extra security. Until then they could hang out in their room. They ate in silence and when they were done went upstairs. Sasha ran them a bath because there wasn't a reason to break their normal routine.

They were both thankful for the hot water. It wasn't that they worked out today; it was due to the fact it relaxed them. It wasn't often a crazed terrorist threatened to blow up a city square. They discussed the possibilities of what happened and how it happened. As they lay in the tub the vapor covered all the glass while soft steam rose from the water.

"Sasha..." Avarie started to speak but cut herself off. She wasn't sure if she should tell him or not. He cocked his eyebrows at her waiting for her to continue. "So, while you were sleeping Mikhail and I had a pretty interesting conversation."

"Oh really?" He sat up in the tub and wiped his face. "Tell me all about it." Avarie told him about what Kirill and Mikhail really were. When she finished he busted up laughing.

"What's so funny?" Avarie asked credulously. He started laughing even harder. "Seriously, Sasha."

"That explains so much." That was all he said on the subject.

A few hours later they were lying on the bed. Avarie was reading while Sasha played a handheld game. Kirill entered without knocking. "I'm back and supper is ready." Kirill's tone was flat and he looked exhausted. His tie was loosened and dress shirt unbuttoned to his chest. Concern spread over his face. Sasha was about to say something then decided against it. Slapping Avarie's leg he motioned for her to get going.

At the table Kirill hardly spoke a word. He ate quietly staring in the distance. Usually dinner was the time that they all had their talk about the day and things that went on. Tonight was not one of those nights. Under the table Avarie kicked Sasha and with her eyes gestured for him to speak to Kirill. Sasha shook his head no and mouthed 'this is not the time'. Avarie glanced outside the windows to see extra guards stationed around the property. They were patrolling in full gear in the darkness. Sirens were heard in the distance but not seen. It felt like Moscow was on high alert tonight. Sadness and guilt washed over Avarie. Something was going on out there and it felt like it had something to do with her.

Hopefully it didn't. She didn't want to feel like a drama queen and think the world revolved around her. It was possible that today's events had nothing to do with her presence at all and it really was just a crazy suicide bomber who wanted to cause turmoil. Either way none of this sat right with her. Butterflies filled her stomach and she set her fork down. Pushing herself away from the table she left without saying a word or a look back. An escort followed her to her room and she thanked him. Picking up her book she plopped back down on her bed and continued reading where she left off. The point was to distract her from the dark thoughts that circled her mind like black ghosts in the mist. They weren't allowed to have a TV so they couldn't watch the news nor were they allowed a radio. Avarie felt like she was completely shut off from the world.

Thirty minutes later Sasha came in. Avarie paid no attention until he patted her shoulder. "Kirill wants to see you." He pointed towards his door.

"What for? He looked like he didn't want to see anybody today and he didn't even talk at supper. Probably the best thing for him right now is to be left alone." Avarie said softly. She knew his job wasn't easy. Being a Prime Minister wasn't exactly a stress free job. She couldn't even imagine the bullshit he had to deal with. Sasha shook her from her thoughts.

"He's waiting for you, now go." Sasha demanded sternly. "Take your iPod with you." He handed it to her. "I charged it up for you." Giving her a wink he smiled down at her. Without a word Avarie walked out of the room.

Knocking on Kirill's door there was no answer. She knocked louder and heard him yell to come in. Upon entering she found him by the bed kicking off his shoes while on the cell phone speaking orders. Closing the door she stood there until he gave her an order or indication to step completely inside. Her nerves were racked. She didn't know if he was upset with her for leaving supper so soon or he just wanted to see her. He hung up the cell phone and acknowledged her presence.

"You can come in." He waved her over. "Remember I promised Sasha that he'd have weekends to have the bed to himself?" She nodded and walked over to him. "Well, weekends you'll either sleep in here or hang with Mikhail." His voice softened a bit. "I'm not mad at you. Today was frustrating for everybody." Her expression must've tipped him off. He patted the side of the bed. "I suppose you're wondering what happened?" She sat next to him on the bed and leaned her body into his left arm.

More sirens were going off while lights of red and blue pierced through the balcony doors. He heaved a great sigh. "Their tactics are getting dirtier, *Mishka.*" *Wonderful,* she thought. "Anyway they know you're with us now and at the FSB. The word is that they were trying to draw you out into the open."

"They don't know about Sasha do they?" Avarie asked quickly.

"It seems they don't. However, they knew your driver. He thought he had the flu. It just so happens that he died earlier today from radiation poisoning." He pulled off his socks and threw them into the hamper. His blazer was already off and shirt unbuttoned. She noticed the tie was already on the dresser. "Neither of you were exposed." Kirill continued but Avarie cut him off.

"You know, I'm getting really tired of this shit!" She jumped off the bed and paced in front of him. "Seriously! Will I ever have a normal life where factions aren't trying to hunt me down? What the fuck is so special about me anyway?" Avarie yelled. "How many innocent people have to die because I exist?"

Kirill stood up and stopped her pacing by placing his hands on her shoulders. "Avarie, even if they had you innocent people will die and you'd be the cause of it. They want you because they know exactly what you are even if we don't." He said sternly. "Normally somebody like you would be shrugged off but you aren't." He pulled her into him and wrapped his warm arms around her body. "Avarie, the reason they want you is because you are special and they'll do anything in their power to reach you."

"Then what the hell am I, Kirill?" Avarie was beyond frustrated. "Normal people can't do what I do and they sure as hell don't have bad guys hunting them down." Tears gathered in her eyes. "For once I want to feel like a normal person instead of somebody who always has to hide behind a façade of guardians." She pushed herself away from him and threw up her hands. "Maybe I should just step out and let them have me. *Maybe* it'll give me an opportunity to destroy them from the inside."

Kirill picked her up and set her on the bed without effort. He leaned into her with his hand pointing into her face. "Avarie, first of all I'm not sure what exactly you are. Second you will never be normal for as long as you exist. Third, you're lucky to have guardians to hide behind. And forth, if you let them have you it would be almost impossible for you to destroy them from the inside. You've been poisoned by fairy tales of what normal is. If you think you've seen the nasty side of the others at this point, believe me when I say you haven't seen shit yet." He wasn't angry with her. In fact, his tone was empathetic. His hands moved back to her shoulders. "You are worth the sacrifice. I wouldn't have said that when I first met you, but I know now." He kissed her forehead. "Even if these people don't know you they fight the same battle. It's been like this for centuries, *Mishka*."

Kirill sat down next to her. The bed shifted under his weight pulling Avarie's body closer to him. "Look, none of this started with you. It started because the Watchers didn't do their jobs right in the first place. I'm just as guilty as the rest of them. Mikhail and I could've done better." He rubbed his hands over his face. "You just happen to be one of the keys to the undoing of the Watchers reign. What exactly your place is I'm not sure."

"What are you talking about?" Avarie turned to him. "I think it's time you explain to me what the hell a Watcher is? You guys keep throwing that term around."

"*Oi Mishka*! We're things of great legends!" Kirill chuckled. "You mean you've never heard of a Watcher?" He stood up to take off his shirt and pants leaving only his boxer shorts on.

"Nobody's ever explained to me about what Watchers are." Avarie quoted with her hands. "You've only talked of them." She kicked off her socks and pants. Climbing further on the bed she made her way towards the usual side. He watched as she fluffed her pillow and readied her iPod. Kirill pulled back the covers and they both covered themselves up.

"Do you like bedtime stories?" He asked seriously.

Avarie gave him a dirty look. "I'm not a child." She quipped. "For Christ's sake I'm almost twenty."

Kirill busted up laughing. "Alright then." He turned over towards her propping himself up on his elbow. "There are many terms for what we are. Some people call us Annunaki, Watchers, Nephilim, angels, seraphim. It doesn't matter because we are not from this plane of existence. There are different groups of us."

"So what are you?" Avarie asked curiously. "You don't look like an angel to me."

"Technically speaking you'd call us extra-terrestrials." He said waving his hand. "If you stepped into another plane of existence you'd be called an ET also." He brushed her cheek with his hand. "They came in three waves. The first wave was supposed to observe humanity like a scientist looking through a microscope. This first wave found that when your species were manipulated they learned that you changed drastically."

"How were we manipulated?"

"You were manipulated first by having your powers given away by an authority figure. They noticed that humans had a need...actually desire to be ruled. With the presence of the first Watchers humans became enthralled and worshipped what we were." Kirill explained. "So with unchecked authority the first wave decided to manipulate humans to their will."

"Are we talking about Bible stuff?"

He waved her off. "Forget about the Bible. That book has been written and rewritten so many times there is almost no truth to it anymore. This is the point that I'm trying to get at; the first wave created the savior myth for their own benefit. That is how humans became so willing to worship us."

"So there's no God?" Now he was confusing Avarie.

"*Mishka*, the only God that exists is the Universe. There is no bearded man in the sky, there was no immaculate conception and this Jesus guy never existed." He breathed deeply. "Now may I continue?" She nodded. "The second wave came directly to the humans. Their job was to give them counsel on how to deal with the first wave. Mostly it was spiritual advice and how to rise above the bullshit. However there was a problem..."

"And that was?" Avarie motioned for him to continue.

"The problem was there were so many different cultures and the first wave of Watchers had such a hold on the humans that the second wave became unbelievable. Some died trying to help humanity, destroyed by their own kind. This is where religion comes in. It keeps humans in a perpetual state of fear and compliance. Cognitive dissonance caused humans stress. When they were presented with something that conflicted with their beliefs they did anything to destroy that idea." He wagged his finger. "So this is where the third wave came in."

Avarie gave him a strange look. Everything that he was saying made sense. She saw the universe for herself. There was no bearded man in the sky and she never saw Jesus. There've been many religious wars and billions of lives were claimed over the centuries by dubious beliefs. "So, the third wave came in to get the first wave of Watchers the fuck out of Dodge. They completely screwed humanity by the time they got there. My God, Avarie, that was one of the largest and craziest battles you've ever seen. It was actually recorded in an ancient Indian text and the Bible managed to get at least a third of it right."

"Interesting." Avarie stated. "So what wave did you and Mikhail come in?"

"We were the third wave. The man you met at the dinner party, Khalid, was in the second. Luscious comes from the first wave."

"So did the second wave help you guys?"

"Khalid sat on the sidelines. He is a spiritual man and didn't believe in violence. The second wave had the purpose of trying to overthrow the first by non-violent tactics. Had it worked we wouldn't have been needed." Kirill said with conviction. "The point of my story is that if you think you feel the weight of the world on your shoulders; believe me when I say we feel it much more."

Avarie understood completely now. "So how did you guys fail? I mean, they're still here and so are you. What happened?"

Kirill ran his fingers along her slender neck line. He was lost in thought as he watched her breathe silently. "We failed." He swallowed hard. "They were too strong for us, Mishka."

Avarie adjusted her head on the soft pillow. "The Bible said you guys won, Kirill. It's in Revelations and in many of the ancient texts."

"Are you speaking of '*Satan*'?" Kirill asked with confusion. Avarie nodded. "He was cast out of 'Heaven' which I guess you could refer to as our dimension, but not from *your* world."

"Can you explain that to me?" He gave her a confused look. "I mean can you explain what happened that you guys were sent here to fight him if you already cast him out?"

He bit at his lower lip. Avarie has never seen him like this. Normally Kirill is a force to be reckoned with and she felt like she made him vulnerable. "The actual concept of Satan is confusing so let's go back a bit…" His eyes roamed the room slowly as if he was thinking about where to start. "In the Bible it seems there's confusion on who or what Satan is. Satan represents the evil in all beings. It's not really a person but it's a what. The first Watchers tainted themselves with meddling in the affairs of mankind."

"That I can understand." Avarie nodded in agreement.

"Good. Now that you understand that concept, the battle in the Bible was a trial not an actual battle in itself. When the third wave came down we had to round up the first wave and bring them to justice. They stood before our courts and were tried and found guilty for their coercion with the evolution of mankind. We said 'fuck you' to them and sent them on their way back to Earth to deal with their mess."

"Alright, so why did you guys come back?"

Kirill tapped his fingers on the bed. He was starting to fidget, still looking for the right words to say. "They didn't clean up their mess. Since they no longer belonged in our dimension we came back down and then had our battle. Why we didn't kill them when we had the chance? It's because it's against our laws. However, once on Earth, it was no holds-barred. We had one of our biggest battles and lessened their numbers. It wasn't enough. The power of their manipulation had at that point spread across the world far and wide."

Avarie sat up a bit. "So what happens if we destroy the Watchers? Does that destroy you too?"

He waved his hand in front of her. "No, *Mishka*. Let's say we destroy the first wave that came, eventually the doctrines that they used to influence mankind will die out. It will take almost a millennia before humans can get back on track. The second and third wave doesn't have to be destroyed at all."

"What will you guys do then?"

Kirill smiled at her. "We can continue to help the second wave of Watchers restore humanity."

"I guess that leaves the question of how many of each side is left."

He worked is mouth back and forth trying to get a number out of his head. "There are fourteen original Watchers that I know of. The second would be at least five and the third wave is just Mikhail and I."

"Those aren't good odds, Kirill." Avarie shifted onto her back. "That's a shitty ratio."

Again, he wagged his finger at her. "That's just Watchers, *Mishka*. We aren't counting the other levels." She raised an eyebrow at him. Rubbing his hands together he explained. "The universe is strange indeed. In the other room, you have an elemental. You happened to name that elemental Sasha. Do you know what that name means?"

"Defender of mankind." Avarie shrugged her shoulders. "So?"

He rolled his eyes at her. "Avarie, we have an Ivan who's living with Courtney and helping Eva with her powers. He's also an elemental. Do you know what Ivan means?" She shook her head no. "Gracious Gift from God." His eyes implored hers for acknowledgement. "The universe is sending help, Avarie. There are no coincidences in life and there are hundreds of elementals out there still." He nodded slowly. "When they're ready, they'll come into the vail and show themselves."

Avarie rubbed her eyes with her left hand. "You're talking about back up?" He nodded cheerfully. "Alright. I'm officially mind blown." She threw up her hands in defeat. "Now where the hell do I come in?"

It was his turn to throw up his hands. "I've been trying to figure that out myself. It's obvious you're special and the others want you. I know of only one person who could help solve this riddle and we haven't seen him in over five hundred years. That fucker is elusive I tell you." He shook his head in frustration. "We've been trying to find him since you arrived here."

"Who is he?"

Kirill heaved a deep sigh. "His name is Lukas. We don't know if he even goes by that name anymore. He was part of the first wave of Watchers but didn't fall for their bullshit. He made good by humans and gave them intellectual tools and knowledge of the universe. Rumor is he still does."

"Hold up!" Avarie said sitting fully upright. "So is he somebody we have to destroy?"

"No!" Kirill said in disgust. "We leave him the hell alone! Without him, there's only thirteen." He waved her off. "Lukas isn't somebody you want to destroy. We need to leave him intact and in good spirits. By God, he's a fucking muse to humans!" he declared loudly.

"Alright Kirill!" Avarie said angrily. "Don't get your panties all wadded up your ass."

He chuckled. "I'm just saying he's off limits."

"Well then let's try and find him." Avarie suggested. "If he's a guy who likes to help humans than maybe the first place to start looking is in Universities or something. Maybe politics."

"He's in neither." Kirill reached out to stroke her hair. "We've already looked."

"He could be a missionary?" Avarie said. He shook his head no. "Customer service?" Kirill busted up laughing. "What's so funny?"

"It's the fact that you don't even know what the criteria are in finding a Watcher."

"Fine! I'll just ask the universe to send me a sign or something." She huffed and brought in more blankets to her chest.

Kirill leaned over and kissed her forehead. "You let me know if you get an answer. For now, the bedtime story is over." He switched off the lamp. "Good night, *Mishka*. Try not to steal all my covers."

Avarie adjusted her iPod and earbuds. At least he wasn't drunk and wouldn't snore. That had the potential to distract her from many thoughts that ran through her head. In honesty his truth put her at ease. Now she understood what was really going on in the world. Before her eyes closed she remembered what Kirill said. *There is no such thing as coincidence.*

CHAPTER EIGHTEEN

The week flew by in a hurry for Sasha and Avarie. By Monday morning they had a new driver. Kirill didn't want them driving themselves anymore. Mikhail worked out a plan where drivers would be switched every now and then as to confuse the enemy. At the FSB it was business as usual. Mikhail and Tori worked the hell out of Sasha and Avarie. They went through a mini boot camp. The snow was gone and they were forced to run obstacles through a muddy cold mess. By the time they were done they were chilled to the bone and caked in mud. Mikhail made fun of Sasha calling him 'Big Foot' because he had vegetation and mud stuck on his clothes. He called Avarie the 'poop fairy'. "Hey *Mishka*! It looks like Big Foot over there took a shit on you!" Mikhail yelled from the distance. Oh God he was rolling! That man was laughing so hard he couldn't breathe. "I shall call you the 'poop fairy' for now on!"

Sasha stood next to Avarie and shook his head. "Think he drank before work today?"

"Even if he didn't, he'd still make fun of us."

"I so wanna kill him right now." Sasha glared at Mikhail. "Look at that asshole! He's laughing so hard I'm surprised he hasn't busted a rib."

"We can pray for a collapsed lung you know." Avarie said sarcastically.

Sasha patted her back. "We'll get him somehow." He knocked off a clot of dirt from his pants and chucked it at Mikhail. It only missed him by an inch. "Damn." He cursed out loud. Mikhail flipped him off in response.

After their fun was done they were taken back to the FSB to shower and change. Tori had to help Avarie get all the mud out of her hair.

"Mikhail is such an asshole sometimes." She said combing through Avarie's hair. "He decided that he wanted to put you guys through that fucking obstacle and he knew it was still too cold."

"Well we passed it at least." Avarie said handing Tori more soap. The hot water felt good on her body. "Sasha says he wants revenge." Tori compressed more shampoo to Avarie's head. Tori was silent for a second and then she busted up laughing. "What?" Avarie asked.

"I have something to show you when we're done." She said. It took another five minutes just to get the muck off of Avarie's hair. With towel wrapped bodies Tori motioned Avarie to follow her. She pulled out a Russian magazine. "So Russia names its sexiest men every year and Mikhail and Kirill happened to be in it." She started to giggle. "This issue just came out last month. I know he was gone for a few days a couple of months ago and he didn't tell anyone why." She flipped through the pages. "Here he is!" Tori squeaked in delight.

Avarie blushed. There he was in all his sexy glory. Wearing his FSB hat he looked seductively at the camera. He stood sideways shirtless with his right hand on the bill of his hat. The left hand was pulling down his combat pants halfway down his ass cheek and you could practically see his pubes. His upper torso tattoo was stunning. "Oh my God!" Avarie managed to whisper. "Is Kirill in here too?" Tori gave her a shit eating grin and flipped to the next page. His picture was a bit tamer. He was shirtless but in blue jeans tugged to his pubic area. "Oh wow." Avarie made her way to a bench to sit down. "They have no shame do they?" Tori shook her head no.

Sitting next to her Tori rubbed her back. "*Oi*, Avarie. What are you thinking?" Avarie put her head in her hands.

"I'm thinking that millions of women are going to throw their panties at them on the streets." Was she jealous or ashamed? A strange mixture of feelings welled inside her belly but it was mostly butterflies. "It's like they said 'Hey world! It's just us sexy black haired sculpted Russians here to show off our good looks and tease your women by showing off a little ass'." Avarie waved her hand. "I'm surprised that they don't have girlfriends and women aren't throwing themselves at their feet." Tori giggled. "What's so funny now?"

"Nothing, it's just that they claim that you're their girlfriend." Tori shrugged. "And as long as I've known them, they've only had flings and it was never anything serious, but with you it's different."

A realization hit Avarie. "Oh my Gawd I'm a whore!" She stood up and circled frantically around the benches waving her hands around like a lunatic. "I have or had Courtney in Germany. Now I'm the plaything of twins! Holy shit Tori I'm a *damn* whore!" She declared.

Tori opened her locker and studied Avarie as she pranced around in her towel. Pulling out her clothes she tried to calm Avarie down. "No Avarie!" She hissed. "You're not a whore! Now stop freaking out and get dressed." Throwing down Avarie's clothes on the bench she grabbed Avarie by the arms. "What you are is lucky. You're lucky to have so many people love you. Now sit down and get your clothes on." Tori pointed at the bench. "So what if you have sex with the twins." She waved it off. "Really it's nothing compared to what people really do these days."

Avarie sat down and threw her clothes on. Her hair was still wet so she threw it up in a ponytail. "How many women do you know date twins?" She asked Tori.

"Who cares?" Tori said in amazement. "You seem to be the only one shocked by it. Everybody knows that you belong to the twins." Tori grabbed her bag from the locker and slammed it shut. "And everybody also knows that you have those two wrapped around your little pinky." She flexed her pinky finger in front of Avarie.

Tying her boots Avarie shot Tori a look of confusion. Shaking her head she stood up and grabbed her bag from her locker and flung it shut. Tori handed her the magazine and Avarie stuck it in her bag.

ϒϒϒ

After supper was finished Avarie showed Sasha the magazine in their room. "Holy shit!" Sasha started to giggle. "These two are just insane." He read their stats out loud. "Mikhail Borowitz; age 41 Lead Direktor of the FSB, 6'4" 220lbs. Kirill Borowitz; age 41 Prime Minister, 6'4" 220lbs." He threw the magazine on the bed. "They forgot to put their hobbies as drinking vodka, snorting coke, and getting head in the powder room at Red October."

Avarie lost her shit and busted up laughing. Sasha had uncontrollable giggles and had to cough through it. Avarie held onto the chair just to keep upright. Suddenly the door opened up and Kirill entered. "What the hell is wrong with you two?" He glanced around the room and they were both pointing at him while laughing. Sasha managed to point at the magazine and Kirill picked it up.

"So this is what you jerk off too huh Sasha?" Kirill joked.

Between fits of laughter Sasha came back at him. "No, that's what I have your niece for."

"*Oi* Sasha, you're perverted! For shame!" He clapped his hands at him.

Avarie was almost on the floor. The chair couldn't help her now. "So it say's you're 41. We all know you're older than that!" She cackled like a witch. Sasha threw himself down on the bed and covered his head with a pillow. He was lost to the laughing gods now.

"*Oi Mishka*! That hurt!" Kirill chuckled. "Who gave this to you anyway?" He threw her an accusing smile and stepped closer to her.

"I'm not telling!" She declared. Losing the laughing battle she was on the floor trembling in her own joy. Kirill threw the magazine on the table and started to tickle her. "I'm not telling you." She said maniacally slapping his hands away from her.

"I already know it was Tori." He held her down to tickle her more. Sasha came to her rescue and wrestled with Kirill on the floor for about five minutes. They were laughing so hard they had to stop and catch their breaths.

"Have you gotten any fan mail yet?" Avarie rolled over to her side. "I'm sure your mailbox is overflowing with sexy single ladies."

Kirill popped his head up from the floor to look at her. "I get fan mail all the time. You should see my filing cabinet at work. I get pictures from ladies and men!" His eyes went wide. "Some of the ladies are scary." He joked. "And the men wish that I would go to their team. That's not how I operate."

"That's not what I heard." Sasha joked.

"*Oi*! What happens in Rome stays in Rome!" Kirill nudged Sasha in the ribs.

"Woah!" Avarie jumped up off the floor. "You did dudes in Rome?"

Kirill sat up laughing. "You weren't around in ancient Rome, *Mishka*!"

Sasha covered his ears. "Dear God we don't want to hear anymore!" He scooted away from Kirill. "Avarie, make it stop!" He pleaded.

"What was that like?" Avarie asked curiously pulling out a chair. Spread across her face was a shit eating grin. "Sasha wants to know." She pointed at him and he shook his head violently back and forth.

Kirill glanced over at him smiling. "I don't want to give Sasha ideas so maybe another time." He stood up and patted Sasha's shoulder. "Not to change the subject; but you guys mentioned at dinner that Mikhail was picking on you both today." Sasha uncovered his ears and took a seat on the bed. Telling the story of how Mikhail made fun of them on the obstacle course and their new nicknames, Kirill asked them, "So, you want *revenge*?" He threw some serious Russian dialect into the last word while rubbing his hands together deviously. Sasha nodded vigorously. "You shall have it!" Kirill declared. "It's been a while since I played a prank on Mikhail."

Picking up the magazine from the table he flipped back to Mikhail's picture. "What are you going to do?" Avarie asked eyeballing the magazine.

"I'm going to borrow this." He winked at her. "Today is only Tuesday right?" They nodded. "Alright, so by Thursday night I'll have everything ready for you both." He headed towards the door. "Now go to bed you trouble makers." Shutting the door behind him they were left alone once more.

"What do you think he has up his sleeves?" Sasha asked eyeballing the door.

Avarie shook her head in wonder. "I don't know but I bet its damn good."

ϒϒϒ

Thursday night at supper Kirill had the biggest grin on his face and declared, "Tonight is the night for your revenge!" He pumped his fist in the air. "*Mishka*, you stay here. After supper Sasha and I are heading to the FSB."

She threw down her fork. "Why can't I go?" she whined. "I'm always up for shenanigans."

Kirill shook his head. "There won't be enough protection for you." He pointed his fork in her direction. "I'll tell you what; you can sleep in my room tonight and if you're awake when I get back I'll give you an early birthday present." He winked his eyebrows at her.

"Fine! But will you at least tell me what's going on?" Avarie hated feeling like she was being left out of this game.

"Kirill blew up the picture of Mikhail from the magazine and we're going to plaster it everywhere." Sasha answered her with a mouthful of food. "Oh sweet revenge."

"Oh dear god in heaven." Avarie shook her head. "He's going to hate us forever!"

"No!" Kirill said wagging his finger at her. "Only for a little bit. He'll get over being butt hurt." After their meal Avarie was escorted to Kirill's room. "Wait here for me, Mishka. It'll be late when we come back so if you fall asleep I'll leave you be." He kissed her goodbye and motioned for Sasha to follow. She shut the door and undressed for bed. Wondering around the room she turned the fireplace on low. The soft glow of the flames filled the room and heat blew around her bare legs. Stalking towards the balcony door she propped her head on the glass.

A soft cold rain had filled the atmosphere earlier. Mist from the street adjacent from the courtyard lifted up into the air. Streetlights spilled their halogen glow through the drizzle, giving off strange shadows through the dark night. Clicking open the door a bit, the scent of mud mixed with water filled her nostrils. Springtime crept upon them. From the right corner of her eye, something caught her attention.

Studying the crowd that passed by in the square a tall man stood still among the throng of people. Avarie waited for a dark and sinister presence to wash over her, but it never came. Finding bravery, she opened the door further and stepped out in only her t-shirt and panties. The cold air penetrated her body while she leaned over the rail to get a closer look. Focusing her vision on him he looked strangely like Courtney. An overwhelming desire took hold for an instant and she wanted to run to him. Her heart beat faster in a panic mode. The man turned and caught her eye. Realizing it wasn't really him she turned away feeling stupid.

"You're an idiot, Avarie." She whispered to herself. "He's got somebody else and he told the twins they could keep you remember?" She stared down at the empty courtyard. Sadness threated to overtake her body. Finding an object to focus her attention on she told herself the color and shape to help her fight back tears. She did this for about a minute. Growing colder by the second Avarie was about to go back inside when she looked over again at the square. The man was still looking at her.

He wore a heavy jacket and a ball cap. She squinted her eyes to focus in more on the details of his face. She couldn't tell what hair color he had but his manicured beard was somewhat sandy blonde. Carefully she studied him but wished he was a bit closer. He had to be at least 6'3". He easily stood above the crowd. Goosebumps covered her skin and she rubbed her arms. She looked back over and he seemed to be moving in her direction. She looked around and wondered how he could even see her. Everything was dark for the exception of the soft glow of the fireplace at her back. That wasn't enough light to make out her figure on the third floor.

He stopped at the sidewalk across the street. The light of the lamp illuminated his figure but the baseball cap he wore shadowed his eyes. Chills worked up her spine. She knew he was looking at her. Cocking his head he smiled sweetly at her. Instinctively she smiled back. He waved at her and shyly she waved back. He stood there for a few more seconds. Tipping his hand on the bill of his hat he nodded and walked off into the distance. Suddenly she wanted to yell out to him to wait, but what for? She didn't know who he was. How did he even see her? Quickly she stepped back into the bedroom and sat by the fire to warm up.

Quietly she climbed into the huge bed and pulled the covers over her. Putting in her earbuds she turned on her iPod. Humming along to *Drive* by The Cars Avarie's mind never wondered away from the man across the street. There was no threat by him. In fact, it felt like he was there to reassure or watch over her. Drowsiness overtook her at last. Closing her eyes, the last image she saw was the strange man nodding goodbye.

ϒϒϒ

Avarie bolted upright to the alarm that screamed in Kirill's room. He sat up shutting it off. "*Oi Mishka.* You slept like the dead last night. You didn't even wake up when I came in." He threw back the covers and walked into the bathroom. "Stanger yet, the time that you're usually fidgeting you stayed asleep. I'm amazed." Sleepily she dragged herself off the bed and into the bathroom. Kirill handed Avarie's toothbrush over at the sink. "You slept so well you're still tired. Are you getting sick?" He asked with concern. He felt her forehead and her cheeks with the back of his hand. "Avarie, you feel a little warm." Opening the filing cabinet he reached in and pulled out a thermometer. "Here, I'm not sending you to work sick."

He gently placed it under her tongue and watched her as he brushed his teeth. It beeped a minute later and he pulled it from her mouth. "Avarie, you're at 99.9. You're borderline at this point." He plucked a bottle of aspirin from the cabinet. "Here, take two of these."

Avarie opened the bottle and popped two pills. Screwing the cap back on she handed it back to him. "I'm just tired Kirill." She said yawning. Swallowing the pills with water she moved him over to brush her teeth. "I can't wait to see your revenge plan in action today."

"You won't see it if you don't hurry up." He quipped. "I'm seriously debating on leaving you at home today, *Mishka*." He leaned over the sink and looked at her. "Your birthday is tomorrow and I don't want you getting sick."

Avarie heaved a deep sigh. "I'm just still tired that's all." She said reassuringly stroking his muscular arm. "My body will wake up eventually don't worry."

"Did you do something last night while I was away?" He cocked his eyebrow at her.

"I just went out on the balcony to check the view." Avarie hesitated. "I noticed while I was out there a guy was looking at me so I think I stayed out there longer than I should have."

"Avarie." Kirill's eyes dropped. "Tell me about this man you saw." She explained the story while climbing quickly into the shower and washing her body. "So you weren't able to get a good look at his face?" He asked as he was dressing.

"No, he had a ball cap on and the shadow of the bill covered his eyes. Plus it was really dark." Avarie answered him. "If he was a threat I would've informed security but it wasn't like that." Kirill motioned for her to hurry up. He threw her clothes at her inside the bathroom.

"How long were you out on the balcony?" He squinted at her while doing his tie. "If you were out there for too long it could explain why you have a mild fever." He grabbed his blazer and put it on.

"I'm not sure how long I was out there." She shook her head while pulling on her shirt and hoodie. "What time is it anyway?" She looked around.

"It's early yet. I wake up thirty minutes before you two. I have Mikhail on an errand right now so you two will be there before he arrives."

"Sasha knows?" Avarie asked grabbing her bag from the foot of the bed.

"He does." Kirill opened the door for her and motioned her to follow. "I'll let Mikhail know you have a slight fever though and to feed you aspirin every so often." Avarie didn't feel horrible, she was just tired. Maybe the cold air last night did a number on her. Secretly she prayed the day would go fast so she could hop back into bed. Hopefully Mikhail won't take them out to the nasty obstacle course today. She was tired of pulling mud from her hair and being called *poop fairy*. Inside her head she laughed. Soon they would have their revenge on Mikhail. She rubbed her hands together in delight.

ϒϒϒ

Sasha and Avarie arrived early to the FSB by only fifteen minutes. Sasha looked around and quickly shuffled Avarie through the corridors of the lobby to show her what they were up to last night. "Here it is!" Sasha declared as they approached a group of people snickering. "There's more around the FSB, too." He whispered in her ear and chuckled. "If we see him coming, we need to hide somewhere so we can see his expression." Sasha glanced around the gathering group of people as a lookout.

Avarie silently made her way through the small crowd. Up on the wall was the blown up picture of Mikhail from the magazine. She spotted Karl towards the front of the group. He was trying hard not to laugh along with the other agents. He stood there studying the picture with one arm crossed on his chest and the other on his chin in semi quiet contemplation. Every now and then the corners of his mouth would form a grin. When he happened to catch himself he put on a serious face. Avarie shook her head in wonder.

Avarie felt herself being pulled from the crowd. It was Sasha and he was leading her away. "He's coming and I found a good observation spot." He rushed her over to a crevice where the water fountains were and shoved her in. "Shh, don't make a sound. He's coming from the other direction." He pointed his finger down the hall. Avarie nodded in response.

Mikhail stalked towards the crowd that seemed to gather more people. Mikhail pushed his way through it curious as to what they were looking at. Avarie was trying not to jump up and down from anticipation. His head was lost in the crowd of people and excitement grew in Sasha's eyes. He muttered, "Call *me* Big Foot you sonofabitch." He rubbed his hands together and he was bouncing on the balls of his feet.

Cheering erupted from the crowd when Mikhail was right in front of the picture. Avarie covered Sasha's mouth quickly because he was starting to laugh. She had to fight back the giggles. From their vantage point Mikhail could be heard slinging around cuss words in Russian. Somebody yelled out "Nice Ass!" Mikhail slinked against the wall blushing. He was defeated. "Revenge mother fucker!" Sasha yelled out cheering. Avarie slapped him on the arm. Losing the battle to the hilarity of the situation, uncontrollable laughter erupted from her body.

Mikhail stood up and screamed at Sasha, "*Oi*! You two shitheads are going to get it!" He took off running towards Sasha and Avarie. They ran down the corridors laughing as Mikhail picked up speed. They split off with Sasha going right and Avarie going left. She knew she could outrun Mikhail any day. Knowing him, he went after Sasha. On the stairwell she made her way towards the classroom at a slower pace. Five minutes later Sasha joined her and the rest of the class.

"He get you?" She asked giggling as he sat down.

Sasha nodded. "He knows you're faster than him. I was an easy target. He put me in a headlock. I couldn't fight back because I was laughing so hard." He started chucking again. "Wait till he finds out that there are at least four of those pictures on each corridor."

"Seriously?" She asked and he nodded. "My god we're dead."

Sasha patted her shoulder. "It's so worth it though." They sat silently in class while Valentin directed them through their course. An hour in there was a knock at the door. Valentin opened it and Mikhail stepped in with a shit-eating grin. He whispered something to Valentin and they covered their mouths with their hands snickering.

"Agent Moeller." Valentin called. "Will you kindly come to the front of the class?" Oh shit, she thought. Hesitantly standing up she made her way around the others and stood next to Valentin and away from Mikhail. "Since tomorrow is your twentieth birthday our Direktor has something to present to you." A mischievous smile crossed Mikhail's face. She looked at Sasha for help but it was no use. He shrugged and mouthed '*I can't save you*'. Avarie's face flushed with embarrassment.

Quickly Valentin heaved Avarie over his shoulder. Mikhail rubbed his hands together and cracked her on the ass in front of the entire class.

"Owwwww!" she screamed. "You *cocksucker!*" She tried to rub her cheeks but Valentin kept her hands away from her backside. Sasha joined in with the other agents in laughter.

"I believe there's nineteen more!" Mikhail declared rubbing his hands together and lining them up against her butt cheeks.

"No!" She tried to squirm from Valentin's grasp but he held her tight. Another crack sent searing pain against her right cheek. "Alright! I give up! Let me down." Mikhail nodded to let her down. Once on her feet Avarie wanted to punch both in their jaws. She muttered to both of them about how they were assholes. She rubbed her backside furiously. That man knew how to land a slap.

"Sasha!" Mikhail yelled. "Why don't you come up here and get your birthday spankings?" Mikhail motioned for him to come to the front of the room.

"Fuck you, Mikhail." Sasha responded back. "It seems you're always finding excuses to touch my ass!" Mikhail rolled in laughter along with Valentin.

"I'll get you later." Mikhail threatened pointing a finger at him. "I'll pound your ass."

"That's what I told your mom last night." Sasha made a gesture of dropping a microphone on the desk. Some of the agents made an 'Ooo' sound.

"Mikhail, he made a 'yo momma' joke." Valentin slapped him on the shoulder. "That's a good agent right there." They whispered to each other and Mikhail left. Valentin winked at Sasha and it took a good fifteen minutes for the class to get back to order.

Twenty minutes before lunch Sasha and Avarie stalked the halls looking at all the pictures of Mikhail. Many of them had graffiti on them. They caught Valentin and Karl putting a Sharpie to one of the posters drawing a huge cock. They added to it in Russian '*Agent Moeller's Birthday Present*' with an arrow pointing towards the member. There was another poster that had another cock directly behind Mikhail's ass. Avarie felt bad. The agents were taking this too far. Sasha told her to remember all the horrible shit he's put them through. After thinking about it she didn't feel so bad anymore.

Mikhail left them alone for the rest of the day. He didn't take them to the obstacle course. In combat he flipped Sasha shit and they wrestled around on the mat. Tori couldn't stop smiling at them. "I know Kirill had a hand in this." She whispered to Avarie. "That is the most epic prank ever in the history of the FSB. It'll be one for the history books."

"We couldn't have done it without you." Avarie told her. "Had you not shown me that magazine this wouldn't be possible." Avarie had been smiling all day. The atmosphere was light today at the FSB. She felt this prank lightened the mood throughout the entire building.

"Are you feeling alright? You've looked flush all day?" Tori asked examining her. She put her hand on her forehead. "I think you have a slight fever. I'll go get the aspirin for you." She left and came back with two tablets and handed Avarie her water. She swallowed the pills down. "Let's just hope it stays a small fever." Avarie nodded in agreement.

"*Mishka!*" Mikhail yelled. "It's your turn to take me on. Sasha keeps laughing too hard. I'm afraid he's going to piss on the mat."

"Nope! Not in the mood today." Avarie yelled back. Mikhail stood up and walked towards her. He felt her forehead and looked her over just like Tori did. Tori explained that she just gave Avarie some aspirin. His facial expression went from funny to concern within seconds.

"Avarie, I think maybe we should just cut this short and go to the pool."

"I'm alright." She said looking him up and down. "Really, I feel fine."

"I don't want you getting sick before your birthday." He said shaking his head.

Avarie gave him a strange look. "Why? It's just another day. If I'm sick, it's best that it's on the weekend and not a weekday." Tori and Mikhail exchanged glances. Sasha came over and asked what's going on. They explained about Avarie's slight fever. "You guys are acting like you have something planned." Avarie broke in. "I told all of you that there's nothing that I want for my birthday. No presents, no cake…nothing." She sliced the air with her hands. "Really, it's just another day."

Mikhail turned to her with sad eyes. "Alright. Then let's get you home so you can rest. Hopefully whatever you have will clear up overnight."

ϒϒϒ

Sasha and Avarie were taken home early. Mikhail followed them back to the house. He'd already called Kirill and let him know they were coming back. As soon as they arrived Kirill was there to meet them at the door. He looked Avarie and Sasha over. He asked Sasha if he was feeling peekish and he responded that he wasn't. They gave Avarie a light supper of soup and bread. They let her head upstairs to Kirill's room. He wanted Sasha to get some rest and he'd watch over Avarie.

She was already in bed when she heard whispering outside Kirill's door. She couldn't understand who or what he was talking about and she really didn't care. With her earbuds in she turned on her music. Her body felt sore and she was cold. Throwing back the covers in disgust she turned up the fireplace a bit and let the warmth blanket the room. Laying back down she snuggled into the think blankets.

Kirill walked in and started to take off his tie. "*Mishka*, it's warm in here." Kirill looked her over. "Are you cold?" She nodded from the pillow. Avarie closed her eyes from exhaustion. She could hear Kirill talking to her but she didn't answer back. It was like her body didn't give two shits what was going on outside of the covers. Kirill nudged her and she didn't respond. He made sure she was breathing and took her temperature again. It was at 102. "Fuck." He scrambled for his phone and dialed a number.

"I need you here right away….it's Avarie and she has a fever….alright I'll see you within the hour." He hung up and went to the bathroom. Wetting down a washrag he folded it up and placed it on Avarie's forehead. Patiently he waited for the doctor to arrive. Sweat started to form on Avarie's body. He grabbed another towel and wiped her off. Within fifteen minutes she sweated through her shirt. He stripped it from her body and threw it on the ground. Kirill was about ready to panic. He checked her temp again and it was up to 103. He paced the room and observed her.

A knock at the door was a welcome interruption. He opened it up and let Dr. Alex step in. "Kirill, how high is her fever now?" he asked. Kirill told him how high it was. "Alright. Let's get her in a lukewarm bath and steadily drop the temperature. I'll give her another fever reducer." The doctor moved to her side of the bed and pulled out a bottle with a dropper. He gently opened her mouth and squirted a pink liquid into the back of her throat forcing her to swallow. Kirill was already in the bathroom running water into the tub.

He came back into the room. "What do you think it is?" Kirill had towels in hand to wipe off more sweat from Avarie's body.

"It could be anything right now. Whatever it is just started. I'd like to take her in for x-rays." He put a stethoscope on her chest. "Right now her chest sounds clear. She hasn't been coughing or anything right?" He shook his head no. "We can knock down the fever tonight, Kirill. Her medical history doesn't indicate serious illness or any illness at all for that matter. Is Sasha doing alright?"

"He's been fine." Kirill shook his head. "It seems Sasha is immune to illness."

The doctor chuckled. "Elemental's usually are. We may need him if her fever doesn't come down a bit. I don't want her to pass it down to him if it's something serious though so we need to weigh our options carefully." He clacked his tongue. "Poor thing gets sick a day before her birthday."

"Mikhail had them run the obstacle course this week. It's possible the weather and muck gave her something."

"Oh I'd agree." The doctor pulled off Avarie's socks. "I'll need you to put her in the tub for me. She may be little but I'm not as strong as I used to be." Kirill took off her earbuds and picked her up to carry her to the bathroom. He stood her up but she was completely limp. The doctor pulled off her panties and they gently lifted her in. "I talked to Matthias when she arrived. He said she suffered severe blood loss and had an embedded IUD device that he had to remove." He propped Avarie's arms along the side of the tub. "Good thing he knows what he's doing." Kirill agreed. "I called him before I came. He said that Avarie never suffered a fever or had an illness. He thinks that maybe she needs to build up her immunity." He continued. "I already know about the car accident a while back and she healed quickly."

"*Oi*, this is a bad time to suffer a fever. We have plans tomorrow." Kirill threw up his hands. "This poor girl just can't catch a break." He leaned back against the bathroom wall.

"We'll give this half an hour. If we don't get her fever under 100 then we'll grab Sasha. He'll at least be able to hold it off over the weekend." Kirill agreed. After half an hour her fever only dropped to 102. Kirill left and returned with a drowsy Sasha. "Sasha, her fever isn't going down. Think you can work your magic and try to lower it a bit for us?"

He heaved a sigh and crossed his arms. "I could try. It would help if I knew what was really wrong with her." He felt her forehead. "Well, if I do lower it, it'll only last through the weekend." He rubbed his face with his hands. "Alright, I'll take care of this for you guys. Just so you know you risk getting me sick too."

"We know." Kirill patted him on the back. "We'll get you both back to Alexander's office on Monday. I just want you both to enjoy this weekend."

"You damn well better make it a good weekend." Sasha warned. "I'm taking one for the team right now. Under normal circumstances I'd just let this ride." He shook his head slowly at them. They left Sasha alone with Avarie. He stripped down and entered the tub. He pulled her body towards his and whispered, "The shit I do for you." into her unhearing ears.

ϒϒϒ

Avarie awoke sometime early morning. Kirill slept next to her breathing softly. She leaned in and brushed the hair on his forehead. The soreness in her muscles disappeared and she didn't feel exhausted like she did yesterday. Flipping back the covers she found herself naked. Maybe Kirill took advantage of her in the middle of the night. Oh well, she thought as she made her way to the bathroom. Finding her panties on the floor she picked them up and flung them into the other room.

After she used the facilities she brushed her teeth. "*Mishka*! Where are you?" Kirill sounded like he was half asleep.

"I'm brushing my teeth. You didn't happen to take advantage of me last night did you?" She asked with a mouthful of toothpaste. "I found my panties in here!" Footsteps approached her. Turning around she saw Kirill had on his sweatpants.

"No, you had a high fever and we had to take drastic measures to bring it down. You almost had a trip to the hospital." Kirill wagged his finger at her. "I hope you feel better." Avarie spit into the sink and nodded. "Good. We have plans today. Your fever will stay away for the weekend we hope but you'll have to go see Dr. Alex on Monday. Sasha has to see him too."

"Alex was here?" Avarie asked confused. "I must've been really out of it then."

"Oh you were. We had to get Sasha to help. That's why he has to see Alex on Monday too. We're going to see what's causing your fever."

"So what are we doing today?" Avarie cocked her eyebrows at him. "I know it's my birthday and all, but we don't have to do anything. It's just another day."

He slapped her bare ass. "Avarie, it may be another day to you, but we're also celebrating Sasha's birthday along with yours." She was about to ask why and he answered for her. "He doesn't really have a day he was born so we decided to give you guys the same day. You two are blood bound so it's only suitable that you share a special day together."

"Fine." She said as she rinsed off her toothbrush. "So what are we doing?" She worked her way towards the shower and turned it on.

"You don't worry about what we're doing. Everything is set up." She glared at him from the glass of the shower stall. "Avarie, you told me that for once you wanted to be normal right?" She nodded. "This weekend you and Sasha both get to be normal." Within seconds he was joining her in the shower. "So, I heard that Mikhail received his just rewards." Avarie busted up laughing. "One of the Direktor's from the FSB called me. He wasn't happy but he couldn't stop laughing at the prank. He wanted you two suspended but I told him it was all me." Kirill turned on another showerhead from the wall for Avarie. "Anyway we collected the posters and my God, the shit those people write." A low growl came from his chest. "They're perverted."

Avarie loved how the twins spoke. Their Russian dialect was extremely sexy. A smile curled on her lips. She knew she had the two sexiest men in all of Russia. "What are you smiling about?" Kirill ran shampoo through his hair. Avarie looked away. "No, you don't get out of this. Answer my question."

She rolled her eyes. "I was just thinking about how handsome you two are." She turned around again trying not to make a big deal out of it.

"Avarie, you've never called us handsome before. I'm amazed that came from your mouth." Kirill's eyes went wide. He studied her movements. "What else?"

"Well, I guess when you guys talk you have a sexy dialect."

"Really?" She nodded. "Is there anything else?"

From under the spray she answered nonchalantly, "You guys also look dangerous and there's a serious appeal to that." She started to giggle. "The universe made you so nice it had to make you twice." She slapped his ass and he jumped away smiling.

"You're becoming very brave. Now that's hot." He eyed her up and down. "I'd like to give you your birthday present." He rubbed his hands together. "I'm thinking you'd like it."

She put her hands out in front of her. "Wait a minute." She looked him up and down. "What if there was something I wanted to do to you?" She cocked her head to one side. "Would you let me do it?"

He pursed his lips together and crossed his arms. "Is it sexual?" she nodded. "It's not overly kinky is it?" She shook her head no. "Then by all means." He opened his arms wide as an invitation.

"I don't know." She teased. "Now I'm put on the spot."

"*Oi, Mishka.*" He shook his head. "You've got me all excited. This isn't fair. For shame." The water beaded up on his body and trickled down through the crevices of his muscles. Avarie did want him but she never initiated sexual contact. Everything was an order or they're the ones who started it. Avarie shot him a seductive look. Slowly she made contact with his body and stroked the soft dark hair on his chest. He didn't lie when he said he was excited. His cock stood erect in the shower.

She stood on her tiptoes and he leaned in to kiss her. His lips felt soft on hers and he let her guide him on the pace. Avarie probed his mouth with her tongue while her hands never left his chest. Kirill wrapped his arms around her lightly stroking her spine. Avarie moved her lips from him and let them linger on his cheek and to his neck. Lapping at his artery she suckled the sensitive skin and moved to his earlobe. Kirill moaned with pleasure in a low growl that came from his chest. Slowly she worked her way back down his neck, running her tongue and grazing her lips along his collarbone and then to his nipples. She nipped and licked at them gently. "Avarie." He whispered. She looked up at him and his eyes were half closed. He was enjoying himself as she explored his body. Her hands brushed his back in gentle strokes. She planted kisses along his abdomen and licked around his hip where his muscles made a V-shape.

His cock reached up to his belly button completely hard and she took it in her left hand. Gently stroking him she worked her way down to his inner thighs. She felt him shutter. He held onto the side of the shower stall. Avarie didn't want him sitting or lying down. She only allowed him to lean his body against the tile while she went to work on his member. She licked the base of his shaft and worked her way up to the head. Rolling her tongue around it a drop of clear liquid formed. Looking into his eyes she lapped it up. His breaths became deep and shallow as she continued running her tongue along his length.

Cupping his balls in her right hand she caressed them lightly. Another moan escaped his lips. Taking as much of him as possible in her mouth she moved her left hand with the motion of her head. Keeping her pace steady she swirled her tongue around his shaft and head. Her nipples hardened at the sound of his deep moans. Wetness formed between her legs. She fought against the sprays of water as it dripped down her head onto her body. He moved his left hand to play with her nipple. She breathed deeply and moaned. He started to slowly lower himself to the floor. She gently slapped his ass and said, "You'll stay standing." His eyes went wide with disbelief. She continued stroking him and he closed his eyes.

Leaving her hand on his sculpted ass, she caressed it. "*Mishka*, you're driving me crazy." Kirill said between breaths. "I won't last much longer." Avarie sped up her pace a bit. He brought his other hand to her head. Feverishly she continued to run her tongue over his head as she bobbed up and down and kept pace. He struggled to breathe as he moaned deeper. She moved her hand from his ass towards his chest, lingering over every sensitive spot she could find.

His hand gathered up her wet hair and he gently bucked against her. Avarie loved the feel of him inside her mouth. His cock was smooth like velvet and filled her wide. She could tell he was close to coming. His member throbbed against her warm tongue. His moans became louder and she picked up her pace. "I'm coming Avarie." The grip on her hair tightened as he bucked into her. Salty hot fluid filled her mouth and she swallowed while still working his member. Kirill trembled and almost doubled over her when he finished. Avarie allowed him to slink down into the shower. It wasn't until he sat at the bottom that she released him from her hold. She planted kisses from his cock all the way up to his lips. She pulled away from him and smiled.

"Where the hell did you learn that?" Kirill pulled Avarie into him on the shower floor.

She giggled and answered, "The Internet." She leaned her body against his and made herself comfortable between his legs. He kissed her shoulders softly. "Courtney allowed me access."

"Thank God for the Internet." Kirill was still recovering from his experience. "My God you made me feel like it was *my* birthday." He said excitedly. "I need some recovery time." He admitted.

"That's fine." Avarie kissed his cheek. "That was more for me anyway."

Kirill let out a deep groan. "What else do you have for me?"

Avarie patted his leg. "I don't know. Maybe you'll wake up in the middle of the night to find me riding you. I'm told I'm full of surprises."

"Please do!" Kirill rolled the back of his head against the tile. His breathing returned to normal and he kissed the top of her head. "I love you, *Mishka*." He whispered into her ear.

"I love you too." She whispered back. Standing up she shut off the water. "So, let's get dressed and see what you have planned for us." She clapped her hands together and he followed her out.

ϓϓϓ

Kirill pulled up to a large warehouse on the outskirts of Moscow. There were rows of cars parked on the outside and heavy security. "What is this place?" Avarie asked as she leaned forward. Loud music banged against the metal walls and vibrated through the parking lot. She got out of the car along with Sasha, Tori, and Mikhail.

"This is your birthday present. You guys wanted to have fun and feel normal so here it is." Mikhail answered her. He guided them to the doors and showed the guards his FSB ID. They were allowed entry and the music was extremely loud. Going further inside strobe lights flashed along with other bright lights. Avarie had to rub her eyes to adjust to the scenery. She smelled food and found a huge buffet table line filled with all kinds of delicacies. Alcohol filled the air along with laughter. She smiled as she realized they turned a warehouse into a party zone for her and Sasha.

Suddenly the music shut off and a crowd gathered to yell *Happy Birthday* to them both. Wild applause and whistling erupted. The twins had the entire FSB here to party. "Where's the powder room?" Sasha asked Kirill.

"*Oi*, there's only one powder room and it's not here." Kirill's eyes went wide in shock.

Sasha nudged him in the ribs and asked, "So there's no place to get blowjobs either?"

"Sasha, you're perverted, for shame." Kirill pushed him further into the warehouse. "Go look around. We have all kinds of fun stuff for you guys." Kirill kissed Avarie sweetly. "I know in America they had a fun zone near where you used to live back in the day." He clamped her arm. "I can't remember what they called it but it's like a trampoline park." He walked her towards the area. When she saw it Avarie felt like crying. There were huge trampolines lined together with safety features. Some had foam and ball pits.

Pandora Rising

Avarie took in a deep breath and couldn't contain her excitement. "Oh my God!" She screamed like a child. "This is freaking awesome!" Mikhail was already on a trampoline and he motioned for her to join him. Kirill waved her on. Other agents were already jumping around them.

Mikhail started showing off by doing flips and running up the side trampolines and launch point. Kirill called him a show off. Mikhail told him to go fuck himself and it was on. Kirill kicked off his shoes and the twins dueled. Avarie had to get away from them because they were getting too rough. They were using karate and Judo moves against each other. One would fly in the air and she felt like she was watching *Crouching Tiger Hidden Dragon*.

She made her way to another trampoline and after a bit grew brave. She bounced higher and higher doing flips and twirling in the air. She was getting dangerously close to the rafters. "*Mishka*! Don't bump your head!" Mikhail yelled at her. She flipped him off and on her next bounce she was able to grab onto one. She let go and fell back to the trampoline. "Stop it, Avarie!" He yelled again. While she was in the air she grabbed the rafter again and pulled herself onto it. Flinging herself backwards she flipped and landed on her feet and went again and again.

She didn't notice Sasha was next to her. "Let's scare the shit out of them." He suggested. He started doing the same thing and the twins stopped wrestling and yelled at them both. A crowd gathered and cheered them on. She felt like a kid. Tonight she knew nothing could go wrong. For now at least. They had adequate protection and this place was filled with FSB agents. Unless somebody planned on bombing the building they were safe. That thought stopped Avarie in her tracks. She grew worrisome and she looked around to study her surroundings. She felt stupid for not following the first rule of being an agent; situational awareness.

"Avarie, are you alright?" Mikhail came up to her. "You're not hurt are you?"

She shook her head no. "I just had a strange thought." He beckoned her to share. "If they knew all the agents were here, couldn't they just bomb the place if they wanted?"

Mikhail was taken aback by her words. "Avarie, we already swept this place and changed the location three times. If they wanted to bomb us, they'd have to do it by air. There's no way in hell that's going to happen." She still looked worried. "Look, we planned this weeks ahead for you two.

You let us worry about the what ifs. Go have fun, that's an order." He gave her a reassuring look. "Go."

Avarie had enough of the trampolines for now. She explored the massive warehouse. Agents came and talked to her and wished her a happy birthday. They had a dance floor set up and people were dancing. She didn't recognize most of the people in their street clothes. The DJ even had a karaoke machine for those who wanted to sing. It was still early in the night. The party started at five and it was only 6:30. Tori found Avarie and led her to the food tables. They ate all kinds of things. When they were done she took her to an open bar.

"I'm not much of a drinker." Avarie admitted. "I've seen Courtney and Matthias get lit and it was too funny."

"You've seen the twins drunk off their asses. It's your night, you can get drunk if you want." Avarie shook her head. "Then let's start off with something small." Tori suggested. She handed her a fruity drink. "The trick is to drink water between drinks so you don't get drunk too fast. I'll help you pace yourself." Avarie thanked her. "That's what mentors are for." Tori winked at her. "Now where is my water demon?" They took off looking for Sasha.

The Direktors found the twins and handed them drinks. They made small talk and watched Avarie mingle and party. "They really deserve this you know?" One of the older men stated. "She's worked through a lot of issues and asking for a normal day isn't too much. Sasha has really come along in his skills too. I bet he'll like our present."

"*Oi*, you got him something?" Mikhail asked him. He nodded. "Is it what I think it is?" He nodded again. "Shit! I'll have to lock it up." He busted up laughing.

Kirill shook his head. "A man never forgets his first sexual relationship, even if it's with a gun." There was a tap at his shoulder and he turned around. "Konstantin! I thought you'd be sleeping." Kirill joked and gave him a hug.

"No, I slept enough today. I decided to make an appearance and bring Viktor with me. He's wondering around somewhere. I last saw him at the bar." Konstantin waved. "Where's the birthday couple?" He asked.

Mikhail pointed towards the buffet. "Sasha's over there stuffing his face and I think Avarie is somewhere with Tori."

"I think everybody will be fucked come Monday." Viktor said next to Konstantin. He held a bottle of vodka. Mikhail took it out of his hands. "*Oi*, I got that from the bar." He reached for it but Mikhail pulled it out of his reach. He ran his hands through Viktor's hair and Kirill put him in a headlock.

"It's our vodka now young man." Kirill joked and kissed his cheek. "You're too young to drink this."

"Fuck you Kirill." He slapped him away. "Where's Avarie?"

"Why?" Mikhail asked giggling. "You don't need to kiss on her here, she's safe." The music pounded in their ears and he had to yell over it. The Direktor's were finding this interesting and laughed along.

"I'll take her back home with me then." Viktor quipped. The other men went 'Ooo'. Konstantin turned red from laughter and patted his son on the chest. "My wife is in love with her." He winked at the twins.

"Your wife is very pregnant." Kirill said back. "Avarie would send her into early labor just standing over her naked." Konstantin had to pull up a chair and sit down. He could barely breathe he's laughing so hard. "Look what you're doing to your father. He's going to die from embarrassment." Mikhail opened up the vodka bottle, took a large swig and handed it to Kirill. After he took a swig he declared, "Somebody get this man an oxygen tank!"

"Somebody get this man a pair of tits!" Mikhail yelled back. "If he's going out tonight it needs to be between a pair of glorious fun bags!" He looked around. "I thought I ordered whores for this party."

"He's standing in front of me." Viktor pointed at Mikhail. "We heard about Sasha's revenge on you."

"*Oi*, he got me good, too." Mikhail placed his hand on his heart. "I have a huge collection of cocks and gay jokes written all over the posters this asshole blew up!" He laughed at Kirill. "Well played." Kirill raised the bottle and took another huge swig in acknowledgement.

The party became wild by the time 8pm rolled around. Everybody gathered to sing Happy Birthday to Avarie and Sasha. After they ate cake the twins decided to have the DJ turn on the karaoke machine. Avarie could tell they were halfway blitzed. They double fisted bottles of vodka. Together the twins sang *I Got You Babe* and it was horribly entertaining. Other agents went up to sing and some of the females were pretty good.

There was definitely talent there. Konstantin found her and held her hand in his.

"I think you should sing. I always loved hearing you sing to the children in your camp." His expression was wistful. "Show all these bastards up." He said taking a drink of his liquor.

"And what do you want me to sing?" She asked playfully. He leaned in and whispered something in her ear. She walked up to the DJ and he put in the song. She walked back to him and took his hand again. "That's an odd song for you to request."

"Oh but your voice could handle it. I knew it was on your iPod and Jace would request it all the time when he was lit." Konstantin chuckled. "You killed it each time." Two songs later the DJ announced her name and cheers were thrown in the air. He patted her hand and motioned for her to go up.

Taking the microphone she gazed upon the wave of agents and their spouses or significant others who looked upon her with anticipation. Butterflies formed in her stomach and at this point she was glad she had liquid courage already in her belly. Most of the time she was shielded by a piano when she sang. The twins stood next to Konstantin while Tori and Sasha were in the front row cheering her on. The first notes of *Only the Good Die Young* by Billy Joel filtered out and the crowd went wild. The agents clapped to the beat and people started dancing.

Avarie really got into the song and the crowd sang along. The atmosphere was awesome and Avarie lost herself in it. She danced around on the stage during the musical breaks. The twins were hooting and hollering her name. When the song finished up they all yelled for an encore. She shrugged her shoulders not knowing what song to sing. Sasha went up to the DJ and threw in another song for her. Coming down he winked. Tori handed him another drink and patted his ass. The screen threw up the words to the song. *Oh shit, Sasha was really testing her abilities.* He requested *Stay* by Shakespeare's Sister. *That mother fucker,* she thought. She knew he listened to her iPod when she wasn't using it and this happened to be one of his favorite songs.

Taking a deep breathe she had to really focus. The DJ lowered the lights and some agents broke out lighters while she sang. She hit the high notes on cue and tore the living hell out of that song. The twins stood there in astonishment. She prayed that she did it justice when it ended. They wanted more but she needed a drink and told the crowd that she'd be back for more. Tori followed her to the bar. The drinks started to get harder and Avarie made sure to constantly carry a bottle of water with her.

Eventually Viktor found her and pulled her aside. He made small talk with her and all Avarie could think was how damn handsome he was. She struggled with the thought of having made out with him in front of complete drugged up strangers. He managed to talk her into going back onto the dance floor. Shit this guy could dance too. Konstantin waved at her from the sidelines and winked at her. Eventually the twins were up again to sing. Avarie wondered what the hell they were going to sing now. Mikhail picked up the microphone and announced, "This song goes out to Agent Moeller." The song started up and Avarie flushed with embracement as *Pillowtalk* by Zayne came on. These guys were killing her but damn could they sing. That song was extremely naughty and it worked her up.

Alcohol buzzed through her body and she was starting to feel brave. She led Viktor over to Konstantin. "Hey, what did I usually drink?" She asked curiously.

He thought about the question carefully. "Well, when you had it, you drank mostly Jägermeister." He said in a matter of fact manor. "Anything else wasn't the same." She bee lined to the bar and had the bartender give her a bottle. She knew something was off with her alcoholic taste buds since she arrived in Russia. The entire night she sucked on the bottle with Viktor following her around. Mainly it was her pulling him around to be honest. They bounced on the trampolines and went around the ball pits. She was at the point of complete giddiness. The twins found her lying on her back on one of the trampolines.

"Viktor, what have you done to our *Mishka*?" Kirill asked him. "She has a huge bottle of that German shit in her hands. She won't survive the night." He declared.

"*Oi*, my father told her that's what she used to drink back in the day. This wasn't my idea." Viktor looked down at her. "I would've given her whiskey but this is her booze of choice." Avarie didn't feel drunk at all. She had a light buzz and half the bottle was gone. Maybe her tolerance for alcohol was put in the system by Matthias. The twins gave her shit about drinking liquid licorice. She waved them off in annoyance. They pulled her off the trampoline and made her sing more songs. After 11pm the night was a blur.

The twins danced with her on the dance floor and so did the Direktors. Mikhail took Avarie out on the dance floor and grinded her right there in front of them, grabbing her ass and pushing her into him as far as she would go. By this time, Mikhail and Avarie were both a sweaty drunken mess and he nor Avarie cared. Their jaws dropped as Mikhail wrapped her legs around his waist and he dipped her lower and lower. Kirill went to break it up, "*Oi*, Bible's length between you both!" he said shoving them apart. "You're both getting too drunk. For shame!"

Konstantin announced he was going home and she hugged him goodbye. He kissed her cheek and bravely kissed her on the lips in front of the twins. Holy shit, she thought. This guy knew how to kiss a woman. He set her back on her feet and walked away. Avarie started to follow him but the twins stopped her. "*Oi Mishka*! You'd kill him." Kirill pulled her to him. "He's like seventy five for Christ's sake. The booze is getting to your head." He shook her a bit. Wow, did she almost try and go home with Konstantin? Alright, she was officially lit.

"When does this party end?" She asked slurring. Viktor handed her a bottle of water and she sucked it down. Tori flipped her shit for breaking her seal hours ago.

"Avarie, this party ends when we say it does. The guard changes at 4am." Mikhail answered her. He had a slight speech impediment himself. "We'll party till we fall down if you want." He burped loudly. "Or until one of us pukes." He busted up laughing.

"Who's driving home?" Avarie looked around. She hoped Sasha wasn't too drunk but she spotted him at the bar getting more drinks. "I think Sasha's getting just as fucked as we are." Damn, just getting out that sentence was hard work on her mouth. Viktor started to laugh at her. He grabbed her bottle of Jägermeister and shook it. The damn thing was empty. "I'm out of booze." She declared and stumbled towards the bar.

Mikhail caught up to her and took her arm. "You're getting silly drunk. Maybe you should stick to water. Let's go get some." He slurred with is Russian accent. True to his word they walked up to the bar and he ordered her another bottle of Jägermeister, *that dirty fucker*. Sasha looked at them with concern. He walked over to the drunken pair and handed Avarie a bottle of water.

"It seems you two won't be getting frisky tonight." Sasha leaned on the bar. "But I will." He nodded and winked. Yep, he was drunk too. "I'm gonna give it to her." His words slurred together. Mikhail and Avarie chuckled deeply at him. Tori wrapped her arms around Sasha's neck.

"You're too drunk to even get it up right now." She slapped his chest. "You'll be lucky you don't puke on yourself at this point." Was everybody blitzed at this party? Avarie thought. Shit Tori's words stuck together like molasses. The scent of food and booze clung to the air. Suddenly Avarie was hungry again. She stumbled along with Mikhail over to what was left of the buffet table. Kirill must've had the same idea because he was making himself a meaty sandwich.

Somehow they managed to sit down at a table and eat sloppily. Sasha and Tori joined them. Kirill tried to hide the fact about how drunk he was but he wasn't fooling anybody. Between the two they counted twelve bottles of vodka. "We are so awesome drunk!" Avarie yelled at them. "Look at us, we're fucking invincible." She bobbed her head around and giggled. Her words were incredibly slurred. The twins agreed with her. They were all awesome at being drunk. "I am the liquor!" She yelled at the top of her lungs. Everybody busted up laughing.

"*Oi*, we're going to pay tomorrow for being so drunk." Mikhail declared loudly. "Nobody's getting laid tonight." They all nodded in agreement. Avarie didn't know if her lady parts would function at this point for the exception of taking a piss. She had trouble keeping her eyes open and the world spun when she stood still or sat for too long. They ate till they were full and made their rounds again. The twins held her up and she did the same for them. Avarie danced more and the twins joined her. They never left her side for the rest of the night. Sasha and Tori were making out on the dance floor and Kirill told them to get a room. Sasha flipped him off and told him to go fuck himself.

Eventually Viktor ended the party for them around 3am. He was drunk but not even close to what they were. He called for a driver to pick them up. Avarie wasn't expecting to be this blitzed. By the time they got home, the hallways of the house confused her because the world was spinning. The guards had to help them all to their perspective rooms and they laughed at them. The twins and Avarie went into Kirill's room. Sasha and Tori went into theirs.

Avarie had a hard time getting ready for bed. She would try and spin in the opposite direction of where her head was spinning and she wrapped herself up in her shirt. The boys helped her get out of her clothes.

Strategically Kirill informed them on how they were going to lay on the bed. Their worlds were spinning too and the trick was to always keep one foot on the floor. Kirill would take one side, Mikhail would take the other. Avarie had the foot of the bed. In theory it worked well. Avarie was able to stop the world from spinning too much. The downside was that she had to lay on their feet. Her pillow was continuously knocked off the bed by Mikhail's right foot. This was going to be a strange night, she thought.

ϒϒϒ

Avarie didn't know what time she woke up, but it was early morning. The twins were snoring and having one foot planted on the floor only helped so much. She sat up a bit as bile rose to her throat and she became sweaty. Avarie's body started to tremble and she knew what was coming. Taking a deep breathe she managed to stumble to the bathroom and hurl the contents of her stomach into the toilet.

To say she felt like shit was the understatement of the century. Flushing the toilet she sat back against the cold tile wall. It was like heaven on her chilled and feverish body. Why the hell did she drink so much? Oh yea, she thought, she had too many enablers. Thank God Viktor got them a ride home. Avarie was in no condition to be behind the wheel and neither were the others. Another wave of nausea hit her and she threw up again. How the hell were these guys still sleeping through this shit? Oh God she felt horrible. How the hell do people turn into alcoholics? The after effects were not fun. Yep, this is how I die.

Three more rounds of vomiting and Avarie was worn out. Her body still trembled and she broke out in a cold sweat. The chill of the bathroom tile eased her feverish body and she didn't want to go back to the foot of the bed. She formulated a plan. After brushing her teeth she went back into the bedroom and snagged her pillow then went into the closet for another comforter. Throwing the comforter into the soaking tub along with her pillow, she made herself a bed. The porcelain cooled her body while at the same time she stayed warm. Feeling better she was able to fall back asleep.

She never went into REM sleep and her thoughts were jumbled quite a bit. Images flashed before her eyes and in no particular order. They went from Kirill to Viktor and then Mikhail. Sometimes they were talking and doing something and she was extremely confused. Was she dreaming or was she awake? She felt somebody next to her and couldn't figure out who it was. Her eyes and brain had a serious lack of communication. She was cold and hot at the same time. Her ears heard snoring and talking. What the hell was going on?

Her eyes flitted open and she willed them to focus on what was in front of her. It was no use. Flashbacks started to occur. *She was in her bed with a young boy snuggled in her arms. He had to have been around six and he held her tight in his slumber. She brushed her hand over his soft brown hair. Planting a kiss on his forehead she folded the covers around him. He rubbed his eyes and asked her, "Niki, do you think daddy will be back soon?" He was so warm and soft with bright blue eyes. She nodded yes. "Niki...I'm glad you're my new mommy." He whispered drowsily and fell asleep again. Avarie, wake up.*

Her eyes shot open. She was still inside the tub with her pillow and blankets. Somehow Mikhail was able to squeeze in with her. "Avarie, are you finally awake?" He whispered with his eyes still shut. His hand reached out and stroked her hair.

"Why are you in my tub?" She asked ruefully. "I claimed this as my drunken haven."

"This is not Sparta, *Mishka*." He chuckled. "Kirill's been snoring so loud Sasha pounded on the door and woke me up. Then Kirill hogged the entire bed." He explained. "When I went to take a piss I saw you in here and decided that you had a brilliant plan so I joined you." Thank God he brushed his teeth, Avarie thought. She could still smell alcohol on his breath but it wasn't as bad as it could've been.

They were both lying on their sides in the seven foot tub. Kirill did a good job finding a tub long enough to fit their tall bodies in. Avarie still had a good two feet lying down inside. Mikhail had maybe half a foot. "I was sleeping at the foot of the bed, Mikhail. Kirill's idea was good in theory but the paper he wrote it on was pretty brittle." Avarie joked.

"You know, I realized that I didn't get to give you my present yesterday." Mikhail opened his eyes seductively. Their attention was brought about by shifting of the mattress and footsteps headed towards the bathroom. Kirill stumbled in rubbing his eyes. He looked down into the tub and giggled. Avarie wasn't tall enough to see what he was doing but she heard a stream of water hit the toilet bowl and a flush. She held back laughter. Kirill washed his hands and brushed his teeth.

"*Mishka*, I see you turned my tub into a bed." He said spitting out the paste. "Maybe that's where you should've been all night. Mikhail is a bed hog." His words slurred a bit and they knew he was still drunk.

"*Oi* Kirill, are you still drunk?" Mikhail asked from the tub. "You sound like you drank more than I did."

"The Direktor's fed me booze all night long. Of course I'm still drunk." He said exasperated. "It's like 1pm and I don't think I'll make it to work tomorrow like this." He put the toothbrush back down. "I'm going back to bed." He stalked off and they heard the bed shift. "I can't believe you fit in that thing with her Mikhail." He said sleepily and within minutes he was snoring.

Mikhail rubbed his hands together. "So, where were we?" He asked with a low growl. "Oh yes, your birthday present." He wrapped his arm around her back. "I've never had sex in a bathtub before so this should be interesting."

Avarie threw up her hands to stop him from going any further. "No way, Mikhail." She was losing a battle to sleep and he could see it in her eyes. "I'm tired."

"Alright, *Mishka*." Mikhail cooed in her ear. "We could sleep." He wrapped the covers around them and snuggled her close. It wasn't long before he was out also. Three hours later they awoke again. Avarie's throat was parched and Mikhail got up to get her a glass of water. As she gulped it down he noticed she looked feverish again. He took the glass and joined her back in the tub.

"Tomorrow you and Sasha have to go see Dr. Alex." He stroked her cheek and gazed into her eyes. "Your fever is coming back and whatever you have Sasha may have now too."

Avarie let her hand glide across his arm in a light back and forth motion. "I know. I don't think drinking last night helped us either." She nuzzled into him further. "I'm hungry. Think you can call the chef and he can make us something?" She suggested. Mikhail nodded in agreement and he stepped out of the tub. She heard his Russian on the other line of the bedroom phone ordering them food. Within minutes he was back inside the tub. "What did you get?" she asked curiously.

"I got some fruit, cheese, meat and bread. I ordered for the other two." He pointed in the direction of her bedroom. "If they aren't awake they will be." He looked around. "Oh, I also had him make coffee. He already knew we were hung over and Vinton makes a mean cappuccino."

A knock came at the door thirty minutes later. The door opened up and they heard somebody say, "Hello? I brought your breakfast in for you drunks." Avarie's eyes popped open, it was Viktor. She heard the cart rolling into the room and the door close behind him. "Kirill, wake up you drunk fucker." He told him. They heard the bed shift and Kirill mumbled something. Viktor came into the bathroom and spotted them in the tub. "Interesting place to sleep." He sniffed a bit. "Smells like booze and sweat in here. For shame." He said as he walked by to use the toilet. Avarie felt the flush of embarrassment and Mikhail flipped him off. "What are you two doing in there?"

"Avarie was sleeping and Kirill hogged the beg." Mikhail stated as he lay his head on her chest. "What the hell are you doing here?"

The toilet flushed and he washed his hands. "I brought back your SUV and decided to make sure you were all alive. My security group said they had a hard time getting you guys in your rooms because you were so drunk." He clacked his tongue at them. "It's almost 3pm and you guys are still lying about."

"Get out of here so we can get dressed or something." He waved him off. "Make sure Kirill is awake."

"The other two are awake. They wanted to make sure Avarie was still alive." Viktor winked at her. "So when do I get to give her my birthday present?" He peered into the tub rubbing his hands.

"*Oi*, you know she's our girlfriend, Viktor." Mikhail made his way out of the tub. "If you work her the way you did at Red October she'd leave us for you." Avarie had to laugh at them both. It was funny how they treated Viktor like a little brother. They picked on him and in the same sentence gave him praise. He handed Mikhail a towel and he headed into the bedroom. Viktor handed her a towel also and helped her out of the tub.

"Avarie, when I picked up the SUV there was a birthday card for you. It was put under the windshield wiper." He whispered and pulled it out of his back pocket. "I don't know why they wouldn't have come inside and put it into the card box." He shook his head. Avarie wrapped the towel around her and took the card. Her name was written on the card in beautiful calligraphy.

She went into the bedroom and placed it on Kirill's night stand. Mikhail started to dish out food and opened the bedroom door to check on Sasha and Tori. He found them already sitting at the table eating. He left both doors open to each other when he came back. Mikhail offered Viktor food but he declined. He'd already eaten before he came but took a cappuccino.

"*Oi*, Kirill! Sit up and eat!" Mikhail yelled from the table. Kirill struggled through the process of sitting up against the headboard of the bed. He gave a plate to Viktor and he set it on the bed in front of Kirill. "Get your hangover cure in!" Kirill rubbed his eyes and burped. Avarie cringed. "Kirill that sounded juicy." Mikhail laughed in his direction.

They made small talk at the table while they ate the salty meat and cheese. Avarie loved the fruit. Pineapple and cantaloupe were her favorite treats. She ate vigorously. Sasha yelled at Mikhail, "Is Kirill dead?" Mikhail shook his head no. "That's a shame." He yelled back.

"Water sprite!" Kirill yelled from his bed. "You're lucky I'm still drunk or else I'd piss on your food." Sasha walked into the room in his boxer shorts. He moved Kirill's food from the bed and started shaking it. "*Oi*, Sasha you're going to make me puke. Get the hell out of here." Kirill slapped him away. Everybody could tell that he defiantly wasn't in the wrestling mood. Avarie smirked at them. Sasha enjoyed picking on the twins whenever he could.

Sasha walked away from the bed and told Kirill he was a pussy. Kirill quipped by telling him to go fuck himself. The back and forth between those two continued until they ran out of steam. They were cracking everybody else up. Viktor had issues controlling himself and he almost spilled his drink. The twins discussed their plans for the week. In the morning, Avarie and Sasha would go to Dr. Alex for a check-up. They'd have Viktor pick them up and drive them to and from the office. Kirill had a meeting with Konstantin about working with the militia in the states. Mikhail had a series of meetings with the Direktors.

Avarie could feel her fever coming back. She peered across the hall at Sasha and he looked flushed as well. She knew she wasn't going to win against a fever at this point. Chills ran up and down her body as she drank her cappuccino. Viktor noticed her changed behavior and felt her forehead. "Shit, it's starting up again." He looked at the twins. "Early to bed for you, *Mishka*." Avarie agreed with that. She wanted nothing more at

Pandora Rising

this point than to crawl under the covers and hibernate. "Sasha doesn't look good either." He pointed out. Mikhail peeked across the hall. His expression became worrisome. Viktor passed out aspirin to both and told them that they need to go to bed early and he'd be waiting for them at the usual time. He left an hour later.

Kirill and Mikhail told her that she was sleeping in her room that night and she needed to get rest. Her body was becoming sore and a thin film of cold sweat formed on her body. That night Sasha helped her shower and he looked to be in about as bad shape as she did. Their sleep was fitful and they couldn't get comfortable. Taking her cue from last night's adventure they both slept in the tub. At least the cold porcelain kept their sweating in check and they stayed warm at the same time.

In the morning Viktor had to come into the house and find them. Sasha was usually in charge of the alarm and nobody heard it go off. Making his way around the room he wondered where they were. He was shocked to find them in the tub. "Sasha, Avarie, we're late and you need to get up." Sasha could barely move and neither could Avarie. Without showering or brushing their teeth Viktor helped them out the door. Avarie felt like hell. Her muscles were stiff and her head throbbed and her chest hurt. They fell asleep on the way to see Dr. Alex.

Avarie felt sorry for Viktor today. He had the gruesome job of getting them to and from the doctor's office. Dr. Alex took turns examining them both and determined that whatever they had was viral. He ran blood tests just in case something came up. He took Avarie in for chest x-rays first and then Sasha. They were there for most of the day. Sasha had a temp of 102 and Avarie was at 104. When the x-rays came back he determined that they had pneumonia. He made them stay at the office while he ran IV antibiotics and fluids through them. As soon as it started to flow through her veins, Avarie felt a horrible pain in her chest.

Sasha coughed up nasty green phlegm and cursed Avarie for getting him sick. She profusely apologized through the pain. Dr. Alex corrected him and informed Sasha that he already had it and Avarie had nothing to do with the virus. "You both are young to this world and have been exposed to different environments. I know you have recently woken up Sasha but it's no different for you. The diseases have changed since you last walked this earth." He explained. "Just because you're an elemental doesn't mean you can't get sick. You have a human body after all." he pointed out. Shit, he had him there, Avarie thought. "You both are going to get plenty of bed rest this week."

Viktor relayed the information to the twins. They weren't happy with the prognosis. Viktor brought them home. The twins came into their room. "Dr. Alex is on call for you both this week. He said that if either of your fevers spike that we need to call him right away. The antibiotics don't work overnight." Kirill told them. They decided to get extra help and called Tori off work and hired an in home nurse.

Tori took the first watch through the night and Sasha stayed steady but Avarie flared up to 105. By the time Dr. Alex was called she was in a feverish sweat and fitful sleep. He decided to hook her up to an IV and pump more antibiotics into her. By Thursday Avarie couldn't keep food down and her fever spiked to 107. They knew they were in serious trouble. Sasha was at 105 and following behind her. He discussed his options with the twins. They needed help and there was only one person who they knew could do it.

CHAPTER NINETEEN

Courtney rushed home passing every vehicle that was in his way. The phone call he gotten sent his heart on fire. It thumped against his chest in panic. Gerhart was the one who answered and told Courtney about what was going on since he was in a meeting. This wasn't good, he kept thinking. By the time he pulled into the garage he bee lined for Matthias' work area. Skidding into the space he caught his breathe.

"Matty!" He yelled. Matthias came out from under a workbench with a soldering iron. "Matty, you gotta pack your bags and fly to Moscow immediately."

"Why? What's going on?" He asked confused. When he examined Courtney's face he knew something was wrong with Avarie. "Is she alright?" Courtney shook his head no. Matthias dropped what he was doing and ran upstairs with Courtney following him. "I'll pack and you explain what's going on."

"Sasha and Avarie have pneumonia. Their fevers are spiking beyond their control and Dr. Alex needs your help. He said to bring anything that you could to help either bring the fever down or get the disease out of their bodies quickly." Courtney stood in the doorway as Matthias flung clothes into his suitcase on the bed. "Their security agency is meeting your plane in their personal hangar." He handed him a piece of paper with all the information. "The twins said the sooner you get there the better but you need to go ASAP."

"What about Eva?" Matthias asked. She was visiting her mother and he didn't have time to tell her what was going on. "She's gonna freak."

"You let me take care of her." Courtney answered as Ivan walked in. Courtney quickly explained the situation and Ivan looked startled.

"I remember I gotten sick too." He told them. "But it wasn't this bad. While you're away I'll try and get in touch with other elementals and see what they can do to help."

Damn, that was a good idea, Courtney thought. Matthias finished packing and motioned for him to lead the way. Ivan went with them to drop Matthais off at the hangar. He called Eva on the way and let her know what was happening. Ivan was on his phone networking with his people

Pandora Rising

about possible causes and cures for what was happening to Sasha and Avarie. Panic never left Courtney as he pulled into his personal hangar. He called ahead to make sure Matthias' plane was fueled up and ready to go.

In three hours Matthias would be in Moscow, Courtney thought. They watched Matthias take off and headed back to the castle. When Eva arrived they explained everything. She broke down into mournful sobs. Not only were Sasha and Avarie sick, but now Matthias was needed as back up and she never felt more lonely in her life. Courtney and Ivan felt for her and they were all worried about how this tirade was going to work out. Hopefully in their favor.

ϒϒϒ

Three and a half hours later Matthias was in a security hangar in Moscow. Security escorted him off the plane and took his suitcase. He met Viktor and he drove him to the Prime Minister's house and arrived around 12am. The twins met him at the door. Matthias was exhausted but he wanted to see them right away. Quickly Kirill led him up to the third floor. When he entered the room it smelled like sweat and hospital equipment. He flicked on the lights to find Tori asleep in a lounging chair.

Stepping to Avarie first he asked her temp. It was holding at 106. She muttered and mumbled things that he couldn't understand as he touched her feverish head. "Shit, she's hallucinating. Are the fever reducers working?" He asked Dr. Alex who just stepped in the door. He shook his head no. The IV lines pumped their fluids into the duo. "Did you guys try an ice bath?"

"We were going to try but afraid that they might go into shock. I took their oxygen levels and Avarie is at 75% and Sasha is at 90%." He handed Matthias his stethoscope. "You can listen to their lung sounds." Matthais went to Sasha first. He heard more noise in the left lung than the right. Going over to Avarie it was the opposite.

"Jesus, why aren't the antibiotics working?" Matthias scratched his head and looked at the deflated bag on the IV pole. "This is the strongest shit out there and they're not responding." He looked over at the blonde on the chair who was still asleep. "Is that Tori?" He asked Kirill. He nodded. "Damn, Sasha's got his hands full." Kirill managed to chuckle. Clapping his hands together Matthias announced, "Alright. Let's start with what we know; this started on a Thursday right?"

"Right, her fever started last Thursday. I believe on Friday night we had Sasha help bring down her fever so she could enjoy her birthday party." Alex bent his head at Kirill. "Sasha warned us that since he didn't know what she had he couldn't take it completely away, but hold it off for a bit. However, when I examined them on Monday it turns out that Sasha was indeed infected first and not Avarie."

Matthias was about to say more when his phone rang. It was Ivan. He answered it. "Ivan, you got anything for me?" He pressed the speaker phone button.

"I spoke to Julia in Brazil and she said that since Sasha and Avarie are blood bound, the disease will get progressively worse. You need to separate them and stop antibiotics." Ivan answered.

Kirill and Mikhail gave each other strange looks. "Why do they have to be separated?" Mikhail asked.

"They have to be separated because they feed off each other. If Avarie is sick so is Sasha and vice versa. In a way they're like twins. This is how Sasha is able to heal her when she's sick. Separate them as soon as possible before they make each other worse." Ivan said sternly. "Sometimes an innocent virus in blood bounds turn into something uncontrollable."

"So if we were to put Avarie across the hall will that do?" Kirill asked him. "Is that enough separation for them you think?"

"It should be. She said they don't have to go far just not in the same room." Ivan responded. "They still need to be watched though." Ivan heaved a deep sigh. "She said if you're running antibiotics through them to stop. An IV line to keep them hydrated is fine. Since Sasha is a water element he needs the fluids. Somehow the force between Sasha and Avarie is stopping the antibiotics from doing their job."

Matthias thought about it and it made sense. "Alright so do we start the medication back up after we separate them?"

"I asked that same question and she said it depended on how much you already ran through them. If you guys feel that whatever went through her system is sufficient than no more is needed."

"What about the fever?" Dr. Alex asked him. "The antibiotics aren't meant to bring it down and everything we tried isn't working."

There was silence on the line. "I didn't think to ask her about the fever. I just assumed once you separated them then everything else would work in your favor. I won't be able to call her until tomorrow afternoon because of the time zone difference."

"That's fine." Matthias answered. "They've survived this long they can fight it out longer." They spoke for a few more minutes and he hung up. "Alright, let's separate them." Mikhail woke up Tori from her deep slumber. She explained that she was up with them for 48 hours trying to control their sweating and fever. She had a hard time trying to get them up to go to the toilet and it was a serious struggle. "Alex, we need to cath them and watch their outtake. Kirill, you don't mind if Avarie takes your bed do you?" He shook his head no. Matthais shot off a set of instructions for all involved and they went to work.

Kirill and Mikhail stripped the sheets off Kirill's bed and put on new ones. They ran a lukewarm bath for Avarie and prepped the room for her. Kirill ordered more towels from the housekeeper and she brought them up immediately. She also took all the sweaty clothes and commented that they need to start throwing the dirty laundry in the hallway so she didn't disturb anybody.

In with Sasha, Tori and Matthias did the same. They couldn't strip the sheets until Avarie was in the next room so they ran him a bath. The twins took Avarie into the next room and put her in the tub. Together they helped lift Sasha into the tub. "Water sprite." Kirill whispered into his ear as he opened his eyes a bit. "Avarie is going to stay in my room until you both get better."

Sasha tried to laugh but managed to cough. "Make sure she keeps her hands to herself. Even with a fever she keeps fidgeting on me." Green phlegm landed in his hand after another cough. "Ew that's gross." He said drowsily. He wiped his hand on a towel that Tori gave him. Looking up his eyes went wide. "Holy shit did you guys send us back to Germany?" Matthais smiled down at him.

"No, I was sent in as backup." Matthias waved him off. "Instead of getting better you guys got worse and they worried." He wet a wash cloth and put it on Sasha's head. "You still have a high fever, Sasha. If you and Avarie were normal people you'd be dead by now." Matthias stated sadly. "I'm going to check on Avarie so I need you to stay in the tub for as long as you can tolerate it." Sasha nodded in agreement and closed his eyes.

Matthais went into the next room and met Mikhail and Alex in the bathroom. Avarie was still unresponsive but she was in the tub without incident. Matthias studied her form. The last time he saw her she had four ab muscles not six. She was extremely toned. Just by looks he assumed she was only at 2% body fat. He felt like he walked in on an older more mature Avarie. The little thing was built like a boxer and probably just as deadly. "Jesus, for being sick she looks damn good." Matthias commented to Mikhail.

"I know it!" Mikhail threw his arm up in the air. "We work the living hell out of her and Sasha. I've never seen a woman shoot a gun like she does. Hell, she can hold a Barrett standing up." His eyebrows furrowed. "She's been out of the research facility for less than a year and look at all that's happened to her. It's like she can't catch a damn break."

Matthias felt frustrated too. There were so many strange events that surrounded Avarie and Sasha that he wondered what it meant. "Maybe the universe is trying to get shit out of their way before the showdown begins." He suggested. "After a shitty disease like this, Avarie and Sasha should both have their immunities up to par."

"There are many times this girl could've died and she didn't." Dr. Alex added. "The same goes with Sasha. I've never seen such an odd pair in my life."

"I don't think any of us have." Mikhail answered. "These two are one of a kind." He stood behind Avarie's head and carefully poured water over her hair. Gently he washed the sweat and oils that coagulated on her scalp and face. Matthias and Alex formulated a game plan. After Avarie was done with her luke warm bath, she'd be dried off and cathed. She was to remain unclothed to make it easier for cleanup. Same went with Sasha. In the morning they would hire more nurses for their care so everybody could get some rest. Sleeping arrangements were made. Tori and Matthias were to go back to Mikhail's apartment and sleep. Kirill and Dr. Alex would manage cares until help arrived.

ϓϓϓ

Avarie continued to have fits in her slumber. There were times when she was responsive and other times where it seemed she was somewhere else. Images blazed behind closed eyelids. Many times she met Sasha at the gazebo by the lake at the castle where it all started. She asked him how long this was going to last. He said that they just needed to be patient. Most of the time they laid on their backs in the twilight watching the stars move about the heavens in silent contemplation. He told her that Matthias

Pandora Rising

was there helping take care of them. Avarie didn't see or hear him. "Where's Courtney?" she asked him.

"He's still in Germany with Eva and Ivan. He's worried sick about us but he couldn't come." Sasha answered her gently. "This will be over soon, *Maus*." He assured her.

"Why's all this strange shit happening to us?" Avarie asked him with concern. Ever since she arrived in Russia it's all been following orders, strange sex, and danger at every turn. Just when things seemed normal it was just an illusion.

It took Sasha an eternity to answer her. "I don't have all the answers. It seems like everything is being pushed in front of us only for us to knock it down." Sasha shook his head in frustration. "I didn't think that things would get this weird either." He stood up and found a flat rock. Pawing at it with his fingers he chucked it across the lake. "I mean you have to admit the twins are strange." He continued to lean down and chuck the rocks. "Truthfully it's nice to have a break. They're taking care of us for once. Neither of us have to put out or take orders." He giggled. "Now that Matthias is here I think everybody will behave themselves."

"Yea, but for how long?" Avarie asked standing up to join him. "Between me and you these guys are always danger and sex." She huffed in frustration. "I need a break. It isn't that I don't love them or anything. I just need something that feels normal." Finding a log she pulled it over to the bank and sat down.

Sasha gave up on his rocks and placed himself next to her. "Avarie, you're not normal." He said patting her shoulder. "These guys aren't normal and neither is this situation." His gaze lingered on the stars. "I'm just as shocked as you about the shit that comes our way. The first time around I've never dealt with Watchers. In fact, I've never dealt with women like Tori or you." He scratched his head. "More and more I think you're right when you say that we should run away. But maybe this will be enough for now." He raised his hand over the purple landscape. "Maybe the universe said 'let's give these two a break from this shit' and that's why we're here."

"I don't mind being here at all." She shifted to sit with her head between her knees. "It allow us to run away mentally." Rocking back and forth she added. "I like it when it's just you and me most of the time."

Sasha turned to her. "Why's that?"

"I think it's because everything we do together is meaningful." Avarie said quietly. Sasha pulled her closer to him and leaned his head on hers. Avarie wrapped her arms around his waist and joined him in his closure. No more words had to be said. There was an understanding between them that allowed silent words to flow from one to the other. Here, there was peace.

ϒϒϒ

Avarie's lids fluttered open. A sharp pain raced through eyes from the light filtering through the window. Blinking away the sting she allowed her vision to clear. Without moving her head her gaze came to rest on every object in the room. Her mind wondered slowly. How long had she been like this? Where was she exactly? It took what seemed like hours for her mind to clear and her body to become aware of her own presence. She was alone in Kirill's room and naked.

Slowly shifting to sit up she coughed up green phlegm. "That's just nasty." She said out loud. Reaching to the night stand, she snatched a tissue and wiped her hand. Without warning, Avarie went into a coughing fit. Every nasty thing that was inside her lungs came up with each heave. She went through an entire box of tissues. With a parched throat, her eyes went in search of water. With none being found she built up the courage to go to the bathroom. Carefully making her way there she bumped into a disconnected IV pole.

Now she remembered. She and Sasha had a fever and they had to go to see Dr. Alex. Everything was a blur after that day. Hell, she didn't even know what day it was. Avarie wondered what she had that was so bad that laid her up. Where was Sasha? The thought impaired her momentarily. It was possible that they separated them and he was in their room. At the sink Avarie took huge swallows of water. Daring a glance in the mirror she noticed her face looked pale. With a washcloth she wiped down her face and neck. It wasn't enough. Her skin still felt sticky and nasty.

She decided to take a shower. The hot water felt wonderful raining down on her body. She washed herself head to toe in an effort to feel clean. Before she left the bathroom she scrubbed the living hell out of her teeth. Feeling refreshed she walked into the bedroom and pulled out her clothes from a drawer that Kirill had for her when she slept in his room. After she dressed she found her combat boots under the table and she laced them up.

Pulling up her now damp hair up she inspected herself in the mirror. Her body felt much better and she felt clean.

Deciding to find Sasha she left the bedroom and went across the hall. Opening the door she found it empty. The same type of IV pole was left unattached and there was nobody there. This was extremely odd. Why was she the one left alone? Where the *fuck* is Sasha? A slow panic rushed through her body. Something wasn't right. Letting her senses perk up she creeped to the window. Looking down into the muddy front yard there were black vehicles lining the driveway. None of them belonged to Kirill or the FSB. She strained to hear any commotion but nothing came through.

Trusting her instincts she went to her footlocker and grabbed her riding gear, motorcycle keys and her short swords. Somebody had scabbards made for them so they could rest on her back. For extra measure she put on her combat gloves. Quickly suiting up and grabbing her iPod she quietly stalked out of the room like a lion on the prowl. There were no guards on the third floor. It was another signal that told her something was off. She decided not to take the elevator and ran to the second floor. Running towards the weapons room she put in the code and went in. The armory was almost empty. "What the fuck?" she whispered. She hurriedly grabbed her Rossi and Beretta. Putting them on the table she loaded them up. Making sure she had extra ammo and loaded up the extra magazine and looped the .45 Colt hollow points into their holders. Her utility belt was in a drawer and she clipped it on.

She left the room and tiptoed down the steps. Carefully opening the door to the first floor she found a guard blocking her exit. She tapped on his waist to get his attention. He looked down at her and said in whispered Russian, "Avarie, go back to your room. It's too dangerous down here for you."

"What's going on?" she asked him with slight panic. Her eyes darted down the hall and found exotic men who didn't belong with Kirill's security team. "Who are these people?" she whispered into his ear.

"Avarie, please I beg you. Go to your room and hide." When she didn't move he heaved a defeated sigh. "*Mishka*…you can't fight them and I fear you aren't well enough." She strained her ears and could hear arguing and yelling. It was one of the twins along with two other men. She breathed deep and steadied herself. "Please…." He begged, but she already pushed past him.

Her heart thumped in her ears until she heard nothing. Using Kirill's security team as cover, she snuck behind each one silently letting them know she was there. Another guard blocked her path, silently signaling her to stay where she was. With her Rossi in her right hand, she cocked the hammer back with a muffled click-click. Never allowing the strange armed men see her, she closed into the parlor and felt an extremely dark presence. She peered behind the guard for a better view. *Holy shit....they're here.*

ϒϒϒ

"Now Kirill." Shimon glared at him while swigging his brandy in the crystal glass. "You didn't play by the rules. You promised you'd tell my colleague here if you had the girl." Kirill rolled his eyes and huffed at him.

"Since when did you fuckers play by the rules?" Mikhail asked slyly in his thick Russian accent. "The last time I checked there was no rule book." He crossed his arms and cocked his eyebrows at them. "She's ours and that's the last of it."

A nasty cackle came from the other end of the room. A blonde haired well-built man walked up to Mikhail and stood face to face with him. "No, she's ours." He smiled arrogantly and Avarie knew exactly who he was…Luscious. "Now, if you'd kindly hand her over we'd be on our way." He waved his hand toward the exit.

Avarie's heart continued to race. These two men wanted her and would use violence to get her. No wonder she was left alone in her room. They needed all hands on deck to deal with these fucktards. Did the twins just let them walk in or was this meeting set up? It didn't matter now. Kirill was right, they'd be at their doorstep and here they were. Her eyes trailed the room as Mikhail continued to shit talk Luscious. Matthias had his arms crossed at the fireplace. Where was Sasha? Maybe he was with Tori? She felt a hand move her back. It was the guard in front of her. Looking up, she found her answer. Sasha was dressed as security in the doorway. They used him as a safety net. Looking further over she saw Tori dressed in the same garb towards Matthias.

Silently Sasha implored her to stay back. "You wouldn't know what to do with her even if you had her." Kirill mocked Luscious. "She's too much for you to handle."

Luscious gave him a devious grin. "Let me tell you what I'd do to her…" He looked around the room. "Once she was in my possession, I'd show her a good time." He moved his tongue against the inside of his cheek to motion a blowjob. "Then I'd tear off her clothes and show her who her master is."

Avarie shook her head. This guy was unbelievable. He had the balls to tell the twins that he'd practically rape her. "Too bad your cock is too small." Mikhail laughed. "She's used to much bigger men than you." *Oh sweet Jesus*, Avarie thought. Sasha grinned at that remark and Matthias' eyes lit up in shock.

"So, you assholes want a showdown?" Matthias said moving from the fireplace. His German accent was welcome amongst the throng of testosterone being thrown around in the room. "I guarantee you shitheads she won't go down without a fight." He walked straight up to Luscious without fear. "If I were you I'd walk away from this battle. There'll be more to come, that's certain, but the girl is off limits."

Luscious turned towards him and peered down into his eyes. Matthias didn't waver one bit. "Tell me Matthias…" he said sternly. "Who the *fuck* invited you into this conversation?"

"I'm the one who created her you stupid *prick*." Matthias rubbed his fingernails against his shirt acting like he was already bored with the conversation. "So, if you want her, you'll need to go through me, not the twins." He looked around the room. His eyes met Avarie's but he didn't acknowledge her. Sasha's hand stayed fast against her side, trying to immobilize her at her spot. "I created her strong enough to destroy your kind. If you want, I'll unleash her on you and I won't do a damn thing to stop her."

The twins looked at Matthais with wide eyes, unbelieving in his bold statement. The moment Luscious looked down while laughing Matthias signaled in Avarie's direction. The twins quickly glanced at her and turned away. "Matthais, is Courtney still your lover?" Luscious asked him while sizing him up. "Because it sounds like you've had a dick stuck in your ass for too long." Avarie quickly hid again behind Sasha as Luscious turned around the room. "You know, I'm curious as to why he isn't here? Doesn't he care enough about the girl to fight for her honor? Or did he just create her to get a good fuck and pass her along to the next person?" Avarie's nerves rumbled with hatred and she started to tremble. She swallowed hard, forcing herself to remain calm.

Luscious continued. "I'm giving you boys five minutes before hell is unleashed in this room to get her down here." He pointed to the ground and spun toward the twins. "She isn't down here, your guards are dead, Matthias is dead and I leave you boys in a pool of your own blood." He hissed at them. "I'll do you like I did that Pandora and others like her." Luscious seethed. "And believe me when I say, that was the most enjoyable experience I've ever had in my life." He cackled. Now Avarie was pissed. If he kept going she was coming unglued. "The best part of that....smashing her baby's head against the wall and hearing her skull crack." He laughed manically. "That worthless cunt..." he said rubbing his hands together. "She balled her eyes out while I killed her family one by one. The best part... I left her alive." His eyes darkened. "Now, I'd love nothing more than to do you like I did her."

    Sasha's grip tightened on Avarie's side. Silently he pleaded with her to not make a move. Avarie shook almost uncontrollably. She wanted this mother fucker *now*. An astonished silence swept the room. All on Avarie's team were aware she was listening to every word Luscious said. Shimon sat back and let him shit talk the twins and Matthias with a disgusting grin on his face.

    Matthias backed up again to the mantel of the fireplace taking his previous position. Luscious stalked the room like he owned it. He poured himself another brandy. Matthias' eyes met Avarie's and he nodded at her. Sasha loosened his grip on her and the twins steadied themselves into a nonchalant fighting stance. They were almost ready to let her fury be unleashed upon this satanic douche nozzle.

    "So…" Luscious said spinning around on his heal with a fresh drink. "Do I need to get her?"

    "No need asshat." Avarie stepped out from behind Sasha. She cracked her neck and knuckles readying herself for whatever was to come. "Nice story by the way…" She stepped closer to him while eyeballing Shimon. "Your first mistake was ever walking into that woman's home." She lifted her Rossi towards his chest. "The second mistake was taking her family." She pulled out the Beretta with her left hand and cocked it against her thigh. Aiming it at his head she stated. "The third was leaving her alive."

    He smiled gleefully at her. "No…it can't be." He sized her up and tried to spin circles around her but she followed his every move, never letting her weapons leave his body. "Nikita?" His eyes were now in disbelief. "They brought you back from the dead…" He clapped his hands in mock applause. "Good show boys."

"It would be a better show to watch you bleed on this carpet." Avarie said in a steady serious tone. Her eyes never wavered from his. Fear was completely gone from her system and she knew she could take him now. "I'm going to give you a choice, Luscious."

"What's that?" He crossed his arms and cocked his chin. "You can't kill me."

It was Avarie's turn to smile deviously. "Oh, I can kill you, but I'm going to give you a choice. If you want to live another day to get a blowjob at Red October, you'll take your bitches and walk away right now." Recognition filled his eyes.

"It was you..." He whispered. She nodded.

"Or, I can tear you apart limb by limb right here in this parlor. It doesn't make a difference to me. Either way, I'm going to get you and I'll bring the hounds of Hell with me." Matthias backed up completely against the wall now. Fear shadowed his form. The twins joined him against the wall. It was time for the showdown and they promised they wouldn't stop her. Kirill shot her a smile and nodded. Mikhail wasn't so sure about this and it showed in his expression.

Luscious looked around like this was some kind of joke and he was enjoying every minute of it. "Alright." He said rolling his head around on his neck to loosen himself up. "How about I take the latter? You aren't strong enough to fight me." This idiot was cocky as hell. He didn't have a single clue what she was capable of.

"I'm strong enough this time." Avarie stated. She looked him up and down, still holding her weapons. She lowered her guns and turned on her heel. Uncocking the Rossi she handed it to Sasha. She put the safety on the Beretta and put it in his belt. He looked down at her and nodded. Avarie was given the green light by all involved. It was her time to shine. Even if she managed to take down Luscious, it wasn't over. There were others. Pointing at Shimon she stated, "After I'm through with him you're next."

"Don't get too cocky." The man spat at her. "You're being a stupid little girl." He swigged his brandy. "You should just come with us and spare your friends your defeat."

She looked at him and eyeballed Luscious. "I don't go quietly into the night." She felt her body change. Thunder rattled the windows. "I am the darkness." Her eyes focused in clearly to Luscious, pulling off her riding jacket and short swords she threw them at Tori. Lighting started to spark and the electricity flickered. "I am the storm in every heartbeat you own." She hissed at them.

The twin's eyes grew wide. Avarie's body started to change before their eyes. Her eyes turned a deep green and pupils went vertical, turning her eyes catlike. When she opened her mouth they noticed her eye teeth grew sharp points. She stood not even five inches from Luscious' body and stalked around him like a tiger sizing up its prey. Luscious didn't move from his spot. She wasn't just sizing him up; she was making sure he didn't have any weapons on him. She grabbed a knife from his boot and threw it straight at a wall. There it stuck to the hilt. Running her hand across his ass and he shuttered. She went to his belt and pulled out a Derringer. She slid it across the floor towards the twins.

Gracefully sliding her fingers up his right side, he holstered another gun. Ripping open his shirt she grabbed the revolver and emptied it of its contents on the floor at his feet and slid it over. Her right hand moved across the front of his pants and found nothing. Being sure he had no more weapons she backed away from him. "Well asshole?" She motioned for him to step forward. "Come and walk through the gates of Hell. They're wide open for you." Avarie opened up her arms to him.

"Then I guess that's where I belong isn't it? In your Hell." He smiled seductively at her. "I'd love to burry myself into you." Luscious peeled off his dress shirt revealing an extremely muscular build. "Once I win, you give yourself to me."

"Hell doesn't give, it just takes." Avarie licked her lips. "And I will never give myself to a demon like you." Without warning Luscious threw a punch that landed straight in her jaw. Avarie recovered and blocked his next blow. Swinging her right leg up she managed to hit his left side but he didn't flinch. He was able to pick her up from the waist and flip her over to her back with a hard thud. "Get the fuck up, Avarie!" Mikhail screamed. She wrestled out from under Luscious and caught her breath. Matthias clenched his fists so tight his fingernails dug into his palms. Naturally he was scared. He hoped that she was strong enough to take him. Right now it didn't look so good.

He looked over to the twins. It seemed as though Kirill was getting antsy and wanted to have at him. He turned right back to Avarie. Blood streamed down Avarie's face and Luscious was still clean. He handed her a blood curdling smile and motioned her forward again. Her heart thumped in her chest. *I can take him,* she thought to herself. *Don't let him scare you. You're stronger than him.* In the quickest motion Matthias had ever seen Avarie jabbed Luscious over and over again. His face turned crimson and it splattered on the floor. He shook it off as he blocked her blows. He threw her off him and spin kicked her again to the ground.

Kirill was ready to join in the fight. As he took a step forward Matthias pushed him back against the wall again. Kirill's eyes turned deadly as he stared at Matthias. "She's got this Kirill." He whispered. "Let her feel him out." Shaking with rage he nodded and leaned into the wall. It was then he noticed something...Luscious was already wearing out. Soon, Avarie may have the upper hand. He cringed when Luscious kicked her in the stomach and knocked her down. She managed to jump back up. Then the dirtiest boxing fight ensued. These two were throwing fists, elbows, knees, and feet. All of their parts collided making sickening cracks against bone.

Both Luscious' and Avarie's knuckles were bleeding. Shimon sat at the table and smiled with glee, rubbing his hands together with a knowing look on his face. Mikhail could tell he was getting his jolly's off on this fight and it made the bile rise in his throat. Choking it back he prayed for some sort of miracle to end this fight. It's already been over five minutes.

With a nasty jab to Avarie's ribcage, she flinched giving Luscious the opportunity to drop kick her into the plaster wall. It gave way with a crunch and she slumped to the floor. Luscious hopped up and down on the balls of his feet in victory. As his back was turned, Avarie was able to swing her leg under his and knock him flat on his back.

Swiftly she was on top of him and Avarie jabbed him straight in the jaw. Her punches kept coming and he was only able to block a few at most. She moved with superior speed and gave him zero opportunity to move his arms. It was like beating on Kirill all over again. Time seemed to stand still as she straddled him only to punch into his heart over and over again. Blood splattered from every direction. His blood shot onto her face and dripped into her mouth. It tasted like sweet nectar and she wanted more. Madness overtook her entire body.

Luscious tried to desperately kick and pull her off him but it was no use. Her legs pinned the inside of his thighs and she held his arms down on the floor. Dark red blood pooled under his body. Without warning she dipped down and sunk her teeth into his neck, pulling every drop of blood out of him. She felt others hands on her body and she shrugged them away.

Their screams filled her ears yet she heard nothing. Avarie drank and drank until she felt his heartbeat fade into her own.

Bringing her head up she watched as the light faded from his eyes. His body still trembled from fear and she wanted more. Large arms wrapped themselves around her and they pulled her off his body. She kicked and screamed at them in a voice that wasn't her own. "Avarie!" they screamed her name in terror over and over again. Images flashed across her eyes. They weren't hers, they belonged to Luscious. She saw *everything* and it only made her rage more. His soul was disgusting and putrid. Her eyes followed his life from the beginning to end. The horrible things he did, the women he raped, the atrocities of his wars, the rape of Courtney over and over again, the babies he killed to drink their blood for sacrifice, the children he flung into deep pits to their deaths. It went on and on.

Kirill kept losing his grip on her. Her blood soaked arms were too slippery. Shimon surrounded himself with his guards for protection from her. Mikhail kept screaming her name and Matthias threw himself on her legs, begging her to stop kicking at them. She was beyond control... she was retribution. She wanted to lick the blood under his body.

Sasha tried desperately to clamp her mouth shut. "Avarie has bloodlust." He yelled at them. "We need to get her contained!" Five more guards joined them and she kept kicking them off. Mikhail was able to get her arms behind her back. Using zip ties he enclosed her wrists behind her. Kirill rolled her over on her back as she continued to kick and scream. Matthias handed him more zip ties. Putrid things came out of her mouth that they never heard before in six different languages. Tori gagged Avarie's mouth with a cloth napkin that was on the table.

Sasha, Matthais, Tori and several guards were able to get her out of the room. The twins watched as they took her to the elevator. Turning toward Shimon, Kirill shook with rage. "You're lucky we didn't let her come after you." He kicked Luscious' dead body. It started to wither away and finally turn to dust before their eyes. "Now Shimon, you go back and you tell the others that they don't *fuck* with us on our territory."

Shimon nodded in a state of distress. He looked down into the pile of putrid dust that was once Luscious. Mikhail added another statement before he was allowed to leave. "You also tell the others that they'll get their war and Pandora will have her revenge."

Did you love *Pandora Rising*? Then continue on with the next book in the saga *Pandora's Revenge: Part One* by Rochelle Purdy! Coming Soon!

Finally returning back home to Germany, Avarie has to come to terms with her fate. With Luscious gone, her work has just begun. Courtney is struck with a horrible illness and while he recovers, Avarie must continue her work for the Twins. She must find a man named Lukas and bring him back with her to Germany.

The real battle of good versus evil takes place from the USA, South America, and all the way to Dubai. However, a problem arises when Avarie gets kidnapped by the Elite. Courtney and the twins need to find her before time runs out.

Pandora Rising

ABOUT THE AUTHOR

Rochelle Purdy is the mother of three biological children and two step-children. She hosted a radio show called "Truth is Treason" on the Oracle Broadcasting network. She also has a Bachelor's Degree in Business Administration. Rochelle resides in a small town near Iowa City, IA. She is also an artist and you can find her work on Facebook at AberyJane Artwork.

CONTACT:

Rochelle always enjoys hearing from readers. Drop her a line at pandoraawakens@gmail.com.

Website:
www.rochellepurdy.com

Twitter: @rochelle_purdy

Made in the USA
Columbia, SC
23 July 2017